PRAISE FOR *BENEATH THE THIRTEEN MOONS*

"A beautifully drawn story filled with lush scenery and an engaging plot. It's a story you'll enjoy reading again and again."

—Romance Reviews Today

"In a single word, 'Wow!'… Kathryne Kennedy's computer must smolder from the power she creates in her stories! I simply cannot describe how awesome or how thrilling I found this novel to be… If you love romance and fantasy… you will *not* be disappointed."

—Huntress Reviews

"A highly original fantasy tale… Kathryne Kennedy has done an excellent job with world building. I really loved this world."

—Romance Junkies

"If you are looking for an extraordinary science fiction romance with a blow-you-away world, give *Beneath the Thirteen Moons* a try."

—Escape to Romance

"What a wonderful story! For a wonderful escape to a new world and a good love story, too, be sure to pick up *Beneath the Thirteen Moons*."

—Romance Readers

BENEATH
THE
THIRTEEN MOONS

KATHRYNE KENNEDY

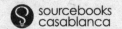
sourcebooks
casablanca

Published by Sourcebooks Casablanca, an imprint of Sourcebooks, Inc.
P.O. Box 4410, Naperville, Illinois 60567-4410
(630) 961-3900
FAX: (630) 961-2168
www.sourcebooks.com

Originally published in 2003 by Five Star, an imprint of Gale Group

Printed and bound in the United States of America
QW 10 9 8 7 6 5 4 3 2 1

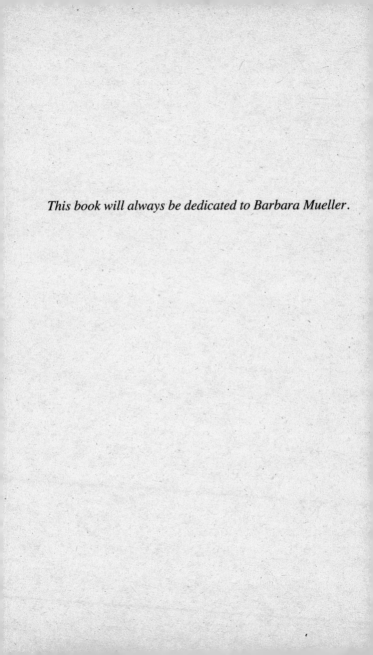

This book will always be dedicated to Barbara Mueller.

Chapter 1

MAHRI POLED HER BOAT AROUND THE BASE OF THE SEA tree, the bone staff she used as much an extension of her body as her own arms. She ducked beneath a branch, a wide one, the limb as straight as the Power of a Seer could make it. The gloom of the evening blackened to inky darkness, the slap of the waves echoed eerily inside the cavern-like arch, and here Mahri chose to anchor her craft.

She flipped her wrist in the pattern peculiar to her bone pole, and it retracted with a sliding hiss; her fingers shook as she slid it into a sheath of octopus skin. She patted the bone grapnel with its length of coiled rope and then dug into the small fish-scale pouch that hung against her hip. Mahri withdrew a small piece of zabbaroot, unsure if it would be enough for her task—she'd never kidnapped a man before, how could she possibly know?

With a shrug, she popped it in her mouth and squeezed it with her molars, releasing the bitter drug of Power that shivered through her veins and allowed her to See. The world turned into bits and dots and she closed her eyes for control. The root burned her tongue and she fought the need to gag, then opened eyes that flickered with sparkled light before fading to their normal green hue. With control returned, she'd now only See when, and how, she wished.

A scurry of sound beneath her collapsed sleeping tent reminded Mahri that she wasn't alone. The tiny face of her pet peered up at her from beneath the rugged narwhal skin. The dark prevented her from making out the features, but she knew them so well her mind filled in the details. Monkey-like, with scales for fur and webbed hands and feet, Jaja had the agility of the native tree dwellers with the slippery fluidity of a sea creature. And the curiosity of a treecat.

"Stay," whispered Mahri, her mind reinforcing that command with such mental force that Jaja moaned.

Mahri breathed deeply, quieting her thoughts so that they didn't project with the equivalent of a piercing scream. *I won't risk you in this, Jaja. I have lost so much already.*

She only caught the most basic thoughts from her pet, but he seemed to understand hers with amazing accuracy, especially when she was filled with root Power. He scurried back beneath the tent.

Mahri leaped from her boat, hesitated a second to adjust to a firm surface beneath her feet, then crept along the narrow ledge formed by the base of the sea tree, emerging from beneath the branch with caution. Mahri looked up at the balconies that spiraled around the tree, watching for guards, but not really expecting any. Not around the Healer's Tree. The Palace, yes, and perhaps even the Seer's Tree… but how could she know for sure, being only an ignorant water-rat?

What did they do, she wondered, with water-rats that skulked around the city at night?

She pulled the grapnel from her belt.

Throw them in prison for later torture?

With an easy swing of arms strengthened by a life of poling, she threw the hook up to the first balcony.

Or maybe force them into slavery as they did the native tree dwellers?

She tugged, and the rope held her weight. Fear fluttered her stomach and was swiftly followed by the inevitable fury at that cowardly reaction, propelling her up the rope with the speed of a silver-fish.

Mahri crouched, listened to the breeze swishing through the leaves, the soft patter of rain that had just begun to fall, the constant rushing, flowing of the water surrounding the interlaced network of sea trees. She studied the row of carved doors that circled the tree, Seeing beyond each door to the occupant within.

She knew if she went up to the top balconies that she'd find the powerful Master Healers. Here on the lower level slept the apprentices and newly learned. But all she needed was the knowledge, she would provide more Power than all of the Masters combined. Besides, if she stole away with someone of importance they might come after her, and she hoped that if a lowly apprentice disappeared no one would take any notice.

So she chose the first person she Saw snug in their bed. To See into the lock of the door, move the latch from here to there, took a flick of her Power. To See into the center of the Healer gently snoring, and to make those unwilling limbs move to her boat, was a different matter.

For a moment Mahri considered waking the sleeper. Perhaps the Healer would be willing to come with her? She crept closer to the bed. She could only make out longish, light hair, a smooth yet masculine jawline.

With a flash the memories of a past she'd tried desperately to forget overwhelmed her, of another Healer with long, pale hair. But hers had been arranged in artful layers of braids and pearls upon her head, and she'd stared at Mahri as if she were some swamp creature that had oozed out of the slime.

"You truly expect me," she said, one eyebrow raised in delicate disbelief, "to get in that piece of scrap you call a boat, travel into the swamps to heal a fever-ridden village of water-rats? And blindfolded, no less?"

Mahri narrowed blazing green eyes. If this woman only knew that those "water-rats" provided the city with more zabbaroot than a year of production from the root farms, she'd be begging to go with her. And that Mahri herself was a smuggler; who defied the Royal's decree that they possess and distribute all the zabba, on the pretense it presented too much danger for the common citizen. But to Mahri's thinking, the only danger lay in lack of knowledge, and the Royals hoarded that more surely than the root.

"Without a blindfold," growled Mahri, "I would have to kill you." Then she almost slapped her hand over her mouth. She spoke the truth, for the safety of the village lay within the secrecy of their location, but it needn't have been said. She never could control her temper.

The Healer's face flickered with sudden fear, then feigned annoyance. "Use one of your own Seers then."

"They don't have the knowledge you possess, as you well know."

The woman rose, presented her back to Mahri, and flung over her shoulder, "I can't help you."

Mahri clasped her hands together, her lifemate's agonized face in her mind, and the cries of their child, the once-perfect little hands twisted in agonized deformity. She swallowed her anger, and her pride.

"Please," she whispered. "Is there no one that would be willing to help?"

The woman hesitated, her posture slumped briefly in response to the desperate appeal in that voice, and then too quickly stiffened.

"No one," she replied, then slammed the door behind her.

The Healer on the bed snorted and rolled over, bringing Mahri back to the present, knowing she was mad to even consider asking for help ever again. Brez and her little boy, Tal'li, had died—even the thought made anger and guilt burn anew—and she'd become a Wilding herself. But the fever had only hidden, to return with a vengeance to strike again that same village and the only family she now had left.

And although this time Mahri had the root tolerance she still needed the healing knowledge. She could See the effects of the illness, could treat the symptoms, but couldn't be sure of the Pattern to cure the disease itself. Only one trained to know the normal body cells could detect the shape of a virus in time to destroy it before it could mutate again.

Her eyes sparkled and she Saw into the Healer's mind, traveling the path that controlled muscular movement, manipulation at least possible with the person unconscious. Mahri lowered her face to his, could almost feel his breath on her cheeks, when a soft knock on the door made her concentration slip and her heart stop.

"My lord?" whispered a man's voice as the door opened a crack.

Light fell across the Healer's face. His eyes flew open and met Mahri's for just a moment, a second of time that felt like an eternity, and there was a flash of recognition, as if she'd known him long ago, perhaps before this lifetime.

Mahri cursed, her Vision shattered and just sufficed to keep the Healer immobile while she spun to face the intruder. She pulled her pole from her belt, flipped it once, twice, and spun a long staff at the light globe. It connected with a sharp thwack, the wooden holder cracked in two, and the globe spun along the floor.

The man, no guard—for on his head lay the bone helm of a warrior—reacted with astonishing speed. She heard the hiss of bone being drawn from a scabbard and danced away just in time to avoid his blow. His advantage lay in strength, but Mahri's in speed, the small confines of the room aiding her even more. And of course, she'd just chewed root, and her opponent looked like it had been days since he'd last felt a fresh flow of Power.

He couldn't swing wide enough for a forceful blow and resorted to thrust and parry. Mahri grinned, drew on the Power, and Saw muscles tense before her opponent could attack. Her weapon flew; the force of the blow cracked his helm and laid him out on the floor.

So, Mahri thought, the Royals don't provide Leviathan bone for their warrior's gear. Her opinion of their rulers sank to a new low.

Then she had no time for thought, for she could hear a cry being raised, and spun to where the Healer lay muscle-frozen on the bed, watching her with a combination of admiration and fury. Mahri tried to Push his muscles, but knew that she'd used too much of the Power in that brief struggle, and didn't have the strength left to fight his own conscious control. And she didn't have the time to chew more zabba.

She flicked her wrist again, in the subtle yet complicated pattern that retracted her bone pole into a short staff. With her foot, she rolled the Healer onto his stomach, and with a muttered apology slammed the bone into the back of his head. Used the Power again to See into her own muscles and adrenal glands, taking that vigor to haul him out of the room, hoist him over the balcony and fling him as far out as she could.

There followed a splash, instead of the thud if he would've hit the base of the sea tree, and she sighed with relief before scrambling over the balcony, rope-burning her hands in her attempt to get below before he drowned. Shouts from above and she looked up, two light globes bobbed on the balcony, the light reflecting off of helmed faces. One of those faces smirked, sawed a bone knife along the top of her rope, then waved at her.

Mahri had just enough time to wonder why so many guards patrolled a Healer apprentice's balcony before the rope went slack and she fell.

And hit the ground rolling. Her left shoulder slammed across an upthrust wrinkle of tree bark and she grunted with the pain of it. She spun over into the water, swallowed a good portion of it, and inhaled enough to make her strain for breath when her head broke the surface. Something bumped her and she turned and flung out her arm to haul the body of the Healer closer.

The rain of arrows that had peppered the water suddenly stopped. They drifted with the current under the branch road and bumped up against the boat. Mahri looped an arm over the side while her other hung onto the Healer and fought the pull of the current, exhaustion making her tremble. Somehow she managed to climb into the boat, but the most she could do was to get the Healer halfway in. With a sob she collapsed, her shoulder throbbed with pain and she knew she fought against unconsciousness.

Through her haze she felt the gentle caress of Jaja's webbed fingers against her cheek, the cool slide of his scales. Something pressed past her lips and she tongued the root between her teeth, bit hard and welcomed the flow of strength from the Power. And tried not to think of the price she knew she'd have to pay for it.

Mahri hauled the man into her boat, Saw into his lungs and convulsed the tissue until water spewed from his mouth, reduced the movement to gentle contractions until he breathed on his own. She covered him with the narwhal skin and positioned herself towards the bow, feet splayed, confidence spreading through her with the comfortable feel of the current beneath her boat. She sensed Jaja weigh anchor, slid free her staff, the bone almost warm in her hands, and twisted her wrist to expand it.

Mahri poled, offering a brief silent thanks to the Leviathan of the deep for the gift of his bone, and the Power that made the forging of it possible, for the structure of it wouldn't yield to any other means. It took great skill to wield a bone staff, and many long years of training to learn the intricate movements that released the hidden locks to expand and contract the pole. But it had been worth it, for the price given had already been repaid with the saving of her life many times over.

Mahri used the current, as only a skilled water-rat could, by sensing its flow and nudging it with the Power.

With long practice she kept her contact shallow, knowing that the sea lay just below, flowing around the roots of the sea trees, unobstructed by the enormous growth that hampered its movements above the surface.

The sounds of alarm grew faint behind her, and she allowed herself to relax. In the maze of water channels lay a measure of safety; the real danger of pursuit would be when she reached the cove, a large stretch of open water that led to the open sea. From there thousands of channels led into the "swamps"—what the city-dwellers called the younger part of their forest—but any direct routes to them were heavily patrolled by the guards.

They occasionally passed other boats. The light globes that hung on their bows, and her Sight, made them easy to avoid, as long as the passage stayed wide. No lights lit her small craft; they crept along the inky water, the rain now a light misting that clung to her eyelashes like dew drops.

Mahri bottom-poled through the city channels, for the roots of this old forest lay thickly woven together, and the sea flowed over them at a shallow depth. She imagined the city as a safe haven perched atop its tangle of roots, protected from the monsters that swam beneath it. In the swamps lurked places of deep water where she'd have to tap her pole against the edges of the trees for steerage, and be twice as vigilant against the dangers that lurked in those bottomless channels.

Mahri sighed. She still preferred the swamps. For although the sea spewed forth some nasty beasts, it also produced beautiful, astonishing creations that never ceased to amaze her. Every journey through those snaking passages resulted in a discovery, made her marvel anew at this wondrous world. She watched the peacefully sleeping city they traveled through and knew that it would bore her to death.

Jaja hopped on her shoulder, his favorite perch when they traveled, and patted it reassuringly. Mahri winced, for her injury still pained her, and used her thoughts to distract her from it.

Somewhere below she knew the sea must stop, and wondered what lay beneath it. Only the trees were solid in her world, they sustained life; animals, insects, and plants all parasites on their bodies. She couldn't imagine what *something* could sustain the all-powerful trees. Perhaps her ancestors had known but that knowledge had either been lost or lay buried within the Royals' hoard of records.

They cruised through a warren of city homes; caverns hollowed from thick bark, or branches twisted into curved structures by the Power of a Seer. Front doors opened onto the water, balconies a few paces wide created small landings which tethered boats in all shapes and sizes. The white gleam of seashells used for decoration reflected the glow of the myriad moons overhead.

The Healer moaned and her attention centered on her unwilling passenger. Now would not be a good time for him to wake. Mahri centered the boat, went aft, and trussed him like a pig-fish. She frowned, remembering that feeling she'd had when their eyes had met, and with a feather touch she brushed the long, pale hair away from his face. Curled from the damp, the silky strands of it wrapped around her fingers, tumbled across his smooth brow. High cheekbones, a strong chin. A straight nose that tipped up at the end saved him from being classically handsome, to just boyishly so.

Mahri sighed, ran a callused finger along the fullness of his bottom lip, and Jaja hopped from her shoulder in apparent disgust. She snatched back her hand as if it'd been burned, tried to think of the nastiest curse she knew, gave up and just spit. She'd never reacted like this toward another man, not even her lifemate. Why couldn't she have stumbled across an ugly, old Healer?

A light globe that hung outside a treehome flared behind them, the phosphorescent creature trapped within giving one last surge before dying. Mahri glanced up, saw the spray from the bow of a craft that pursued them with deadly stealth and this time swore aloud.

She retracted her pole, used only the Power, Seeing the tiny particles that composed the water, shaking and stirring them until foam erupted around the sides of her boat. Unfamiliar with the city, Mahri still sensed the pathways of the sea and her smaller vessel surged between channels that formed the back alleys of the homes. The odor of raw sewage made her gasp from the stench; the waves she'd created butted against garbage that she deliberately refused to See.

When she felt the cove just ahead she gratefully eased the agitation from the foam. Her shoulder pounded in agony when she started to pole again, the root's Power that had drained with their flight had let the full pain of that hurt through. She wished she'd Seen to it when she'd had a chance. Hopefully when they reached the cove they'd be lost in the blackness and she wouldn't have to paddle but just drift with the current.

Her passenger grunted.

Mahri armed sweat from her face. First guards, then determined pursuit. Surely, a bit too much attention for a novice.

"Who in the-thirteen-moons are you anyway?" she snapped over her shoulder.

No answer. What had that guard said when he'd come into the room? Had he called the Healer "lord"? Only Royals were addressed by that title—her luck couldn't be that rotten! Besides, what would a Royal be doing learning the art of a Healer? Usually a selfless task, certainly knowledge not required for the ruling of the Forest. Perhaps he was the youngest son of a low-ranked Royal?

Mahri breathed a sigh of relief. That's it! A few loyal guards, easily shaken. A token show of interest for a barely worthy relation.

Thunder growled and the rain that fell every night thickened to a deluge when they reached the cove. She traded pole for oar—with regret for the alien feel of wood instead of bone in her hands—and paddled into the middle of the black water.

She had to squint against the downfall which obscured the lights of the wharf and the myriad moons. Between rolls of thunder she could hear in which direction the wharf lay, for even at night the taverns and trading houses spewed forth laughter, chanties, and the occasional scream. The temptation to hide out at Vissa's for a breather came and went. Although it might help shake any pursuers, the complications it could cause...

The image of daring black eyes and clever hands made her grin.

She hadn't the time for anything but a direct route to the village, and if she tempted death by abusing the root in order to get there, so be it. If she arrived too late, she might as well not return at all.

The seashells entwined in her long, braided hair tinkled gently when Jaja climbed up to hop on her shoulder. He chattered in her ear, his tail half-spread into a fin from his excitement and she reached back to smooth it down.

"What is it?" she whispered.

Her hand froze, muscles paralyzed in a grip she struggled to break. She could feel the Touch through the rest of her body, the tingle spreading through her legs, snapping her spine rigid. Again Jaja pressed root between her lips and with a surge of Power she broke that other's grip.

Master, she thought. Not as powerful as she, thank-the-moons, but strong enough that it couldn't have been a casual encounter. Her pursuers had found them, and now enlisted the aid of a Master Seer!

Lightning flashed and she saw a large, black shape bearing down on them. Only a warrior ship would be that big—had she the entire fleet after her? Mahri went aft, stood over her unwilling passenger, and nudged him with her foot.

"You're not a low-ranked anything, are you?"

As she suspected, he'd been awake. Large, round eyes looked up at her, caught the reflection of the lightning when it flared again. And exposed their position to their pursuers, for a slew of arrows tipped with the poisonous spikes of an anemone suddenly fell around them.

Mahri crouched, winced when an arrow thudded home next to the Healer's ear. "Whoever you are," she said, "It seems like your rescuers don't care if they get you back alive."

His words floated through the black night. "Your actions have made me vulnerable to my enemies."

Mahri felt a shiver run through her at the sound of his voice. Something about it, the deep timbre, the cultured words, sparked something inside of her that she hadn't known existed. A longing that... ach! What was the matter with her? She'd never responded so idiotically to anyone before.

Still, she wasn't sure if she questioned him just to hear his voice again. "Who are you?"

Lightning flashed, another volley of arrows, and this time the black shape loomed closer. Her captive's eyes widened. "Korl—" he managed, then began to spasm on the deck.

Mahri rocked back on her heels. Couldn't be, she thought. After all, a lot of people went by the name of Korl; her luck just couldn't be...

"Not *Prince* Korl!" she groaned.

Chapter 2

INSTEAD OF ANSWERING HER, HE TRIED TO HEAVE himself overboard.

The Seer has control of his muscles, thought Mahri, struggling to hold him down. But the Healer didn't have enough Power to fight the invasion and kept trying to lock his muscles against that other's control. She tied the ends of his bindings to the tent anchors inside the boat, hoping they'd hold him down. She knew that if she gave him root he could fight back, but she couldn't risk it because she needed him as helpless as possible.

Lightning crackled a jagged pattern across the cove and she looked up at the looming bow of the warrior ship, felt her own small craft begin to tilt from the wave that had swelled from its thrust. When they plummeted down it, they'd be sucked beneath that huge ship, shredded against the bottom of it into pieces of so much flotsam.

Mahri shook her head to clear the terror, dug into her fish-scale pouch and snatched out the biggest piece of root she touched. She'd never taken this much for such an extended period of time, yet she had little choice. She bit it again and again, shivered and gagged, felt her body expand with released Power. Then Saw the wave, let it grow, the foam cradling her craft atop it like a mother with a newborn babe.

They towered above the warrior ship for a second which allowed her to see the lantern-lit deck. A tall figure shrouded in a luminescent cloak of birdshark feathers stood like a statue midship, fists clenched at his sides. Mahri felt his Sight crawl through her, the same dirty Touch that had tried to attack her before. Then she smiled when she sensed his recognition and immediate withdrawal, watched those fists lift and shake up at her.

The Healer moaned and her concentration slipped, her craft spinning as if caught in a whirlpool. Jaja shrieked in her ear and catapulted onto Korl's chest, the spin slamming his small body so that it took several attempts for his webbed hands to push a small piece of root into the man's mouth.

Mahri Saw into the Healer, recoiled at what the Seer attempted to do, and didn't rebuke her pet for his actions. She couldn't afford to protect the man and flee at the same time, and she needed the Healer alive… with his insides in one piece. Hopefully, he'd use most of the root's Power to protect himself instead of trying to escape her.

She didn't envy him his enemies.

She Saw back into the foam, steadied her craft, barely heard a scream of rage over the roar of the swell as they surged forward. They rolled atop the crest of the wave, the tower of water now their valiant steed, brief flashes of lightning allowing her to see that they'd left the warrior ship far behind. She desperately tried to steer the flow of water, but she'd built it too high, the particles so agitated that they'd have to gentle naturally. Luck would determine which channel they'd flow into—she could only hope it would be familiar to her. The swamps were full of dangers and even a water-rat couldn't know all of the passages.

Wind buffeted her face, loosed tendrils of red hair from her braid and smacked them against her cheeks with a sting. For just a moment she grinned, for this had to be what it felt like to fly, skimming across the water on the wing of a wave. Let it take her where it would, she hadn't expected to make it this far anyway.

"You've no control over it," shouted the Healer behind her. She glanced over her shoulder, saw him sitting up, his eyes narrowed against the wind of their flight. "More root—I can help you."

And I'm a water-rat and therefore lack a brain, thought Mahri. Royals had such a high opinion of themselves that they underestimated everyone else. She made a rude gesture at him and imagined she heard a gasp of indignation, and tried hard not to giggle like a little girl.

The lightning saved them. Just a brief flicker, but enough to reveal the tree that lay in their path. Mahri renewed her struggle to direct the wave; her mouth opened and she panted, the spray of saltwater stinging her tongue. She directed Power again to her Sight, half aware that she sank to her knees, her trembling legs no longer able to support her. She grasped the sides of her boat and leaned forward over the bow to see better, for the rain had stopped and the clouds had dispersed to let the light of the moons guide her through this channel. Finally, a little luck.

But then the aft hull struck the side of a tree, her teeth jarred with the impact, and her passenger grunted behind her. Jaja had grabbed her braid and she felt him swing sideways, chattering in angry fear. The wave rode them too high, she could see a channel of water about a ship's length below being drowned by their own passage. They weren't even close to being high enough to ride over the tops of the trees and too many branches spread out at this height. Mahri ducked and swore, tried to steer around the obstacles with her Power, using the ineffectual paddle to slap leaves away from her face.

With sudden, bruising force a limb slammed into her chest and threw her backwards on top of the Healer's trussed body. She heard the breath whoosh from his lungs and hoped Jaja didn't get squashed between them while she tried to get her own breath back. Pain ripped like knives through her chest and her shoulder throbbed anew. Korl's body burned beneath her, the warmth of it begging her to curl up on it and go to sleep. To give up the fight and let the water do with them what it would.

"Get off me," gasped Prince Korl through clenched teeth, his voice tinged with what sounded like fear.

Because he sensed that she might give up, or could it be something else? Could he be as drawn to her heat as she was to his? And where did these foolish thoughts come from anyway? The moment she'd met him she'd felt an irresistible chemistry.

"Root," he continued. "I can control the wave."

Mahri steeled herself against the agony and sat up. Her craft slammed into the trunk of a smaller tree and knocked her sideways, her head bounced off the side of the boat and she couldn't tell if they actually spun or if it existed only in her now-jangled skull.

This time she crawled to the bow, anger the only thing that fueled her. Just because he had the knowledge of a Healer, he figured he could control water better than a rat? He who knew nothing of swamps and currents and the younger forest? And what perverse fate let her be drawn to a Royal anyway?

Mahri peeked over the bow. Their progress slowed but they still rode high. She couldn't control the wave but maybe she could throw more obstacles in its path. With a concentration that sucked up the remaining Power in her body, she focused her Sight on the channel of water that flowed beneath their onslaught, churning up humps of water that created a counter-force against the wave. But she knew it wouldn't be enough.

How long before they hit a big limb or tree trunk dead-on? Before the sides of her sturdy boat caved from the impacts that continued to beat at them? Mahri fumbled in her pouch for another bit of root. The pain of her injuries could no longer be held at bay from the dregs of Power she retained and if she lost consciousness they would die. But still she knew that the bit of zabbaroot in her hand might result in a coma she couldn't be sure of waking up from.

"I can't do it," shouted Korl. Mahri turned in surprise. "I've tried, but I don't know the strings in the water—how they're put together."

Well, of course not, she wanted to answer him. Just because you're a Royal you think you know everything? But she held her tongue because his face showed genuine shock, as if this was the first time he'd ever failed at anything, his self-confidence shaken. But Jaja had only given him a small bit of root, not enough for him to See unfamiliar patterns. And she surely wouldn't give him anymore.

Mahri crunched the piece in her mouth and let the Power flow again. But so sluggishly this time, following

pathways through her body that had already been traumatized by too much Power. With a groan she fished in
her pouch again, brought more of the green tuber to her
lips. She felt the slight weight as Jaja pounced on her
shoulder, the smooth feel of his webbing as he tried to
cover her mouth with his little hand. She could almost
hear the actual words in her head: *no-no-no*.

"I've no choice," she said aloud, and for just a moment several moons cleared of clouds and she met the
eyes of the Healer. Still too dark to see their color, she
wondered if they'd be the olive green shade of hers or
some lighter hue, for those of Power always had green
eyes, if not from birth then from use of the zabbaroot.
Mahri frowned. She might never know.

That feeling she'd felt before, as if she'd known him
forever, again shivered between them and she knew he
felt it too. The moons cast angled shadows across his
features, played their soft light along the pale strands of
his hair. Mahri swallowed a sigh.

"Don't do it," he said in that deep, soul-wringing
voice. "That's too much root for a Master, much less
the likes of you."

She could've slapped him, if she'd had the strength.
Instead she closed her eyes so he couldn't trap her any
longer with that charismatic stare and defiantly popped
the tubers into her mouth. Jaja whined and hid his head
under her braid, waves of fear emanating from his mind
to hers.

"I'll get you out of this," she promised the pet, even
though she knew his fright wasn't for his own safety.

Mahri's head felt stuffed with cotton, then it cleared
and she stood with the rush of Power, her eyes sparkled

with light and she dropped the paddle, drew her staff and flicked her wrist. With a natural agility she batted away lesser twigs, Saw the wave and made it guide her craft around the larger branches and trunks.

She no longer attempted to slow down, instead she navigated her boat through the channels. Mahri didn't know the path they traveled yet she sensed the direction in which the village lay, knew she'd waste precious time in unfamiliar waters, and with this surge of Power she'd cover as much ground as she now could. For the longer it took to reach what was left of her family, the greater chance they had of dying from the swamp fever.

She refused to consider that she'd be too late. And if—no when—she lapsed into a death coma from the root...

"Jaja," she whispered. His tail slunk around and caressed the back of her neck. "When I sleep, take this man to our village. He won't know the way so guide him there to heal the people. Don't let me die for nothing. Promise."

He patted her cheek in reassurance and she felt his agreement, breathed a sigh of relief. Then rode the wave as if it were some great sea beast, made it follow her commands, reveling in the feel of Power even while she cringed at the thought of the certain consequences.

But it ended too soon. The wave shrank and they descended to the normal level of the water in the channel. An unnatural silence surrounded them, compared to the maelstrom they'd just come through, and the wind softened to a gentle touch. Mahri continued to See into the current, pushed them to a speed she couldn't equal with her pole. She drained herself until she fell to her hands and knees, head hung between her shoulders, convulsions starting to rip through her body.

Exhaustion so intense she almost cried from it, an alien response that she hadn't resorted to since her life-mate and child had died. Pain so severe her quivering muscles cramped against the feel of it. Yet she still tried to See until her arms and legs collapsed and curled her into a fetal position on the bottom of her boat.

Jaja squeaked and pattered aft when her eyes closed, and though unable to keep them open she could still hear enough to know that he untied that Royal.

But was he? He'd never answered her, and suddenly it became necessary for her to know before she slipped into the blackness of a coma. The thought that she could die without ever knowing who she'd kidnapped seemed... unfair somehow.

A warm palm caressed her cheek and by slow degrees she opened heavy eyes. His face lay so close to hers. A strong chin, the barest hint of a cleft. A mouth that she could see curled up slightly at the corners, yet somehow didn't give the impression of a perpetual smile. A full bottom lip. Then the nose that tilted up at the end. Mahri didn't have the strength to let her eyes wander up his face any farther, where she knew she'd be captured by his gaze.

"Who are you?" she whispered.

"Shh," he replied, his breath the lightest touch against her face. Mahri breathed in the scent of him; clean, masculine, compelling.

"Prince... or... not?" she demanded, fading to that empty blackness.

She felt his grunt of exasperation. "Prince," he answered, "Prince Korl Com'nder, at your service. And who might you be, my ferocious little water-rat?"

I'm not your anything, she wanted to reply. Royals and their assumed superiority. Why did he have to smell so good? "Mahri Zin," she sighed, and succumbed to oblivion.

Yet not a total emptiness, for Mahri dreamed. Jaja hopped from one of her shoulders to another, his excitement making her nervous as she walked along the branch road. A road she'd never seen the likes of before, a sea tree many times larger than even the Palace Tree, the branch seeming to stretch straight toward the horizon. And the bark looked odd, almost as if it breathed in slow undulations, a living animal instead of the plant she knew it to be.

"Where are we, Jaja?" she asked with hushed wonder.

Mother Tree, he replied within her mind, for the first time not just with abstract feelings but in actual words. *Source of all zabbaroot.*

For just a moment Mahri could see the trunk of the mammoth tree, a dark mass of twisted bark that would take many moons for her to even walk around, if that was even possible. The limbs that splayed out from it stretched into infinity and she shuddered at the sheer majesty of it.

Tendrils of fog wreathed her face and blocked her view, as if mere mortals were allowed only a glimpse of the tree. The mist thickened as their route dipped down to meet the surface of the sea, and through another break in the whiteness she could see beneath a parallel branch and stopped in stunned amazement.

"Zabbaroot," she breathed, and felt Jaja nod his tiny head in excited agreement. Not just one but hundreds of roots grew from underneath the branch, long tendrils that dipped their tips into the water and curled back up and around each other. The pale green tubers sparkled with suppressed Power. The natives that tended them reflected that light in their black eyes.

Mahri frowned. Although many natives hovered around the fringes of her own village, frequented the wharves and were said to tend the Royal's root farms, she'd never paid them any notice. Similar to Jaja, they stood larger, perhaps half her own height, possessed the webbed hands and feet, the scales that looked like fur until closer examination. But their heads were much larger in proportion than her monk-fish, and their eyes glittered a uniform black instead of the soft brown orbs of Jaja.

How could she have never noticed them? Like the sound of the sea they existed on the fringes of the conscious but never drew attention to themselves, never spoke, just appeared from the forest to take over a task that needed doing. Why had she never questioned their existence before?

She felt rather than heard the laughter in her mind, met Jaja's eyes but he shrugged in negation.

"Who?" she mouthed, and a tiny webbed finger pointed toward the trunk of the Mother Tree.

Mahri lifted leaden feet, hesitant to walk away from so much root without harvesting just a bit. Yet she had a feeling it wouldn't be allowed, that she'd be upsetting some kind of balance.

Then she almost smacked nose to bark, if Jaja hadn't tugged on her braid, pulling her up short as mist unfolded to reveal a door set into the trunk before them. A door unlike any she'd ever seen, one solid piece of bone carved with scenes of the natives, arms opened to the sky and something falling from the heavens, an impossible bird with a tail that spewed fire. Mahri knew she should understand this, something tickled at her mind, like an old memory…

Jaja shook her braid, the seashells entwined in it tinkled in muted tones, and her hands rose of their own accord and pushed open that door. When her fingers touched the bone she knew it to be Leviathan; impossible really, for something that large. But she felt her retracted pole in its sheath of octopus skin and knew they were of the same substance.

They're wealthy, yet they serve humankind as willing slaves, fetching and working with such unobtrusiveness that most of the time they go unnoticed. Why would the natives of the sea forest pretend to be unintelligent animals—and to what purpose?

To learn, to guide, answered that same voice that had laughed in her head earlier.

Mahri stepped into the room, then reassessed that definition. A room had sides and a ceiling that she could see, yet this place stretched beyond sight. What could she call this surround of blackness? An abyss? And she shuddered with more than fear.

"Where are you?" she asked, searching for the source of that mind contact. She'd never heard of a coma inducing such vivid dreams. Then again, she'd never met anyone who'd survived an overdose of the root.

Enter, sit, replied the voice inside her head.

A cushioned pallet of the skin of an unfamiliar sea creature appeared at her feet, and Mahri sank with a sigh. A pool of light surrounded her but couldn't penetrate the recesses of the inner trunk of this tree, and when a native stepped into the seeming brilliance her mouth dropped open in stupid wonder.

Natives didn't often wear clothes, but this one sported layers of spider-silk scarves, a crown of birdshark feathers, jewelry of carved bone and iridescent shells. Even slippers of sharkskin covered the webbed feet.

"Who are you?" breathed Mahri.

The native female, judging by her size and the thick head of fur-scales, tried to imitate a smile by the baring of sharply pointed teeth. At Mahri's alarmed expression, she shrugged and squatted down next to her, black lips quickly covering those deadly incisors. Jaja hopped on the native female's shoulder.

I'm the Speaker, she thought-answered while she rubbed scaled cheeks with Jaja.

Mahri fought down a sense of betrayal at her pet's abandonment and frowned at his contented little expression. "Speaker for who?"

The female waved a webbed hand negligently in the air. *For all.*

It felt peculiar to hear words without a mouth moving. Jaja hopped back onto her own shoulder and Mahri grinned with satisfaction. As if this had been some kind of signal the female almost-frowned and met her eyes with her own black, intense native ones. Eyes that weren't truly black, Mahri noticed with a start, but such a deep green that they darkened to black.

Hard to speak to your kind, began the native. *Still learning… odd thought directions.*

Mahri rubbed the top of her bone staff. "Am I dead or just dreaming?" she wondered aloud. The native leaned forward, she could almost feel the slight wind from the flutter of those impossibly thick alien lashes.

No matter. No time. Root allows speak… but danger to you if long. Heed me. Black lips thinned with determination, the feathered headdress fluttered in agitation.

Mahri had a sinking feeling. This dream took on an aspect of importance that she suddenly didn't care for. "I'm just a water-rat, a rootrunner that only cares for her village. I don't know what you want from me, but your people had better choose someone else to speak with, someone who cares what you have to say."

The native widened her eyes and slowly blinked. *You only one. The HALF. Protect… nurture, the Prince of Changes. Make whole.*

The prince of what? wondered Mahri. She didn't know any princes… then she groaned. "You don't mean Prince Korl, do you?"

The native nodded her head, clapped webbed hands that made a soft popping noise. *We guide your people, you help. Prince of Changes must rule with you. The beginning of… peace, brotherhood, for all of Sea Forest.* And she stood, as if she'd made Mahri understand her wishes and didn't doubt they'd now be followed.

"Must rule?" shouted Mahri, springing to her feet. "Listen, I'm a smuggler, I stand against everything the Royals want—control of root and knowledge. I wouldn't help anyone rule, even if I knew how!"

The native fluttered her hands and began to pace around their circle of light. *When your people come from above… different. Want, demand. Either fight or help. Choose to guide, see long future. Understand?*

Mahri shook her head, a bit dizzy from following the

native circling around her. "You're telling me that old tale of our people traveling through the stars, coming from another world, is true?"

The native stopped in front of her, looked up into Mahri's face, nodded slowly. *Need Prince of Changes*, she shouted into Mahri's mind, making her head ache. *Path to peace. But he needs you*.

"Even if that were true," she replied, stroking Jaja's tail for comfort. "I don't see how I can help him to rule. A water-rat could never be Queen of Sea Forest."

If the native had been human Mahri would swear the look she wore reeked with a sly, subtle humor. *You. Bond. With Prince of Changes*.

That seeming demand made Mahri freeze with shock. A Bond! She wouldn't enter into that state with her chosen lifemate, and by-the-thirteen-moons she'd never even consider it with a Royal! To link Power through the zabbaroot with another took far more trust than most people were willing to give, much less someone like her.

Mahri's only comfort lay in the thought that this was a root-induced dream, albeit of the highest caliber. "You want the impossible," she replied.

The circle of light they stood in began to shrink. The native eyed it with alarm and grabbed the taller woman's forearms. *Not impossible. You… the half*.

The light now encompassed only Mahri, the native's grip had loosed and disappeared into the blackness. "The half of what?" she demanded into the growing abyss.

The answer in her mind tickled faint as a whisper. *The other half… of his soul*.

Chapter 3

MAHRI OPENED HER EYES WITH A SCREAM IN HER throat that couldn't be voiced. The noise that did come from her mouth sounded like a fair imitation of Jaja's squeaky chatter and made her snap her lips shut, swallow hard against the sandy feel of her tongue. Her eyes flew open onto daylight, and she became aware of the rhythm of the water beneath her and a body that felt bruised all over. And felt an amazed gratitude that she seemed to be alive.

She tried to tense her muscles to sit up. Nothing happened. They wouldn't—or couldn't—respond; useless strings that now sufficed just to hold her bones together. Mahri lay immobile with what felt like swamp fever, watched the interlaced tree branches above, the shafts of sunshine that managed to filter through the canopy, and hungrily eyed the krizm vines that dangled their swollen globes of stored water from the night's rain.

She couldn't see him, but heard a whistled tune, knew that Prince Korl guided their passage through the channel by the unnecessary splashes from his inept paddling. They'd be better off if he just let her boat drift. Her mouth opened to ask for water when she realized that the Royal wouldn't know a krizm vine from a dedo, would most likely pluck a pink globe instead of the red, accomplishing what the coma had not.

But thank the-thirteen-moons for the mind closeness of her pet. Jaja must have felt her need for his sweet little face appeared above her, brown eyes huge with concern, then the blessed relief of wetness flowed into her mouth, down her parched throat. When she'd had enough Mahri managed to turn her cheek into her pet's hand, rubbing skin to scale in a silent thank you.

"So, the water-rat wakes," drawled the Royal.

Mahri gritted her teeth at his patronizing tone. The brief flare of anger allowed her to lift her head and she gasped at the result, her vision red with the pain that pulsed through her skull.

I'm proud to be a water-rat, she reminded herself.

"You're lucky to be alive," he continued. "That much root would've downed many a Master Seer I know." He dropped the paddle and turned, his face in direct contrast with the voice, for his forehead narrowed in concern as he studied her.

"You've still got a nasty lump on your head, but I've Seen to your shoulder and, er, chest." His face reddened and Mahri fought back a smile. "The effects of the overdose, well, there's nothing I can do about that. But it looks like time ought to heal you."

He crouched beside her and Mahri stared in mute wonder. His eyes sparkled with root, eyes that glowed the palest green that she'd ever seen, their color and large, round shape making them jump out from the rest of his face, impaling her with their brilliance. She couldn't look away.

"I thought about tying you up," he continued, his face reddening again, "just to return the favor. But you'll be too weak to give me much trouble anyway."

Mahri could only stare and listen to that strangely deep throaty voice, unaware of the words he spoke, only responding to the feeling that shivered through her at the sound of it. Her heart thudded erratically and fish-fins fluttered through her stomach and she wished he'd keep talking forever.

The Royal's mouth continued to move and she continued to stare at him until his words just trailed away, his eyes locking with her own, caught up in the same spell that gripped Mahri.

His pale hair absorbed the filtered sunshine and made each strand shimmer with gold; tendrils that had loosened from the strip of mosk-leather around his forehead curled lazily against his jaw and neck. Thick, brownish-gold lashes framed those startling eyes, high cheekbones sculpted an otherwise boyishly round face. Pale, creamy skin, the envy of any woman, allowed a blush to betray his thoughts and made Mahri want to run her hands along his face, to see if that perfection were real. And absently made her wonder if he spent any time out-of-tree.

She broke the trap of his gaze and trailed her own over to his mouth, that full bottom lip. Mahri could feel the sudden pull like a tangible thing, a taut rope that tugged her own lips to his, to barely touch that warm fire and allow her to breathe in the scent of him.

The sudden roar of rushing water, the spin of her little craft, broke the hold he had on her.

"Stop it," she snapped.

"Me?" he growled, jerking his head back. "You're the one who…"

Mahri raised her eyebrows and watched him blush in confusion. She could still feel the bare brush of his lips on hers, knew she couldn't help the draw he had on her, that he'd done nothing she hadn't asked for. Everything about him, every feature of his face, seemed to be made to fit her idea of perfection. He was simply the most beautiful thing she'd ever seen. And her body wanted him.

Although still young in years, she'd been married and knew lust when she felt it. Yet she'd only been with Brez, despite Vissa's creative attempts at seduction, and even after her lifemate's death had never even considered another. Until she'd met this Royal. This attraction went beyond her scope of experience, this demanding, hungry… she needed to touch him, crush him, overwhelm her senses with the taste and feel of him. Mahri nearly panted aloud with the ache of it.

She refused to believe she could behave like such a wanton.

Korl had grabbed the oar and attempted to stop the boat from spinning, his muscles bulging through the thin spider silk of his shirt, and Mahri closed her eyes against the sight. Immunity, she thought. I'll just keep looking at him until I'm immune to this attraction, until his power over me fades with increased familiarity. Simple.

"Water-rat," he shouted over the increasing roar of the current. "There's whitecaps ahead."

Mahri tried to rise but her muscles still refused to obey her. Where are we? She wondered. What channel had they been thrown into? Root-fried, yes, but she never should've relaxed her guard—those that did seldom survived the swamps.

"Jaja," she whispered. "How far?"

The monk-fish hopped to the bow of the boat, made a show of shading his eyes with a tiny webbed hand.

Then he undulated his fingers for entirely too long. The whitecaps went far down the passage.

"Zabbaroot," she demanded. Her pet bared his teeth and didn't budge. *Now*, she mentally screamed. He winced but held his ground.

Mahri moved her hand just enough to feel the loss of her mosk-leather belt from around her waist. Raised her head long enough to catch a glimpse of it now encircling Korl, the fish-scale pouch containing her root supply hanging against his hip.

So their positions were now reversed. But she wouldn't lower herself to begging for root as he did. Either he'd get them through this or come to his senses and ask for her help. She felt around again, sighed with relief when her fingertips touched the warmth of her bone pole. At least he'd left her the staff, although without the root to fuel her muscles it wasn't much help.

Mahri felt the boat buck beneath her, fought down impotent frustration at being powerless to act. She clenched her fists and occasionally raised her head to see how Korl fared, and those actions were all that her body allowed.

Jaja continued to perch atop the bow, the thrash of the waves too forceful for him to risk jumping down. His tail fanned out in fear, the fin waving back and forth like a banner. When the boat rocked with a force that almost threw Mahri from the deck, Jaja barely had time to scream before a swell swept him into the channel.

Mahri screeched the vilest curses she could think of, struggled to a sitting position and flicked her staff. The bone extended and she used it to support herself to her feet, only to have her body betray her and sag back to the deck. Jaja swam like the fish he partly was and he needn't come up for air for hours, but if he slammed into a rock, or slipped into the maw of a wide mouth skulker... She didn't know this passage, couldn't know if any skulker's had staked this territory, but any smuggler knew that where the water ran swift, skulkers usually hunted.

"What's wrong?" That deep, strong voice at her ear.

"Jaja," she cried, struggling upward again, locking her muscles when she reached hands and knees. By-the-moons, she'd asked too much of her body, it wouldn't respond to her demands. She reached out a hand and tried to wrest the root pouch from him.

He swatted her hand away as if it were a pesky insect. "No more root, water-rat, do you want to die?" And then he did the most selfless, idiotic thing she'd ever seen. He jumped over the side of the boat after her monk-fish.

Now she'd have to save both of them, she thought with more than a little disgust, and started to crawl aft. Typically arrogant of him to think that the only zab-baroot she had lay in her pouch. Mahri pushed then twisted, and exposed the secret compartment in the deck—standard, although hidden differently, in every smuggler's boat. She reached far into the cranny and pulled out her supply.

The Royal's also a Healer, she reminded herself. What if he's right about more root being fatal? She'd never pushed her tolerance this far.

Yet Jaja is more family to me than those in the village. There's really no choice here. Mahri crunched zabba.

The oddest sensation shivered through her veins, as if the overdose of root had forged new pathways through her. When the flush reached her head she remembered the vivid dream that she'd had from her coma. That the natives were intelligent, that they could communicate through the mind and had done so with her. The Speaker's demand that she Bond with the prince.

Mahri grimaced. That she'd Bond with anyone, much less a Royal, was laughable. She'd given up her freedom once, and although not Bonded she'd given her heart to her lifemate and her soul to little Tal'li, and lost them both. If she thought that there was even the slightest chance that this physical attraction could develop into something more—she'd never risk that kind of despair again.

She shook her head, stood and splayed her legs on deck, Saw into the water, the strings and bits and dots, and cradled her craft along the surface of the froth. Scanned the channel for a pale head, an even smaller brown one, and noticed with alarm the several odd humps that weren't rocks.

They'd stumbled on an entire nest of skulkers then. She shuddered with a moment of weakness at the fear that she'd been too late for Jaja and Korl. That they'd already gotten sucked into one of those powerful maws that waited just below the surface, were sliced and flayed by the rows of jagged teeth that encircled the mouth of the beast.

Mahri couldn't even curse, the terror swelled so strongly within her. She frantically Saw into the water, kept the boat steady, Looked through the skulkers for the Patterns that meant Jaja and Korl. And realized the fear for the one was as strong as her fear for the other… but of course, she needed Korl to Heal the village.

The boat listed to the side and she swayed with the

movement, glimpsed the hand that flailed at the rail before disappearing again. Shifted her sight to norm and saw them; Korl struggling to get a hold of the boat, his silk collar clutched in a death-grip by Jaja's fingers. With a mental heave Mahri used the water to fling them onto the deck. She watched with anxiety as they both lay gasping and choking up enormous amounts of the channel, but seemingly unhurt.

Jaja shook the water from his scales, crawled to Mahri and slowly climbed the braid of her hair, curling his tail around her neck and huddling on her shoulder. Korl sat back, head bowed, arms slung atop his bent knees, and just breathed. With profound relief she switched to the Sight to use the Power to steer around the humps of skulkers, through the white rapids until they reached calmer waters.

Mahri Saw where one body of water mingled with another, knew they traveled far from any mapped passages or any of her own routes. Currents flowed and shifted in opposing directions; she could glimpse other channels within a stone's throw of their own through the massed trunks of the sea trees, yet still recognized nothing.

If I can find one familiar passage, she thought, I'll know the way to the village—but how long before that happens when I know only the general direction to go? A full night and half the morning gone, and a journey with unknown hazards ahead. While the fever spreads through my village.

The water gentled to a blue mirror and Mahri had to churn it to move the boat along. She couldn't pole, had locked her joints just to keep her standing upright, using only enough Power to blunt the pain in her body.

She felt Korl's eyes on her—how could she not? But

took her time before she met them. Water still clung to his lashes, making them thicker, the pale green of his eyes even more vivid. By-the-moons, she thought with a groan. My body's in too much pain to respond to that face.

"You're a Wilding," he said, his deep voice making the title sound like an accusation. "No water-rat can chew as much root as you have and still be standing to wield the Power. How much did she pay you, anyway?"

"Who? What do you mean?"

His eyes narrowed. He looks incredibly sexy, thought Mahri helplessly, when he's angry.

"Don't play stupid," he snapped. "It doesn't suit you. How much did S'raya pay you to kidnap me? Enough to buy a whole lot of root, apparently." Korl gestured towards the pouch at his waist. "And why bother to save my life—unless you intend to try and ransom me back. Hate to disappoint you, but…"

Mahri's eyes widened with surprise. How many enemies does a prince have anyway? But she asked the only question that mattered at this particular moment. "Who's S'raya?"

"She didn't tell you she's my sister, did she?" he asked, and then did the most extraordinary thing. He pulled the thong from around his head and shook back the hair from his face. Shimmering droplets sprayed about his feet and the move whipped the curled strands of hair away to expose his throat. A gesture that surely many a man had made, but by-the-thirteen moons he turned it into the most provocative thing Mahri had ever seen. Her lower half throbbed in response and she gripped the bone staff until her knuckles showed white.

She'd have to stop doing this to herself. Focus, she thought. S'raya isn't a scorned girlfriend, which could be a good thing. But his sister? What kind of family did he have, anyway?

"This has nothing to do with politics," she managed to say. "I needed a Healer and I just happened to pick your door."

He reached up and tied the thong of mosk-leather back around his head. "You expect me to believe that?"

Mahri felt the root's Power ebb from within her. Blast it, she'd need his help if they were going to make it to the village. She needed to rest.

"Believe it!" she snapped. "I had no intention of kidnapping a Royal. I would've dropped you over the balcony of the Healer's Tree if I'd have known it."

Prince Korl stood, the thin material of his spider-silk sleeping clothes still wetly clinging to every part of his body. "If I remember rightly, that's *precisely* what you did."

Mahri tried not to smile at his words or pant at the ridges of his body. "I... I couldn't think of anything else." She shrugged. "Sorry."

He steadily advanced toward her and she tried not to admire how quickly he'd gained his sea legs.

"Why exactly," he asked, "did you need to kidnap a Healer? Couldn't you have knocked on the door and asked for one or is that too easy for you?"

You patronizing, thought Mahri, arrogant, ignorant... Prince! How her lust for him turned to anger. "Tell me, Healer. Had I come to your door and asked you to travel in a rootrunner's boat to a village in the swamps, to cure a virulent fever, what would've been your response?"

His mouth dropped open. He had even white teeth, she noted. Of course.

"You're a smuggler?" he asked, with a hint of wicked admiration. He stepped back and eyed her up and down, as if seeing her for the first time.

Mahri fisted hands on hips. Why did people who lived in luxury think that those who didn't made them somehow exciting? She had no false illusions about what he looked at. Her vest of snar-scales with its matching calf-high leggings exposed most of her dark, freckled skin. Although impervious to water and of rugged endurance, she couldn't imagine that snar-scales would be the fabric of choice for most of the women at Court that he'd be used to seeing. He slept in spider-silk himself!

Mahri knew she had a nice face, heart-shaped, with slightly slanted olive-green eyes and freckles across the bridge of a narrow nose. She stood tall, lean, and too muscular; her biceps bulged from constant poling. Her dark golden-red hair refused to be tamed by the long braid down her back, constantly escaping its fetters and flying around her face. Her feet had never known shoes.

And although her lifemate, and recently that rascal Vissa, marveled at the expanse of her chest, she knew it would be too… much for a cultured Royal.

Yet when she stared defiantly at him the look on his face told her he liked what he saw.

Oh sure, thought Mahri, something different. A peasant water-rat that had dock-side language and fish clothes. If he'd passed her in the street, he'd sweep his robes aside to keep them from getting sullied. Well, she was just as good as any silk-attired, powdered-faced court lady, whether he knew it or not.

He stepped closer and she could smell him again. That indefinable scent that made her want to crawl into his skin.

With a gasp of surprise she sagged to the deck. The root in her veins had spent itself and the pain from her injuries, and the overdose, made her whimper. Jaja had hopped down when she collapsed and chattered up at Korl in accusation.

"I'll take care of her," he assured her pet.

Mahri gritted her teeth. "I don't need taking care of," she ground out.

Korl ignored her and picked her up, which set the boat to rocking and almost capsized them into the channel. Mahri would've vented her disgust at him but her traitorous body had already responded to his arms around her. She instinctively snuggled her face into his neck, remembering the sight of him shaking his hair. The muscles in his arms tightened shellhard but his skin felt soft and warm, radiating a spicy scent.

She melted into him and would have been horrified if he'd recoiled from her reaction. But he didn't. Korl just froze with her in his arms, the boat gliding down the narrow channel, the soft swish of the current and their harsh breathing the only sound in the sudden stillness of the morning.

"I believe that you don't know S'raya," he whispered in her ear. "But I definitely don't trust you."

Mahri groaned inwardly at the sound of his voice when it gentled. The hair rose on the back of her neck at the feel of his breath against her ear. "Nor I, you."

"But we need each other," he continued. "Even if you're telling the truth, S'raya will take advantage of my absence. She's enlisted a Master Seer—I felt his filthy

Touch from that warrior's ship—and she'd be stupid if she didn't try to make her move now."

"Mmhhm," agreed Mahri, not knowing what he spoke of, not particularly caring as long as he continued to hold her and this feeling that shivered through her went on.

"I don't suppose," he mused, "That you'd return me to the city—get another Healer?"

She went rigid in his arms.

He sighed. "I didn't think so." He took the few careful steps over to the narwhal tent and gently laid her in it. Their eyes met, pale to dark, and his hands lingered on hers. "I know I'm right about one thing—you are a Master, aren't you?"

Mahri shrugged.

"Why don't you heal your own people?"

She bit her lip then sighed. "All the Power, all the zabba, but none of the knowledge."

"Of course," he replied, all arrogance. "A Wilding! Amazing though, that the Seer Tree Masters haven't captured, er, discovered you before this."

She feebly pushed his hands off her own. "Yes, amazing isn't it?"

And how long, she wondered, is it going to take you to realize that I can't ever bring you home? That I could never trust you enough? Even if you didn't remember the location of the village, you could still describe *me* to them, a Wilding with non-Royal blood that can tolerate the root to a Master level. They'd hunt me down and kill me, for not only must they control the supply of root but those who can use it as well.

Then an alien voice sounded in Mahri's mind,

something about the Prince of Changes… that he must rule and she had to help make that happen. Stop it, she told herself. It was only a dream.

Korl rose to his feet, fished some of her zabbaroot from her pouch that still lay down his hip. "The quicker we get to your village, the quicker I can heal your people and return to the Palace Tree, right?"

She nodded up at him again, watched in fascination as the tiny curls at the corners of his mouth fleshed out into a full smile. A shallow cleft appeared in his cheek, his nose tilted up even more, and small wrinkles radiated from the corners of his eyes. When would she stop noticing every little detail about him?

"I can help Heal you again," he said, popping a small piece of root into his mouth. He hesitated a moment. "Or I can hurt you even more, force you to tell me the way out of this maze of a swamp, back to the city."

Mahri felt her heart stop. A skilled Healer could inflict creative types of pain, with little damage to their victim. But only a Dark Seer would dare such a thing, and she'd thought—no she *knew* he wasn't of that ilk. Besides, she'd endure whatever it took to save what was left of her family from the agonies of the plague. Again, she really had no choice.

"Hurt me," she said, her gaze locked on his, challenging him to do it. His eyes flashed with sparks of Power and a quick rage. He leaned over her and she couldn't be sure what he intended to do, yet still when he ran his hands over her body she responded, arching her back towards him, groaning at the shafts of pain that resulted from the movement. The anger faded from his face to be replaced with that indefinable something that existed between them.

And the pain ceased, to be replaced with the warmth of his touch. His large hands moved up her abdomen, across her ribs, slowly inched higher with the definite absence of a Healer's dispassionate touch. A moan rose from the back of her throat. She thrust her breasts at him when she felt the warmth of his hands cover them and heard him gasp in response.

His fingers trembled up to her neck. He traced the strong curve of her jaw and the sweep of her nose then plunged his hands into her hair, jerking her face up to meet his. This time when their lips met, it wasn't a slow, gentle touch. Hot, soft flesh met her own with a fierceness that left her weak, aware that she'd wanted to taste him in this way, but unable to match his strength. The root, and his touch, combined to sap what remaining stamina she had.

And he did hurt her. His mouth ground into hers with numbing force, his tongue plunged into her mouth again and again. Mahri tried to respond, frustrated that she couldn't, for she wanted to hurt him back. It felt incredibly good.

Korl let her go so abruptly that her head snapped backwards. She would've taught him a new dockside curse but for the look on his face. A drowning man coming up for air. He sat back on his heels, let that mask of arrogance he constantly adopted fall back over his features.

"That shouldn't have happened," he said, avoiding her gaze. Korl rose to his feet, hands fisted at his sides. "And won't again—I promise."

Is that right? wondered Mahri. The High Born Prince shouldn't have lowered himself to kiss a filthy water-rat? As if it weren't already hard enough to resist him, now he'd thrown a challenge like that at her! As her body gave in to exhaustion, she vowed to see how easy it would be to break the promise of a prince.

Chapter 4

MAHRI BECAME AWARE OF KORL'S WHISTLED TUNE and pretended to continue sleeping just so he wouldn't stop. She'd never heard such a melody before, the rise and fall totally unlike a dockside chanty, the low tones of it making her shiver. The soft splash of his paddling blended with the rhythm of it, and although she felt the urgency of her task she hurt all over, and didn't open her eyes until she felt a soft brush against her cheek.

She blinked when another gentle something fell across her brow, attempted to flick it away but her muscles were still too weak. Mahri lay still while clouds of white petals rained from the branches above, covering her with a blanket of soft perfume.

The whistling stopped. "What kind of flowers are those?" asked Korl.

"How should I know," replied Mahri. "I've never seen anything like them before."

She studied the vines overhead, the way they twisted and snaked from one tree to another, creating a tunnel out of the channel they drifted through. Thousands of large buds hung from every lavender vine, pulsing out balls of pure white which exploded into flowers that dropped their petals before they could hit the surface of the water.

The faded sunshine that filtered through the branches told Mahri that she'd slept most of the day, and since the flowers didn't seem to pose an immediate threat she concentrated instead on just standing up.

"Jaja," she muttered. The little monk-fish scampered to her side, batting at the petals with obvious delight. "Root," she told him. He splayed his empty webbed hands in front of her face.

Mahri frowned. "What d'you mean, you can't find any?"

Jaja spun and pointed an accusing finger at the prince.

She looked at him and he raised an eyebrow. "You're not getting anymore," he said, and patted the bulging pouch that still hung at his hip. "I'll get us to the village, you just show me the way."

"Nobody gives me orders," snapped Mahri, and with a surge of anger managed to lift her upper body off the deck, tumbling a pile of whiteness into her lap.

Korl regarded her as if she were some rude courtier. "I just gave you a command and expect you to follow it. If you won't respect that coming from your prince, then consider it advice from your Healer."

"I don't need your advice. I don't need anyone telling me what to do."

He laid down the paddle and crossed his arms over his chest, catching petals of white in their crook. "Everyone's got someone telling them what to do, even a prince. What makes you think you're so special?"

He's patronizing me, thought Mahri, like I'm some kind of spoiled brat. And her anger at this man who'd grown up with everything she lacked loosened her tongue. "I grew up on the water, had only my father to guide me until I was ten. Then even he left me and I was on my own. With no one to tell me what to do."

Korl looked taken aback, his arms fell loosely to his sides, scattering his own bounty of flowers. "What about this village? Don't you have family there?"

"My lifemate's," she murmured. "For a time, I did have someone who cared enough to try and tell me what to do."

But not for long, Mahri thought. Not long enough to get used to that sensation, to appreciate it. So that when it was gone she could only feel relief at being free again. And a terrible guilt because of that feeling.

Korl's face reddened and the curls at the edges of his mouth turned downward. "I've had plenty of people telling me what to do, but that doesn't necessarily mean they cared. In the palace everyone has a hidden agenda."

Mahri's arms trembled and she sank back. This conversation had become dangerously intimate and she'd end it now. "I can't even move. I just need enough zabbaroot to stand and pole." She truly hated justifying her actions to anyone. She blew petals away from her mouth. "You have to save your Power for Healing the village. I'll make sure we get there." It was absurd, really, that he thought she'd put her trust in him. He'd never even been in the swamps much less navigated through their dangers.

Korl stood, put his hands against his lower back and arched it, his eyes closed against the falling whiteness. Mahri groaned. He looked like some god accepting homage from the heavens.

Quit trying to distract me, she thought.

He looked down at her and grinned, as if he knew exactly what she was thinking. "If you chew anymore root you won't make it to the village."

Conceited… "I didn't know you cared," she snapped.

He came over and squatted down next to her. "You're my only way out of this swamp—you bet I care."

Mahri refused to be caught in his gaze and instead watched Jaja pile up mounds of petals then gleefully dive into them. Of course he doesn't care, she chastised herself. You kidnapped him, put his life in danger, forced him to do your will. Worse, an ignorant little water-rat had done it!

Korl sighed and looked up over the bow. "Still, it'd be a shame if you didn't see this."

Mahri stared down the smooth line of his throat, to where the top of his spider-silk shirt had been torn open. She wondered idly if the rest of his chest was also speckled with dark-gold hair.

"Here, monk-fish," he called, his chest rising and falling with each word. Mahri swallowed hard.

Jaja managed to look indignant at the way he'd been summoned but hopped to the man's side anyway. Her pet accepted a small piece of root and held it over Mahri's mouth. She opened and wondered why Korl hadn't just given it to her himself, until she saw him swallow. Hard. With a grin she accepted the piece of tuber, wrapping her tongue around it, closing her mouth ever so slowly. He reached out and traced the outline of her lips with a finger that trembled. Mahri grinned wider and crunched the root.

He jerked back like he'd been struck, shook his head as if to clear it. Mahri tried to rise to her feet, accepted his hand when he offered it and stood close beside him, using his body to anchor herself. Their eyes met, almost on a level, and he looked away down the length of the channel. She followed his gaze, acutely aware of the heat of his body.

She gasped and felt him grin in response. The lavender vines wove walls between the trees, a ceiling over the snaking passageway of the water. Those exploding buds grew tightly layered together and masses of white flowers flew from every direction. The farther they drifted down the channel, the thicker the cloud became. The stronger the perfume. Mahri filled her lungs and lifted her face, felt the barest breath of a touch from each downy-soft petal.

"It's beautiful," she sighed.

Korl's voice sounded very close, compellingly deep with emotion. "Yes, beautiful," he agreed. But when she turned to face him he wasn't looking down the tunnel of white, but at her. "Beautiful," he repeated, his voice gentled to a whisper but intense with desire.

His hand rose, with aching slowness, and he brushed her wayward hair from her cheek, his fingertips burning like fire against her skin. Mahri reflexively turning her head into his palm, cradling it there with a silent moan. She watched him through her lashes, through the white down that fell between them.

"I don't even know you," he said, his hand dropping to his side, the absence of his palm a cold ache on her skin.

"Nor I you." And Mahri dropped her staff, set her own palms on his shoulders, the muscles hard beneath the pads of her fingers. The silk of his shirt bunched, then dropped with a sigh as she slid her hands toward his neck, reached beneath that pale-gold hair, curled it around her fingers. So incredibly soft.

His head lowered and her mouth rose to meet his of its own accord. "Yet," he breathed, his lips so close she could feel their heat. "It feels like I've known you forever."

Mahri inhaled, pulled his breath deep into her own lungs, relished the thought of that mingling even as she closed the gap between them, met the firm softness of his mouth. Dry warmth, wet heat, she strove toward him, aware of nothing but this furious need to taste, touch, crush him to her.

As if a rope had snapped she felt him move, his hands grip her lower back, pull her hard against him, smashing the falling petals between their joined bodies, releasing a fresh wave of perfume. Mahri ground her hips into his in response and he groaned, the sound rumbling through her own chest, making her smile beneath his mouth.

She arched her back and he followed, lowered her to a bed of flowers, ground his own hardness against her. He thrust his tongue into her mouth and she stroked it with her own, fevered, hungry for all of him. When he ripped away from her lips and tasted the skin on her cheek, trailed the hot fire of his mouth to her ear, she tried to follow, grazing the side of his face. In the madness of her desire she plunged her tongue into his ear, felt him shudder and impale her in the same way.

An inarticulate cry tore from her throat and he pulled back and stared at her. She could only pant as they gazed at one another, transfixed by the reflected mania of their desire.

"Who are you?" he demanded, looking at her as if he could see into her very soul, search it for an answer.

Mahri didn't know what he meant, didn't care. "It

doesn't matter," she whispered, and ran her hands beneath the silk shirt across his back. Smooth hardness, coiled strength.

"Ahh, but it does." He smiled sadly, making the shallow dimple appear in his cheek. "Royals," he recited, "do not consort with water-rats."

Consort? Thought Mahri. He sounded so ridiculously pompous. "Not even to tumble?" she invited, still in the grip of her fired senses, ignoring his ridiculous words for the hunger that still emanated from his face.

His chin jut into air. "I do not 'tumble.'" Korl sat back on his heels, shook the hair from his face. That mask of arrogant hauteur settled again over his features and he lectured her as if she were an ignorant child. "A Royal, especially a prince, has to keep the line pure. It's our duty to strengthen the blood by producing children of master-level root tolerance."

Mahri sat up, slapping away the petals that covered her. "By-the-thirteen-moons who said anything about having kids?" Desire faded and was being replaced by fury. She just *had* to be physically drawn to an up-tight, morally-conscious… snob!

"Are you denying it's a possibility?"

Mahri made a strangled noise. "I've got more," she ground out, "root-tolerance in my little finger than all your simpering courtiers put together."

The man had the nerve to smile at her with feigned indulgence. "Aah, but you're a Wilding, a freak of genetics that can't be counted on to run true, like the original line of heredity."

Mahri shook her head. What had happened? One minute they were on their way to oblivion, and the next…

"You take things entirely too seriously, Prince Korl." And she made the word "prince" sound like a curse, and his handsome face fell into a frown. She paused a moment and thought, don't be too hard on him, he's only repeating what he's been taught.

"It's just that a prince can't waste himself on—" he began.

This time she did curse, a vile word that made him blush clear up to his headband. "Don't worry, oh-great-one, I barely sullied you!" she spat.

He froze, the arrogant mask dropped for a moment and Korl regarded her with lustfully curious speculation. "Really?"

Mahri choked, momentarily speechless, not knowing whether to laugh or scream. Then she stood utterly still, her mouth wide with horror. That he could make her forget all else…

"We're not moving," she cried, scrambling to her feet. "Why aren't we moving?"

Mahri looked over the bow of her craft. The vines had spent most of their buds, only a few late-bloomers remained. And flowers now choked the channel, huge mounds of white petals that mired their boat and slowed the current to a crawl. She spun. Except for the depression where she and Korl had lain, the boat overflowed with the white mass, and she dropped to her knees, searching for her bone staff.

"This is all your fault," she scolded.

"My fault?"

"Aya. Why couldn't you've been old and ugly?"

Korl quit searching for the paddle and stared at her in astonishment. "But most apprentice's are young."

"But you didn't have to be so handsome," she exclaimed, turning an accusing look on him. They both balanced on hands and knees, almost nose-to-nose. He didn't even have the good grace to look flattered, and Mahri could've bitten her tongue. His smirk told her he knew he was good-looking, enjoyed the fact that she thought so too. She gritted her teeth against the fury that boiled inside of her. He was so arrogant.

"And you," he drawled, that deep voice pitched to send shivers up her spine, "didn't have to be so provocatively... exotically... gorgeous."

Mahri reeled as if he'd slapped her. One minute he made her furious and the next he made her want to melt against him—and there he goes, she thought. He's doing it again. Making her forget everything but his existence.

"Jaja," she called, her gaze still trapped in his. "Where are you?"

A muffled squeak for an answer, and Korl's eyes released her, turned to watch the monk-fish's progression across the deck by the petals that puffed up from his movements. Another muffled, fairly disgusted squeak, and a brown ball of scales exploded from the whiteness, landing unerringly on Mahri's shoulder. With an almost human display of dignity, he brushed off any remaining petals from his scales.

Her hand touched bone and she pulled it from the fluff, stood and swung it with unnecessary force to beat the flowers out of her boat. Korl accomplished more with the paddle, and when the deck was relatively clear he looked up at her with a grin.

"Now what?"

Mahri opened her mouth to reply when something shook the boat, a tentative wiggle that didn't come from any current. Korl's grin faded and they both looked out across the expanse of white. Something fast, long—like a tentacle, yet not—speared through the water, snagged a mound of petals then disappeared with a quiet plop.

Mahri Saw into the water, down past the upper roots of the sea trees, her Vision dull with lack of root but able to discern the huge shape that lay around and underneath them. Her craft wobbled again.

"Do you See it?" she asked him, knowing that he'd taken more zabba than her, hoping her own Sight proved wrong.

But he shook his head. "I can barely make out the water, much less See anything in it." His brows drew together and he shrugged. "I don't understand it, it's like I'm in some kind of foreign land. I can't See the Patterns clearly and when I do they won't rearrange the way I want them to."

The boat rocked again, this time with enough force that they both squatted and grabbed a side of the hull.

"You have to use their nature when you Push, not bend them to your will. The swamps are young and vital." Mahri heard several "plops" around the boat. "It's not like the tame city that you're used to."

Korl flushed. "I didn't think it'd be this different."

"And I don't have time to give you lessons. Give me my pouch, Korl."

He shook his head, that golden hair catching the dying rays of the sun and throwing glints of light at her. "You can't push your tolerance this far. The next piece of root may be your last." He turned and began to paddle furiously. "Pole, water-rat!"

Mahri flicked her wrist and the bone retracted. "I can't pole, Korl. Don't you get it? The water here is open straight down to the bottomless sea." The boat suddenly shot straight up, plummeted so quickly she felt her stomach in her throat. "This creature's huge, straight from the deep, come up for a snack of petals. The swamps don't have all the thick, woven roots of the city trees. Sea beasts can break through them. Give me the pouch!"

Her craft near tipped over.

He quit paddling, turned to face her, his hand hovering near the pouch. Then his brows rose, his mouth dropped open, and Mahri felt a wet sticky rope wrap around her neck. Jaja lay trapped within that noose also, squashed against her ear, grunting with the effort of breathing. She tried to scream, only issued a strangled grunt before her feet left the deck, her bone staff falling from nerveless fingers. She hung in the air, her feet dangling a man's height above the deck, scrabbled at the slimy thing that choked her but couldn't break its hold.

Korl lunged for her legs and she tried to kick him away. By-the-moons he's doing it again, she thought. Reacting before thinking about the risk to himself. Korl caught her legs, tried to pull her down, nearly hanging her for good in the process. She held on to the sticky thing, her bones cracking from the weight of the man as the monster flung her higher, then pulled her down into the water with a loud splash.

Prince Korl held onto her legs with stubborn strength.

Mahri closed her lids on the swirl of white petals, used the Power to See instead. Not enough root, and she'd have to use most of it to hang onto consciousness for lack of air, but in her panic she Saw clearly their destination, the black mouth-slits that the beast stuffed the petals into. That they'd be stuffed into.

It's a tongue, she realized. That's what's wrapped around my neck and it's bringing us to the beast's mouths. She could See thousands of the slimy things, wiggling through the water's Pattern. Think, think.

The water roared past her ears.

Tongues are sensitive, she thought. Well, at least human ones are, but Korl had her bone knife because he had her belt. And the surface of this thing felt tough as mosk-leather.

Suddenly the drag stopped, her ears rang in the silence as the creature's tongue hesitated for a moment.

Perhaps he's full, wondered Mahri with maniacal hope. The lack of oxygen's making me giddy. And what's that Royal doing anyway?

He crept up her body, hugging her closely, never releasing more than one hand at a time from his hold on her. She'd be covered with finger-bruises.

He locked his legs around her waist when he reached it, his hands finally letting go of that punishing grip. Mahri's eyes flew open. Through the darkness she could make out the pale strands of his hair waving like grass in the wind, the fist of his hand around her knife as it plunged forward. The tongue jerked down again and Korl flew backward, his legs like a vise around her waist, holding on, then they were flung in the opposite direction and he slammed into her body.

Mahri's grip slackened. Too much, all this squeezing and pummeling. Her lids drifted down, she reached out almost lazily with the Power and the most amazing thing happened. She Touched the beast, not just the Pattern of its body but that of its mind. Like the native, she thought, in my dream. *And maybe this is a dream, so why not let us go, sea beast? Dreams are too insubstantial to make a good dinner.*

And she drifted free, only the arms of Korl now held her, pushed her back to the surface of the water, dragged her into the boat and forced the water from her lungs. Mahri breathed in the perfume of bruised petals and wondered if she still dreamt.

"Jaja?" she whispered from a throat too painful to be anything but reality. No chattering reply and she opened her lids to see Korl searching the boat.

"Where?" he asked, then cursed one of Mahri's favorite words and flinched in self-disgust. "You are a bad influence, water-rat." He stood, swayed just a moment, and dove over the side of the boat.

He took my pouch with him, thought Mahri, too tired to be angry, unaware that she'd even fallen asleep until the splash of rain in her face woke her up. How long had she been out? Moonlight glowed inside her empty boat and the feeling she had in her chest made her want to scream beneath the weight of it.

"Korl!" Silence. She didn't notice her tears that mingled with the rain. "Jaja!"

A tiny squeak of acknowledgment. She let out a ragged breath, saw the fingers that clutched the edge of her craft and crawled over to where Korl's body floated in the water, his pale hair haloed around his head. Jaja tried to squirm out of his arm but the man held him with the same frozen grip he had on the boat.

"Prince Korl, let Jaja go." He didn't answer her, seemed to be in some kind of stupor. How long had he been floating there, anyway? She tried to peel away his fingers, gave up and jumped into the water next to him. She could still hear the plops of those feeding tongues amid the patter of rain and hurriedly untied her belt from around Korl's waist.

Mahri had to swim to the other side of the boat so that it wouldn't tip over when she climbed in, barely escaped another seeking tongue and swore under her breath. She opened the fish-scale pouch and selected a large piece of the zabba and eagerly chewed it, gagged, shuddered, amazed at how the Power now flew through her system.

It seemed that the coma had changed her in more ways than one. Her pathways seemed enlarged, able to let greater Power flow through her. She could still remember the pain when she'd had her first bite of zabba, when the poison had forged the beginnings of small pathways to her brain. She'd thought she hadn't the immunity to the poison, that she might die like so many others who'd tried the root. Instead, after that first initial agony, she'd felt the changes in her head, the chemical reaction that allowed her to really See the world around her.

The overdose of root had felt the same. Only now her pathways had enlarged and Mahri Saw things that she didn't know anyone was capable of Seeing. Like other minds.

She repressed a shudder of terror for the unknown, and with the ease of long practice, banished the unwelcome speculations of her altered condition from her thoughts.

Mahri tied the belt around her waist, more confident with its familiar weight around her, and retrieved her bone staff. Saw into the water, Pushed it under Korl and hauled him aboard. She managed to release Jaja from his clutches and between the two of them, dragged the prince into the narwhal tent. Then she carefully Saw into Korl.

He's only tired, she decided. And assured of his recovery she roiled the water and propelled her boat through the clogged channel, wondering about how much easier it seemed, the Power in her system barely tapped by the Seeing.

When they emerged from the flower-tunnel the channel narrowed; the now unhindered rain flooded the half of her boat not protected by the tent. Mahri bailed, continued to Push the current, and sang the bawdiest chanty she knew. The downpour shrank to a light mist and as she reached for the pouch again a pale head emerged from the tent.

"Food," the prince demanded. "Water."

She had Jaja fetch her journey sack while she reached for more root, stilled when he spoke again. "Another of the dangers from zabba is that it kills your appetite—and eventually you. From starvation. Eat, Mahri."

So they sat together and ate by the glow of the moons, and drank fresh rainwater from the buckets attached to the boat for that purpose.

"That's the second time," she said, noting the damp and tattered condition of his clothes, "that you've rescued my monk-fish. You don't need him to get home. So why'd you do it?"

Korl frowned, his face all soft angles in the moonlight, and answered without hesitation. "Why wouldn't I?"

And Mahri knew then that he was a dangerous man, that she'd have to be very careful. He was of that rare breed that not only seduced the body, but also the heart.

Chapter 5

MAHRI CONTINUED TO SEE INTO THE CURRENT AT occasional intervals, to nudge it along, make sure they followed the water's path and protect her boat from any obstructions. Before the coma, that would've taken all of her concentration, and she tried not to wonder at her capacity for the Power now.

She'd never heard of anyone surviving a zabba-wrought coma, although many had taken the root to their death. Some were more immune than others, Wildings like herself, and of course the Royals—that carefully cultivated line of heredity. Most had such a low tolerance level that they could See into the nature of things but not Push or Alter them; some could do small magics, and most would die from even the smallest piece of zabba. So, as Korl would say, what made her so special?

Cool rain misted her face and the interlaced branches above cleared to give her an unobstructed view of the evening sky. Stars glittered like morning dew around the moons, small and bright.

Could her dream have had some truth? Did her people come from the sky and settle on this planet like tribal wanderers? And if so, where had her ancestors come from—those twinkling lights or even the moons? How powerful they must've been to fly from place to place!

The branches crowded together again and ended her stargazing. She could hear Korl's gentle snores with an occasional nasal squeak from Jaja within the tent, the rolling of the water, and the constantly changing song of the forest.

Mahri knew this to be her reality—how it had come to be didn't matter. Yet, why would she dream such a thing? And if it wasn't a dream... could the natives have helped her to survive the overdose so that she'd help this prince to rule? And why her—and forget about being the other half of someone's soul. That had to be nonsense.

Mahri groaned aloud. Her head ached from all this thinking, stupid really, since she didn't have any answers for anything that had happened to her since she'd kidnapped a prince from his bed. Like why a sensible woman like herself could act so ridiculous over a handsome man. She'd never acted this way around Vissa. He was undeniably attractive; a prosperous tavern keeper who had a charmingly crooked smile and tempting rakish eyes. Mahri acknowledged his appeal, might even have felt herself tempted once or twice, but had never succumbed to his single-minded pursuit of her. She was too level-headed, too independent. She didn't want to be tied to anyone ever again.

Mahri's thoughts came to an abrupt halt when she Sensed deep water below. She didn't like what had come up through it the last time and thank-the-moons she had plenty of root now. She Saw into the water and recoiled from the barrage of colors that exploded in her Sight. She quickly readjusted and blinked at the water with normal vision. And gasped at the wonder of it.

For the water glowed in clouds of multi-colored light, in layers that spiraled down to a depth she couldn't even guess at. Plankton, she thought, but those of a peculiar phosphorescence. They didn't glow with the bright whiteness of a sun slug—those barnacled creatures that lived happily in a light globe—but with a muted rainbow of gleaming sparkles.

A display like none she'd ever witnessed before, Mahri stood in transfixed delight for so long she felt dizzy from the sheer pleasure of it.

This is why I'm a water-rat, she told herself. To live on a boat, not up in the trees, and to be a discoverer of so many of the sea's treasures. She couldn't wait to get to the village, to tell Caria of this new phenomenon, to see the delight on her sister-in-life's face as they racked their minds to name this new…

Mahri shook her head and clenched her fists. If she's still alive. *If I reach her in time. Brez and Tal'li had counted on me, too. I watched them die and a part of me felt relief that I'd be free again, with only myself to worry about. Ach! Can my selfish need for independence be threatened by even this sister-friend?*

"Stop it," she said through clenched teeth, her hand inching toward her pouch. Mahri dug out a handful of root and bit it with furious determination. She'd never wanted her lifemate and son to die—she'd loved them! And she'd save Caria this time regardless of the cost. The flow of Power made her spasm and slam into the deck with bruising force, her muscles convulsing in sudden uncontrollable jerks.

"Water-rat?" mumbled Korl sleepily, the husky timbre of his voice making her shiver even harder. "What did you do?"

She opened her eyes and the sparks of Power that emitted from them reflected off of Korl's face, made

him sit back on his heels and shake his head in horror.
"Woman, you've done it this time."

Mahri crossed her arms, tried to hold herself together
by hugging tightly. "Then don't let me waste it," she
stammered. Her teeth chattered like it was the cold season, instead of the warm. "Help me up."

Jaja scampered up her chest, stroked her face with his
webbed hand and made a low crooning noise. For just
a moment Mahri could swear she heard his thoughts as
clearly as she had during her dream: *No, no spirit-friend.
Can't help you with so much Power. Crazy, crazy friend.*

"Jaja, I'm not crazy. The only thing that matters is
getting to the village in time."

The monk-fish's soft brown eyes widened in surprise.
He put his tiny black nose close to Mahri's face. *You
hear me thinking to you, spirit-friend?*

"Aya," she breathed, "just like in my dream."

Her pet splayed his fingers over his face, covering
it with webbing. *You shouldna' be able to. No-no
ready, friend.* And it felt as if a wall of black slammed
down between them and she could again only sense
Jaja's feelings.

"Help me up," she repeated to Korl, as he stood staring down at the two of them, his mouth agape, his pale
hair agleam in the moonlight.

"You were talking to him," he said. "I mean, not just
you talking to him, but like he was talking to you, too."

"You're babbling, Prince."

With hands that trembled he wiped rainwater from
his brow. "It's not possible. Nobody can See into another mind unless they're Bonded, nobody can wield
the kind of Power you have. I'm going to ask you again

and this time I want a straight answer." He took a deep, steadying breath. "Who are you?"

Mahri's head pounded with waves of untapped Power, although thankfully the convulsions had stopped. She was a fool, yes, to take this much root. Her immunity to the poison could only go so far. But she didn't want to live if she failed her family this time, so it wasn't the dying that scared her, but the Power-changes that had happened to her since the coma. That they might be permanent, that she'd be this powerful for the rest of her life. The thought frightened her, because with great power came great responsibility and that's something she'd never purposely seek. "I'm just a water-rat, Prince. And as scared as you are by what's happening to me. I can't hear him anymore, if that makes you feel any better."

He must have read the genuine fear in her face and for some reason that reassured him, because he adopted his superior attitude and raised one pale eyebrow. "Of course, just a temporary anomaly, probably from the accumulation of so much root in your system."

Reassured by his own superior logic, he bent over and picked her up, set her on her feet. Mahri swayed like the breeze, so the man stood behind her, his chest pressed to her back, his arms wrapped around her to hold her steady. His breath stirred the curls of her dark red hair as he spoke again, as if to himself. "I could do a thesis on this. 'The Aberrant Affects on Root Overdosage' by Healer Prince Korl. I like the sound of that."

Mahri understood about half of what he said as she melted against him. He felt deliciously warm.

"Wait a minute." He stiffened. "You can't—you've never heard my thoughts, have you?"

"No," murmured Mahri, her fingers raking through the hair on his arms. "But I've heard your body."

Power whipped through her like bolts of lightning, her every nerve afire, her skin sensitive to the slightest of touches. It made his nearness practically unbearable. All he has to do, she thought, is come near me and I can't think of anything else but getting closer. I just have to have him—all of him—and then maybe this craziness will stop.

Korl turned her in his arms and impaled her with those mesmerizing eyes. "What do you mean, you can hear my body? Are all Wildings as powerful as you?"

"I don't need the Power to hear it." Mahri stared, could see the fear in his face. No, she couldn't hear his thoughts but she could imagine them well enough. If there were other Wildings like herself hidden in the swamps, what a threat that would be to the Royal line's dominance. For if they banded together, they'd have a good chance of defeating even the Royal's numbers, invading the Seer's Tree, learning the guarded knowledge, allowing access to the root to any that could tolerate it. A Royal's worst nightmare.

Mahri then knew for certain that she could never let him return home. He'd start a Hunt like the one that had taken her mother; with his tales of her Power, his fears that there could be more like her. But she knew of no other Wildings like herself. It'd taken her years of exposure to the root to attain the level of tolerance she had for it now and most of the zabba she'd eaten this trip belonged to the village. She'd used it because it would save their lives, and although they'd lack for food and warmth in the cold season, at least they'd be alive to see it.

Mahri grimaced. "I know of no other Wildings, and by the time we reach the village even I will probably cease to be. Like you said, Prince, I'm a freak of nature, not likely to be repeated anytime soon. And as for hearing your body," she snaked her hands down the ridges of his chest, circled them around his waist to his lower back, slowly inched down until they rested on the sloping curve of his bottom. "I hear what any woman would when a man wants her." And with a brazenness that reflected in her olive-colored eyes she caressed those mounds of muscle, tight beneath their thin layer of silk, pushing them towards her, grinning when she felt his hardened response.

Korl froze. "You're purposely baiting me."

"Aya."

"Do you mind telling me why?"

Because I can't help it, thought Mahri. Because every time you come within touching distance, I just have to touch. "We of the lower classes," she replied, "Handle a physical attraction like we do all other things."

"And that is?" He stepped back, moonlight playing around the tightness of his curled lips, those round eyes narrowed to slits. She'd insulted him, somehow.

Mahri shrugged. "We let it happen. Let it burn itself out, then go back to work."

"But what if," he growled, "it doesn't burn itself out? What if," and he took a menacing step towards her, "the flame just gets hotter, and you just want more? And more?" His voice lowered to a huskiness that made her blink. He traveled the same path with his hands that she had earlier but cupped her bottom, lifted her off the deck, and with harsh angry movements rubbed her against him.

Undaunted, Mahri wrapped her legs around his back and grinned. "But then you're talking love, Great Prince, and we both know that between us, it's an imposs…" She grabbed her head.

"What is it?"

"Hush, let me See." For although she'd had little difficulty maintaining their passage through the channel with her Power, as if to Push had become as natural as breathing, this new ability to See into the thoughts of creatures demanded her full attention. And she dared not say anything to Korl about it.

Slow thoughts reached her. Contented peace, a wisdom that could be detected but not understood, a language that could be interpreted just barely in her own words.

"A narwhal," she breathed.

Korl peeled her off his body and spun. "Where? There's no place big enough for it to be beached."

Mahri sagged to the deck, her head still held in her hands. She couldn't tell him that the whale lay far below in deep ocean, too far to See its body but not its thoughts. The only time a narwhal could be seen was when it blew a spout on the open sea, or dying, washed amongst the trees like a mountain of black oil. What would he think if she told him she could hear one of the great beasts? He'd called her a freak and although she'd never admit it the remark had stung.

"No, I meant my tent. My narwhal tent. I need to lay down."

He looked at her with sudden concern. "A little zabba, Mahri. Let me Heal you, if I can."

At least it would keep him occupied so she nodded, offered a tiny bit of root and let him See into her while she communed with the great creature. It swam far down the roots of the trees, sucked up the glowing plankton in a lazy, contented way, made clicking sounds to its brethren. There were more. Mahri shuddered.

"The root's already taken care of your bumps and bruises," Korl murmured. "But there's so much Power in you I can barely See further. There's—something." He sat on his heels and shook his head. "You've developed new pathways, I've never seen anything like it, and I couldn't mess with them, anyway. Your nerve endings are traumatized—I've repaired as best I can, but expect the shakes."

Mahri barely heard his words, instead she concentrated on pulling away from the creatures below. They knew the leviathans! Those ancient ones that left their bones within the trees. Bones that could only be shaped by the Power, that were stronger than any substance known, that seemed, at times, to retain the life of their owner. She shuddered again. She was an ignorant water-rat. She'd have no connection with such as those, no matter how remote.

Jaja suddenly snatched up her braid and played with the shells in her hair, whipped the dark red rope around and tickled her nose with the bottom strands of it. She looked up and although he scampered playfully, making Korl laugh, she saw the serious looks he threw her way, the question in those alien eyes.

Why can't I hear you anymore, she thought at him. *Yet I can hear the narwhal, and even the small pathetic mind of a sea slug. It's getting worse, the noise. And I can't stop the Seeing. Help me!* And she felt another black wall slam across her mind, this time blocking all thoughts from her Power. She hadn't even been aware of the tiny mind flicks of the plankton, the crazed hunger of a night stalker, the slow preponderance of a seastar, the contented thoughts of roosting nightwings. Until they stopped. Mahri breathed a sigh of relief.

"Feel better now?" Korl asked, as if his healing were responsible for the sudden lack of tension in her shoulders.

Mahri nodded, locked gazes with her monk-fish. She'd always thought of him as her pet, albeit a particularly sensitive one, the way he seemed to respond to her needs and desires. Yet the black wall—she knew Jaja had done it, had not just sensed her thoughts but read them as clearly as if she'd spoken aloud. And had the Power to block them for her.

Too many questions festered in her mind. Monk-fish chose their masters, not the other way around and although not particularly rare, their companionship was much sought after. Why had he chosen her? He'd called her a spirit-friend, what did that mean? She couldn't deny that she'd read his thoughts until he'd created that wall, couldn't deny that he read hers, even now. It frightened her, somehow, like he'd been spying on her. But to what purpose?

"It wasn't a dream," she murmured.

Jaja patted her face, nodded with slow deliberation and then climbed onto the triangle of wood on the bow, occasionally glancing back at her with forlorn looks of apology.

"What's that?" asked Korl, pointing at the plankton that had risen to the surface thick as soup, their colorful radiance lighting the channel far through the trees.

Mahri rose to her feet. "Tiny, glowing sea creatures. A ribbon of light."

"I don't suppose there's another monster lurking around to feed off it, right?"

She stared at him, afraid he knew about the narwhal, but his lips were curled into a smile and so she just laughed. "I hope not." Their shoulders touched and he jerked away as if stung.

"It's a little late," said Mahri, "to be insulted by the touch of a water-rat."

Korl shook his head. "It's not that, it's just... well, I think it'd be better if we just didn't touch each other, that's all."

Mahri grinned.

He continued to stare in wonder at the glowing water. "The swamps aren't what I'd imagined. They're dangerous, yes. Certainly uncivilized. But beautiful, too."

She felt an unreasonable surge of pride. He'd grown up in a palace, surrounded by the finest beauty that Power could fashion. She'd grown up on a boat; ignorant, poor, and for most of her life, powerless. Yet at this moment she felt their place in the world to be equal, that her advantages could somehow match his.

Mahri couldn't help it. The Power thrummed inside of her, hammering to be free, only a trickle needed to keep her craft moving forward, the barest thread used to Seek familiar waters. She raised her hands, Saw into the glowing water, and Pushed.

Pillars of rainbow-hued water grew to staggering heights beside them and flanked their progression down the passage. Erupting fountains of light threw showers of glittering droplets, balls of color burst from the water

and exploded high above them, thin streams of mist
curled in fanciful shapes through and between the sparks
of lavender, ruby and emerald.

Korl crossed his arms over his chest and raised an
eyebrow at her. "Not bad."

Jaja hopped up and down, clapped his hands in delight. An occasional fish or crab would be thrown from
the swirling water onto the deck and he'd investigate,
munching with relish or throwing the catch overboard
with disdain.

Mahri stalked the man, grabbed his hand when he tried
to pull away, and flung it into the air with her own. A
narwhal grew from the glowing mist of water, its mouth
opened and the boat traveled into it, surrounded by colorful ribs. A sea flower waved its graceful, deadly, sting-
ers at them. A phoenix burst from the water, its feathers
gleaming scarlet fire that consumed it into a drizzle of
rain. A skulker formed and opened its huge maw, closing
onto the bow in a shower of exploding light.

She dropped his hand but he wouldn't let go. His
mouth, that full bottom lip, hung slightly open and when
he pulled her against him she could feel the hammering
in his chest. His skin sparkled with reflected light…

"You're just like your swamp," he breathed.
"Beautiful—and dangerous."

Her lips sought his of their own accord and he responded, but too tenderly, beyond a mere physical desire,
and Mahri almost melted against that unexpected onslaught
of affection. Then she froze in sudden terror. He pulled his
lips from hers but still held her tightly. "What is it?"

"Look behind you."

He glanced over his shoulder. "What?"

Mahri let the water fall back into the channel with a sudden splash. She couldn't be sure what scared her the most; that look on his face or the natives that watched them from the bank. "Don't you see them?"

Korl turned, kept his arm around her waist. "I don't see anything but the blackness of the trees."

"But they're standing right there!"

Natives lined the stream, watched them from no more than a stone's throw away, and they wore clothes just like the speaker in her dream, and nodded in obvious pleasure at the couple on the boat. Jaja had turned his attention to them also, waving in their direction as they passed.

Mahri Pushed against the black wall surrounding her mind that she'd so welcomed earlier, until a bare crack split it open. And she could hear them like the barest of whispers. *Don't see us, we're not here, don't notice us, look elsewhere…*

Korl put his hands against her cheeks and turned her face to his. "Are you all right?"

"You can't see them," she choked, "because they don't want you to. That's why they live among us and we don't even question their existence. Because they don't want us to."

His forehead crinkled and he frowned at her, the curls at the edges of his mouth now faint lines. "What're you talking about?"

"Don't you get it? They can manipulate our thoughts, make us see what they want." Mahri poked his chest with her finger. "They're making you fall in love with me."

Korl gripped her shoulders. "Who?"

Mahri pointed at the line of fur-scaled bodies. "The natives, of course!"

Korl raised an eyebrow and one corner of his mouth tipped dangerously upward. "And why would the natives want me to fall in love with you?"

"Because," said Mahri with exasperation, "They want me to help you rule."

He threw back his head and howled with laughter. "You?" he sputtered, "Help me to…" More laughter choked him. "A water-rat?"

She pushed him away and he fell to the deck, holding his stomach, still howling idiotically. Mahri faced the line of watchers and shook her fist at them. "I can see your thoughts," she yelled. "As easily as I can see you. I won't be manipulated, do you hear me?" And she roiled the water and the boat shot past them with a spray that drenched those not quick enough to dart back.

Mahri plunged them through the maze of passages, hoping she sped towards her village but just wanting to get away from *them*. Her craft bucked and tipped, for she could still hear the Royal chuckling and didn't care if he was thrown overboard or not. Jaja held on and whooped with delight, his fanned tail whipping like a banner, the fresh deluge of night rain not bothering him in the least.

They narrowly escaped two low-lying limbs when Korl pulled himself together enough to stagger to her side. "Water-rat," he shouted into the wind. "I'm sorry, I shouldn't have laughed at you."

The Power sang in her limbs and Mahri spurred the boat faster. The bow soared upward and Korl grabbed her waist with his hands to keep from tumbling backwards. As angry as she felt, she still welcomed the warmth of his fingers and fought to lean back against him. It felt so incredibly *right*.

Natives, she thought. But she still held that wall of black around her mind, had repaired the chink she'd broken before. So they couldn't be influencing her thoughts, making her feel this strange attachment to the man. But he had no such protection.

Korl tried again. "Mahri, listen. You've had so much root, it's possible you're hallucinating."

"You can only See true with the zabba," she shouted back.

"But you're a Wilding, with no discipline. Isn't it at least a possibility?"

"No."

Branches and vines slapped into the boat and Mahri used her bone staff to fend them off. Jaja had hunkered down beneath the bow, kept shaking his head and trying to catch her eye.

"It's all nonsense, Mahri. I'm not falling in love with you, okay?"

The boat slowed and she felt the sigh of his relief warm the top of her head. She turned in his hands and at that moment dawn broke, surrounding him in a cloud of soft golden light.

"Are you sure?" she demanded.

He put his palm over his heart. "I swear to you, I am absolutely not falling in love with you."

"But I thought I saw—in your eyes…"

And she saw it again, as the sun touched those faceted orbs and lit them with fire. But he shuttered them, that mask of arrogance fell over those perfect features, and he shook his hair back from his face. "Maybe a little lust, water-rat. But that's all."

Chapter 6

"Thank the-thirteen-moons," breathed Mahri.

Korl scowled. "It's not very flattering, you know, when a water-rat's grateful that a Royal *doesn't* love her."

She laughed, her face aglow, threw pole-strengthened arms around those broad shoulders and hugged him hard. To his credit he held the air in his lungs.

"No, it's not that," she laughed. "Although I'm relieved, but that doesn't mean what I told you about the natives isn't—oh, never mind. I've found the trail!"

Korl hadn't released her from her hug. "What trail?"

His eyes were bottomless depths of... "Stop looking at me like that. I've found the way to the village, a hint of familiar water." Mahri tried to wriggle out of his arms, gave up, and just turned to face the bow, his warm body pressed against her back. A small part of her marveled at his reluctance to let her go, how her own body tried to meld with his, despite the disparity of their minds and hearts.

She zealously followed that hint of the village, lost it once when it got overwhelmed with other water Patterns, but finally reached a channel that she recognized. "We've gone too far," she murmured. "I'll have to Push the water against its natural current." She tried to open her pouch when strong fingers wrapped around her own and squeezed.

Mahri sighed. "Listen, Great Healer, you've already told me I've taken enough root that I won't survive after we reach the village. So what's the point in stopping now?"

"How much zabba have you got left? How much am I going to need to Heal your people?"

He's got a point, thought Mahri. But we're far from the village and to Push against the current takes a lot of Power. She Saw into his hands and took control of his muscles, made them release her fingers so she could dig into the fish-scale pouch. She pulled forth root and ate.

"Stubborn wench," he growled into her ear. "Give me back my hands."

"Bossy brute," she flung back, shuddering from the bitter taste of the zabba. "I just did."

"Then how come they're running up the front of your vest, like they've a mind of their own?"

Mahri choked back a laugh and Pushed those wandering hands back down around her waist. Had she done that to his muscles unconsciously, or did Korl really have a sense of humor? "Stop it, I need to concentrate." And she forced the water to do her will, made it go against the natural flow and felt the enormous drain of Power.

This is what Royals do all the time, she thought. Shape things to their will regardless of the natural order. No wonder they require so much zabbaroot.

The sun crawled higher into the sky and she armed sweat from her face. Korl had taken up permanent residence behind her, as if he thought she'd collapse at any second, and only tore himself away to bring her a drink. At noon he forced her to eat and Mahri kept it down by sheer force of will, the normally bland dried fish and seaweed nut-cakes now too potent for her heightened taste buds.

She fought the current with the Power and her will, created wave after wave that flung them through the channels like porpoises arching above the water. They flattened to the deck several times to avoid low-lying tree limbs and Mahri spun the waves higher to flow over those they couldn't squeeze under. The Power drained from within her at an alarming rate, but when she tried to ingest more zabba her throat tightened up and she gagged it out.

The rays of sun that filtered through the canopy had begun to fade when they reached a passage thickly webbed with vines. Afraid to drain any more of her root reserves, Mahri fought an opening through the curtain by physical strength alone using her bone staff, almost crying with the need to get them through, for the boat had slowed against that barricade of plants.

Korl laid a gentle hand on her arm and grasped the staff, his forehead wrinkled with concern. "You look awful."

"Thanks."

"I meant tired. Let me help."

"No thanks."

"What're you trying to prove?" Korl's face flushed with exasperation, his mouth turned down and his eyebrows lowered. "Much to my father's regret, I consider myself a Healer first, prince second, and I'll be drowned before I'll watch someone kill herself, no matter what the reason."

Mahri stared at him through eyes dreamy with fatigue. His anger didn't bother her; if anything, it made her want to touch his brow to smooth away the lines, kiss his lips to take away the frown, caress the skin that flushed with such color. She sighed and lowered her head, knowing not to argue while she looked at him. Her mind always seemed to turn to mush.

"I'll atone for my sins in my own way," she said.

His voice softened to that husky timbre and her heart skipped a beat. "What sins?"

She felt the coiled strength in his fingers as he laid them under her chin and raised it, focused his brilliant gaze on her and seemed to see into her soul.

"Brez and Tal'li, my lifemate and child, died of a plague."

He sighed. "I see."

"No, you don't," she snapped. "You still don't get it. Just because I want to… just because I *want* you, doesn't make you any less an enemy. I don't need your help."

His brows rose nearly up to his headband with surprise. "Without my help you'd be fish-monster food."

"You saved me because you knew you needed me to get back home."

"And Jaja?"

Mahri pulled away from the heat of his fingers beneath her chin. "I haven't figured that out yet." She turned and started smacking away the vines, cursing between each blow of her staff. Everything between her and Korl had gone terribly wrong. They'd had to rely on and take care of each other and it'd created some kind of responsibility between them that she'd never desired. Now that they neared the end of their destination she needed to break that confining tie. But she didn't know how.

Mahri's arms had begun to tremble when Korl gently pushed her aside and fought the plants with the paddle, not even bothering to argue about it. She felt the onset of withdrawal like the weight of a narwhal dropped on her shoulders and sagged against the side of her boat. The root had almost wrung her dry, she could feel her very life force start to fade, and realized that Korl could be right. If the poison overwhelmed her immunity she might not survive this trip.

"Korl," she whispered. He turned to her and without a word traded paddle for staff. Mahri let him take it. She felt so very tired. When she started to resume his attack on the vines she placed a trembling hand on his arm, even that slight contact making both of them jump from the chemistry it created. It made her words all the more confusing, yet none the less true.

"It's not you, so much, that I despise. It's what you represent."

He flung back his hair, his face stiff with arrogant pride.

Mahri sighed. "You're a Healer, like the one that had refused to help me save Brez and Tal'li. And a prince, who denies the people their right to knowledge. And worse, a Royal, so fearful of losing their Power that they not only control the root but destroy any that may match their in-bred tolerance to it."

"And you," he countered, his deep voice laced with contempt, "are an ignorant water-rat, a Wilding and a smuggler of zabba—the worst kind of criminal."

"Aya. I am what you've made me."

And he stared hard at her, those brilliant green eyes clouded with conflicting emotions, as if he'd never questioned himself before and it confused him.

At least now we're even, thought Mahri.

He opened his mouth to speak when Jaja jumped on Mahri's shoulder and chattered excitedly, pointing his little scaled finger at the limbs above them. They both looked up into hundreds of pairs of soft, brown eyes peering down at them through the interlaced vines. Jaja grasped the nearest plant and scampered up it, his tail fanned wide. The humans watched with smiling fascination as Jaja embraced, then frolicked with his brethren, swinging from the vines, leaping into the water only to clamber up them again.

Then a heated discussion seemed to ensue, for the monk-fish surrounded Jaja and displayed their fanged teeth, shook fists at him, then nodded hundreds of tiny heads in reluctant acquiescence. Then the curtain of greenery parted before them like a slowly expanding tunnel, webbed hands pulling up each hanging vine.

Jaja swung on a vine back into the boat and settled on the bow, his chin in the air, and imperiously gestured at the humans to go forward with a curt wave of his hand.

Mahri met Korl's gaze for an instant, their differences forgotten as the chemistry between them snapped in the air when they smiled at each other. The shallow dimple appeared in his cheek and her heart tripled its beat as she stared at him in open-mouthed fascination. That pale, smooth skin crinkled at the corners of those eyes, that narrow nose wrinkled at the bridge and that full bottom lip curved in a tempting smile. Golden-white hair tumbled over his headband and she pushed it off his brow with a trembling hand.

"Criminal or not," he murmured, "you're quite simply the most fascinating creature I've ever known." And he captured her hand with his own, brought her fingers to his warm lips and kissed them.

He'd make a wonderful king, thought Mahri. With that charm his subjects would lay down their lives for him. And she wondered how much of his flattery had to do with his desire to return home. Did he think that she might fall in love with him and use it to control her? Did he actually confuse lust for love? She laughed and he smiled wider, flashing those even white teeth. Well, two can play at this game.

She brought his fingers to her own lips, kissed them in turn, but closed her teeth over his index finger and held it there, firm but gentle, and watched his eyes widen with alarm. Mahri's smile turned wicked and she closed her lips around the tip of his finger, to replace teeth with tongue. She sucked that part of him deep into her mouth, eased the pressure so that he started to pull out then sucked even harder, again and again, until his fascinated gaze began to smolder and he drew his lower body toward hers.

Two can play... but two also pay, thought Mahri as her lower half began to throb with the rhythm of her mouth. Jaja gave an impatient disgusted snort and she reluctantly released Korl, took back her staff, and began to pole by using the weight of her body to do it. She channeled the root left in her system to her own muscles, for although she could See she didn't have enough Power to Push, and she'd have to get them to the village with what little strength she could glean from her own abused body.

She glanced back at Korl only once. He stood frozen, staring through the trees, hands fisted at his sides and trembling with suppressed fury, as if he fought for control of his own body and it wouldn't, or couldn't, submit.

They reached a channel that flowed in the right direction and Mahri flicked her wrist, partially retracting the bone, and leaned on the staff. The sea trees grew larger here, not the size of the city's but their width at least ten times a man's height. Krizm vines grew in abundance along this route and she plucked a swollen globe, drank the sweetened water, then shared with Jaja and Korl.

Dedos lurked within the foliage, mimicking the plants, and when Korl reached to pluck one of that animal's globes she slapped his arm with her staff then poked at the one he'd chosen. It burst at the contact and the animal swarmed its vine-like arms around the globule, formed a hellish cage, and contracted shut. Sharp, thin tubes pierced the air, searching for its intended victim. A squeal of outrage, and the animal spread out again, dangling its own imitation bait among the krizms.

Korl flushed scarlet. "Thanks."

Mahri shrugged. How many times could you save someone's life, she wondered, and still not feel responsible for them?

"I guess I'm the ignorant one, after all," he laughed in self-deprecation, then straightened those broad shoulders. "At least in the swamps."

Mahri knew that they'd come from different worlds but only now realized what a wide gulf that was. "You're as out of place here as I would be at court."

He raised an eyebrow, as if picturing her in that very place. Then grinned.

Her little craft floated through the twilight.

When Mahri saw the village's cluster of trees her knees buckled as if, now that she'd reached it, her will could support her no further. She slid gracefully to the deck, her staff rattling against the wood, and gave in to the shakes that rippled through her body. She'd never been so tired in her life.

Korl poled them to a flat limb the village used as a dock, climbed from the boat and pulled Mahri out. They both stood for a moment, getting used to the absence of movement beneath their feet, Mahri trying to stop the quivering in her legs.

"Where is everyone?" she wondered aloud.

The skeleton of a boat under construction lay on a limb parallel to the one they stood on; the fire shell that melted the glue lay cold and abandoned. Various sea animal's hides were stretched on racks but had only been scraped clean halfway. Shell utensils, woven baskets of laundry, tools, even toys were strewn haphazardly along the branch paths around and above them. All the signs of human habitation, but not the face of one person anywhere.

Mahri let her legs have their way and collapsed to the ground. "They can't all be dead. The fever couldn't have taken them so quickly!"

"Of course not." The prince squatted down beside her. "They're probably fishing or something." He gathered Mahri in his arms and stood, looking around uncertainly. "Show me where your family's house is and I'll take you there."

"Along this limb, over to the next one intersecting, then across the rope-bridge. You can see it from here."

"Really," Korl muttered, peering through the riot of leaves with a puzzled expression. But he followed her directions, stopped in astonishment when he stood before a piece of otter skin that resembled a door. What at first glance appeared to be a burl in the tree was actually a cleverly crafted dwelling. Mahri watched him pick out the other homes in the surrounding trees, tucked in natural twists of the limbs, hidden in hollows and forked branches.

"They let the tree choose their homes, not the other way around."

He only nodded, ducked slightly, and pushed his way past the otter skin. Almost as dark inside as out, Mahri struggled out of his arms and crossed the main room to the fire shell. She added seafire clumps to the husks already laying in there, found the shell of oil and doled it over the lumps. A sizzle, a puff of stink, and the seafire grew red with heat, basking the room with its warm glow.

Mahri looked around. Caria's shell collection adorned every available surface; hung in strings from the wood roof, lay piled in grass baskets or wooden platters placed on the table, on the shelves. "Caria?" she called.

A mumbled string of syllables that could've been her name and Mahri staggered to the bedroom, exhausted, root-fried, but so grateful when she looked on the flushed face of Brez's sister. Still alive, thank the-thirteen-moons.

"Mahri, is that you?" Caria knelt beside the moss-padded bed, her blue-green eyes bright with fever, her hand laid possessively on the arm of little Sh'ra.

"Aya. My niece, she lives?" she replied as she crept closer to the bed.

Caria nodded, her face crumpling into a mask of agony. "But she's so weak, so tiny. Her hands have begun to twist with the deformity . ." She covered her face with her own hands and sobs wracked her small frame.

"I've brought the Healer, Car. Hush, now."

And for the first time her lifemate's sister really looked at her and the man who shadowed behind. "What've you done?" she asked with horror, wiping the tears from her face.

Mahri frowned. "What do you mean?" Could she tell that Korl was a Royal?

"You look worse than I feel and I've got the fever."

Mahri almost laughed with relief. "It was a journey I'd rather never make again. And I've used most of the root to get here. Have you more, for the Healer?"

Caria swayed to her feet, rummaged in a cupboard that stood next to the bed. "It's where they've all gone, those that aren't sick. To harvest more root."

"Wald is with them, he's not..."

"No, my man is fine. Says it'd take more than some little bug to down the ox that he is." She handed Mahri a small bag of zabba. "We hoped that you'd find a Healer willing to help us." Tears rolled down to the corners of her mouth as she threw a look of gratitude at Korl. He didn't even have the decency to look sheepish, instead he half-bowed to Caria. Sh'ra moaned weakly from the bed and she flew back to her daughter's side, missing the look that passed between Mahri and the Healer.

Mahri gritted her teeth. Korl acted like he'd come of his own free will, as if he were some self-righteous savior. She threw the bag at him. "Eat it," she hissed. "And heal every last one of them or I swear you'll never see the palace again." Empty threat, really, since she never intended to bring him back anyway. But his face lit with hope, as if she'd made him some kind of promise.

Mahri dug into her own pouch, a dread in the pit of

her stomach at how empty it seemed. She brought the root to her lips and willed her body to take more, to keep it down this time. To her relief she didn't gag it out but felt the Power shiver through her and groaned with relief.

Korl's eyes sparkled with their own Power, met hers in a shower of mingled light. "What d'you think you're doing?" he whispered, "You're already half-dead from root!"

"Do you think I'd trust you to do this alone?"

Korl slapped a hand to his forehead. "What could I have been thinking?" And he took swift angry strides to the bed, then let out a loud breath.

"She's bad," he murmured as he laid gentle hands along the small body.

Caria's face lit with panic and Mahri could've kicked Korl. Instead, she asked her sister-in-life to make them tea, had to practically force her from the room. "We'll take care of her," she promised.

Mahri laid her hands on top of Korl's and even her concern couldn't dull the feeling that swept through her at even that innocent contact. She heard him take another deep breath as she Saw into the child, knowing that the dark things eating at her body needed to be destroyed but unable to determine where to even start.

"You See them?" he asked.

"See what?"

"Those spiked shapes—See how they attack and change the normal, healthy cells?"

"Aya, I... I think so. How do we stop them?"

His gaze met hers, intense with purpose. "We Push them to here," he pointed with his finger to the organ that cleaned out the body. "You start here, me here."

Mahri nodded and began to Push. She felt no satisfaction when her Pushing exceeded his, no pride at her
superior Power, for she had little control, root-fried as
she was; whereas Korl had total control but little Power.
In the end, there were too many of the buggers, they
clogged the organ and spread back out too quickly. She
cursed. In silent agreement they then tried to Push them
out of the body altogether but like grains of sand slipping through fingers too many eluded them, and then
they multiplied even faster.

Korl caught his chin in his hand and frowned. "We
can attack them directly."

Mahri shook her head. "How? They change their shape
and by the time you've got 'em cleared out, you need to
go back in and do it all over. That's if you can recognize
their new shape in time." She turned on him, hands on
hips. "What d'you think I needed you for? You're supposed to have the knowledge to deal with this."

"Listen, water-rat…"

Sh'ra moaned from the bed and her long-lashed eyes
opened to stare blindly at her aunt. Sea green eyes, just
like her own Tal'li. Mahri smoothed back the chestnut
curls from the child's forehead, felt the silky down
of a rounded cheek and was overwhelmed by a sharp
memory of her son.

Tal'li had loved to catch fly-fish, his little hands clap-
ping at air while they swirled around him in columns
of delicate wings. When he laughed she would always
laugh with him—so infectious, that staccato chuckle.
And if he managed to catch one, he'd carry it straight to
her, his little back stiff with pride, and lay it in her lap as
if he presented her with the rarest of treasures.

"Do you like to fly-fish?" she whispered to her niece. Her voice strangled against a sob. "But I've never taken you, have I? Make it through this, little one, and I promise I will."

But those lids closed, like Tal'li's had closed, with a sweep of finality. Mahri looked up at Korl, caught him staring at her as if he'd never seen her before.

"Save her," she whispered.

He nodded. Once. "We'll attack them indirectly, then."

"How?"

"Look at it backwards. Instead of killing them off, we stimulate the antibodies, make them stronger." He pressed her hand against the child's chest. "See into her system, here? The virus is surrounded by these white cells, the body's defensive system, and they're killing 'em—but too slowly. There aren't enough of the antibodies."

Mahri struggled to understand. "They're like warrior's—but they're outnumbered. Can we stimulate them enough so that they make more?"

"Reproduction? We don't have that kind of knowledge, Mahri. But," the Healer snapped his fingers. "We could give her some more antibodies, that might work."

"Reinforcements!"

"Yes. The mother's antibodies might have a better chance of working, being more compatible. The same blood type."

Mahri's head spun with questions. Antibodies… and what's a blood type? To have access to such knowledge, what she wouldn't give for that! She turned to fetch Caria when a touch on her arm stopped her. He stared sadly at her. "Wait, water-rat. I… I don't think I can do it."

"What?" she hissed, her own olive-colored eyes wide with disbelief. To offer her a shred of hope and then to crush it so quickly!

"It'd take a Master Seer to do something like this and the girl doesn't have the time for you to go kidnapping one."

Mahri shook with frustration, weariness, and too much zabba. "Are you saying you're not powerful enough? But what about me? You know I am."

"You're also a root-fried Wilding and don't have the control I do. I saw what happened when you tried to Push the virus. What if you accidentally Pushed harmful bacteria or something into that little girl?" They both glanced down at tousled chestnut curls, the innocent face of that sleeping child.

Mahri dropped her head, stray wisps of dark red hair fell to cover her face. "There has to be some way."

Sh'ra moaned and barked a weak cough.

Warm strong fingers tilted Mahri's chin up, brushed the red strands away from her face. "Even a water-rat knows," he said, "that there's only one way to tap another Seer's Power."

Mahri lost herself in his eyes. "A Bonding," she whispered.

Chapter 7

MAHRI BLINKED AGAINST HIS CHARISMATIC LURE AND had to force herself to look away. "I knew it!" She cursed viciously. "I knew they'd find a way to make this happen."

Korl crossed muscled arms over his broad chest. "What're you talking about?"

"The natives…"

His full bottom lip curled into a smile and Mahri snapped her own mouth shut. She remembered his reaction the last time she'd told him about her dream. He didn't believe it for a moment and neither should she. Yet, why were the natives watching them at the river? Although it could be hard to determine the facial expressions of those scale-furred humanoids, she'd sensed smug satisfaction as they watched her and the Prince. As if they knew that the two of them would be drawn together.

"There has to be another way," she muttered. "A Bond could only be as a last resort—it's too permanent, we could never break it."

Korl's eyebrow rose in that arrogantly superior manner and Mahri knew that he was about to spout off something that would make her angry. "You didn't think I was suggesting that we Bond, did you? A prince and a water-rat?" He barked a short laugh.

She'd been right. Anger flared inside of her. "Spare me your ego, Oh Great One. I'd risk twice as much as you, considering I've got more tolerance than you could ever hope for."

He near sputtered with surprised indignation. "Well it works both ways. You could tap my Power too, maybe use that to influence me—or keep me weak—or try to control the throne."

"You haven't got the throne, at least not yet. But you could use enough of my own Power to secure it."

They stared at each other, sparks of unleashed Power flashing between them, and recognized the mutual distrust. And fear. No wonder a Bonding is so rare, thought Mahri. The risks far outweighed the advantages.

Sh'ra moaned and Korl took Mahri's hand when her face crumpled in response to that pitiful mew. "I don't trust you," she whispered.

"Nor I you."

Mahri shook her head. If only there was someone else who could tolerate the root as much as she did. Someone who could feed enough Power to Korl to save her niece. "But I don't know any other way to do this thing—there are no other Wildings in the village."

They both stood frozen with indecision, the silence in the room only broken by the rattled breath of the child.

"A prince can't Bond with a water-rat," muttered Korl with the finality of a command.

Mahri snatched her hand from his, tried to cool the burn in her fingers from that brief contact with his skin. He didn't want to Bond anymore than she did yet that only slightly reassured her. The natives had wanted this to happen and she didn't like the feeling of being manipulated, even if Korl shared that distinction.

She looked at Sh'ra's pain-ravaged face. While they stood here arguing, worrying about their own selves, her niece could die. She'd have another death on her conscience, another life she could've saved if she'd been strong enough. How could she stand here and refuse the very thing that could help this child?

Mahri looked into Korl's eyes, watched the sweep of those incredibly long lashes when he blinked at the furious resolve in her face. "We have no other choice," and her own words rang with the finality of a command.

He blinked again. The tips of his lashes were edged with the same pale-gold color of his hair. "Mahri, we have no idea how this would affect the rest of our lives. I won't take that kind of risk."

Had he ever spoken her name before? she wondered. The sound of it in that husky, deep timbre made her shiver with pleasure. "No risk, Korl," she replied, purposely rolling his own name over her tongue.

If anyone had told her that she'd try to convince someone, much less a Royal, to Bond with her, she never would've believed it. And that she'd use feminine persuasion, well, she would've laughed until it hurt. Nevertheless, she curled her arms around his neck before he had a chance to know her intent, molded her body against his, met the firm softness of his mouth and kissed his breath away.

"You already told me," she whispered, after running the tip of her tongue along the fullness of his bottom lip, "that I'd never survive the zabba I've taken. I'll die anyway, after we save them, so you needn't worry about the Bond."

His arms had somehow managed to wrap themselves around her and they tightened when she spoke. "Not if I can help it," he muttered. And then louder, "You don't know very much about a Bond, water-rat."

Mahri didn't know what he meant, didn't care. "You'll do it?"

"I can't."

She sighed. She couldn't be sure that it would work if she forced him to form a Bond, for it took a mutual intent to meld the Power, but she had to try anyway. "Unless you save this child you'll never see the Palace Tree again."

Korl looked at the expression on her face and gently pushed her away. "I can find my way back."

"You think? It's possible, although I doubt if you'll make it back alive." Mahri's voice lowered with exasperation. "You can't even tell the difference between a krizm and a dedo."

"I'll get someone to take me back." Korl stuck his tipped, arrogant nose in the air.

"Right. After you let this little girl die. You'll be lucky if they don't throw you to the leaf wolves." She could tell he didn't even know what a leaf wolf was and knew he was dying to ask but wouldn't give her the satisfaction.

During their whispered argument Jaja had crept into the room, his head whipping back and forth between the two of them. When Korl opened his mouth to fling another retort the monk-fish chirped with disgust and leaped onto the bed. He took Sh'ra's hand, reached for the Royal's larger one, and clasped them together. His soft brown eyes widened to enormous proportions as he gazed at Korl with sad indignation.

Mahri smiled at her pet. "I think he's reminding you that you once said 'I'm a healer first, a prince second.' And while we argue, *Healer*, my niece is dying."

He contemplated the three of them, then sighed in exaggerated defeat. "What do we do?"

"I'm not sure." Mahri blinked. She felt so taken aback at his sudden agreement that she forgot to wonder why he didn't seem so terribly angry about being forced against his will.

Caria spoke from the doorway. "Jaja knows."

How long has she been standing there? wondered Mahri. And why does she think the monk-fish knows anything about Bonding?

"Jaja's always been more than a mere pet, sister," answered Caria, as if Mahri had spoken aloud.

Mahri started, watched the monk-fish with suspicion when he leaped on Korl's shoulder and imperiously waved her closer. She took the step that molded her body against Korl's, the consequences of that action so different this time she couldn't help the shudder of revulsion that rippled through her. Korl frowned so hard his eyebrows almost met.

"Never react to my nearness like that again," he commanded in a fierce whisper.

"I'm not sure if I can do this."

"If I can do it, so can you."

She nodded, felt a small, webbed hand press her forehead to Korl's and suddenly knew what Jaja wanted them to do. Mahri Saw into Korl, could feel his own Touch inside of her, and together they roamed every inch of each other, memorizing the individual cells that made them unique. Any novice of the Power knew to avoid another's pathways that zabbaroot had carved into their system, for the Power's natural defenses would either burn the intruder's lines or shrivel their own closed. So Mahri and Korl avoided them instinctively.

Jaja slapped both of them in the back of the head. It seemed that they must deliberately probe each other's pathways.

Mahri felt the tentative Touch of Korl as he slowly probed her old root-paths, skirting the stronger new ones that she'd blazed into her system over the past few days. She carefully Touched a sparkling green line that crackled inside the center of his chest, felt Jaja Push her Power into it and quickly pulled away.

Power can be Pushed? thought Mahri in panic. "By the… no," she groaned.

"Do it," demanded Korl, his breath a hot flame against her face. And aided by Jaja he plunged into her pathways with an almost physical sensation of entry, mingling his Power essence with hers, claiming each flowing green line as his own. Mahri cursed and responded in kind, felt him shudder as the greater Power at her command overwhelmed the root-paths in his body.

She felt Jaja pat her cheek as if to say, "go easy on him." Knew with a vague sense of detachment that Korl gripped her shoulders with flesh-numbing force. But her anger ruled and when they reached the nub where the paths joined at the base of each of their minds, she plunged into his with reckless fury. Although distantly aware that the wall Jaja had created around her mind had shattered, that Korl probed her as well, that he now knew her more intimately than her own lifemate had, Mahri didn't care.

She was too intent on her own discoveries, for his memories and experiences lay open to her with no veil of dishonesty. She felt him read her carefully but she felt no such compunction, ruthlessly grasping at whatever bits his thoughts revealed. Pieces of memories like a puzzle flashed before her, raising more questions than answers.

A pale face surrounded by pure white hair with eyes squeezed shut while Korl spilled his seed into her in near desperation. The haggard face of the king, mouth open in fury. The frightened face of a child; the black form of a feather-cloaked man looming menacingly over him. The flash of a bone knife in near-darkness.

Then Mahri saw herself. A heart-shaped face—which glowed with a beauty she couldn't possibly possess—alternately cursing with fury or whispering in passion. Muscles rippled through a lean, long-legged body that she knew didn't look as perfect as he pictured it. Round smooth swells of her flesh strained at her vest in ways that couldn't be that provocative.

He'd lied to her, sort of. When he'd said that he wasn't falling in love with her, he'd meant it. But only because he thought he *already* loved her, had from the moment he'd watched her beat his guard to the floor of his room.

And she'd chucked him over the balcony.

Mahri groaned. I'm going to try to pretend, she thought, that I never saw myself from his perspective. She Pulled out of his mind, vowing to never return again, felt him do the same, but seemingly reluctant to leave. She heard Caria gasp from behind her, knew her sister saw the green aura that briefly surrounded Korl and her; that settled to a pulse that could no longer be distinguished one from the other.

"How long has it been?" Mahri asked her.

"Only an instant," Caria answered in a puzzled voice.

"It felt like a lifetime." Mahri lifted her head and leaned forward, her mouth close to the Royal's ear and whispered as quietly as she could. "How much did you See?"

He seemed to just realize that he held her shoulders in a punishing grip and dropped them. "Not as much as you did, if that makes you feel any better."

"It doesn't."

He grinned and Mahri's heart skipped a beat. She wished he didn't think he loved her. It made him even harder to resist.

"Can you heal her now?" asked Caria.

"Aya. Where's Trian? Has he the fever?"

"No, but what do you want my cousin for?"

"We'll need to... how do I explain?" Mahri looked at the prince but he just shrugged. She went over to Caria and took her hand, felt the heat of the fever and the weakness in those lax fingers. "We need to take blood from you, the parts of it that fight the illness. But you're already so weak that we'll need to also take from Trian so that you won't wind up as sick as Sh'ra." She spun and faced Korl. "Am I right?"

He nodded, flipping back the strands of golden hair that had curled over his face with the gesture. "I didn't think about the effect on her, but yes, you're right."

While Caria fetched Trian, Mahri and Jaja searched the house for tools that Korl felt were needed for the healing. Mahri avoided Korl's gaze, noticed that he did the same, and it made her wonder what bits of her memories he'd Seen.

"Mahri!" exclaimed a familiar male voice, and Trian stepped into the house, swept her into his arms and gave her a resounding kiss.

"Let me down, you big oaf."

Amber colored eyes stared downed at her, thick curls of mahogany hair swept across a broad forehead that wrinkled with dismay as he studied her. Trian's wide, generous mouth shrank in a frown. "Doesn't look to me like you could stand on your own."

"She does just fine," snapped Korl. His sudden appearance at the bedroom doorway had made them both start guiltily. Mahri couldn't figure out why.

"Now, and who are you," asked Trian, setting Mahri carefully on her feet, "and what've you done to my girl?"

Korl raised an eyebrow. "Your girl? If you mean the water-rat, she did it all by herself."

His tone reeked with disdain and Mahri could feel Trian swell up beside her, like a whale-spout getting ready to blow. Caria stepped between them, gave in to the illness a moment so that she swayed on her feet. Both men immediately grabbed an arm and took her into the bedroom. Mahri stood in shocked silence, wondering at the sudden hostility between the two men and grateful that Caria knew how to diffuse the situation.

"What happened?" she asked Jaja. He shook his head at her and scampered after the others.

When Mahri entered the room Korl had already pierced the arm of her niece with a thin hollow bone, took the other end and put it into Caria's arm. He then took another bone and stood before Trian, the sharp knife in his hand still wet with scarlet. The darker-haired man seemed to loom over Korl for a moment, a little taller, shoulders a bit wider, but something about Korl's manner made him nod his head, take a seat, and bare his arm.

When Korl finished connecting her sister-in-life to Trian with the tube, he gestured at Mahri to come closer. She stood at his side and when Trian glared, the prince flung an arm carelessly around her shoulders. She winced, for he'd bruised them when they'd Bonded. By the moons—were they really Bonded? 'Twas odd that she didn't feel any differently.

Korl lowered his head and whispered in her ear. "You don't have to do anything. Just let me tap your Power."

Mahri shivered, whether from his words or the touch of his breath against her ear, she couldn't be sure. He smoothed his knuckles across her cheek and turned her face to his. "I won't drain you, I promise." He looked at her so intensely, imploring her to trust him, at least in this.

Mahri nodded and she Saw with him when he Looked at Sh'ra, then Caria. Watched as he Pushed the antibodies from one to the other, admired his skill when he Pushed Trian's antibodies through to Caria when her own body started to weaken. Like a juggling act he skillfully kept the balance between the three, until the virus shrank to the point that he could flush it from Caria's and Sh'ra's systems.

Through it all Mahri felt him take her Power, the Bond that now existed between them allowing him to access it, but without knowing what reserves she had. Korl removed the bone tubes from all their arms, Healing the slight punctures with a negligent wave of his hand. Mahri could see the Power strengthening him, for she'd fed him as much as he needed to heal her family, as fast as she could. And still continued to do so.

"I can't stop," she gasped, and collapsed to the floor.

"What's wrong?" demanded Trian. Mahri could hear the concern in his voice, although her normal vision had faded to black. But she felt the tingle that told her it was Korl's arms that lifted her from the ground. She snuggled her face in the crook of his neck and sighed. He still smelled faintly of the white flowers that had almost buried her boat.

Trian near growled. "What can't she stop?"

"She's force-feeding me her Power. Water-rat, listen to me." Korl jostled her gently in his arms; she could feel the rise and fall of his muscles. "You shouldn't have Pushed your Power at me, should've just let me tap it. Now I'm going to have to Push mine back at you, understand? Don't fight it."

She opened her mouth to speak but couldn't. She felt tired unto death. Korl had been right all along. With the Power gone she had nothing to keep her going, could actually feel parts of her body shutting down from overstimulation. Then she could feel him Touch her inside, knowing where to feed the Power first, what to heal.

"Jaja, get back!" Korl snapped, his voice more furious than Mahri had ever heard it.

"Let him, Healer. Her pet knows what he's doing," coaxed Caria in her gentle tones, stronger now with the absence of fever.

"She's already root-fried!" Exclaimed Korl… or Trian? Mahri couldn't be sure which of them spoke. The smooth coldness of zabbaroot touched her lips and she opened eagerly, the bitterness making her throat swallow in little convulsions. She opened her eyes and could only See the bits and dots of particles that made up her physical world, tried to refocus to normal vision and couldn't. Would she see the world like this forever, now? Could this be the price of her abuse of the root, a total loss of control?

But there were others in the village in need of the Healer and he couldn't do it alone.

Mahri took a deep breath and drew on the will that had sustained her through the deaths of her loved ones. "Caria's right, Jaja knew what to do." She wiggled out of Korl's arms and struggled to stay upright. She tried to concentrate on the larger mass of lumps and when they moved she could identify each person in the room by the arrangement of their individual particles. Barely.

"I'm fine," she reassured them. "And there's others in the village that need our help."

So she walked in a daze by Korl's side, feeding him Power when needed, ingesting the root that Wald had recently harvested. Young, exceptionally bitter stuff, she forced it down, listened to Korl when he told her to just let him tap the Power, not force it at him. She did what he told her; even when he insisted that he keep hold of her hand as they made their rounds.

By the time they returned to Caria's home the night had gone and Mahri Saw the rising sun in bits of glorious sparkles.

I did it, she realized as Caria ushered them inside. I saved all of them. And she waited for the guilt to leave her while her sister-in-life tucked her into Sh'ra's tiny bed, but it stayed like a tight knot of pain in her heart. She'd never be free from the loss of Brez and Tal'li.

"Where's the prince?" she asked Caria.

"The who?"

"The Healer."

A long, thoughtful pause. "We're going to have a long talk, Mahri, after you recover."

"If I recover."

A warm hand felt her forehead. "What d'you mean, if?"

Mahri closed her lids and could still See bits of tiny matter. She'd hoped she could remain in control long enough to say goodbye properly, but by-the-thirteen-moons she no longer cared. Every nerve in her body felt afire, every muscle burned in agony. The last remnants of the root in her system had faded and the pathways that it had forged shivered through her like knives ripping out her insides.

And she still carried the guilt of those two deaths.

Mahri began to scream.

"What's the matter?" mumbled Korl as he staggered into the room, his voice drugged with sleep.

Mahri kept screaming.

"I—I don't know!" wailed Caria. "I put her into bed and she just started shrieking."

Korl shouted to be heard. "Did she say anything?"

"No, yes. Something about not recovering. But I thought she'd be fine, after Jaja had taken care of her."

"Mahri!" growled Korl, trying to break through to her, his fingers hot brands along her cheeks. But the screaming continued, until Caria fled sobbing from the room. "Why didn't you tell me you'd lost all control, water-rat?"

Thank-the-moons, thought Mahri, that I'm so weak. For as her shrieks faded to a hoarse moan, she could hear little Sh'ra crying in the other room. She'd probably scared her niece to death and if Mahri didn't hurt so bad she might even be ashamed.

Korl laid Healing hands on her and she could only feel his Touch on the parts of her body that hadn't already gone numb. He swore softly, curses Mahri knew he'd learned from her, and she couldn't help but smile.

"More zabba," he flung over his shoulder, and she could hear the heavy footsteps of Wald as he rummaged through the front cupboard, the sound of seashells shattering.

Caria will be mad at him, she thought, and started to giggle.

"Hush, water-rat," commanded Korl, and then she heard the crunch of root. Felt his Power rushing through her pathways until he reached the nub of her mind. But this time he couldn't shatter her firmly placed mind-barrier.

Mahri cracked that black wall herself. "Come on in," she sang between giggles.

Losing one's mind didn't feel too bad, she thought.

Then the Sight began to narrow, she Saw into the cells of her eyelids, opened them but it didn't help. Her Vision kept going deeper, into the things smaller than the stuff that made up her world and she longed to ask Korl if he knew what it was she Saw.

He answered her inside her head. *No one's ever Seen this deeply before. Not that I know of.*

Mahri could hear his voice within, even the deep huskiness that could make her shiver. *Can you hear me, too?*

Yes, water-rat. I can also See what you do. So no matter how hard it gets, I'll be with you.

Like an anchor?

Yes.

Mahri hesitated. *And if what I See makes me go mad? Then we'll go together.*

He'd gotten more than he'd bargained for when he Bonded with me, thought Mahri—or had she seen aright, could his love for her have prompted this selfless aid? Or could it be that he dove in after her with the same unthinking heroics that had made him save her monk-fish? When he didn't respond to her speculations she felt grateful that he could only hear what she wanted him to.

Then Mahri couldn't think anymore, for the Sight continued to spiral into smaller fragments until nothing but pure white remained. Her mind tried to grasp the concept of this void and failed. She could Sense Korl battling likewise, felt his will like a tangible thing grab hold of her and keep them close, for as long as they stayed together they had a reality to hold on to.

Tiny particles pierced the whiteness, the world gone backwards, and now the Sight grew, creating from this reverse nothingness another world, where travelers of their kind dare not venture. Mahri felt Korl fight again, try to stop the Sight from continuing on.

What could lie beyond the opposite of reality?

She heard Korl's mental growl of rage. The mere thought of plunging into that unknown had the power to whip him into a frenzy of panic. And this time Mahri fought too, for she could let her guilt destroy her... but not him.

She matched her will to his and it grew even stronger. What they couldn't accomplish separately they could together and for one breath-taking moment it felt as if their souls fused together, created a force that not even the universe could stand against.

The Sight slowed to a crawl, reversed, then began to grow so abruptly that they passed again through the white nothingness in the blink of an eye, then through the rest until Mahri could See the familiar world that she knew.

She refocused her Vision, and with relief it responded, the bits disappeared, and with normal sight she looked on the flushed face of her prince. He knelt beside the bed, his hands folded around one of her own, dark smudges beneath those light-green eyes, lines etched in his forehead and along the corners of his mouth. He had never looked more irresistible.

"Do I look as bad as you?" she croaked.

He smiled and sat back on his heels, removed the headband from his brow and shook back his hair. "You look even worse," Korl replied as he raked his fingers through the golden strands.

Mahri bit her lip, ignoring the comment. Did he know that it made her crazy with wanting him when he shook his hair back like that? Did he glean that memory from their Bonding? She tried not to stare at the smooth line of his throat, the expanse of his chest that lay naked beneath her gaze.

That moment when their souls had united still echoed in her mind and heart, scaring her silly. How could she fight something like that? Yet, how could she not, when the thought of that kind of connection with another could overwhelm her own identity?

"Put your shirt on," she said through the sandy feel in her throat. "And stay out of my head."

Korl staggered to his feet. "As you wish," he replied with bone-weary exhaustion. When he turned to leave, Mahri stared with hypnotic fascination at the line that ran down the middle of his back, the bunch of muscles that shifted with each step he took. The smooth gleam of his skin. She called his name and he glanced over his shoulder, froze at whatever he saw in her face.

"Thank you," she whispered.

He grinned and the shallow dimple appeared in his cheek. Mahri sighed. Since I'm not going to die, she thought, I'm really going to have to do something about this obsession I have for him.

Chapter 8

THE AROMA OF GRILLED PIG-FISH AND CHAKA EGGS filled the tree home, made Mahri wake with a mouth that watered and a stomach that rumbled. She carefully stood, stumbled to the pot shell, and smiled at the muffled sound of a childish voice. She emerged from the room, blinked at the late afternoon sunshine flooding through the open door and watched her niece string a necklace of pearls, feathers, and whatever else suited her fancy, while her mother tended the fire shell.

"Where is he?" croaked Mahri.

Sh'ra's eyes widened and her rosy mouth formed a silent "O" of surprise. Caria froze and studied her sister with a speculative gleam in her blue-green eyes. "If you mean the Healer, and somehow I'm sure you do, he's hunting with Wald and Trian. And Jaja went with him." She added the last comment as if it were a question, for the monk-fish never went with anyone but Mahri.

Mahri ignored the implication and frowned. "For what?"

"More zabba, of course, and any game they might flush that can be put on the grill for dinner."

Caria laid a platter of food on the rough-hewn table and gestured at Mahri to eat, who collapsed into a chair and wolfed down a chaka egg before she could even taste it. She slowed down to savor the salty taste of the pig-fish.

"S'good," she mumbled through a full mouth. "I'm beyond famished—how long've I been asleep?"

Sh'ra giggled and covered her grin with a chubby hand. Caria ignored the little girl and continued to study Mahri. "Don't talk with your mouth full," she admonished absent-mindedly. Sh'ra gave her aunt a sympathetic grimace. "You've been out for three days and I've been near bursting with curiosity about this Healer you brought."

Mahri lowered her head and concentrated on her food. A gust of wind set the seashell chimes that hung near the door to tinkling, carried the sound of women gossiping while doing their wash, men whistling as they constructed a new boat, and children laughing between and betwixt them. It was good to be home.

"I brought you some new shells," she said, hoping to avoid a conversation about Korl as long as she could. Caria's face lit up and Mahri's lips twitched. She'd never understand her sister's fascination with the common things, the way she studied and categorized them, spent her evenings scratching her findings onto soft bone tablets. But she knew Caria couldn't resist a new find.

"Snail, clam, oyster, which?"

"Mostly snails."

Caria sighed. "Those're usually the most beautiful. They in the boat?"

"Aya."

Caria gave the child instructions and sent her along to fetch them, but before she left, Sh'ra approached her aunt shyly and placed the finished string in Mahri's lap. "T'ank you," she stuttered. "For healin' me." Then she turned and stumbled out the door, still weak from her illness but rapidly recovering like only the young could.

Mahri tied the string around her neck, then fisted a hand around the beads and feathers, pushing against her chest as if that would stifle the pain that lay within her heart.

"She's the same age as Tal'li, when he..." began Caria.

Mahri stiffened. "Don't go there."

"You've never mourned them, sister. Perhaps if you could, it'd stop tearing you apart."

"Leave it be, Caria."

The blonde woman stood and began to clear the dishes, stacking them with intentional clatter in the woven basket she always used when she carried them to the river. Mahri shook her head and rubbed an un-comfortably full belly. Her sister-in-life preferred to take an issue and flay it open like a fish, picking apart the innards and exposing the bones. For some reason she thought that it would somehow make things better and couldn't understand why anyone would be reticent about sharing her methods.

Mahri took the bittersweet memory of her son and buried it again. She stretched until the joints in her arms quietly popped. "Traveled some new channels, this trip."

The noise stopped a moment, resumed with much quieter clinks. "Oh, really,"

Mahri leaned back in the chair, fought down another smile at Caria's feigned nonchalance. "Aya. Had plants and animals living in them that I never saw before."

Caria shrugged. "Like what?"

"Oh, flowers that exploded. Waters that glowed with rainbows. A big old creature with lots of tongues."

That did it. Caria dropped the last bone spoon and near landed in Mahri's lap, peppering her with questions. Mahri answered them all as best she could, even helped her sister to name them when she insisted on adding them to her bone tablet "records." And when Sh'ra returned there followed another round of questions, until the exhaustion again began to creep into Mahri's abused body.

"Enough, now," Caria said, removing her daughter from the redhead's lap, where she'd insinuated herself during the conversation. "Your aunt and I will have a bath, while you run along and play with Zerik."

Her niece's mouth dropped in horror. "You going to wash in the daytime?"

Whether she feared an actual bath or birdsharks, Mahri couldn't be sure. But as for the winged monsters, she didn't really care, for just the thought of clear fresh water to soak her aches made her willing to take on a flock of the huge beasts.

"We'll stay beneath the leaves, darling. Run along, now."

Sh'ra looked at them both with an expression of genuine puzzlement. When she bolted from the house the two women exchanged a maternal grin.

Mahri began to rummage through the trunk Caria kept for her and forced herself to hum a bawdy tune until her sister-in-life quit examining her with that frown of suspicion. Mahri sighed in relief. She no longer thought of anything but the need to get out of her dirty traveling clothes. Her hand brushed across the softness of green spider-silk, the only true dress she owned. Brez had bought it for her shortly after they'd been mated, said the hue brought out the dark-gold highlights in her red hair. She'd worn it once. With an angry grunt Mahri

shook the mass of spider-silk out, refusing to acknowledge that she wanted to wear it just to see the look in the
prince's face when he saw her in it.

"How'd you know?" asked Caria.

"Know what?"

"That we're planning a celebration tonight. A party
to honor you and Korl."

Mahri rolled the dress into a bundle and strapped it
with the belt of her bone staff. "So he told you his name.
Does it mean anything to you?"

Caria started for the door, tossed her sister a bow and
quiver of arrows, then waved her through the threshold,
a frown of puzzled annoyance marring her clear skin.
"No, should it?"

"Course not." Mahri followed Caria around the base
of the home tree, then up slanted branch-paths. In the
backwoods they wouldn't recognize that rare name as
belonging to the prince and apparently he hadn't enlight-
ened the villagers as to who he was. Not that it would
matter. Swamp villagers didn't care much for Royals,
one way or the other. They usually kept to themselves.

When they reached the smaller limbs near the very
top of the tree Mahri dropped her bundle and began to
strip, avoiding Caria's curious gaze.

"Something's going on," said the blonde woman,
"Between you and this mystery man."

Mahri strapped her weapons around her bare waist
and eyed the sapling that grew next to the home tree.
"Why do you keep thinking there's something mysterious about the Healer?" She grabbed the rope ladder that
hung down the side of the small tree and started to climb
without waiting for an answer. "Do you have the soap?"

"Yes," snapped Caria, her voice already far below.

Mahri scrambled over the crown of newly budded leaves and scanned the late afternoon sky with caution. Although the sapling's fresh water cache didn't have the dangerous depth, nor the perilous garbage-skimmers that the older trees did, they grew so tall to find the sun that they rose above the forest growth—growth which usually hampered the attack of birdsharks. She didn't spot any dark specks against the clouds and relaxed. All dangers being relatively equal, the villagers preferred the small ponds of sun-warmed water to the frigid lakes of the older trees.

She allowed herself to enjoy the view. Here atop the canopy the sky stretched on forever, the treetops creating a blanket of bumpy green beneath. The crystal blue of the sea lay even farther below, its incessant waters flowing around and through the trunks of the forest, until it spread out to the very edge of the horizon.

Mahri tore her gaze away. A leaf from the home tree had reached over to partially cover the sapling and she hunkered beneath the edge of it. "All clear," she shouted, setting down her weapons on the dry lip of the treetop.

"I'm right here," panted Caria, her blonde head popping up over the edge. She removed her belt and set down the soap root, spread the drying cloths over the leaf to warm. Her eyes squinted against the bright sunlight that reflected off the water as she immersed herself, quiet grunts of pleasure sounding from the back of her throat. She walked to almost the middle of the pool before she had to tread water.

Mahri scooted down the shallow bowl until the water covered the top of her breasts and let the warmth of it soak the aches from her body. The bark felt smooth beneath the skin of her bottom, the air smelled spicy and light, and the wind made a gentle roar through the canopy. She might've dozed, listening to Caria swimming around the pond, if not for the sudden splash across her face.

"No you don't!"

"Caria," she sputtered. "What's your problem?"

"If you think you're gonna get out of answering my questions by pretending to sleep..."

Mahri wiped water from her lashes. She might as well give in now—from past experience she knew the woman would pester her to death until she'd told her everything. "Let the flaying begin," she grumbled.

"What?" Caria sat behind her and began to unbraid Mahri's long red hair.

The gentle tugging on her scalp felt wonderful and she sighed. "Nothing."

"Good. Now first things, first. Who is this Healer, anyway? And why'd he agree to help us, and what's going on between you two? Hold out your hand." Mahri obeyed and Caria deposited one of the shells that'd been strung through the braid. "Well?"

"What do you mean, what's going on between us?"

Caria yanked the red mass, hard. "Don't play games with me, sis. I saw the way you two looked at each other. Now don't make this anymore difficult for yourself. Fess up."

Suddenly the words tumbled out and Mahri near stumbled over them. "Nothing's going on, I swear. It's just that the journey kind of threw us together in ways that I couldn't... and I refused to let him get to me... even though I wanted him... but not in my *heart*? You know?"

"Uh huh, right. Let's make this easier. Where did you find this Healer?" Caria added another shell to the pile.

Tell her all, tell her some? wondered Mahri. "In the Healer's Tree."

"And he agreed to come with you to the swamps?"

"Not exactly."

The hands untwining her hair stilled. "You didn't, I mean, have to, give him something to come with you?"

"Not exactly." Caria tugged hard enough this time to bring tears to Mahri's eyes. "Oh, all right. I kidnapped him."

She heard the air whoosh from Caria's lungs. "You *what*?"

"I stole him from his bed, chucked him over a balcony and trussed him like a pig-fish."

Mahri smiled at Caria's muffled giggle. "But why?" the blonde woman managed to ask.

The wind lapped at the water, made Mahri's full breasts bob gently. They felt wickedly free from the tight constraints of her vest. "You remember what happened the last time I tried to ask for help, don't you?"

Both women sobered for a moment, remembering the loss of brother, nephew, life-mate, child. But they both knew it wasn't a subject they could discuss and allowed the wind to sweep their memories out to sea.

"And I thanked him for agreeing to help us," said Caria, voice low with disgust. "Why—he'll be honored at the party tonight!"

Mahri turned her head, met the blue-green eyes with her own olive ones. "Don't discuss what I tell you with anyone. Swear, or this talk ends now."

Caria blinked. "I swear. You know you can trust me."

"Aya."

"Tell you what; I'll wash your hair if you explain why this Korl is so... strange."

"What do you mean?"

Caria spun the redhead around and finished unplaiting the mass of thick hair. She spread it out and Mahri moaned in pleasure.

"I thought I recognized my work," said Caria. "You haven't washed this mess since I last braided it, have you?"

"I didn't exactly have the time."

Caria snorted.

"I stood in a rain wash for hours."

Caria snorted louder. She waded over to the thin dry edge of the tree, pounded some soap root into foam and brought it back to Mahri's head, scrubbing it in with vigorous pleasure.

"Ouch. So what's so strange about the Healer?"

Caria's hands gentled as she replied. "He acts so odd, like every time he says something, people ought to jump to do it. And I know city folk aren't used to the swamps, but he seems downright ignorant of the sea forest... and yet quite intelligent about things we barely understand."

"He's a prince."

"So?"

"That's what they're like—used to having everyone bow to them, take care of them. And they focus their talents on the old records."

"What I wouldn't give to see a real library! Aah, the envy. No wonder you don't like Royals."

"Aya. Worse though, is that this prince has many enemies, many powerful enemies."

The hands working their way through strands of dark red froze. "You weren't followed?"

"No."

"Does he know what you are?"

"Aya."

"Oh, Mahri, this could get very complicated."

"You don't know the half of it." She stood, so that Caria could wash the rest of her hair. The wind curled around her body and raised gooseflesh, the lavender scent of the soap filled her nostrils and nearby something hooted and growled. "He saved my life, more than once, and did agree to Heal Sh'ra when I promised to return him home."

"Uh oh."

"Aya. If I take him back, he could tell them about me." She sank into the water and leaned her head backward, let her hair spread around her like a dark halo.

Caria worked the soap from the strands. "But he wouldn't."

"And why not?"

"Because you're Bonded to him now." Caria's voice lowered. "I meant to thank you before, but words just didn't seem enough. Still, thank you Mahri. I know what a sacrifice it was for you to tie yourself to anyone that way."

Mahri sat up, her head tingling with cleanliness. She stuck her face in the water, rubbed briskly, and came up sputtering. "I didn't think I'd survive it."

Caria wet her own short locks and fetched more soap. "Well, if anyone strips you of your Power, or if you should die, he'd likely die as well. Or worse, be utterly Powerless. 'Till death do the Bonded part' is literal."

Mahri gasped. "It's worse than I thought. I can't believe that I'm tied to that arrogant Royal forever. I'd thought a Bond only a myth, until a few days ago, so I wasn't sure what it truly meant. Not that it matters now." She sighed. "Anyway, I haven't decided what to do about him yet, I'm still trying to figure out what happened before we got here."

Mahri started to soap her body while Caria rinsed her own hair, smoothed the blonde curls back and eyed her sister-in-life with a speculative gleam. "You should cut off some of that," she said, gesturing at the heavy red hair.

"You know I can't. Your brother loved it."

"But he's... oh, never mind. What happened before you got here?"

"I, um, tried to seduce him."

"You?"

Mahri nodded.

"The same woman that's never even looked at another man since my brother—you actually tried to—I don't believe it."

"Would you lower your voice?" Mahri spread the lather down her legs, whispered dreamily as she spoke. "I can't believe it either, but when we were alone together on my boat and he stood near me, he just smelled so good. Looked so good. And then he did this thing with his hair." She stroked a foamy hand across her abdomen. "It was an innocent gesture... but the way he did it." She washed her breasts absent-mindedly, thinking of his broad shoulders, that full lower lip. Her hands slowed and she became aware of her painfully hardened nipples, the way Caria stared at her in open-mouthed shock. She dove in the water, stayed under as long as she could to regain control of herself. She'd thought it was his proximity that affected her but the mere thought of him had her acting like an idiot in front of Caria.

"I can't believe the way I threw myself at him," she admitted as she swam beneath the leaf.

"Oh, I can," Caria stood frozen, knee-deep in the water, her hands cupping flaming red cheeks, "after that little display. Don't look so embarrassed. I'm not. I just got all caught up in your passion. Frankly, I'm glad you've finally, er, fallen for another man."

"I haven't fallen. I'll never love again, you know that."

"All right, call it what you will. But you've got it bad Mahri and you'd better decide what to do about it."

"I thought if I bedded him, it'd take care of it. Now I'm not so sure."

"You're right, it could make it worse—" Caria's mouth dropped with sudden horror as wind buffeted her shoulders and she felt the scrape of talons across her back. Reflexes honed by living in the swamps allowed her to dive forward before the birdshark had the chance to get a good grip on her. The creature shrieked with rage and circled for another attack.

Mahri cursed and lunged for the weapons. Just the thought of Korl could distract her from the dangers of the swamps. She should've seen the thing coming; if Caria got hurt it'd be her fault. She grabbed the bow, nocked an arrow and let fly just as the bird plummeted toward the blonde woman swimming beneath the water. The shaft hit a wing, knocking the creature off balance, spoiling his angle just enough so that Caria could swim beneath a leaf.

If it gets brave enough, thought Mahri, it'll land and attack and we won't stand a chance. She joined Caria under the dubious protection of the leaf. "Did you bring any root?" she demanded.

"No, your body needs to rest, and you know I haven't the Sight. What good would it do me, and we haven't seen a birdshark in so long…"

"You're babbling," hissed Mahri, knowing she didn't stand a chance against the thing without the Power, just that she had to try.

Another swoop and the leaf above them slapped their heads. Caria started to scream for help. Mahri nocked another arrow and shoved through the water until she stood ankle-deep. "That's better—only louder."

Caria took a deep breath and complied as Mahri sprinted from beneath their cover, searching the skies as she ran around the rim of the pond. The birdshark had already lunged for the leaf, saw Mahri and screeched as it swooped upward again, barely grazing its target. It circled once and dove straight for her, beak open to reveal jagged rows of sharp teeth, beady red eyes intent with primordial hunger.

Mahri stood stock still, feet splayed, arrow level with her eye. She could hear Caria's screams for help as if it came from a great distance, for her world narrowed to the tip of her arrow and the red of the creature's eye.

Not yet, she told herself as the bird loomed before her. He's not close enough yet. The arrow wavered and she forced her hand to stop its sudden tremor. Not yet.

The thing squawked and she almost jumped out of her skin, heard Caria yelling at her to shoot.

Not yet.

Odd, how a few seconds can seem an eternity.

When the red of the bird's eye grew to the size of a sun fruit Mahri let fly and the shaft sunk into the slitted pupil. The squawk of outrage made the leaves on the trees shudder with the force of it and silenced the usual noise of the sea forest. It swiped at her with its scaled talons as it beat wings to climb back into the sky.

Mahri sprinted back under the leaf, tossed Caria the bow, pulled her bone staff from its sheath and started back for the open.

"What do you think you're doing?" demanded Caria.

"No way I'll get lucky like that again—"

Caria saw the bow in her hands and snatched up a few arrows. She emerged from beneath the leaf shelter and sighted against the deceptively clear sky. "Maybe I will," she yelled.

Mahri flicked her wrist, extended the bone to almost poling length. I don't stand a chance, she thought, but swung the staff around her head. I won't be an easy meal, anyway.

The forest lay too quiet around her. From the side of her vision she saw Caria backing her up and increased the odds a bit. Where had the monster gone? Did it know the waiting was killing her?

A pale, golden head appeared over the edge of the sapling, her monk-fish perched atop those broad shoulders.

"Water-rat, what do you think you're…" began Korl, then those impossibly light-green eyes widened and Mahri remembered that she stood as naked as the day she was born. That drops of water which sparkled with reflected sunlight barely covered her in their jewel-like cloak. That she stood like some kind of savage with her weapon trained on the sky. That her breasts jutted freely before her, the size of them no longer camouflaged beneath her vest. Their nipples hardening under his gaze.

Korl continued to stare in stunned amazement; he seemed to feast on her body as his gaze traveled slowly up and down. She could feel the intensity of his look as if it were a tangible thing, raking her skin with fingers of flame.

Mahri heard Trian's voice come from farther down the ladder. "What's the matter with you? Get up there!"

Jaja slapped Korl in the back of the head, fluffing up strands of golden hair. Korl blinked, then scrambled over the side to crouch like an animal, as if waiting to spring. "What is it?" he croaked, while hefting a spear.

"Birdshark. Have you eaten root?"

"Some." At Caria's cry of alarm they both turned as the monster appeared from behind a cloud and began another descent. "Not enough," he added.

"Feed the Power to me—now." Mahri's knuckles whitened where they gripped the staff. She couldn't believe that she'd just given that command, that she'd rely on someone else for anything. Still, he could refuse, and she half-hoped that he would, that she'd die here instead of becoming further entrenched in this Bond between them. If she could only forget that with her death, he would die as well.

Korl responded without hesitation, draining himself until his shoulders slumped with weakness. Jaja patted his cheek. Trian scrambled over the side, tried to take in what was happening, his head swiveling from the Healer to Mahri, then up to the attacking birdshark.

It works, marveled Mahri, as she felt the Power enter

her pathways, shiver inside her head. And it feels so incredible, this Power without the price of root-fever. Suddenly she knew what to do and extended her pole even farther. She only hoped that her staff would be long enough to keep the talons away from her, and that she had enough Power to strengthen her muscles.

The birdshark plunged down at her, talons first, beak open with a scream of fury. Trian threw his spear, Caria let loose her arrow, and both struck the creature's wing, although it didn't acknowledge the score. This time such puny weapons would be no deterrent to the rage of the thing. It swooped with single-minded determination. Mahri anchored the pole between her feet, angled toward the path of its flight, and at just the right moment pulled it up, straight into the feathered chest.

The creature struck the bone with enough force to almost shudder the pole from her numb hands, but she held on with Power-enhanced strength, continued to pull the staff upwards so that the bird swung over her head, talons just grazing her shoulders. The creature hit a neighboring tree branch, landed with a thud behind her, its neck snapping on impact.

"It worked," she breathed, her knees trembling with relief.

"Of course it did," answered Korl, appearing at her side. His voice dripped with arrogant pride, but she didn't care, just flung her arms around his shoulders, including Jaja in her hug.

"We did it."

Korl slid trembling hands down her naked back. "We can do anything together."

Mahri wanted to melt against him, but she pushed him

away and said the first thing that popped into her head. "Well, you managed to get out of your sleeping clothes."

Korl smoothed the snar-scale vest that sleekly covered his chest, adjusted the leather belt that hung around his waist. "Trian loaned them to me, until I can make my own." He raised an arrogant chin, but Mahri could tell he struggled to maintain that imperious facade, for the sudden drain of Power had weakened him.

She felt an irrational surge of respect for his stubborn pride and ignored his weakness as well. "Start a new fashion at Court, aya?"

He grinned and crossed muscled arms across his broad chest. "I don't know, I think I prefer your suit to mine." Jaja copied his movements, grinning with his own sharp pointed little teeth.

Mahri felt her face grow hot, realized that several other villagers had joined Trian at the edge of the pool and that their eyes kept drifting in her direction. She dove into the water, where Caria had already taken refuge.

"Shows over," called out Caria. "We're all right, and there's a new feathered cloak laying on yonder tree branch that I'm sure Mahri would appreciate being fetched for her." The men scrambled back down the ladder, Trian threw a departing scowl behind him, and Korl followed with the slowest of steps.

"I drained him," whispered Mahri.

Caria shushed her. "He'll be fine."

Korl looked at her one last time before he went over the edge, those eyes near burning into hers. Mahri couldn't look away. "You'll be okay?" he asked.

"One birdshark a day is the usual limit."

Jaja clapped in appreciation but she didn't blame

Korl when he didn't smile at her lame joke. He seemed to want to impress her with his serious expression, that he had something to say of the utmost importance. She waited, heard Caria beside her holding her breath.

The wind stirred his hair, the pale strands curled over his forehead and swung into the hollow of his cheeks. "Of all the palace treasures," he said, "there's none as stunningly beautiful as you looked today, wielding your staff."

Chapter 9

CARIA LET OUT HER BREATH IN A SUDDEN WHOOSH. "I feel almost… scorched from the fire between you two."

"Aya. Now you know why he scares me."

"I'm just grateful," continued Caria, "that his eyes weren't looking at me like that—married or no, I'm not sure I could resist that sort of magic. Oh Mahri, what're you gonna do?"

The redhead shrugged, swam to shallow water and began to angrily swish water drops from her skin. Thanks to the birdshark their drying cloths now lay soaking in the pond.

"It's not like we have any future together, even if I wanted one. A prince and a water-rat! Why, the entire world would have to change before that could happen. And this charm he has, what did you call it… magic?"

Caria nodded, a look of bemusement still on her face.

"Well, what if it's his way of manipulating women to get what he wants? And he wants to go back home, believe me!"

Both women gathered their belongings and scrambled down the ladder when they heard male grunts and laughter. The villagers had come to collect the carcass of the 'shark, and they'd already gotten enough of an eyeful already, as far as Mahri was concerned. When they reached the bottom she pulled an anemone spike-brush through hair already half dried by the wind, and then struggled into the silk dress. The fabric clung to her like a second skin.

Caria began to twine a small string of black pearls into a thin braid down the left side of Mahri's face. She made another on the right and gathered them together behind the mass of red curls, tied another string around the slightly freckled forehead and stood back to survey her handiwork.

"Do you honestly think he can turn that chemistry off and on for any woman?" she asked, pulling a lock of dark red over the green silk and twisting it into a spiral curl.

Mahri shook her head. Tiny black pearls dangled from the string across her forehead and danced across the edges of her vision. "Who knows? They're used to getting their way—don't you understand? They're the haves, and we're the have-nots. 'Tis as simple as that." She spun, felt the pearls bob lightly against her brow and the silk flow in waves of soft green across her skin. "They dress like this every day," she murmured.

"They do not," said Caria, while she pulled her own best dress of supple otter skin over her shoulders. Tiny seashells were stitched along the hems of the ivory leather and around the neckline. They tinkled softly whenever Caria moved.

"Aya, they do."

Caria layered her throat with seashell necklaces, her arms with like bracelets. She unwrapped a headband of delicate paper shells and gestured at Mahri to tie it for her. "How do you know?"

Mahri tied the knot and watched in amazement as her sister-in-life pulled out more strung seashells and wrapped them around her ankles. "They parade through the city nearly every day—Caria, how many seashells are you going to wear anyway?"

Her sister-in-life chuckled in response, the sound accompanied by the clatter of her ornaments. "Wald says if I keep adding to my collection I won't be able to stand up and he'll have to carry me around. But really, sis, they're all so beautiful I can't choose between them." And with that said Caria pulled on a girdle of shells that graduated in color from pink to red, lavender to purple.

"I'd like to go to the city, just once," she added.

"I'll take you, anytime you want."

Caria sighed, gathered up their dirty things and clasped Mahri's hand. "I'm not brave, like you are. I love to hear your adventures and marvel at the things you bring home. But I like familiar things around me, and besides, I'm afraid to be without my family."

She thinks I'm brave, marveled Mahri, as they made their way down the tree through the thickening dusk. She doesn't realize that I'm just as afraid to be with a family as she is to be without one—that it's too dangerous to rely on others.

Mahri stopped and untangled her dress from the claws of a snatcher vine, smoothed out a little pucker in the silk and frowned. Caria admires me for the same thing I despise in myself, she thought. "You're the sister of my heart but we'll never understand each other, will we?"

Caria stepped lightly across a rope bridge, seashells tinkling in time to the sway of her hips. "I hope not! Then we'd never have any fun."

Mahri laughed, saw the glow of fire shells through the leaves and felt the beat of the drums through the trunk of the tree before she could even hear the music. Caria pulled on her hand and together they crossed the threshold from the privacy of the dark forest to the light of the villager's celebration.

People surrounded them and Mahri shrank back, only the pressure of Caria's fingers keeping her within that circle. A loner by choice, brusque by nature, the villagers usually kept their distance from her. She figured that they allowed her in their midst only because of her connection to Brez's family.

Yet tonight they vied for the chance to shake her hand or just touch her shoulder.

At first Mahri felt puzzled by their attitude. She'd come and gone from their midst as quietly as possible; the men admired her lifestyle but thought her strange, the women jealously envied her looks but were usually content to just ignore her. This sudden display of affection had taken her completely by surprise.

Yet, she'd saved their lives, and perhaps they felt she belonged to them now.

Beyond Trian's shoulder she glimpsed another group, surrounding another hero. As if at a silent signal a path opened between the two and her gaze met Korl's, and the laughter she'd shared with Caria over their mutual misunderstanding of each other felt suddenly hollow. Looking into his eyes made her need someone to understand her, made her yearn for a kindred spirit to share her life with. Mahri cursed softly, even while she took a step towards him. Why did he always make her feel things she didn't want to?

Korl strode toward her, those brilliant eyes still fixed on hers, brushing off any hand that tried to stay him. He wore a vest and leggings that she recognized as Trian's, but it'd never fit her cousin the way it did him. With every step he took the thin pelt of smink rippled with the movement of his muscles. The front of his vest cracked open to reveal the ridges of his taut stomach and that fine line of hair that disappeared beneath the waist of his leggings down to… Mahri swallowed.

He stopped a hair's breadth from her face—she could feel his breath against her skin and smell the musky clean scent of him. She retreated a step. He laughed, a low sound that rumbled in his chest, the stretch of those firm lips revealing the shallow dimple in his cheek as if to taunt her to smooth it with her finger.

"My lady," he whispered. "Your loveliness would grace any court of Sea Forest."

Did he make fun of her? wondered Mahri. She dipped in a graceful curtsey, having seen it done only once, but a good imitation nonetheless. She batted her lashes at him. She could give as good as she got. "Even that of the Queen, Great One?"

Korl looked taken aback a moment, then laughed again. "You've got me there, water-rat. The Queen's vanity is well known—but I'd risk offending her just to tell you…" He closed the distance between them again and Mahri could only fervently hope that he didn't touch her. If he touched her, she was lost. His breath caressed her ear as he leaned close to whisper to her. "That no other woman's beauty could compare to that of a Wilding with only her staff for adornment."

And as Korl pulled away from her his lips brushed her cheek and she shivered from the heat of it. Her eyes lowered to escape the lure of his, and the leggings he wore covered him like a second skin, and the glow of the seafire shells revealed physical proof of his desire for her, and...

"Caria?" she called weakly.

A feminine giggle responded, but not her sister's. A narrow-fingered hand, nails sharpened to almost a point, snaked over the bare bulge of Korl's shoulder, traveled slowly down to play with the hair on his forearm. Another woman—with the blackest, frizziest hair she'd ever seen—leaned against his other side, purposely smashing the side of her breast into his arm.

Mahri blinked. Where'd these women come from? Whenever Korl looked at her the world shrank and she could only see the two of them. Were they the source of his brief display of desire? For he looked as if he enjoyed the attention.

She tried to smile. She should be grateful, after all. They'd saved her. Another moment longer and Mahri would have dragged him off into the night. Yet she didn't feel gratitude. Oh no, more like an urge to pop them in their artfully pouting mouths.

Mahri felt a tug on her dress and looked down into the impish face of her pet monk-fish, grateful for the diversion. "Where've you been, Jaja?" she murmured as she settled him onto her shoulder. He spat out a fish bone that fortunately landed right onto the hand of the sharp-nailed woman, who withdrew from Korl's arm with a grimace of disgust. "At the food already, eh?"

Jaja responded with one of his best fierce animal imitations, a cross between a shriek and a howl, and Mahri laughed.

Frizzy-hair jumped, her breast finally peeled away from

Korl's arm and Mahri relaxed her shoulders, unaware that she'd been so tense. Jaja gave a satisfied chirrup.

"Don't worry, he doesn't bite," said the prince. The woman managed to look even more frightened and Mahri frowned in disgust. All of the villagers were familiar with Jaja—most of the time he played with the little ones and usually *he* got hurt during the tussles. The woman was obviously feigning fear just so Korl would pat her reassuringly. Like he did now.

"I'd never be afraid," she cooed, "with such a strong man like you around."

Mahri bit her lip. Did women really say such rubbish? And did men really fall for it?

Korl's chest puffed up and he flicked back his head. Both women closed in now, sharp-nails playing with the ends of his fine hair, the other one leaning against him. Korl smiled with unbelievable arrogance, watched Mahri with a look that flickered with more than firelight. Amusement, challenge, and for some reason, a hint of self-satisfied revenge.

Mahri couldn't figure that last one out, didn't even try. She just turned to walk away but his arm lashed out, those strong fingers near bruising her. Their eyes met and magic shivered between them as he held her put—with more than just the muscles in his hand.

Frizzy-hair watched the two of them with compressed lips. With the speed of an eel she reached out and fingered Mahri's shoulders. "Ooh, my," she drawled, sarcasm dripping from her voice. "Look at the muscles in your shoulders, why, they're almost as large as Korl's!"

Sharp-nails grinned and nodded her head with

enthusiasm. "All that poling, and your… how can we put it? Oh, yes, your masculine ways. It'll make you a great provider someday."

Mahri gasped. They insinuated that she wasn't even a woman! She felt no satisfaction when Korl's full lips narrowed into a thin line and his jaw hardened with anger. He'd basked in their attention and encouraged them to continue it. She blamed him more than the women, although the game had gotten more dirty than he'd probably intended. Or had it? It didn't matter, for she'd had enough.

"You might want to wash that hand," Mahri suggested to the woman whose hand the fish bone had landed on. "You never know what my pet might've eaten lately."

Jaja grinned.

Then she turned to frizzy-hair. "And my pet's never bitten anyone yet, but you never know, you could be the exception."

Jaja obligingly bared his teeth.

Korl threw back his head and laughed, a deep-throated sound that made Mahri's lips twitch even while she wanted to slap him. He disentangled himself from the clutching women and gallantly held out his arm to Mahri. "A dance, my lady?"

Mahri put her hands on her hips. "You've got to be kidding. I wouldn't dance with you if you were the last—"

"I only suggest it," he interrupted, "to save the lives of these two unfortunate women who dared to tangle with a water-rat." His arm snaked around her waist and Jaja clapped little webbed hands, then jumped onto Korl's shoulder and mimicked the beseeching look the prince impaled her with.

"They're not worth the trouble," snapped Mahri, trying to pull out of the circle of his arm. She'd never admit to him the humiliation they'd made her feel with their comments. She threw Jaja a baleful look but he just blinked at her innocently, clasped his hands together and shook them imploringly.

Little traitor, she thought, and saw him blanch from the force of it. *You're supposed to be on my side*.

Jaja squealed and hopped back onto her shoulder.

"Maybe *they* aren't in any danger," Korl replied. "But what about him?"

Mahri turned and saw Trian standing nearby, watching them intently, a shell of quas-juice in his hand. "Why would I hurt my own cousin?"

"Not you, me."

"All right, why would *you* hurt my cousin?"

"He isn't really your cousin, now, is he?"

Mahri shrugged in exasperation. "By Brez, but not by blood."

"That's what I thought." Korl began to drag her toward the dance circle, his arm like a vise around her waist. He glanced at Jaja. "Thought you were supposed to help me out, buddy."

Jaja squealed in disgust and hopped back to his shoulder.

Mahri tried to pull away, felt Korl's muscles hold her in place, and a primal thrill went through her at his incredible strength. And disgust at herself for such a foolish reaction. He entered the circle of dancers and yanked her against his chest. His eyes glittered, the pupils so huge they overwhelmed the light green at their border. His pale face seemed carved of bone, his jaw stiff with suppressed fury, the flickers of firelight playing along the high angle of his cheeks.

Mahri felt slightly intimidated. "Jaja," she whispered, "you're *my* pet, aren't you?"

The monk-fish laid a weary hand on his scaled forehead and his feathery fin-like ears drooped as he shook his head. He crawled back onto her shoulder.

Korl watched Jaja and half-smiled in pity. "Would you leave him out of this?"

"Out of what?" Mahri made herself breathe. She was losing herself in his eyes again and hastily focused on his mouth. "I have no idea what you're talking about."

"Liar," growled Korl. "Trian called you his girl."

Korl moved her in his arms, guided her across the smooth bark beneath their feet with practiced skill. Mahri had never danced the courtly steps but knew the pattern as if she'd partnered with him her entire life. His body language spoke to her far easier than his words ever could.

"Trian's always called me his girl, especially after Brez… became sick. It doesn't mean anything."

"Like those women didn't mean anything to me?"

Mahri shook her head, the black beads on her headband twinkling with the movement. So, he'd been jealous of Trian and had sought revenge for some imagined tryst. What had living in the palace been like, that he'd learned such ways? "You played a game."

Korl's hand caught a stray lock of her hair and smoothed it back into the mass behind her head. As if it had been snared in some web he kept it there, filling his palm with the dark red strands, letting it flow through his fingers. "Life is a game."

His fingers through her hair created shivers of pleasure along Mahri's scalp. She moved her hand over his shoulder, curled it around the soft skin of his neck, and caressed the fine ends of his hair with the sensitive pads of her own fingers.

"Ach, my fine prince. Is that what we're doing?" Mahri melted against him, the top of her breasts overflowing the green silk to brand his chest with a gentle heat. "Just remember, two can play at any game."

They stood so close that Jaja managed to put one foot on Korl's shoulder while keeping the other on Mahri's. With a triumphant chirrup he beat his chest with two webbed fists before he hopped to the ground, gave a nod of almost human self-satisfaction and scampered away.

Korl ignored the monk-fish and Mahri felt his hand tense as he cupped the back of her head and forced her mouth close to his. She made the mistake of looking into his eyes and her steps faltered, slowed, until they no longer danced within the circle of people, just swayed to the rhythm of the drums, the haunting melody of the bone flutes.

Mahri felt the beat of his heart against her own. His nose flared and his breath pounded across her mouth and she opened, inhaling the life of him as he lowered his head and set his lips on her own. For a brief moment his mouth lay unmoving atop her, that full bottom lip warm and quivering over her own. Then he groaned and sought to devour her, his tongue grasping at her, demanding her own in his, sliding back and forth as if he couldn't get near enough, couldn't taste her fully enough.

Korl tore his mouth away. "I've wanted—I've needed to do that all day." Then dipped his head down to hers again.

Mahri felt like a jellyfish, trembling and pliant in his arms. If he laid her down and took her in front of the entire village, she wouldn't have the will to resist him. Her mind kept screaming of danger but her body won with its insistence of pleasure. When she heard the clatter of hundreds of seashells she wasn't sure whether to curse at Caria or hug her in gratitude.

"May I cut in?" Caria insinuated herself between the two of them. Korl looked at her in dazed confusion. "For a prince," she whispered, "you have absolutely no sense of propriety."

Mahri choked back a giggle. Caria sounded so stuffy! But then she looked around and realized that none of the villagers were dancing, eating… or talking, for that matter. They stood and stared at her as if she'd broken some taboo. Well, she'd been to enough celebrations to know that the villagers weren't ordinarily a shy group. Why, she'd seen Caria and Wald near attack each other in the heat of a dance.

"What's the matter with everyone?" she asked.

"It's Trian, you fish-brain," hissed Caria.

"Trian?"

"Everyone's been watching him, waiting for the explosion. Now, dance with me Healer." Caria waved at the musicians and they struck a lively tune, and she spun Korl away.

Mahri snapped her mouth shut. Truly, she and Trian were fond of each other, but she'd never thought—

"May I have this dance?"

Mahri looked up into the face of her cousin. Without waiting for an answer he swept her up in his arms and danced her as far away from Caria and Korl as the circle allowed. He stumbled and Mahri knew he'd had too much quas-juice this night.

Trian concentrated on his steps, that broad forehead wrinkled in a frown, his amber eyes almost hidden beneath thick curls of dark brown hair. "I've been waiting," he said, his voice slightly slurred, "until I thought you were ready. After what I seen tonight, I'm thinking it's time."

Mahri didn't want to have this conversation. All the villagers had decided to dance, crowding into the circle and huddling around the two of them, their ears tuned toward their words.

"Trian—"

"Now, do not interrupt, girl. You know I care for you, always have. But you weren't done grieving, wanting to be alone, and I left you. But seems like I need to be asking now, before you get yourself into any trouble. What I'm saying is… that I want you for life, to belong to me."

Mahri stepped on his foot. Hard. He blinked, that smile still pasted on his dear face. She sighed. "Trian, I don't want to belong to anyone. Not ever."

His arms tightened on her shoulders. "What about that Healer?"

"That's different. It's just—a game, Trian. That's all. I only want to belong to me. After Brez, well, it hurts too much, tangling your life with someone else's, then having it ripped away. Do you understand?"

Suddenly he hugged her to him, picking her up off her feet and dancing her across the floor as if she were one of Sh'ra's rag dolls. Mahri saw a flash of blazing pale-green eyes as she spun.

"I want you to know that I love you," whispered Trian.

"And I love you too, but like a cousin, that's all. Now let me down."

He stopped dancing and set her on her feet, raked strong fingers through his mahogany curls in frustration. "All right then, I'll let it be. But you best be careful with that Healer, something's not right with him."

Mahri nodded, grateful that Trian hadn't pushed his suit any further. She'd had no idea that he'd wanted her in that way. "I'm sorry, Trian."

Trian's generous mouth split into a grin. "You're still my girl, that's sure. And being family means I'll have to protect you from anyone whose intentions aren't honorable. You hear?"

Mahri threw her arms around the big man's shoulders, grateful after all, that they'd talked. She hadn't known how much he cared. "I'm a Wilding, Trian. I don't need anyone to watch over me."

"I know," Trian whispered into her ear, "but that man's peculiar, girl. You're playing with fire."

Mahri nodded. "Aya, I'll be careful," she promised. Then she kissed him, a small part of her wondering why it felt so different when she placed her lips on Korl's. With Trian, it felt the same as if she'd just touched his hand.

Then she felt herself torn from his arms, glimpsed a blur of pale hair and raised fists that slammed into her cousin like a wave of white water from a storm. Trian grunted, rolled, and came up smiling. Then the prince went down in a flurry of fists.

The villagers surrounded the combatants, almost stepping on Mahri in their haste to see the action. She

heard them calling out changes in wagers and realized
that they'd been waiting for this all night.

Caria dragged her to her feet. Wald glanced to make
sure she was all right, then pushed his way through the
crowd, already yelling encouragement at Trian.

"Wald thought you'd ruin it," muttered Caria.

"What?" Mahri craned her neck to see over the
crowd. Taller than most women, she could almost see
over the men's heads.

"Said the whole village knew there'd be a fight
tonight. Either a cat- or fist-fight, they didn't care, although they wagered on that, too. Wald thought you'd
spoil their fun."

Mahri bit her lip. In the swamps they worked rough
and played the same. So she wasn't surprised. She just
didn't appreciate that she'd been a part of the wagering.

Jaja! she mind-sent. Her pet scampered up her dress,
almost tearing it in the process. "See how Korl is faring,
will you?"

He nodded briskly and hop-skipped across several
shoulders to the innermost circle. Mahri saw him clap
his hands with delight, shake a fist and swing it in mock
fighting, then bound back to her own shoulder. He nodded, bared pointed teeth in semblance of a human smile,
then went back to the action.

"Has Korl had any zabba?" asked Caria.

Mahri shook her head. She would've Sensed any
Power within him.

"Then it's a fair fight and they won't kill each other,
so let's go get some food."

Mahri trailed behind the clatter of Caria's shells,
glanced back once at a particularly loud thump, and

cringed. They fought over something that neither one could have.

At the mention of food, Jaja had left the pleasure of the fight for that of the table. The little scamp stuffed sweets in his mouth at an alarming rate, and Mahri watched in fascination while she nibbled on farnuts and redshoots.

Shells clattered and Caria nudged her arm. "The fight's over. And I think Korl won."

"How do you know?"

"He's coming to claim his prize."

Mahri looked up in alarm. Korl strode determinedly toward her, his golden hair in wild disarray, that gorgeous smink vest torn to shreds, the beginnings of a swelling in his right eye and a line of scarlet running down his full mouth. Every inch the conquering hero.

He grabbed her arm. "Come with me. Now."

"I'm not going anywhere with you, you arrogant…" sputtered Mahri.

The muscles of his face tightened hard as bone and Caria drew in a breath. With a negligent sweep of his arms he tossed Mahri over his shoulder and stomped out of the clearing, villagers stumbling over themselves in their haste to get out of his way. The frizzy-haired woman and her friend glared envious daggers at Mahri and even though she cursed Korl viciously, she paused a moment to give the women a grin of smug satisfaction.

Then resumed cursing, crying out for some root. If somebody would give her some, she'd show Korl that he couldn't just toss her around like a bag of seed. But the villagers didn't interfere and she had a feeling Trian couldn't.

"Put me down!"

Korl plunged into the forest, the sounds of the village party dwindling behind them. "Not a chance." He paused for a moment, as if getting his bearings, and Mahri heard the unmistakable sound of root being crunched. When he resumed his purposeful stride she tried to take the Power shuddering through his body but this Bond thing was so new to her. She hadn't yet forced the Power from him and wasn't quite sure how to go about it without him Pushing it to her.

By the time she thought she'd figured it out he'd reached wherever he'd been taking her and dumped her into a carpet of fallen leaves. While the blood drained back out of her head she looked around and gasped at the sight before her.

In the middle of a road branch grew one of the largest, most beautiful flowers she'd ever seen. Taller than two men's heights, wider than four, it grew from a vine that twirled around the trunk of the tree and along the branch. At the bottom of the red blossom small petals puffed out like feathers, but the larger, silken ones gathered up to a peak at the top. She'd never seen the like before.

"What is it?"

Korl grasped her hand and lifted her to her feet, his grip firm and final, pulling her toward the scarlet flower. "Wald showed me. He said this vine blooms once every thousand moons. It's called a xynth flower."

His voice had dropped to that deep timbre. Mahri shivered, thinking of the man who'd saved her life, the jealous feelings that those two women had aroused in her, the Bond and the fusing of their souls. And the smell of him that mingled with the spicy scent of that red flower. "What are you doing?"

Korl had dragged her next to the bloom, reached out and forced an opening through the huge petals, revealing a crack just large enough for a person to squeeze through.

"Get in," he commanded.

"I think not."

He sighed, picked her up, and tossed her through that curtain. She landed with a bounce and a curse. The spicy scent was stronger inside the flower; it filled her senses as she noted the small opening above her where the petals reached in a peak, allowing the light of the moons into this nest, the soft, powdery surface she lay on, which had a golden glow of its own, and the feathery fronds of stamens that encircled the inner wall of the petals.

Mahri filled her lungs with that wonderful perfume and it seemed to flow into every muscle of her body, through the channels of her root-paths, relaxing yet stimulating all of her senses. She sighed. A feathery touch brushed her cheek, then the sides of her arms, the top of her breasts. Yet it didn't startle her, even though it took a few seconds to realize that those gentle caresses came from the flower itself, that the stamens surrounding her swayed with almost sensuous undulations, stroking and releasing even more of that marvelous scent.

"Korl," she whispered.

His voice came back at her muffled through the petals. "What?"

"Come in."

"I think not."

Mahri shifted on the cushiony surface, trembling

from the feel of the glittering powder that covered this chamber, the constant strokes of the feather-like stamens against her skin, the languid heat that increased every time she breathed in that spicy scent. She stretched out full length, the silk of her dress sliding across the tiny hairs of her body, the glowing powder filling her pores and making her skin ache with the want of a touch. What was happening to her?

"Korl," she groaned, and she heard him respond with a grunt, a rip of petals as he plunged into the giant flower, overwhelming her with the sudden heat of his body, the touch of his hands against her sensitized skin. "By-the-moons, what's happening to me?"

Korl's voice felt hard. "I take what I want."

"Aya, aya," she agreed. "But why don't I care?"

His hands slid up her ankles, the powder a smooth catalyst for his motions, catching the hem of her silk dress and scrunching it up to her thighs. His voice when it answered had changed, a distracted sort of throatiness. "The perfume of the flower, and the pollen it exhumes, releases your inhibitions."

There he goes again, thought Mahri, using words I can't understand. Forcing her to remain clueless or display her own ignorance. But it didn't matter. She giggled and lifted her bottom so Korl could slide her dress underneath her. The sweet, sweet feel of cool air against her naked skin made her long to stretch like a treecat and wriggle the rest of her way out of that blasted silk.

Korl growled when she did just that, his eyes for a moment flashing with root-Power, illuminating the planes of his face, the intense longing in his soul. The nightly rain began, drops hitting Mahri's exposed breasts; sudden slaps of gentle pain. The flower responded by closing the petals above them, plunging them into darkness illuminated only by the golden glow of the pollen, which heightened her senses even further, straining to hear his breath, the beat of his heart.

She jumped at the sudden loud sounds of ripping smink fur. Held her breath, waiting for him to touch her again. Mahri couldn't think of her past, nor of the future. The present was all that mattered.

Having the man that saved her life quenching the fire that burned between her legs, in her heart, throughout her soul.

She cursed him when he didn't come to her quickly enough, when he teased her with only the touch of his tongue, licking the drops of rain from her breasts. She could feel him smile when she arched her back, a silent command to touch her that he ignored, letting her writhe shamelessly, until she managed to clutch his hair, bring his mouth over her own, sucking at his tongue until he writhed as well.

Love is grand, thought Mahri.

Their bodies entwined, covering them with pollen so thickly that their skin began to glow with a golden light.

Finally, Mahri had the freedom to touch him anywhere she wished, without the fear and confusion that usually followed. She brushed the hair away from his face and allowed her hands to linger in it, traced a path to that full bottom lip, along his cheekbones and across his brows, down his neck to the swell of his shoulders and the rigid planes of his stomach.

Korl explored her as well, with a less than gentle

hand. He touched her with a fierce possessiveness, pulling her against him so that she felt the hardness of his want for her, and she let him… let him push against her own wet heat, consumed by a frantic desire that satiated her soul and allowed her heart to soar.

Yet, in a tiny corner of her mind lay the knowledge that he had manipulated her, using the gifts of Sea Forest to get what he wanted. When he drove into her she screamed aloud in joy and anger, and as the rain began to pound in earnest against the petals of their shelter, so did Korl pound himself into her, trying to lay a claim and Mahri fighting it all the way.

She sensed the undercurrent of violence that lay in this night and somehow knew that when the rain brought a storm that shook the foundations of their xynth flower, it damaged the root vine and killed the blossom for another thousand moons.

Chapter 10

"CARIA," WHISPERED MAHRI, SHAKING THE SLEEPING woman's shoulder.

The blonde woman cracked open an eyelid. "What?"

"I wanted to say goodbye."

Caria slapped a hand over her face and rubbed at her lids. "Goodbye? What do you mean? It's the middle of the night!"

Mahri readjusted the pack slung over her shoulder. It'd been two weeks since the night of the party and Korl's use of the xynth flower. And she'd tried—unsuccessfully—to avoid Korl since. But it seemed like every time she turned around, there he was, making her long for something that could never be.

"Shh," she commanded. "You'll wake him up."

Wald snorted and rolled over. Caria blinked. "He sleeps like a snar-fish."

Mahri shook her head. "Not him, the Healer." And she glanced around the room, expecting that handsome face to materialize from any corner.

Caria sat up. "So that's what this is all about. Well, Korl hasn't slept in the house since the night of the dance. I don't know where he goes at night but I thought you would."

"I've been too busy trying to avoid him."

The blonde woman stifled a yawn. "And now you're trying to sneak off and leave him behind, is that it?"

Mahri nodded. "Aya. I can't stay here any longer, with him around. It's like there's some kind of force that pulls me to him and I'm just plain tired of fighting it."

"I'm sure if we talked about this…" Caria swung her legs out of bed, shivered in the cool night air as she uncovered a light globe, and blinked up at her sister.

"It wouldn't change my mind. I've decided to leave him here, see if I can get any news from the city about his disappearance and if they're still looking for him. I can decide what to do after that."

Jaja bounded into the room, hopped onto the bed, and eyed Mahri's traveling clothes with something akin to humor.

"I still think," muttered Caria, reaching out to the monk-fish, "that you can trust Korl to keep our secrets." She hugged Jaja to her and smoothed the silky scales in a parting caress.

"You have more faith in him than I do. The Royals would kill to know the source of our root and would love to hunt a Wilding. I can't trust him not to betray us." Mahri swept up Jaja and settled him on her shoulder. "Now, give me whatever zabba the village needs me to trade and let me be on my way. I didn't wake you for another argument."

Caria humphed, but fetched the supply of root that had been harvested in the past few weeks. She handed it over with a sigh, then grasped Mahri in a desperate hug. "You will come back, won't you?"

"Aya. The Forest willing."

The blonde woman handed Mahri a light globe and studied the heart-shaped face. "Running from him won't help, you know."

The Wilding shrugged, chewed a bit of root, and lifted the flap of otter skin.

"Jaja thinks something's terribly funny," added Caria, as if that would make her think twice about leaving.

Mahri's sparkling eyes met the soft, brown orbs of her pet. He did seem to be in the throes of some private hilarity. She shrugged, not upsetting his balance on her shoulder in the least, and walked into the night.

The air felt thick with moisture, a prelude to the predictable rainfall, and the perfume of evening blooming flowers, their petals open for their supply of fresh water, mingled with the musky odor of wet undergrowth. The moons lit her path around leaf shadows, so Mahri covered the light globe until she might have need of it when the inevitable storms darkened the sky. She tried not to tiptoe like some kind of thief… or coward, she thought to herself angrily. But she still kept glancing around, expecting to see pale hair lit by moon-glow, a strong mouth that challenged her to kiss it without saying a word.

Mahri breathed a gusty sigh of relief when she reached her boat. Jaja suppressed a snort of laughter. She glanced at her pet and he snickered, holding a tiny webbed hand over his mouth. She might as well quit pretending indifference and give the little scamp the satisfaction of knowing that he'd got to her.

"All right, what's so funny?" she whispered.

Jaja hopped from her shoulder and leaped into the boat, skipping along its length, occasionally disappearing into the erect narwhal tent. Mahri frowned and stepped onto the deck, felt the heaviness of their anchorage and swore. She lifted the end of a blanket that protruded from the tent opening and kicked at the bare feet that lay beneath.

"How long've you been sleeping on my boat?" she demanded.

Prince Korl crawled out and stretched, his chest expanding to gorgeous proportions. "How long've you been avoiding me?" he countered. Then he shook the hair from his face, finger-combed it back and looked at her with hungry eyes.

"Get off my boat."

"Why? Where're you going in the middle of the night?"

Mahri shook with frustration, the bit of root she'd taken playing along her pathways like music waiting to be sung. "None of your business!"

He stood, barely swayed against the movement of her craft. He'd slept in nothing but snar-scale leggings, his chest bare and smooth and taunting her with the play of muscles beneath. "You wouldn't be planning on leaving me here, would you?"

Mahri opened her mouth but couldn't speak.

"But then, I've only your word that you'd take me home and what's that worth, coming from a water-rat?" He'd stepped near her, his face bare inches away and hardened with anger like a rigid sculpture.

She hadn't been this close to him since the dance, had avoided the mere sight of him. Mahri groaned. She had hoped that staying away from him would dull the chemistry between them but it only made being close to him again worse.

If he had looked at her hungrily a moment ago, she devoured him now; the tilt of his nose, the sweep of his brow. Without his headband on, the pale strands of his hair swept across his cheeks, along his jaw, like glowing fibers of silk. She'd missed the sight of him, acknowledged the feeling with self-disgust, then cast it away. She couldn't look away if she tried so she might as well enjoy it. Mahri licked her lips.

He gritted his teeth. "Stop it," he said, grabbing her shoulders and giving her a shake.

She knew what he meant and didn't pretend otherwise, but she had no control over the way her body invited his to touch her. And his anger didn't deter her, she reacted to it the only way her body could react to him at all—with an ache in her groin and a fever in her breast.

Mahri bit her lip. Think with your mind and not your heart and soul, she told herself. He's using your attraction to him to get what he wants. "I can't take you home because I can't trust you not to betray the village... or me."

Warm rain began to fall, the sound of it overwhelming her senses, for it seemed to enclose them in a cocoon of privacy from the rest of the world. His strong hands relaxed and lowered down her arms, the wetness making them slide erotically across her skin. His voice lowered to a timbre that made her heart skip. "That explains why you won't take me home but not why you've been avoiding me."

Mahri tried to pull away from him. If he'd stop touching her, she might be able to think straight. "Because I couldn't trust myself."

He grinned, anger gone as if it'd never been, that shallow dimple piercing his cheek and curving a drop of rain that traced along his skin. His pale hair now lay flat against his scalp, curling and twisting across his forehead, and he blinked against the rain, lashes darkened and thick from the wet. "If you took me home, you wouldn't have to worry about it."

"Aya."

"But then you might never see me again." His voice gentled into a tease. "Sure that's not why you won't take me back?"

"You conceited—that's not it at all."

He slid his palms into her own and held them together, his gaze focused on their entwined fingers, not daring to look at her, as if he knew she couldn't concentrate when their gazes locked. Or as if he couldn't. "Listen to me, Mahri Zin. It's imperative that I return to the palace. Not for my sake, but for my people."

She felt the warmth of his hands enclosing hers and frowned. He'd touched her more in the past few weeks than she'd been touched in years. Mahri kept her distance from others, even Caria; they seemed to sense it and rarely tried to invade her space. Yet every time he came near her he reached out as if it were the most natural thing in the world for their skin to meet, and her own traitorous body invited him to do it. How could her mind and heart be so at odds with each other?

"Did you hear me?"

"Aya."

"Do you understand?"

"No, but I can't wait for you to explain." She couldn't keep the sarcasm from her voice. His body might be irresistible, but she knew his mind and found it not the least bit attractive. She used that thought like a weapon. He was arrogant, proud, conceited beyond reason…

Korl squeezed her fingers. "Believe it or not, I've

changed." She snorted. He continued without skipping a beat. "These past few weeks, hunting and working with your people, I've come to realize that they're my people too. And that the only help for them is if I inherit the crown."

Aya, thought Mahri, conceited beyond reason. "Because you'll treat them as equals? No longer control the use of zabba? Allow them access to the same knowledge that Royals possess?"

"Well… no."

Mahri sighed. At least he was being honest.

"But, I *am* different than other Royals. I'd try to make their lives better."

"And I should believe that because…?"

Korl growled. "What do you think I was doing in the Healer's Tree? I was learning the art! And do you think my father encouraged me? Not on your life! He almost chose S'raya to rule, because of my 'weakness for others' as he called it. Not until he saw that it could… be of benefit to the Royal line did he approve of it, or me."

Mahri feared to ask what benefit they derived. That flash she'd read in his mind, of a bone-knife plunging at him—could he have used the healing knowledge to defend himself? And what kind of guilt would that cause in his mind?

She tried to twist her fingers from his hands. He tightened his grip. Then she used the Power to tweak his muscles but it didn't work. Another result of their Bond?

Mahri became aware of the rain beating down on her as strongly as his words. She sighed, and supposed that she should just be grateful that he cared to explain himself to an ignorant Wilding. "You mentioned S'raya before."

His gaze snapped upward and traveled the contours of her face. "I thought you were in league with her—but you could never... S'raya's my half-sister, the eldest of Queen P'erll's children, while I am the eldest of my mother, A'nem."

Mahri nodded. A'nem died years ago, but it was said that she was King Oshen's one true love, that P'erll had used guile and trickery to gain her crown. And that her children were just as cunning and ambitious. Dockside rumors held more truth than she'd have credited. "And S'raya wants to rule?"

"She has half my tolerance for root but she plays my father well. The woman has no pride."

"And you've got an overabundance." How often had it caused him strife with the king? She watched as his brow furrowed in worry, the water skipping across the wrinkles, running a path to the frown that curved his lips. He relaxed his grip on her fingers and she freed them, only to miss the heat of his hands.

Korl swiped rain-soaked hair from her forehead. "I would've said the same of you." He cupped the sides of her face and ran his thumbs back and forth across her cheeks. "S'raya considers hunting Wildings her favorite sport. She's tried to convince the king of the need for another hunt. With my absence she might even succeed. Considering the alternative, wouldn't I be a better choice?"

Mahri stiffened. Ach! Another hunt, like the one that had taken her mother. Would they track her down as well, toying with their prey, torturing her until she screamed for the mercy of a quick death? She shuddered. "It's not up to me."

"Oh, but it is water-rat. I felt the Touch of a Master

from that ship that pursued us through the cove. If S'raya has somehow formed an alliance with the Seer's Tree, there's no one to stop her, except for me. And now, through our Bond, you."

He lowered his head and raised her face to meet his own. Mahri saw his lips part, the rain making them glisten in the moonlight, and knew that if he kissed her she'd be lost.

"No," she whispered, pulling away, fighting against that allure with more than physical strength. Did he think that she was so smitten with him that he could use it to influence her decision? Well, her heart didn't rule her mind, for she'd learned the hard way that therein lay disaster. Brez had made her all sorts of declarations, but in the end he'd left her alone. She couldn't count on anything… or anyone.

"Words can't sway me to risk family and friends. You'd say anything to convince me to take you back, don't you think I know that?"

Korl closed the distance between them. Mahri took a step back. With a roar of frustration he caught her in his arms, strong bands of muscle enclosing her with a heat that took her breath away.

"You won't believe my words," he ground out. "Maybe you'll believe this." And he replaced the cool wetness of the rain on her lips with the moist heat of his own mouth.

Mahri's mind screamed at her to make him stop… she even managed to pull her face away from his. He growled deep in his throat, she felt the muscles of his chest quiver with it, then grabbed a handful of her sopping hair to hold her head still.

"Listen to me," he rasped, but didn't speak another word, just swooped down on her again, drinking the fresh raindrops from her lips, plunging his tongue into her with fevered passion. Mahri felt overwhelmed by his desire; it was as if he'd held a part of himself back before and had now allowed himself to open the floodgates.

By-the-thirteen-moons! she thought as she panicked beneath the onslaught. Could she even hold all that this man offered her?

His mouth seared her face, his teeth tracing across her cheeks, threatening nips of hunger. He whispered into her ear, his breath sending shivers down her spine, his voice husky with an ache that went beyond any yearning that Mahri imagined she'd ever felt for him.

"I want you like I've never wanted anything before." He licked the water dripping off her ear. "My obsession. I'm hiding nothing from you now."

His hand slid from her hair to her upper back, arching her body so that his tongue could slide down her neck and he could drink the rain that cascaded between her breasts before traveling back up that same path.

"Since the moment I saw you," he whispered again, and Mahri's heart pounded, thudded in her ears until she could hear nothing else. She wrapped shaking arms around his neck and held on, her knees too weak to hold her, the feeling that his words aroused and the ardor he radiated shuddering through her until all she could feel was him.

He devoured her mouth again, panting as he sucked at her lips, curling his tongue around her own. The cool rain mingled with the heat of their own wetness and Mahri absorbed it all, fear of his overwhelming desire still tangled in her belly, but holding on to that part of her that was separate from him.

His hands traveled down her back, slid beneath her snar-scale leggings, and cupped her bottom, pulling her lower half against his hardness. He moaned into her mouth and Mahri went limp, the heat of his hands branding her, making her burn, consuming her in that fire. He held her with a strength that made her stomach flutter anew, and she was dimly aware that while he cupped her roundness with one hand the other had escaped the confines of her leggings and traveled across the tautness of her belly. Korl shifted, flattened his hand beneath her navel, the tips of his fingers poised atop the waistband of the front of her leggings.

Mahri had to turn her head sideways to look at him, for he'd trapped her between his arms, his pelvis at her hip. Moonlight reflected off the pale whiteness of his hair, created shadows along those sculpted cheekbones, danced along his rigid jaw and across the fan of his lashes. His eyes should've been shadowed but they burned with an inner light, glazed with a passion that went beyond mere sexual desire. Obsession, thought Mahri.

"It's too much," she whispered.

His fingers slid down, as if he couldn't stop them, but his gaze stayed locked with her own, trying, at least, to seek her permission. Mahri felt his palm burn between her hipbones and she just wanted to thrust upward, to feel his fingers possess her and stop the agony that caused her to whimper his name. "Korl. No, I'm... losing myself in you. You take too much."

"You are mine." He ground it out through clenched teeth.

Mahri shook her head in denial but feared that right now, if he wanted to—for she couldn't, wouldn't stop him—if he touched her there, with this desire that he'd overwhelmed her with, she would be his. Worse, that she'd be so tangled up in him she'd be forgotten and lost in his own needs and desires. She had to stop this—now.

"Do you drug all the girls you want to sleep with?"

"I normally don't have to."

Mahri clenched her fists. "Well, you don't have a xynth flower with you this time to use my body to over-whelm my mind."

His sigh of frustration fanned her temple with warmth and when his mouth nuzzled her there it set off a chain reaction of tiny shivers that made the hair on the back of her neck itch.

When he spoke his words were muffled against her skin. "When we Bonded you Saw into my mind, Mahri. You know what I feel for you."

"You think you love me."

"I know it."

With those words the terror that Mahri had managed to hold at bay unleashed inside of her with a fury that numbed her. She could no longer feel the heat of his hands, the warmth of his lips. Fear of being made the fool, of losing what little pride and dignity the world had man-aged to leave her with helped her to see clearly. She knew in that moment that he'd only needed her, which was a selfish emotion, whereas love was the total opposite.

Poor Korl—did he even know the difference? He'd saved her life more than once, had followed her into the madness of overdose and thought himself in lust with her because he could use her. Like a tool.

Mahri glared at him. "Ach! You don't know the meaning of the word."

His face, by-the-moons she'd never forget the look on his face as he lay open and vulnerable before her and she rejected him. She felt his withdrawal like a tangible thing, heard him close himself off with the finality of a door slamming shut. Mahri's heart squeezed painfully as she realized that he might never offer her the gift of his true self again. But she felt it as such a small regret in an ocean of fear.

Carefully, he removed his hands from her body and stepped back, letting her go. Mahri swayed. She burned with more emotions than she could name, throbbed in places that might never be eased again. A sudden deluge of rain washed the sweat off her body and the tears from her face. In disbelief, she noticed that the river gurgled and the forest sang its leaf-song as if everything were normal with the world.

The rain had slowed to a sprinkle when Korl spoke again. "You must believe me now," he sighed, while he ran shaking fingers through his sodden hair.

"Aya. I believe that you want me, even though I'm not of Royal blood."

He looked at her with astonishment. "And that I'd never betray you? You realize that now, don't you?"

"What has one got to do with the other?" A stray lock of white-gold hair crept back over his brow and she longed to smooth it back, and ach, how even that scared her now. He confused need with love, would he cause her to do the same with lust? This was truly the most formidable man she'd ever met.

"How can you think that I'd ever do anything to

hurt you after, after I…" The passion that had softened his face began to change to a very controlled fury. He grabbed her shoulders and Mahri trembled like a leaf in the wind. With calculated ease his arms snaked around her waist, rubbed slickly against her lower back, forcing her closer by small degrees. "We're Bonded water-rat. Once that happened, you didn't have a choice anymore."

"What choice?" Mahri raised her hands against his chest and tried to push him away. He couldn't be budged and she gave up the futile attempt, amazed that even now her willful hands smoothed over the hardness of his muscles, feeling the water turn his skin into warm silk.

"The one whether to trust me or not." His hands stilled and she felt his body go rigid. "I've tried everything else," he whispered. "Forgive me." And then she felt his mind plunge inside of her.

He invaded the pathways of her Power before she had a chance to defend herself, drawing on all that shivered through her, sucking her dry from one breath to the next. Mahri watched in horror while his eyes changed, slow sparks of her stolen Power making them flicker with green fire. Her legs buckled and only the strength of his arms held her up, and she thought—for just a moment—that he'd drain her until she died.

Then he fed the Power back to her by slow degrees, letting her know he was in total control of the act, of her life. Mahri breathed and let the strength flow back into her limbs, pushed him away and felt him allow it.

"You… you…" With a wealth of dockside slurs to choose from, she still couldn't think of one nasty enough to describe him.

He raked his fingers through his hair, his gaze unable to meet hers. "I can do that at any time. But so can you."

Sparks of renewed Power flew from her own eyes.

"I wouldn't advise it though." Korl fell to his knees. "It would be what rape would feel like."

His shoulders slumped forward and his head hung down, that pale mass of hair falling wetly to cover his face. "The Bond of Power we share has no room for distrust, it passes beyond the scope of any ceremony that lifemate's may perform, beyond any legal binding a king can perform, beyond any physical act of joining. Do you understand that, now?"

Although Mahri burned with the rage that his violation had created in her, she felt a sudden kernel of sorrow for him and quickly smothered it. He'd made her face something that she didn't want to see. "Was that necessary?"

"You knew it already but still failed to acknowledge it. Did I have another choice?"

Mahri stood with hands on hips, her mouth open in shock. She felt as if he'd thrown her into a whirlpool and waited until she was good and dizzy before he yanked her out. "By-the-moons! You'll go to great lengths to get your own way, won't you?"

She spun, unwound the rope from the dock, flicked her wrist and poled away from the village. Jaja emerged from wherever he'd been hiding and patted Korl on the shoulder. But the man still slumped over, refusing to lift his head.

The rhythm of the current beneath the deck made Mahri feel almost normal again. She'd had enough. Somehow she'd have to get free of him and break the connection of their Bond that felt like a noose tightening around her neck. She took a deep, steadying breath. Right now she could think of only one way to be safe from him and that meant she'd have to get him as far away from herself as she could.

"I learn my lessons well. You go home, Great One, and you'll stay out of my life and pathways forever, do you understand?"

Chapter 11

THE SUN'S RAYS PENETRATED THROUGH THE CANOPY and laid warm fingers across Mahri's cheeks. The rain had continued throughout the night and although her new cloak of birdshark feathers had protected her from most of the deluge, her hair felt like a wet blanket and she welcomed the sunshine to dry it. She imagined steam rose from her head just like it swirled above the channel they traveled through.

Korl had shared the poling so she'd slept more than if she'd been traveling alone, but he didn't know the waterways like she did so she didn't trust him at the helm for long stretches. Still, having a companion—even an unwelcome one—made the journey easier.

Channels gorged by the rain let them ride higher than usual, and as Mahri ducked beneath yet another branch Korl emerged from the narwhal tent, stretching tendons and snapping muscles from the cramped quarters. Jaja chirruped a welcome but she ignored the man, trying not to look at him yet sensing his presence with every other part of her being. Hating him and wanting him at the same time made her incredibly frustrated.

"Where are we?" he asked, voice gruff and laced with something she couldn't quite name. Perhaps humiliation—if a prince could even succumb to such a foreign emotion.

"Even if there were a name for this channel I wouldn't tell it to you." Mahri rummaged inside the tent and pulled forth a strip of thick, pliable octopi skin. "As a matter of fact, you'll be wearing this in the daytime, just in case."

She tried to tie the blindfold around his head, but that pale hair of his, like some kind of silken trap, kept tangling in her fingers until she swore with annoyance.

Korl looked at her, making her hands tremble, her chest ache. "Do you really think," he demanded, "that I'll remember all these twists and turns through this swamp?"

Mahri shrugged. "I'm not taking any chances."

"I suppose I deserve that," he muttered, snatching the skin from her and wrapping it around his head himself. He sat where he'd stood, in the middle of the boat, head erect and shoulders squared, his back so stiff and straight that Mahri smothered a smile before she realized he couldn't see it.

Or could he? With practiced skill she swung her bone staff straight for his face, stopped a mere fingers-breadth from his nose. He hadn't moved, although he raised his brow at the sound the staff had made as it whistled in the air.

"Just testing," she murmured, flicking her wrist and inserting the pole back in the water.

Mahri sighed with relief. She could protect the village at least that much, for if he remembered any particular group of trees or had a good sense of the direction they traveled, he could remember the way to their swamps, or at least have a basis to begin. He'd had no root and she'd know if he tried to steal her own so he wouldn't be able to use the Power to track them.

Mahri gripped her staff until her knuckles whitened. He'd invaded her mind once before, they'd joined in that way too, however briefly. Perhaps the Bond allowed him to not only tap into her pathways of Power but also her thoughts as well. So that it wouldn't matter what he saw, he could just read her memories for the way to the village!

Yet, she'd know if he got into her head, wouldn't she?

Jaja must've felt her panic, for he hopped onto her shoulder and poked one tiny finger at her temple. Of course, remembered Mahri, he'd set that mind-barrier up for her. Now that he drew it to her attention she became fully aware of it. A black wall set around her thoughts, sealing her off from any tampering. And although Jaja had let Korl in her mind when they'd Bonded, they'd had her consent. She felt sure that Korl couldn't do it against her will, especially on his own.

Satisfied, Jaja bounded from her shoulder and settled himself in Korl's lap. The Royal felt for the silken mound, began to scratch a few favorite places until the monk-fish purred. Mahri kept glancing at those strong fingers, the way they gently stroked her pet with a hypnotic rhythm, and she couldn't stop from remembering her own skin beneath them. She gave a guilty start when Korl spoke.

"You don't trust anyone, do you?" he asked, his jaw thrust out and that veil of superiority settled securely over his features.

"Not particularly."

"Ha!"

"Ha, what?"

Mahri waited, but he wouldn't answer her.

Jaja clapped his webbed hands for her attention, then pointed at the shell of fishing gear, wiggling his eyebrows up and down in appeal. The channel they drifted through did have an abundance of tasty spotted trasks and if she didn't pole they could drift with the current and throw out a few lines.

Jaja wiggled his eyebrows faster, his upper lip even lifting with the movement. Mahri laughed and nodded, saw Korl flinch at the sound.

"Jaja wants fresh fish for dinner," she explained, finding it easier to look at him when he wasn't looking back at her. "I'm going to anchor a while. You can remove the blindfold while we hunt for worms."

Korl folded his arms across his chest and made no attempt to remove the strip of skin from around his head. Mahri shrugged at his stubbornness and then happily rooted through dead leaf muck, her and Jaja crooning with delight whenever they discovered one of the blue worms. She glanced back at Korl occasionally—the swamp was no place to be blindfolded—and once sprinted back to the boat when a vine-snake decided to investigate such a warm unmoving snack.

"Something wrong?" he asked, his head cocked to the side, listening to her grunts and the smacks of her pole.

Mahri flung the snake that hung from the tip of her staff into the water. "Er, not really."

When they'd collected enough worms, they baited the bone hooks and threw out the lines and Mahri watched her pet dance from string to string, waiting anxiously for a tug. A breeze kicked up and carried the salty tang of the ocean through the forest, made the leaves sway and sound like the roar of waves.

Mahri knew this stretch of water like the back of her hand. It presented little danger and therefore a great deal of boredom. She sat with her back to the bow and smiled with a private glee. She could sit and stare at Korl all day long and he'd never know it. Better yet, she wouldn't be trapped by his eyes, made to feel things she didn't want to.

Mahri could just enjoy the flesh.

Wouldn't that be nice, she mused, studying the way the muscles in his chest moved as he breathed. Just to join with him again on a physical level without the complications of his "love" for her or the constraints of their Bond, or the fear of an involvement that could lead to the loss of her self and the pain of separation. There was something to be said for the gifts of the xynth flower.

The sun made his hair glow with shimmers of gold, highlighted the planes of his face and shadowed the curve of his lips. Fine, golden hair traced a path down the middle of his chest and disappeared beneath the top of his snar-scale leggings. When she took him home, would she pine away for the sight of him? Would she try to discover ways to get a glimpse of that golden hair, that sculpted face? The thought filled her with self-contempt, that she'd let anyone have that much control over her. Yet, she feared that more than anything, that she'd ache to touch him but wouldn't be able to. Like Brez.

Mahri shivered and rubbed her arms. What to do? She wanted to be with him with every fiber of her being, knowing that they had no future, that in the next few days she'd never see him again. Thank-the-moons she didn't love him, at least she wouldn't go through that kind of agony again.

But she had to admit, her body did ache for him. Would it be better to ignore it, or give her flesh the satisfaction of his touch? Which would cause her the least pain? Yet, why should it? She had to keep reminding herself that she didn't love him, there were no risks here. Nothing could ever take away her freedom again.

Mahri stared at the blindfold and sighed.

"Getting an eyeful?" asked Korl.

She started, felt her face flush with warmth. How had he known that she was looking at him?

"I can feel your eyes on me," he replied, as if she'd asked the question aloud. "Like invisible flames..." Goosebumps rose on his flesh and he rubbed his arms. "Stop it, woman."

Mahri cocked her head and grinned. "Not a chance."

He frowned. "So what were you thinking?"

"When?"

"When you were undressing me with your eyes."

"How do you know... by-the-moons you're conceited." Mahri stood so abruptly she rocked the boat. "If you must know, I was thinking of the best way to gut the fish Jaja's caught."

She turned her back on the arrogant man and snapped at Jaja to let go of the line. That fish wouldn't go anywhere, the line lay secured to the boat, but her pet seemed determined to haul the trask in himself. He'd heave it up, the fish would yank, and overboard Jaja flew, to crawl up and do it again.

With a snort of disgust Mahri flung the fish on the deck and whacked it with her staff. She pulled her knife from her belt and began to gut the thing, her annoyance at Korl causing her to make a fine mess of it.

That evening they anchored and she hauled her fire shell to the tree shore—like any water-rat reluctant to have a flame on her boat—and they ate tender, grilled trask.

"Fit for a king," announced Korl, his smile lighting up the night. When the sky darkened and Mahri had removed the blindfold, he'd blinked at her like a man starved for the light of the sun. He hadn't taken his eyes off her since, and when they went back to the boat she immediately crawled into the privacy of the tent. She wouldn't admit to the goose bumps that his own stare kept raising on her skin.

The next morning the sun had barely trickled through the canopy when Mahri demanded that he put back on the blindfold. She sighed with relief when it lay firmly in place and her spirits rose as she poled through the narrow channel. Moss hung in great sweeps of lavender-blue from every limb, like scarves of fine silk adorning the massive sea trees. She poled around and through the maze of them, reluctant to tear the beautiful stuff.

She glanced at Korl. The palace couldn't compare to her own home and it was high time she proved it to him. With a grunt of determination, Mahri channel-hopped, taking them in a new direction. The tidal draw of the planet's thirteen moons made the direction of each channel of running water different, so that even parallel waterways could move in opposite directions. But even then they could change and only experienced water-rats could hope to predict their ways.

Toward dusk she stopped poling, rolling her shoulders to remove the soreness. A bit of root to augment her strength and See into the water and she'd made it just in time. Mahri stepped behind Korl, who sat with his back to stern and his sightless face held up to the wind. She untied the strip of octopi skin.

He blinked. "It isn't dark yet."

"Aya. Keep your eyes closed for just a bit."

He obeyed as she hunkered down beside him and when she brushed against him she could swear she felt each individual hair on his arm tickle her skin.

"What's going…" he started to ask, then his voice rose to be heard. "By-the-thirteen-moons, what's that racket?"

Mahri smiled at his use of her favorite oath. They'd spent too much time together. "Open your eyes."

He did. And they continued to open wider, and wider. She snickered at his expression, but not unkindly. She knew what he felt.

The channel widened before them into a small cove, with nothing but sky for a ceiling, allowing the birds that roosted here unhindered access. Parrots, parakeets, shakaans; every type of bird that possessed brilliant-colored plumage seemed to settle here. Feathers of color that boggled the imagination—ruby red, deep purple, screaming yellow, bright orange—graced thousands of wings and tails and crowns. Flocks of birds flew from tree to tree, swooped down to circle just above the water, huddling in groups among the branches until it seemed that the entire world was one huge, moving kaleidoscope of color.

And sound. Birds shrieked and squawked and cawed. Mahri covered her ears and stared, saw Korl do the same. Their boat drifted through the cove, feathers floating down to cover the deck with a blanket of clashing hue. The birds preened and displayed their plumage, fully aware of the watching intruders, yet secure in the force of their own numbers. A few curious groups swooped down to inspect the boat, a wave of blues and pinks and scarlets, and caused Jaja to make his own dive into the tent.

As the boat left the cove the sky darkened to full night, yet Mahri and Korl continued to stare blindly forward, their minds full of color, ears still ringing from the clamor.

His arm had snaked around her waist, Mahri wasn't sure when, nor how she'd managed to wind up half in his lap. When she tensed to move, his hold tightened with implied stubbornness so she snuggled closer and just let herself feel him.

His hand played with the curls of her hair. "Why'd you take me there?"

She slapped his hand. "Stop it. I... I'm not sure."

He continued to play with her hair. And waited.

"Oh, all right. Maybe to prove to you that my world's just as good as yours. Better even." Mahri could feel him grinning. Arrogant man.

"Why would you care what your enemy thinks? That's what I am, right? Your enemy. Someone you can't trust. Yet you show me all of your secret places, Mahri Zin. Why is that?"

She turned her face to his and watched the moonlight play in his hair.

"You'll always be my enemy," she whispered. "Not that it seems to matter."

And this time when her hand crept forward to brush the hair away from his forehead she didn't stop herself. Felt the softness of the strands against the back of her hand, the silky slide of it between her fingers. Curled her palm around the back of his neck and brought his lips to hers, smooth warmth that hardened into demanding, wet hunger.

He allowed her to lead, and when she pulled away he allowed that too. "Tomorrow, there's another secret place I want to show you. Does the Great One wish to see it?"

Korl smiled at her sarcasm. Actually smiled. "The man who loves the woman would like nothing more. But the prince who loves the Wilding…"

Mahri gritted her teeth. She wished he'd stop talking about love when he couldn't possibly understand the depth of it.

"A Bond is above the laws of man," he recited, "acknowledged by all and denied by none. Even a Royal."

"What're you talking about?"

"Even a King."

"Korl, if you don't speak plainly, I'll dump you over the side." Mahri felt for her pouch. "Where's my zabba?"

He laughed, a full-throated sound that echoed through the dark trees, set a few night creatures to squawking. "You make me laugh, water-rat. Perhaps that's why I love you."

"Would you stop prattling on about love as if you know what you're talking about?" she snapped.

His face grew serious, the angles harsh and grim. His voice vibrated low and controlled. "That's the second time you've accused me of not understanding what love is. So, why don't you enlighten me, Wilding?"

It doesn't matter, Mahri scolded herself. After a couple of days she'd never see him again anyway. Would it hurt him to keep his illusions? Why did she have to say anything? But the words were out and his nonchalant attitude about his feelings infuriated her.

"You want to know what love is?" Now that she'd started talking, the anger took control. Her eyes flashed fire, a fire more brilliant than any root Power could produce, and her dark red hair danced around her face in a fury. Mahri knew what a sight she looked when truly angry.

Korl stared at her as if mesmerized.

"Love is giving all of yourself until there's nothing left to hold onto, doing for another day after day, feeling their aches and joys as if they were your own. It's entwining your life with another's until there's no separating them." Mahri rose to her feet and towered above him. "It's a loss of freedom. It… It's soul-crushing agony when it… when it dies."

Mahri looked wildly around. No place to go, nowhere to hide. She'd told this man more in that one burst than she'd ever told Caria in her months of grilling. Why could this man do this to her? Why'd she let him? She backed away in horror, watching the changes of expression on his face.

Korl held out his hand to her and she backed up. He sighed and raked his fingers through his hair. "So, that's how it is," he murmured.

Mahri felt like she teetered on the edge of an abyss, any wrong move and she'd fall. And keep falling.

Korl looked up at her and smiled, that rakish half-grin that made her chest flutter every time. "I like my definition better," he said into the silence.

Mahri's mouth dropped open in disbelief, and then she slowly, almost painfully, began to laugh.

<hr />

Korl sat in the stern, his knuckles white where they gripped the sides of the craft. "I command you to let me take off this blindfold."

Mahri grinned and had to shout to be heard over the roar of water. "All right, but remember, you asked to see this."

They'd almost reached her most secret place, the place that she thought of as all her own, where she'd taken no one else before. Not even Brez. But in order to get there she'd had to chew zabba and pole with her utmost skill, and even then they'd still almost capsized in the rough waters.

Mahri danced from one side of the boat to the other, red hair sodden from spray and whipping around her face, muscles tense and rippling as she pushed against one obstacle after another. Humps of seashell, backs of widemouth skulkers, dead limbs and gnarled roots threatened her small craft and yet allowed her to pole against them to change direction. She didn't have time to hold on, the water flung them through the wide channel with a speed that made her skin tingle. The deck bucked and dropped beneath her feet so that at times she hung suspended in air, nothing but her bone pole to hang onto, nothing but skill and timing allowing her to stay in the boat.

She whooped and hollered while she fought the current. Such terror, such excitement... such fun!

Korl stared at her as if she were a madwoman. Jaja shrieked from somewhere beneath the collapsed tent. Mahri ignored them both, ready for what came next.

The boat shot over the edge of a drop off, hung suspended for a split second of infinity, then plopped back into the water with a gut-wrenching splash.

Mahri glanced around and sighed with relief. It hadn't changed.

The roar of white water could still be heard above

them, yet somehow muted now by the gentle waterfalls that surrounded this small pool of calm. Insects skittered along the mirror-like surface, purfrogs basked in the sun atop pallets of green moss pads, and swanies paddled gracefully along, stretching their long necks and singing their "tra-lee-lee" songs to each other.

Korl blinked. "How?" he managed to ask.

Mahri shrugged. "The only thing I can figure is that this entire channel is over one large tree root, or maybe a collection of dead ones. So there are dips that create these pools and we're below the surface of the natural sea right now. Of course, I'm just an ignorant water-rat, so I can only guess."

Korl raised his chin and gave her a look that said he felt the barb but it was beneath his dignity to respond to it. "The sea is flat, so there aren't many places that could produce these magnificent waterfalls. We have fountains in the palace gardens, though, that create the same effect."

Mahri flushed. He knew how to deliver a backhanded compliment, all right. "What about flutterflies?"

"My cousin has a collection he's quite vain of." Korl shrugged. "But they're common enough insects. Why?"

"The swamps have their own kinds of gardens." Mahri sat on the collapsed narwhal tent, cradled Jaja in her lap. "I'm bushed from fighting the white water. Would the Great One mind paddling for a while?"

He stretched his arms. "Where to?"

"Beneath that waterfall, second on the right."

"Beneath?"

"Aya."

Korl paddled while Mahri admired the way his

muscles bunched and spread through his back. Why hadn't he put his vest on today? His bare torso would drive her to distraction. His skin glistened in the sunlight, as if tiny crystals lay embedded in every pore. Over the past few weeks his pale complexion had darkened to a light gold, his hair now had pure white strands running through it. He'd been muscular before but now they bulged at the shoulders and rippled along his spine.

A deluge of cold water doused the fire building within her and made her splutter from the force of it. They'd drifted beneath the waterfall and Mahri tensed in anticipation while Korl looked around quizzically.

"Which way?" he asked.

"Let the current guide us through the tunnel to the other side."

"Interesting place," muttered Korl, peering into dry tunnels that water had carved eons ago. "Like a maze through the roots. Have you ever explored where these led?"

"Some," admitted Mahri. "But not all. It's easy to get lost in them and things live back there in the dark," she shuddered, "that I'd rather not see closer."

Their pupils had adjusted to the dusk of the tunnel so that when they emerged into the bright sunlight they both squinted and blinked. Mahri scanned the open sky above. No canopy sheltered them from winged predators here; a vista of open water stretched before them, unusual for Sea Forest, unless one ventured into the open sea. She knew it bothered Korl too, from the way he hunched his shoulders.

But Mahri knew from experience it'd be worth the risk. "The water's shallow here. I can pole." So she pushed from the stern and he paddled from the bow, through a meadow of grass that grew up through the still water.

"The grass is moving by itself," hissed Korl.

She grinned and turned to Jaja, nodded her head. He winked at her and strutted to the bow, scurried up the side until he sat on the front vee of the boat, pounded his little chest, and let forth an ear-numbing shriek.

Korl jerked backward as the field of grass erupted. Little brown birds chirped angrily and flew from their nests, rustling the grass with the beat of their wings. Hoppers as big as a fist jumped into the air and bounced across the deck of the boat. Snakes of all colors slithered forth to land with plops into the water, and for a few moments he became occupied with batting a few away from the boat with his paddle.

"Now, Korl, watch," demanded Mahri.

He flicked the last snake from the boat, a lethal looking variety that sported bright crimson spots of color along its skin. Korl looked at her a moment, his eyes meeting her own. She felt his annoyance at her—he must not like snakes—but it faded into that soul-searching gaze that made her heart skip over and her knees go weak. His stare traveled to her flushed cheeks, across her breasts and down the length of her legs.

He saw her excitement and responded to it.

Mahri shook her head at him, told herself to remember to breathe. Either she must be careful not to annoy him, or to contain her excitement. It did peculiar things to both of them.

Jaja hopped on Korl's shoulder and slapped him upside the head. The man shook the hair from his face and grinned sheepishly, caught movement from the corner of his eye and his mouth dropped open.

The field convulsed in one giant heave, threw half of itself upward, and left naked stalks of greenish-brown. The fluff in the air swirled and undulated and although Mahri knew what to expect she still sighed when it happened.

A cloud moved toward them, close enough to see that what had looked like one mass actually contained thousands of flutterflies. Some with wings larger than an open hand, others as tiny as her fingernail, all of them colored in shades of rose, with either spots of gold or purple, brown and yellow.

They eventually settled back in their grassy homes, but some stayed to twirl around their heads, alight like breaths of air on her boat and across her shoulders. Mahri held out her arms until she had her own wings of flutterflies.

She looked at Korl and giggled. He had a crown of flutterflies in his hair. One had settled on the end of that tipped nose, fanning its elegant wings in graceful homage. He slid the insect onto his finger and stared at it a long time.

"You have a crown, my prince," laughed Mahri.

He grinned crookedly and she knew the image of him surrounded by wings of softness would stay in her mind forever. He executed a courtly bow, barely rocking the boat, losing only a few of his winged passengers from atop his head, and pierced her with his gaze once again.

"No better one," he replied, "could I ever hope to wear, my lady."

Mahri thought for a moment that she'd swallowed some of the flutterflies, her insides trembled so softly.

And then she knew she'd take him to one other place.

Chapter 12

MAHRI WATCHED KORL'S MOUTH DROP OPEN WHEN they emerged from beneath yet another waterfall, and she nodded with satisfaction. She'd heard of the wonders of the Palace Tree, the many rooms filled with skillfully crafted treasures. But nothing could match the creations of nature.

The boat traveled through a narrow channel of water surrounded on all sides by crystal coral that had somehow been sculpted over the eons into massive towers of lace. It glittered in the sun with multiple prisms of fractured color and in places joined over the canal to form delicate bridges.

"Do you know how rare crystal coral is?" asked Korl in stunned amazement.

"Aya." Mahri imagined the Seers taking the coral, using the Power to shape it into their own man-made trinkets. "But I'd die before I'd let anyone destroy this for their own profit—or pleasure."

Korl studied her with scepticism, and then smiled. "I believe you would."

Mahri shrugged and scanned the way ahead, looking for a particular shape of crystal, then anchored onto the coral shore when they reached the bubble-like structure. She grabbed a satchel and stepped out of the boat. Jaja bounded ahead and disappeared into the maze of lace.

"Careful," warned Mahri when Korl hastened to follow her. "The soles of your feet aren't as tough as mine."

He reached out and stroked the side of the translucent stuff, felt the pitted but smooth surface warm beneath his fingers. Then took a step and winced.

"When it breaks it's sharp as a razor," she explained, pointing at the shards littering their path.

Korl nodded and stepped where she did, concentrating so hard that when she stopped he bumped into the back of her, his apology fading away as he looked up in wonder around him.

They stood under a bubble of coral, the lacy stuff creating a ceiling of shimmering light, surrounding them in a cocoon of translucent crystal. In the middle lay a pool of clear water, curls of vapor rising from it to dance with the shafts of colored light from above. Around the pool grew several types of almost colorless flowers, as if they knew they couldn't compete with the rainbow that the crystal radiated, and instead grew within the beams of it and mirrored it back.

Mahri turned and watched the brilliant points of light shimmer through Korl's hair and dance along his golden skin. She memorized the way he looked standing in her secret place, so that she could remember every detail of him whenever she came back here. Alone. Her sigh broke his trance with the magical place and when he turned to her he frowned.

"Why do you look so sad? This is the most wondrous place I've ever seen!"

"Better than your palace?"

He reached out and brushed a strand of hair from her cheek, even that feather-light touch making Mahri tremble. "Why's it so important to you, water-rat, that the place you grew up in should be better than mine?"

She withdrew from his touch. "Because you think you're better than me."

"I'm a Royal," he proclaimed, as if that answered everything. He threw back his head, his chin up in that oh-so-familiarly arrogant manner.

Mahri reddened with anger, flung her satchel on the ground and reached for the ties of her vest. He'd always think he was better than her, with his learning and wealth. But she knew of a way to shake him out of that superior self-confidence.

She felt so angry and sick at his arrogance that she didn't hesitate. Didn't stop to think of the consequences. Mahri would bring him to his knees.

She untied the top of her laces where they tightened across her breasts. The strained ties whipped free, releasing the mounds of annoying flesh that always got in her way if she didn't keep them bound. For the first time in her life she felt grateful for them as Korl's mouth dropped open in wonder. "Wha... what do you think you're doing?"

Mahri slowly unlaced the vest down to her navel. It'd been so dark in that xynth flower, with only the glow of the pollen to light each other, that they hadn't truly seen each other's bodies. Or so she hoped. "The pool is freshwater and I could use a bath."

Korl swallowed hard, his handsome face white with shock. He turned his back on her, then spun right back around. She watched that magnificent chest heave and his leggings tighten and tried not to giggle. She was sure that proper ladies of the court never behaved this way.

Her vest hung open in front, the edges of it barely covering the tips of her breasts, and he watched as if mesmerized while she let the laces fall from her fingers to the ground. Mahri reached behind for the laces of her leggings, fumbling at them while Korl gaped, for her movements had bared her chest fully, jutted her breasts upward.

The open air on her nipples tightened them to hard points and Mahri heard him suck air like a beached fish and she smiled. Her leggings sagged. She pulled the laces from behind her back and held them before his face, and again, slowly let them fall from her fingers while he watched them flutter to the ground as if in slow-motion.

"Mahri," he choked.

"What?"

"Don't… you have to stop."

Her brows rose in feigned innocence. "What's the big deal? It's not as if you haven't seen me naked before." She wiggled her hips out of the snar-scale with slow, undulating motions.

"You're baiting me and you know it."

Mahri frowned. So he knew she was purposefully using her body to… to what? What did she think to accomplish? She only had to breathe and he wanted her, what she did now almost… It was too much.

Good, she thought, he'd know how it feels.

The leggings puddled around her feet and she gracefully stepped out of them. With a gentle shrug the loose vest joined them on the ground. Mahri reached behind and pulled the braid of her hair in front, began to unwind it with slow, fluid movements. Korl's eyes started to burn and she hastily looked away. This time she'd stay in control and she couldn't if she continued to look into his soul.

Mahri raked her fingers through her now loose hair and as usual it billowed around her with a mind of its own. She reached down to her satchel, felt the long strands of red slide slowly over her bottom until her smooth rounds lay bare and she purposely bent further over.

Korl groaned while she fumbled for a bit of soap root.

She ignored him while she went to the edge of the pool and stuck a toe into the water, aware of the way the muscles tightened in her calves and upper thighs. The water felt warm, as it usually did here, whether from the sun or some undersea source of heat she couldn't be sure. With a grin of anticipated pleasure Mahri dove in, her hands sweeping the hair from her face when she surfaced.

She blinked and looked to Korl. He stood frozen on the shore, his hands fisted at his sides, the muscles bulging in his arms and shoulders. Mahri walked toward him, using the water to again reveal her body, the contrast of the warm pool and the cool air making her skin shiver with tiny goose bumps.

She felt a ripple lap the very tips of her breasts and she had to pause for a moment to quench the fire that feeling kindled between her legs. It's his fault, she thought, that my skin becomes so sensitive beneath his gaze. If she wasn't careful she'd be caught up in her own seduction and Mahri tried not to ignore that warning.

Don't look in his eyes, she cautioned herself as she walked toward him. You've lost a bit of your control and lay vulnerable to *him* overpowering *you*.

The brilliant sparks of light from the coral reflected

in the water drops on her skin as she bent down to retrieve the floating soap root, the pool now only up to her ankles. She lathered it up in her hands and started at her calves, rubbing the foam across her skin with seductive, caressing movements, moving up her thighs, curving her hands to the inside of them but not daring to touch that part of her that could shatter her control. Her fingers played across her breasts, then she lifted them up with her palms, rubbing over her nipples when they fell back down.

She glanced up at Korl beneath her lashes. He still stood like a statue but she was close enough now that she could see the muscle that clenched in his square jaw, the sweat that trickled from his forehead. The enormous bulge beneath his leggings.

Mahri could feel his transfixed gaze on the reddish triangle of hair between her legs as she likewise stared at that bulge of his flesh, and couldn't stop the moan that ripped from the back of her throat. Their eyes met and Mahri shuddered at what she saw. His arrogance had been replaced by something far stronger.

Korl fell to his knees.

Mahri did likewise. Only by gritting her teeth did she manage to get back to her feet, wade into deeper water, and dive into the middle of the pond, trying to wash away her sudden shame. She'd played with this man and it wasn't fair of her, for she knew she couldn't finish what she'd started. Terror filled her at even the thought of the way she'd be consumed if he possessed her now. Yet at the same time a fire burned inside of her; Mahri ached and throbbed and cursed herself for she knew there'd be no relief.

She surfaced just as Korl started toward her, his face turning rigid as he read the look on her face.

He knows, groaned Mahri inwardly, that I started this with no intention of finishing it. She'd never seen him look so furious, and belatedly vowed never to be the cause of such anger again.

He strode right into the water, the muscles of his legs playing beneath the wet leggings, and came straight for her, his face intense, his jaw rigid. It took every ounce of courage that she possessed not to turn tail and swim for her life.

He expressed no surprise at the warmth of the water, it seemed as if his entire being concentrated on her and nothing else. When he stood close enough to her for Mahri to smell the musky scent of him, he released her from his gaze and let those pale-green eyes travel over her breasts, caressing them as surely as the water did as it lapped over and under them.

Don't let him touch me, prayed Mahri.

Korl reached out, his trembling hand poised just above her right breast, so close that she could almost feel the heat of it. "I vowed," he whispered, "never to violate you, in any way, ever again." His hand dropped and Mahri trembled. "But you started this and you'll finish it."

She blinked at the hardness in his voice, the deep, alluring threat of it. He leaned closer, his breath caressing her face, strands of his golden hair falling across his brow and the sculpted plane of his cheeks. Mahri could smell his heat.

"Kiss me," he commanded.

It never occurred to her to refuse. His mouth felt hot against her own and she impaled him with her tongue until she felt him shiver. But he didn't hold her, even when she wrapped her arms around his neck and pulled at his fine hair with fingers that trembled from the strength of her passion. Mahri flung her head back and saw that he stood with arms straight at his sides, the muscles in his shoulders and chest rigid with strain.

"Don't stop," he growled.

She had no intention of stopping, at least not yet. Whatever code of conduct he felt compelled to follow didn't extend to her. She might've seduced him, but she'd seduced herself as well. For some reason his resolve not to reach out to her made her feel safer, as if she controlled what could be given. Or taken. Need overrode fear, without the drugging influence of a xynth flower, and she wondered if that had been his intention.

Mahri flung herself at him with an abandon she'd fantasized about, trying to make him touch her, run his hands across her breasts, rake his fingers through her hair, anything that would quench the longing she felt. But the stubborn man stood firm. When she swept his mouth with her tongue in an invitation to do the same to her, he refused, until she sucked it into her own mouth and released and sucked until she near screamed with the want of his own strength behind it.

Korl growled and groaned but refused to touch her. Mahri's body soared with passion and she touched him everywhere.

Almost.

Her hands explored the hard muscles of his chest, her fingers played with the fine golden hair that ran down the middle of it, fluttered across the ridges of his stomach until she heard him suck in his breath. She reached behind his back and pulled herself against him, felt all that warm, golden skin against her breasts and went mad, rubbing them back and forth until her nipples shot flames of desire down between her legs.

Mahri's want of him became unbearable.

She pulled back and looked at him, saw the anger still etched in the lines of his face and wished she'd never put it there, for he'd proven to be an exceptionally stubborn man. Mahri opened her mouth to apologize to him—the game she'd played was unforgivable. He hadn't deserved it no matter what the provocation. But before she could say a word, he spoke.

"Touch me."

Again, a command. And she knew exactly where he wanted her to touch him, so that his words made her tremble and pant as she buried her face in his neck; against that pale, oh-most-softest of skin that she licked between breaths, like an animal in heat.

Mahri laid her palm flat against his chest. "I want you," she whispered into his ear.

Korl pulled back his head and stared at her.

"If I thought you really meant that," he growled, not bothering to finish his sentence, looking at her as if he probed her very soul. "But you don't love me yet, you can't. And I won't settle for anything less."

She moved her hand down, across his navel, to the top of his leggings. Oh, she wanted him all right, just not the same way he wanted her and what was wrong with that?

"I still want to touch you," she whispered. When he said nothing she impaled his ear with her tongue, ran it down his neck and across his chest, played with his own nipples until they hardened under the assault. With one hand she pulled the waistband of his leggings open and then ever so slowly, she slid her other hand down inside.

Korl gritted his teeth. Mahri flung her head back, all of her senses focused on that one hand, interpreting the prickly feel of hair; the hot, smooth, throbbing warmth of him.

By-the-thirteen-moons he felt absolutely enormous.

"Touch me," she demanded, with the same authority that he'd used when giving her that order. She wondered if he'd follow the bidding of a lowly water-rat or just chastise her for daring to speak to a Royal that way.

Korl blinked in astonished wonder, then a slow lazy grin spread across that handsome face and made her heart jump with excitement.

"I'll take what I can get," he muttered, and his hand moved between her legs, replaced the warmth of the water with the fire of his fingers. Mahri realized then that Korl had been right in one thing, for even though they'd already made love it obviously could never be enough, for she burned for his touch even hotter than before, had aroused herself to a new fever by the mere thought of him watching her, so that it wouldn't take much to drive her over the edge. He stroked her once, twice, and Mahri screamed, the cry of ecstasy rebounding through the bubble of lace that surrounded them.

Through her haze she felt him tense, then shudder with his own pulsing release.

They stood for a long time just holding each other, trying to make the world return right side up.

Mahri sighed. She'd never felt anything like that before in her life; such overwhelming, all-consuming pleasure. Yet, she still felt empty and her loins ached with it, her heart throbbed with the pain of it. She tried to squelch the fire still inside of her, a smoldering that could ignite if she let it. If he continued to touch her.

Korl absentmindedly stroked her cheek with his strong hand, slid it down to lay alongside her neck. His eyes sparkled with his own private pleasure, erasing the last vestiges of any anger he'd felt toward her.

"Uh, water-rat," he mused, "if it was that good just touching each other, it could be even better when—"

"Aya," snapped Mahri. "It might." And she shuddered to remember through that haze of pollen the glory of having him inside of her and the thought that it could even be better without that scent-induced haze.

Fear fluttered like a wild thing in her belly. She'd vowed never to let it happen again, to break both bonds that held them together, in every way. But he'd made her forget herself, lose all control, with just the strength of his presence and the touch of his hand.

Mahri tried to wriggle out of his arms. Korl let out a loud sigh of his own before he let her go. She felt an irrational surge of gratitude that he let her escape from the lure of his skin and when she spoke she gentled her voice.

"I need to get you home. I can't imagine why I dragged you all over the swamps when you so desperately need to get back." There, she made it sound as if this were all her fault.

"Can't you?" He raised golden eyebrows and shook the hair away from his face.

Mahri groaned inside and wished he'd stop doing that. How a man could take such a simple gesture and turn it into the most provocative movement she'd ever seen—the way he exposed that soft neck, the arrogant tilt of his head, the incredibly masculine allure of it—still astonished her. She started to throb again.

She raced out of the water and pulled a drying cloth from her satchel and wrapped it around her body. Korl continued to stare at her in complete silence, the water lapping at his chest and making it glisten like a fisjewel. A rare diamond one.

For all that they'd just been intimate, and just moments ago she'd invited his stare, Mahri felt suddenly shy and refused to even try to get dressed. She picked up her discarded clothing, slung the satchel over her shoulder and began to back out of the coral bubble, stumbling and cursing like some kind of idiot. She'd never felt so much confusion before! Did she want him or not? Did she lust for him, fear, or hate him? How could it be all three? Look what the man did to her!

"You can run but you can't hide," said Korl.

Mahri glanced up. He stood at the edge of the water, his leggings plastered to him like a second skin, outlining every curve beneath them. She dropped her clothes as the hand that had held him began to throb from the memory of it.

"What?" asked Mahri.

"I always get what I want."

"Huh?" she asked again, fishing around for her things and totally unable to take her gaze off that part of him. Aya, she knew exactly what he felt like, but could it possibly look that huge... er... beautiful? Powerful? Satisfying?

By-the-moons what had happened to her? She'd gone from a frigid widow to a promiscuous wanton in the presence of this man. Would she ever be the same again?

Korl reached behind his back for the laces of his own leggings. "And I will have you."

What he'd been saying penetrated Mahri's brain. That egotistical, spoiled little brat. How dare he stand there in nothing but his skin and tell her that he'd have her whether she liked it or not?

"In nothing but his skin," she muttered as her eyes widened. His leggings now lay around his ankles and his renewed desire for her stood proudly before her gaze.

He's magnificent, thought Mahri, just as stunning as I imagined he'd be, only better. The hazy outline of him glowing from pollen couldn't compare with the filtered sunlight shining on his bare skin. The ghostly memory of him that night faded to be replaced by the startling clarity of the vision before her.

She found herself walking forward, transfixed by the sight of him.

His face froze with that arrogant mask, yet he held out his hand to her and his voice pleaded his demand. "Come to me, Mahri Zin."

She stopped.

As if he'd willed it a shaft of sunshine blazed through the crystal above and created a shower of sparkling light that fell on his body to outline every perfect inch of him. The beam lit his hair with flecks of gold and danced along his skin like a lover's caress, revealing the fullness of his lower lip, the tilt of his nose and the strength of his jaw. It outlined the muscles along his shoulders, chest, and legs. Tiny points glowed on each strand of hair that lay on his arms and legs, that traced a path down his chest to surround and illuminate that part of him that beckoned the strongest.

She was powerless against such magic as this.

Mahri took a step forward, her breath coming in little pants and the oddest flutter in her breast. Her hand reached for his and her feet hurried to close the gap between them. She felt him then, inside her head, asking to be let in, not just wanting her body but the rest of her as well.

He warned me, she thought. The Bond allowed a joining that he'd never be able to achieve with anyone else; the melding of mind, body, and Power. Either she gave him all or none, and she wanted him so badly that she fell over the precipice and risked her soul. She pulled zabba from the satchel before letting it drop off her shoulder, then quickly chewed the root.

Mahri fought to swallow against the bitter taste while the Power sang through her veins. An errant breeze stirred her hair and the strands stroked her back, tickled across her flat belly, made her skin prickle with shivers. Her vision twisted for a moment, the Sight in full force, then faded to normal.

Korl's face lit with anticipation, the sparkling beam of light he stood in seeming to whirl with his desire.

Her toes felt the warmth of water and Mahri realized what a short distance separated them now. His hand still reached for her but he no longer stood with legs splayed, chin thrust upward. His stance now reminded her of a treecat; tense, coiled and ready to spring.

Mahri shook her head. Two steps forward and she'd be able to touch his hand. The Power sang for release and she shared it with Korl, smiling when he shook back his hair and groaned with the feel of it.

When he snapped his head forward that glitter of pale hair fell over his brow, brushed against the hollows of his cheeks. He looked hopefully at her and she laughed, a reckless kind of thing that made her feel wild with abandon.

Let me in, he said in her mind, and the Power made her aware of the wall that Jaja had thrown around her thoughts and she Saw the blackness of it and cracked it like an egg.

Thoughts rushed in, but not Korl's, he held back as if now that his path lay open he wasn't sure how to proceed. But the others, the tiny insects and animals and even Jaja's faint hungry thoughts of prey overwhelmed her. Mahri struggled to control the sheer weight of all those clamoring needs when she recognized a chant that sounded all too familiar.

We're not here, don't see us, look elsewhere…

"No," gasped Mahri, staggering back from Korl, her eyes searching the pool. She rebuilt that wall of blackness around her mind, sighed with relief when it held firm, heard his answering exhale of disappointment when he felt that barrier again.

He reached for her. "Don't be afraid, water-rat. I won't hurt you."

He'd misunderstood and she ignored him. Where were they? Had they been watching them all along, even when she and Korl… Mahri blushed. What right had they to invade her life?

"I know you're here!" Her voice rang against the crystal walls. "Show yourselves."

Korl lunged and grabbed her arm in a bruising grip. "What is it? Who are you talking to?"

"The natives, of course. Who else has been following us and trying to manipulate us?"

"Aaah," he breathed, his face clearing and taking on the look of someone who must humor the mad whims of another. "The natives who schemed to arrange our Bond? The ones that made me fall in love with you?"

"Aya," snapped Mahri. "And they were quite successful, weren't they? Their plan goes along just as they wished, doesn't it? Well, I for one will not be used. By you, by them, by anyone!"

"Mahri," said Korl, his voice gentle with sadness.

She backed away from him, spinning, looking for the natives. She'd heard them in her head, they had to be here. How did they do it? What were they capable of? And then she admitted her most inner fear, that what she felt when Korl looked at her, that his "love" for her that sprang so quickly in him, that none of it was real. That the natives could manipulate feelings as well as dreams and circumstances.

What Mahri had tried to do before and failed, she now did without thinking. With almost physical savagery she pulled the Power from Korl and used every ounce of it to See.

They ringed the farthest half of the pool. Hundreds of them! Standing with hands clasped and parodies of smiles revealing their fanged teeth. All of them watching the naked couple that stood at the edge of the pool.

Korl staggered from the abrupt drain of Power and let go of her arm. Mahri's skin crawled and she ran to grab her clothes to cover her nakedness, picking up the satchel and holding it like a shield in front of her.

"Mahri?" Korl's voice came out as a low growl. The man looked as if he'd been spun in circles and then let go. "What happened?"

She took a deep breath. "I know you don't believe me, but we're being watched by the natives right now. I can See them, even if you can't. And they're using me to get to you, that's all I can figure, and I won't be a pawn for anyone! You understand?"

Korl struggled into his damp leggings. "No."

Mahri refused to look at him. Instead she watched all those smiling natives. "All right, this love you feel for me, don't you question the suddenness of it, the rightness of it? Isn't it odd that a prince could let himself fall in love with a water-rat—a smuggler, the lowest of the low?"

"I wouldn't exactly call you the lowest…"

Mahri almost screamed with frustration.

"Royals don't 'tumble,' remember that? Since when did it no longer bother you?" She calmed her voice by sheer willpower, tried to make him feel the force of her next words. "You should be more frightened than I am. It's your kingdom that they're after."

Korl frowned and straightened, flipping back his hair.

Mahri moaned. He'll never stop doing that, she realized. It's as natural to him as breathing and just as natural for me to react to it. She turned her back on him.

"We're taking you home, now," she flung over her shoulder. "And that'll be an end to it!"

"Will it?" he mused.

Mahri pretended not to hear as she broke into a run.

Chapter 13

THEY DIDN'T SPEAK MUCH AS THEY CLIMBED OUT OF the waterfall cove, both of them so clean that their skin looked puckered. They struggled out of the old roots, in places having to carry her boat in order to reach familiar waters. Although lighter than it looked, her bulky craft still made them both pant with the exertion of hauling it.

Jaja skittered up vines, hopped between their feet, and threw both of them glances of extreme puzzlement. When they shoved the boat into the channel and collapsed inside with muscles aching, the monk-fish sat between their prone bodies looking back and forth, as if wondering what had happened between them.

Mahri realized that she'd been purposely communicating with Jaja for some time. That she took for granted that her pet could not only understand her emotions, but her words as well, even with that wall of black around her mind. Were all other monk-fish as intelligent as her own? Could it be that her overdose and new pathways allowed her to communicate more fully with Jaja? And most importantly, were monk-fish tools of the natives? She shrugged and winced from a cramped muscle.

It was your friends, she thought at him. *They have their own agenda and I won't play along, do you hear? I won't be their pawn.*

Jaja shook his head.

Tell them what they want's impossible. She nodded at the prince. *Him and I… can never be. Never.*

Jaja stuck out his chin, held his palm out at her and nodded his head up and down. Mahri bit her lip. He might be agreeing with her but she had a suspicious feeling that his gestures were an attempt to humor her. She could almost hear him saying: Sure, sure. It'll never happen.

But she didn't dare crack that black wall around her thoughts to find out what he really might be telling her. They would just have to continue this one-way communication. At least until she thought she could face the barrage of thought that had flooded her mind before the barrier.

"Sometimes I think you're Bonded with that monk-fish," drawled Korl as he raised himself to one elbow beside her.

That handsome face loomed over her and Mahri stiffened. "Better him than you. It's time to put back on your blindfold."

"Not yet." He grimaced down at her, his face lowering close to her own. "You've a nasty streak, woman."

His lower lip pouted and Mahri licked her own, unaware that she did so. Then his face changed, a slight quirk of his mouth that made him look like very young. "You know, I've never had a woman run away from my nude body before." His voice teased with a huskiness that made her swallow.

Mahri felt the boat sway beneath her as they caught the current and knew that she'd best get up and pole him back to the city as quickly as she could. Instead she lay trapped beneath his gaze, those eyes looking through her, into her soul.

Stop it, she told herself. He's doing it to you again and you're such a weakling that you can't fight it. Just imagine how many other women he's charmed like this, using those lips, that voice…

Mahri caressed the handle of her bone staff that lay at her hip. "And just how many women have you been naked with?"

Korl threw back his head and laughed.

She tried not to imagine another woman's hands on that golden skin, another's mouth giving him the same pleasure that she had. It made her stomach turn.

"Well?"

"Does it matter?"

He looks too smug, she thought. "Of course not! I was only curious, that's all."

Mahri relaxed the grip she had on her staff. Although they looked the same age, she'd somehow felt older than him, more experienced. Sometimes he acted as if he'd never been kissed before, never been stroked or held or even seduced. It just surprised her that he might've been with lots of other women. That's all.

"You complain too much."

"Huh?"

He smiled and lowered his face a breath away from hers, his muscular arms trapping her beneath him as he leaned over her body. "I am going to kiss the corner of your mouth."

"No."

"You've just parted your lips and they're trembling."

"So?" Mahri felt the soft warmth of his mouth at the corner of her own and resisted the impulse to turn toward those strong lips.

"Now I'm going to lick your ear."

Mahri screamed inside but all that came out of her throat was a moan. "No."

Korl's deep voice vibrated with humor. "You've turned your head to the side, arched your neck so that I can reach you easier."

"I did not."

She felt wet heat slide along the outer edge of her ear, clenched her fists when he suckled the lobe. He could make her go hot anytime, anywhere. He had too much control over her body, played her like a harp. When she'd first met him—what now seemed a lifetime ago—she'd thought that the only way to get over her attraction to him was by familiarity. Just keep looking and she'd get over it.

That hadn't worked, thought Mahri as the wet heat slid down the side of her neck, traced a path to the shallow dip at her throat. *The only way I can save myself is to get as far away from him as possible. To never look at him again.*

"No," she moaned when she heard him take a breath to tell her what he intended to do next.

"You complain too—" Korl broke off and growled. "Jaja, go away."

The rest of the world flooded back to Mahri's senses. Her pet whispered a screech, as if too terrified to make his lungs work fully. A rumble of sound overrode the normal hoots and clicks and squawks of the sea forest. Korl's hair flew into her face from the repeated slaps of Jaja's webbed fingers against the back of Korl's head. With a final chirrup her pet dove beneath the collapsed narwhal tent.

Mahri froze, placed her hand across his mouth when he tried to speak again. "Shh."

They stared at each other. Korl's face looked puzzled, then alarmed. The rumble grew louder, shivered in Mahri's chest as surely as it must be doing in his own.

"Move," she whispered. "Slowly, just your head."

Korl tilted away and unblocked her view. Her boat traveled beneath the gnarled branches of purplish-brown sea trees and she swore quietly. When had they reached this grove? One of these days her attraction for him, this ability he had to make her totally absorbed with him, would get them both killed. She just hoped it wouldn't be today.

"What is it?" he whispered, wisely not turning around to look.

The noise had increased in volume, a roar that rose and fell with the rhythm of breathing, interspersed with loud coughs and purring rumbles.

Mahri twisted her lips. "Treecats," she hissed. "As you value your life, don't move again, no matter what."

Through their territory lay the quickest way to the City and she'd planned to use enough zabba to put the cats asleep while she poled past. Her hand twitched toward her pouch and a roar of sound shook the air. She froze. It was too late. He'd made her forget about the danger until they were in the thick of it.

They drifted beneath a large branch, the bark gouged everywhere with parallel lines, and Korl looked up. Mahri fought the urge to jump as a huge cat looked back down on them with sleepy interest; long, red tongue frozen in the act of licking a paw. Silver eyes with pupils slit sideways narrowed, triangular furscale-tipped ears popped up and a long, golden-scaled mane shook lazily back and forth. The cat's head followed them from one side of the branch to the other as they drifted beneath, switched its tail that hung over the side, the scaled tip of it near brushing Korl's nose.

Sunlight shone down through a sudden clearing in the canopy overhead.

"That's not a treecat," whispered Korl, "it's a whale cat, the father of all cats. The biggest son-of-a—"

"Shush," snapped Mahri. "There's more."

His mouth shaped the question "more?" and he looked up again in absolute horror. If Mahri hadn't been so scared herself she might have laughed at the expression on his face.

At least half a dozen of the animals lounged within the trees around them, the combined sound of their satisfied purrs shivering the leaves of catclaw vines and the delicate petals of sky flowers. Mahri was grateful for the sound, for it meant that the cats were content— which meant that they'd just gorged themselves—and that meant that she and Korl might float through their territory with their skins in one piece.

They reached another low-lying branch and this time two cubs playfully fought along its length. They would have been cute but for their size, and the length of their fangs, and the wicked gleam of their razor-sharp claws. Intent on their game they paid no attention to the boat that drifted toward them, but the mama cat did. She kept her feral gaze on the craft as it neared her kits and although she continued not to move Mahri could tell the cat tensed, ready to spring at the first sign of threat to her babies.

The larger kit pounced in mock play and tumbled over the side of the branch. He should've just dropped into the water, the loser of round one, but the bow of her craft had just drifted beneath him, and the other kit had the larger one's tail in his jaws, pulling and worrying it in a new game of tug-of-war. So the cat held on, his fore paws clawing for a hold, his powerful hind legs occasionally finding purchase on the deck to lunge back up at the branch, making the boat lurch and bob.

Mama cat had risen to her feet, scrutinizing the two humans. Mahri knew if they so much as blinked, she would pounce.

The boat drifted forward, bringing nearer the kicking legs and slashing claws of the kit. Mahri lay frozen on her back, Korl still half over her body, his gaze locked on hers. He knew what would happen if he moved, that Mahri would be disemboweled from the slashing claws of the cat, that the mother of the kit would attack if he even raised his arm to protect himself.

She inwardly cursed. With root in her system she could've tweaked the kit's muscles to give him the strength to climb back up the stupid branch. Those claws could slash open the soft skin of Korl's neck and—she needed zabba!

But he read the intent on her face and leaned over to pin her arm and pouch against her side with a frown of command.

Mahri heard the mama cat growl at even that slight movement.

Korl's eyes burned into hers when the kit flailed at his shoulder and used it in a last desperate attempt to push himself back onto the branch. Mahri heard flesh rip, felt wet warmth splash across her stomach and still the man didn't move, just stared at her until she thought he could see right through to her heart and its violent constriction in response to his own pain. Crimson dripped from two parallel lines along his cheek and jaw, a final, glancing blow from those claws—and he hadn't even winced.

Mahri hadn't known the definition of true bravery until she'd watched this man stand firm, unable to fight back, while his skin was flayed apart.

The boat drifted out from under the other side of the branch and Mahri looked up at the kittens with relief, for they'd curled around each other for a quick nap, the mother treecat the only witness to the boat's departure from their territory.

"You're beautiful when you're terrified," rasped Korl.

He continued to stare into her olive-green eyes until the rumble of the cats faded, then his face lit in sudden surprise. "By-the-moons, I hurt like…"

And his eyes rolled back in his head as he collapsed on top of her.

The night's rain pattered on the sides of the tent and although Mahri knew she'd have to bail water soon she hesitated to leave Korl's side. She shifted in the cramped space, and he woke, the gentle glow of a light globe softening the angular lines of his face.

"How do you feel?" she asked, as Jaja clapped his hands in relieved joy.

He blinked for a few moments then shrugged his shoulders. "Better than I should, Healer."

Mahri flushed with pleasure. Not water-rat, but Healer. It was a beginning. "But not as skilled as you. There'll be scars on your shoulder—and I tried—but there'll still be scars on your face."

He felt along his cheek, down to his jaw. Only a slight pucker of the skin, Mahri noted with satisfaction, that would smooth with time. And the two scars would be very tiny, but still, for such a vain man as he to be scarred in the face at all…

"The skin's still pink."

Korl dropped his hand and turned his face away from her. "Why are you so worried?"

"Because it's my fault you were hurt and I couldn't Heal it completely."

"I look that bad, huh?"

Mahri sighed. "If you're worried about the ladies at court, trust me, they'll think you more handsome than ever." She couldn't help the mocking tone of her voice.

"There's only one lady I worry about." He turned and arched an eyebrow at her.

Mahri looked at him in confusion. What this man did to her equilibrium should be a sin. Her voice gentled to almost a song. "Aya, well, it'll make you look more rugged. Not so…"

"Soft?"

"Aya, and not so…"

"Pampered?"

Mahri smothered a smile. "Aya, that too. And…"

"Spoiled?"

"Definitely. And…"

"Enough already." Korl scowled.

"Not so beautiful," she finished.

He reached for her, wincing from the tightness of not-quite-healed skin. Mahri couldn't back away, there was nowhere to go, her bottom was plastered against the wall of the tent. His big hand curved around her hip, tugging her forward.

"But it doesn't matter what I think," she hastened to add. "Morning is dawning and you'll soon be home and we'll never see each other again."

Korl pulled his hand away from her and raked it through his hair. "That's what you think?"

"Aya. There's no other way *to* think."

He smiled at her. "For you, no, there isn't."

Mahri didn't ask what he meant. She had to concentrate on fighting this sudden hollow feeling in the pit of her stomach at the thought of never seeing him again.

It's because he's such a pleasure to look at, she thought. And then followed that thought with another: Vissa's just as handsome, although in a darker sort of way, with those black eyes and curly dark hair. She'd visit the tavern keeper when she needed release—he'd been begging her for years—and Korl had awakened something in her that she knew wouldn't go away without a struggle.

And Vissa didn't threaten her soul the way Korl did.

Mahri backed out of the tent and bailed until the sun brightened the green canopy overhead, knew when Korl rose and washed with the fresh rainwater but refused to look at him. If he threw his head back, with that freshly scarred face making her shiver with the memory of his courage, making him look even more appealing, she wouldn't be able to help herself.

I'm too close to being free of him to imperil myself now, she thought.

"How many enemies do you have, anyway?"

Korl's deep voice was muffled in a drying cloth. "Why do you ask?"

Mahri fisted her hands on hips. "How do you think I'll get you back in the palace? You going to just walk up to the front door and knock?"

He stood silent for so long she glanced back at him. He threw the cloth over Jaja, who squealed in mock protest and fought his way free, only to be covered again and again. The crazy pet looked like he enjoyed the game.

"You're right," Korl admitted. "I'll need the protection of my personal guard, but who knows where they'll be assigned now? If S'raya finds me before anyone else knows I'm alive, she'll just make sure to kill me."

Mahri shook her head. To be threatened by your own sister, half or not, made her grateful she had no real family.

"It's what I thought." She sighed. "I'll have to take you to Vissa's. He'll be able to hunt your guards down for you. We can hide you there until they're found, and bring them to you."

"That should work," he mused.

For some reason Mahri thought he spoke about something more than his return to the city. Then he reached her side in one purposeful stride and grabbed her arm in a bruising grip.

"Wait a breath, who's this Vissa? Some fat, old friend, right?"

Mahri tried to shake him off. "What's it to you? As long as he helps and gets you home, that's all that matters."

"So." He just stood there and stared at her, tapping on her mind barrier again. As if she'd let him in.

"Well, then," he said, "I'll just have to kill him."

"What?"

"He's your lover, isn't he?"

"No!"

Korl smiled. He'd gotten her to tell him what he wanted to know.

He thinks he's so much smarter than me, she thought in frustration. "But I plan on making him my lover—not that it's any of your business."

"What for?" he choked.

"Let's just say," she said, feeling empowered, "that you've awakened urges in me that were too long buried."

"Oh, so it's my fault?"

Mahri shrugged.

"Fine. I'm sure I can find some cozy prison farm to ship him off to. I don't necessarily have to kill him."

"You wouldn't."

"He's your—" Korl snapped his fingers. "What do you criminals call it? Your distributor? I'm sure he's wanted by Royal Law just as much as you are."

Mahri clenched her fists, her face tight with anger.

He smiled. "You're beautiful when you're furious, too."

She spun around so fast her hair slapped him in the chest and she began to pole vigorously. Korl gave an exaggerated sigh and stroked the middle of her back.

"I'm only teasing, water-rat. There'll be no reason to send him away, or kill him for that matter."

Mahri tried not to show her relief. When they were in her swamp, she'd forgotten about how much power this man could wield, not through zabba, but through an army. As they neared the city she realized that any kind of threat coming from a Royal couldn't be taken lightly, and lover or no, she counted Vissa as a friend.

"I'll have your promise on that, Great One. Or I'll dump you here to find the rest of your way as best you can."

"Consider my promise given."

She pulled the strip of octopi skin from her belt and shoved it into the hand that just wouldn't stop caressing her otherwise. "Put it on and keep it there. I'll let you know when it's safe to remove it."

"Will you now?"

He's sarcastic, too, grumbled Mahri to herself. But at least for the next few hours he sat quietly in the middle of the boat, his head held high, somehow managing to look dignified in that blindfold, the scars on his cheek pink against that golden skin.

He'll make quite an entrance when he returns to the Palace Tree, that pale skin now gold from the sun, the physical exertions from his time in the swamps evident in the developed muscles in arms and legs. Hair untrimmed, his jaw stubbled, he cut an entirely different figure than the man she'd kidnapped in silk sleeping clothes.

She'd miss him, and ach! How she hated him for that.

Towards nightfall they'd reached the city cove and Mahri had him remove the blindfold, knowing that the trick now would be to avoid looking into those eyes. She knew she'd do something stupid if she let him enchant her with his gaze.

He put on her birdshark cloak and threw the hood over his face as Mahri paddled to the docks. Rain fell and obscured the light of the moons, aiding their stealthy advance, making the glow from the pleasure houses shine like beacons of warmth. She anchored her craft and bid Jaja to protect it as she led the prince into Vissa's tavern.

One of the few real structures—actually carved into a tree rather than a rickety construction of dead wood—it lay within the heart of the docks, a carved bone door testifying to Vissa's prosperity. Mahri knew it hadn't been purchased by the selling of any quas-brew, though. His real wealth came from smugglers like herself.

She opened the door and light spilled across the threshold, laughter rang in her ears, the smell of fish stew and too many unwashed bodies near overwhelmed her. Mahri sighed and strode across the room, aware of Korl following, of the curious glances of patrons. Of the sudden strained silence.

She caressed the top of her bone-staff.

"Mahri Zin!" bellowed a familiar voice. "Crawled from the muck at last, eh?"

She heard whispers of "'water-rat" and "swamp dweller," the sound of badly played harps being started up again and she relaxed. Then Vissa reached her and swung her around, enveloped her in a seabear hug that left her gasping.

"Hoo, woman. I know ya' stay away from me so long just so I'll want ya' even more," crooned Vissa, dark eyes sparkling.

Mahri glanced pointedly at the woman, hands on hips, pouting at the sudden abandonment of the tavern keeper. "I don't think you're very lonely while I'm away," she mused, a smile at the corner of her mouth.

"Ach, but darling girl," he murmured, skillful hands

reaching out to caress her cheek. "If ya' will only be mine, I'd pledge to be true."

"Liar," laughed Mahri.

Vissa looked hurt, his sensuous mouth turned down into a frown.

"Ya' do me an injustice, when ya' mock my feelings." He lowered his face to her ear, his breath warm and inviting. "Who be yer friend, darling?"

Ever watchful, her Vissa. While he had seemingly devoured the sight of her, she'd caught that flicker of awareness for the cloaked stranger.

"No fear, the Healer can be trusted."

It'd been so long since she'd thought of Korl as Healer, not Prince. But that title would be much safer than the other, for she only trusted the tavern keeper so far.

"Get your hands off of her," growled Korl, flinging back the hood of the cloak. His chin jut at air, his eyes narrowed at the clever hands of Vissa. Hands that caressed Mahri's waist from hip to underarm, flicked over the sides of her breasts as if by accident, then fondled the arc of her bottom with an innocence that didn't seem to fool Korl in the least.

The tavern keeper stilled, his body rooted next to hers with a tree's strength. She'd seen that strength tear a man apart and threw Korl a look that told him how stupid she thought his words were.

"Vissa, I've come to ask for a favor, if you'd be so kind."

Black brows rose in surprise. Mahri had never asked him for a thing, knew that it'd shake him out of his urge to strangle Korl, and wondered with a sigh what he'd ask in return. In her experience, people didn't do favors for nothing.

Vissa glanced from her to Korl, decided to ignore

the blond man, and enfolded Mahri in his arms. "For ya', darling, anything. Ask and ya' shall receive." Soft, warm kisses feathered her brow. "What's mine is yers," he promised. "I only hope it's a really big favor."

Mahri heard Korl growl and tried to wiggle out of the black-haired man's arms. "Can we talk in private?"

"Ach!" Vissa slapped his forehead. "I've been trying for years to get ya' in my privates and here ya' are just begging for it."

Mahri had grown used to Vissa's blunt ways and didn't take them too seriously.

But Korl did. "That does it!" he growled, lunging for the larger man.

The tavern keeper smiled and stepped out of the other man's path. "As I thought, ya' brought me a rival, darling." Korl spun and swung a fist. Vissa ducked. "'It'll be my pleasure teaching him who ya' belong to."

Mahri opened her mouth to protest that she'd didn't belong to anyone, when Korl's punch accidentally hit a bystander, who then swung at the man standing next to him. Then someone yelled, "Fight, fight!" and the tavern erupted, and she stayed busy for the next few minutes fending off thrashing fists with her staff.

She cursed with the swing of her weapon, catching glimpses of Korl and Vissa. The prince held his own, but seemed to be getting the worst of it. The tavern keeper knew how to fight dirty.

Then another cry could be heard—"Guards, guards!"—and the place emptied as if by magic. Mahri stood panting as uniformed men flooded the room and surrounded the remaining combatants, who seemed unaware of anything but each other.

"Ya' fight like a woman," bellowed Vissa, his huge fist slamming into Korl's stomach.

The prince let out a whoosh of air, then uppercut the black-haired man's jaw.

"You fight like a water-rat," he replied.

Black hair slapped forward and he licked his lips at Mahri. "Then ya' admit it man, she belongs to me."

Vissa's leg snapped up and slammed into Korl's groin. He moaned with pain, the watching guards echoing the sound in amused sympathy.

Why didn't they stop them? wondered Mahri. The guards just stood with arms crossed, as if enjoying a show.

Korl stayed bent over with pain. Vissa smiled in premature victory just as the prince rammed his head into him, sending both of them crashing into the bar, toppling bottles of quas-juice down around their heads.

A full bottle hit Vissa squarely on his crown. He blinked, shook his head, then fell over, unconscious.

Korl got shakily to his feet and shook the hair from his face, making Mahri freeze in response to that sensual movement.

"She's mine," he hissed at the prone man.

One of the guards gasped. Mahri glanced at him. He looked like that guard that she'd fought when she'd kidnapped the prince. And he'd recognized that arrogant movement of the head. They'd brought him to his personal guard, or at least one of them, but not in the way she'd planned.

"Your Highness?" queried the guard.

The rest of the uniformed men looked at the tall, rough-looking man before them. Mahri could see them peering at Korl with dawning surprise. When they saluted their prince, she sighed and edged her way to the stairs, toward the back door.

They wouldn't even have time to say goodbye, she thought with regret. But perhaps it'd be better this way.

She saw that veil of arrogant superiority fall over those handsome features and barely heard Korl's command to the guards to arrest her. His voice, that deep, husky timbre, no longer sounded familiar to her. At first he'd spoken to the villagers with that air of assumed command, but he'd lost it over the past few weeks. To hear it again reminded her of the gulf that lay between them.

Mahri's mouth fell open as Korl's command penetrated her senses. By-the-moons, had he told his men to arrest her? They all looked from her to him, confusion etched on their faces. But as he barked the order again, it confirmed in their minds that this must indeed be their prince, and as one they converged on her.

She sprinted for the stairs. Thankfully, she'd chewed root before reaching the docks and it sang in her system, danced through her muscles to give her speed and agility. She knew they'd never catch her. Behind her, she heard him again, all arrogance gone, with what sounded like an actual plea.

"Water-rat. Mahri! Are you sure you never want to see me again?"

She shouldn't do it. Keep going, urged her mind. But her heart, that silly thing that melted whenever he spoke, made her hesitate. And she'd known as soon as they'd reached the city that if she looked into his eyes she'd be lost. But she couldn't help turning around for one last look at him, to drink in the sight of that pale hair curling over his strong forehead, those wide shoulders rippling with hardened muscle, that line of dark gold hair that snaked its way beneath his leggings to that promise of pleasure.

Mahri moaned. Full lips, arrogant nose, sculpted, scarred cheek. Thick, dark gold lashes.

Eyes that stole her very soul.

Chapter 14

IMAGES FLASHED THROUGH MAHRI'S MIND. KORL... surrounded by white petals, dripping wet after he'd saved her from the water monster... his mind melded with hers, pulling her back from the brink of madness... feeding her Power to fight the birdshark, his eyes hungry as they danced in the village circle... prisms of color glittering across his skin as he stood vulnerable before her in a pool of warm water.

If I leave now, she thought, I might never see him again. Is that truly what I want?

How dare he make her question herself! If only they hadn't all this history between them now, these ties that seemed almost visible to her, linking them mind, body and soul. If he'd been a cowardly selfish man, she wouldn't be having this problem. For her attraction for him now went beyond the physical, she knew it. It terrified her. And ultimately, it's what made her decide to run.

But she'd hesitated too long, trapped in his gaze. The guards had reached her position on the stairs.

Korl knew what she'd just decided and still, she could tell, the stubborn man wouldn't let her go. He struck quickly, sucking what little Power she had from her system so she couldn't use it in her attempt to escape. Mahri recouped and fought back, in a silent tug-of-war, the Power flowing back and forth between them so that she couldn't use it.

So be it. She flicked her staff, made it longer, ready to fight the guards with her skill alone.

"If any man hurts her," snarled Korl, "I'll have his head in exchange."

The guards hesitated on the stairs, looking at each other in confusion, from their drawn bone swords to her staff. Mahri almost laughed at their expressions. How to catch her unharmed? Korl had just made her escape possible.

She swung her staff in an arc and they ducked, allowing her to turn and advance up another stair. She did it thrice before they caught on, that eventually she'd reach the top and they'd lose her. On the fourth swing she caught the man closest to her across the temple and he went down like a tree in a storm.

Since the stairs were only wide enough for one man abreast they stepped over their fallen comrade to advance. Mahri felled another. And another. Her arms began to ache from the blows.

"What in the blazes is going on?" shouted the tavern keeper. His hand rubbed his head, he swayed unsteadily, but managed to stay upright, watching Mahri on the stairs. She thunked another guard upside the head. "Ach, what a swing! You've always been a woman after me own heart."

Then Vissa turned and sucker-punched Korl.

Mahri heard a screech from the doorway. Jaja hunkered there, his tail fanned out, silhouetted against the dark outside. Her pet looked from Korl to her then scampered up the stairs, shoulder-hopping, occasionally biting a guard's hand if he was foolish enough to try and stop him.

She knew that although he'd fight to the death, he'd still be little help against such numbers, and opened her mouth to tell him to run when another movement from the doorway stopped her. A native stood there, with the black band of a dock worker tied around its neck, watching the scene with a curious detachment.

Then Mahri had no time for anything below, for she'd reached the landing and kept trying to turn to flee but she wasn't fast enough to do it before the guards could spread. She now faced five abreast and knew she was outnumbered. Her arms felt like they had weights pulling them down and her fingers ached where they gripped her staff. And the guards realized that not only did their prince no longer watch them with threatening looks, but that too many of their comrades lay strewn along the stairs from the blows of one filthy water-rat.

One of her enemies grinned, revealing a large gap between crooked front teeth, and lunged at her. Quickly she flicked her wrist and her staff shortened barely in time to deflect his sword. She half-spun, using the weight of her body to slam her bone into his side where something crunched sickeningly before he fell to his knees.

"Hold steady men," ordered a voice, and Mahri looked up into the face of the man she'd beat to the ground at the Healer's Tree. Admiration and anger etched his harsh features. "Don't underestimate her—on my count, one, two, three, now."

And the rest of them closed in on her. Hands clutched at her staff, held firm, and she had no strength left to fight so many off. The guard she'd recognized smiled while she struggled against so many hands, then lowered his voice when next he spoke.

"If you struggle, we might hurt you, so in your best interest," he took her staff and butted it against her head.

As blackness closed around Mahri's vision she heard him finish, "time to sleep. I owed you one, love."

And then faintly, "Now we're even."

———~~~———

Mahri awoke half-smothered. She tried to sit up, but the thing she lay buried in the middle of wrapped around her and foiled every attempt she made to crawl out of it. She tucked her arms to her side and rolled out, fell onto a polished floor and stayed in a half-crouch as she looked around the room.

Her mouth fell open. Couches of carved wood with silk cushions, chests of sculpted bone so old it had yellowed, fur rugs combed to fluffy softness, tapestries so painstakingly woven that it would take her days to discover every detail of the artist's skill. All of these riches lay around her with wear indicating everyday use. Who would dare even touch such masterpieces?

Mahri rubbed the bump on her head and looked over her shoulder. It had been a bed that had near smothered her, the headboard inlaid with a mosaic of pearls—a black dolphin cresting a wave—and the mattress a huge bag of something soft and light. She yanked a feather out of the loose weave and marveled.

She felt afraid to move amongst such treasures, but not so Jaja. Her pet sat perched upon a pink shell table, polished to such a gleam that she could see his little behind in the reflection, and picked out tidbits from among an array of dishes spread out before him.

His belly bulged from his gluttony.

"Where are we?"

Jaja's chirrup exploded into a belch.

Palace? she thought at him.

His little scaled head nodded enthusiastically. She rose, strode across the room, somehow feeling that she disgraced the very floor with her dirty bare feet, and tried the handle of a double door. Then shook it. Then pounded on the relief engraved in it; a man fighting a swordfish, with his own sword of inlaid bone.

"Let me out!" she screamed, knowing the futility of it. If they'd wanted her out the door wouldn't be locked. "I demand to see that rotten, no-good, son-of-a-king!"

Mahri thought she detected muffled laughter but couldn't be sure. Belatedly, she reached down and felt for her pouch. No zabba to help her See anything and no dregs of Power left after that tug-of-war with Korl.

She decided further screaming wouldn't accomplish anything, and besides, it made her head ache even more. So when Jaja yanked at her legging and held up a half-eaten piece of fruit, she shrugged and took the offering, wondering what it was as it dissolved in her mouth with a spicy-sweet flavor. Mahri stifled a sound of delight, followed Jaja back to the pink table like one in a trance, and began to sample one delicacy after another.

I'm starving, she thought. All that fighting made me hungry. And sore, I can barely lift my hands to my mouth.

But she managed, then curled up on one of the floor furs and slept again. The next time she woke she felt much better, rested and alert. And allowed herself to remember his betrayal.

Of course, she'd never trusted Korl, she told herself. Not really. But still she'd thought him to be honorable. A prince, after all, should be a man of honor. Yet, she'd kidnapped him—the Royal's couldn't allow such impunity to go unpunished, whatever the reason—and had allowed herself to get caught. He didn't have much choice but to arrest her.

Mahri shook her head. Don't make excuses for him, she scolded herself. A part of you had believed that he could be as attracted to you as you were to him. Not just the body but also the soul. That his mind had revealed the truth when she'd glimpsed that he loved her.

She fought an empty feeling, the sense that her world had again crumbled around her, and began to pace the room. She'd felt this way once before, when Brez and her son had died. Her lifemate had betrayed her by his leaving, for he'd sworn he never would, and thus proven to her that no man's word could be trusted.

Mahri shook her head and winced from the pain of it. Brez had no control over his death—she had. If it'd been up to him, perhaps he would've managed to bring a Healer to the village. She'd failed him, not the other way around.

Jaja hopped to her shoulder and stroked a webbed hand across her cheek, crooning tiny syllables of sound at her.

"See what that man's done to me?" she murmured to her pet. "All the agonies I've buried now rise to haunt me." She couldn't let grief overwhelm her. With a mental shrug Mahri focused on her one weapon: anger.

So, he half-convinced me that he did love me, using his bravery and good looks to sway my mind. How many other women had he used that irresistible charm on? Did he laugh at my doe-eyed looks at his incredible physical beauty? Did he grin with triumph when I wasn't looking whenever I melted at his touch? Oh, how I hate him!

Mahri cursed and raved until she remembered her saving grace. She'd not wholly given him her heart. Her mind, yes, but only until Jaja had created that barrier around it, and her Power with the Bond, but only because she had to in order to save the village. The important thing, the one that truly mattered, she'd not given him.

Why then did she still feel like a fool?

And soon to be a dead fool.

She stopped pacing and Jaja hopped down from her shoulder to pick at the food. So this is prison, she mused, looking around again at her elegant surroundings. And the feast on the pink table, is that my last meal? Before they… what? Hang me? How far would Korl's betrayal go? Did he tell them she's a Wilding? By-the-moons, what did they really do to a captured Wilding? It'd be worse than a hanging, she felt sure.

Mahri fought the weakness of panic as it rose in her chest.

She cursed him again, this time leaning out the only window while she screamed her rage. Then hastily withdrew inside when she looked down. Not particularly afraid of heights, the abyss that lay below her was another matter. How high up in the tree were they? How would she ever escape?

With unthinking fear and rage she began to tie together tapestries, bedding, rugs—only cringing a little as she ruined some of the beautiful fabric with the making of her rope. Mahri knew it wouldn't be long enough but the window was her one avenue of escape. Perhaps she'd hit a branch… or something.

A knock on the door and she spun, for the moment saved from what she knew to be folly.

Did one knock on the door of a prisoner?

Jaja quit ripping apart the cushions, dismayed at the interruption of this new game, and chirruped at the door. An impossibly old man entered, long hair and beard that merged into a mass of white, a beaked nose that hovered beneath intelligent faded-green eyes that sparkled with cunning and shot sparks of green Power. Behind him hid the most graceful delicate women Mahri had ever seen, decked in cloth that billowed and swayed with every nervous movement they made.

Mahri became aware of her bare feet and tangled hair. She dropped the cloth in her hands and almost smoothed it before she caught herself, lifted her chin, and planted hands on hips. A Master Seer, she thought. Korl overestimated her abilities. Or perhaps he just wanted to humble her.

He betrayed you. Who cares what he thinks?

The old man assessed the damage she'd done to the room, settled an almost amused gaze on her flushed face. The women tittered and Mahri caught whispers of "water-rat" and "savage."

She scowled.

"I'm tempted," said the old man, "to give you zabba, and then see what you'd accomplish." He sighed and shook his head regretfully. "A Wilding. Hmm. Well, we haven't the time. His Highness is most impatient."

Mahri swallowed. To see her hang? If she hadn't been so enraged she would've drowned in this grief Korl made her feel. Her face tightened with anger and the old man didn't miss it.

"My name's Master R'in. You can cooperate on your own," he paused and Mahri could feel the promise of his threat. "Or I'll control you completely."

She felt his Touch in the muscles of her arms just as her hand flew up and slapped her face a stinging blow.

"Do we have an understanding?"

Mahri nodded. She understood completely; he didn't mess around. But what did he want of her?

Master R'in hobbled across the room and pressed a panel. A door sprang open and Mahri silently cursed that she hadn't discovered it herself. But even if she'd found it earlier it only opened on another small room, this one without windows.

The three women scurried past her and into the room, pulled some levers and the sound of running water made Mahri follow them. She gasped in surprise. A miniature waterfall poured into a large basin of mosaic shell, steam rising from it upon contact. The women looked at her bemused expression and tittered.

For some reason Master R'in took it upon himself to explain. "Seer's heat the water and it's carried through small tunnels dug into the tree."

"Won't it hurt the tree?" wondered Mahri aloud.

The old man's winged eyebrows rose. "No more than it hurts them for us to carve our homes in the outer bark. As long as we leave the heart pure, no harm will come to the sea tree."

Mahri sighed with relief and the old man appraised her again. She didn't like the way he kept evaluating her, like an animal that had shown a spark of unexpected intelligence.

"Anyway, it'd be easier to heat the tub rather than the water," she muttered.

The Master Seer stifled a smile. "Perhaps."

Her ignorance of the water-thing seemed to make the women less frightened of her, for they surrounded her and began to unlace her clothes. They picked at the dirty snar-scale as if it were a dead carcass.

"I take it I'm supposed to bathe?" Mahri kept her voice even. If he thought to completely intimidate her, he could think again.

Master R'in nodded.

"Well, I don't need any help."

She tried to push away the hands of the women. One had hold of her vest laces and managed during the struggle to pull them all the way out. Mahri's breasts sprang free, and old man or no, his eyes near popped out of his head. The women gawked at her as if she were some kind of freak, comparing her body to their white skin, small bones, and delicate, almost boyish figures.

"Barbaric," mumbled one of the women.

"Positively vulgar," whispered another.

Mahri wondered if Korl had thought the same as these women when he spewed his charming compliments to her. Wishing it could be the prince, she shoved the women hard, a tumble of frothy material and flying feet.

"I'm sorry," she hastily told the old man, remembering the sting in her cheek. "But I'll bathe myself, thank you."

Master R'in cleared his throat, face flushed bright red. "See that you do," he muttered. Then quickly, "I'll overlook it this time."

The smallest woman wailed and clutched her elbow, but Mahri knew she couldn't be too badly hurt. The old man ushered them over to the shredded bed and glanced over his shoulder just as Mahri bent to strip off her leggings. His eyes bugged again. "For the love of... shut that door, woman!"

Mahri complied then hugged her naked chest and shivered in the privacy of the bath. She'd never be able to continue this brave act, she told herself. They'd undressed her in front of a complete stranger and she'd had to put up with it, no, actually pretend it didn't bother her. How many more humiliations would Korl put her through?

Did all the Royals think that Wildings were savage animals?

Mahri immersed herself into the hot water until the wrinkling of her skin was near painful, until the sharp smell of the scented soap and the fruity aroma of hair dressing near overwhelmed her. She tried not to think of the reasons they had for letting her bathe while she dried off with some abnormally fluffy cloth.

Would they give her to the guard to "play" with before they hung her?

Stop it, she commanded herself.

Mahri took a deep breath and left the room, feeling she'd just had her last moment of privacy on Sea Forest. She'd have to be strong now, put on a mask of arrogance like she'd seen Korl do so many times.

After the hot water the air stabbed her skin with frigid fingers and she clutched the cloth tighter around her. The women were still there, the one she'd hurt now looking at her with daggers. The old man sat with his back to the room, small purrs of contentment coming from his lap.

Jaja, you little traitor, she thought with half-hearted anger.

Master R'in tweaked her muscles once, just to let her know that he Saw with the Power. "Don't harm them again."

"I should let them insult me?"

"When it's from envy and spite, yes."

The small woman stuck her nose in the air. The other held up a concoction of white lace and advanced on Mahri with the air of a trainer handling a tigershark. They stuffed her into the frock while avoiding her gaze.

"Do you dress all condemned Wildings with such finery?" asked Mahri, fingering the tiny pearls that hung from the tiers of lace that cascaded down the skirt.

"Eh," grunted the old man. "What's that you say?"

The women stepped back and eyed her with something akin to horror.

Mahri struggled for composure. "The Royals want me to look good, I suppose, for the hanging. Probably consider it an enjoyable event, like entertainment."

It was the only thing she could think of for putting her into such an outrageous garment. The dress billowed so far out that the women had to stand a few paces away and lean forward to brush her hair. A train of cloth lay draped along her back and spread behind her like the plumage of a peacock-fish.

The small woman gasped at her words and her face softened somewhat. Her hands gentled as she lay a circlet of pearls around Mahri's dark red hair and began to weave tiny braids here and there among the mass of it.

The old man jerked around, tumbling the chair to the floor as he stood. "You'll not be hung, woman." His mouth lay open to say more when he focused away from the Sight and he saw her with normal vision. Those faded eyes traveled from the crown of her softly brushed hair to the hem of white lace and he sighed with what almost seemed like longing. "I understand now, the madness of my prince."

"What… what do you mean?" Mahri struggled with fear and confusion. If they weren't going to hang her, what then? She tried not to speculate on her fate. It might be better not to know.

"She's ready, Master," whispered the taller woman.

"Hmm, yes, I see that. Let us go then, it's best not to keep him waiting."

The executioner?

Mahri had to ask.

"Who?"

"Why, the prince, of course. Never seen him so eager," continued the old man, hastening her out the door. "Youth, I suppose. Hard for me to remember what it felt like, although you reminded me for a heartbeat there."

Mahri concentrated on not falling on her face. How did women walk in these things, much less work? She grabbed handfuls of the lace and lifted but still more cloth tangled up her feet. She kept her face lowered and blinked back tears. It'd been ages since she'd cried, where had they come from? It couldn't be from hearing that Korl couldn't wait for her death, could it?

Mahri sniffed.

They traversed through high-ceilinged tunnels of polished wood, hundreds of light globes creating a soft brilliance that hung like stars above them. Guard after guard saluted as they passed, the shell adorning their uniforms polished to a high sheen, their swords of bone sharpened to a wicked glint. Other doors opened off their corridor, allowing Mahri's curious gaze a glimpse of their interiors. Myriad treasures sparkled at her, yet the blackness of her own death lay over all she saw with each step they took.

Master R'in stopped before huge double-doors, easily four times his own height. He signaled the guards to open them and they creaked and groaned with their massive weight. And opened onto a room of such brilliance that Mahri blinked, half-blinded by the sight of it.

More people than she had ever before seen assembled in one place milled along the sides for the entire length of the room. Not room, she hastily corrected, more like the biggest channel she'd ever seen. Instead of water, a carpet of red ran down the middle of it, to a dais that was so distant it looked no bigger than her thumbnail.

The roar of sound hushed when the people caught sight of her, then rose again like a ripple as farther down the room faces turned to stare at her. Mahri swallowed. So many, just for the execution of one lowly water-rat?

Wait, she needed more time, it couldn't be happening this quickly.

She wanted to scream for help. Instead she stiffened her spine and lifted her chin although she couldn't seem to stop the spasms of fear that trembled through her.

"Go on," whispered Master R'in. "I'll be right behind you, so you'd best do what's expected of you properly. Or remember, I'll do it for you."

Properly? wondered Mahri. How did one die properly? And although the old man's words had threatened, she'd also sensed that in some ridiculous way he'd tried to reassure her. Could he be letting her know that if her courage failed her, if she screamed and babbled like the savage she was, he'd take over for her and at least give her the comfort of a valiant death?

"Thanks a lot," she muttered.

Then took a deep breath and stepped on that blood-red

carpet. Jaja screeched from where he perched on the old man's shoulder and sprang to her own. Master R'in reached out at first, then smiled and nodded as he saw the monk-fish wrap its tail around the back of Mahri's neck and stroke her cheek with tiny caresses of encouragement.

Is it possible, wondered Mahri, to feel the stares of people as if they were little pricks of ice shards? For her entire body burned with a coldness, the back of her neck prickled with an awareness, that made her want to turn around and run screaming from those hundreds of eyes.

I don't want to die, thought Mahri. Not like this.

Although she'd faced death every day in the swamps it seemed an abstract thing. But to know it lay before you with a finality that couldn't be changed—worse, to walk toward it without a fight!

She feared it would take more courage than she possessed.

Mahri stumbled. A sigh of apprehension rose from around her and drifted up to the cavernous ceiling. She regained her footing and lifted her head even higher.

If only she had her staff! Just the thought of it in her hand made her feel stronger and as she walked down that hall of gleaming crystal ornaments and plaques of sculpted bone she visualized fighting her way out of the room.

That smiling woman, with purple feathers stuck in her hair—she'd flee from the look on Mahri's face as she wielded her staff. That man, watching her with a speculative frown, reeking of some musky perfume that reminded her of sea grass—he'd pull out his ceremonial sword and find it just as quickly broken in two. And those natives, furtively peeking over the shoulders of the humans with a curious delight on their faces—she'd teach them a lesson for trying to manipulate her!

It gave her courage, pretending to fight back in the only way she knew how. So she wished for zabba. Let the Royal's see what a Wilding in full power could do!

Something trickled through Mahri's fantasies, an insidious suspicion that pounded away at her blind fear, that forced her to wonder. Now that she looked back at the crowd, the expressions on their faces weren't what she'd expect from people waiting for an execution. And this room, why it looked like it could be a ballroom, large enough for a dancing throng. And did the court dress in such finery all the time, as if they witnessed a matter of state?

Mahri, although uneducated, wasn't stupid. Even if she'd never stepped foot inside the Palace Tree she'd know something smelled wrong.

She'd come near enough to the dais to see the king and queen enthroned, their regal expressions curious, but in no way threatening. And Korl, attired in the most ornate costume she'd ever seen, holding out his hand to her.

Mahri's eyes widened to enormous proportions. So if this wasn't an execution what, by-the-thirteen-moons, was going on?

Chapter 15

MAHRI CAME TO A DEAD STOP, HER SKIRT SWISHING around her until settling in a billow of lace. The pale-green of Korl's eyes stood out from his face as if to capture her own within that vortex, and of course he succeeded, her heart doing a small flip when that chemistry flared between them. She read in their fathomless depths his intention, the purpose of this ceremony, and her mouth dropped open. It couldn't be possible.

Korl intended to take her as lifemate!

Relief flowed through her, enough to make her tremble with the force of it. She wouldn't die today. At least, she thought with sudden anger, not physically. But *he seeks to bind me to him even more, until I can never escape, never be free of him.*

Korl strode toward her, long strides of rippling muscle revealed by the fluid fabric of his leggings, his brow furrowed in concern and one hand caressing the pommel of a ceremonial sword that lay along his hip. Within a heartbeat he'd reached her side, grasped her elbow in a none-too-gentle grip and began to urge her forward. Mahri stayed rooted to the carpet.

"I won't," she hissed at him.

He bowed over her hand, leaned down as if to kiss it. She could feel the warmth of his lips as they moved across her skin.

"You have no choice," he murmured. "This is the only way I can protect you, Mahri Zin."

She swallowed. Either take him as lifemate, or face the consequences of being a Wilding and a smuggler of zabba. She snatched her hand away from his lips and heard a sigh of dismay from a hundred mouths. Mahri glanced up at the crowd of onlookers, her gaze drawn to the face of a woman, a bit younger than herself with the same pale hair as the king, but with the blue-green eyes of the queen. She knew, somehow, that the woman was Korl's half-sister, S'raya. And blinked against the hatred that shone on her face.

Mahri stepped toward Korl and placed her brown hand into his larger, golden one. "I'm not a fool," she whispered.

Korl half-smiled, that shallow dimple appearing in his cheek. "No, just afraid."

Mahri stiffened but continued to walk forward. He slowed his stride to hers. She turned her head and pretended to smile at him, as aware as he that hundreds of eyes watched their progress.

"I'm not afraid to die," she lied.

"That wasn't what I meant." His voice lowered to that deep timbre that never failed to make her want to touch him. "You, my water-rat, are the bravest woman I've ever met. So it saddens me to realize that the one thing you do fear is me."

"I don't…"

He stroked her lips with the callused pad of his finger, instantly quieting her. "Shh, not me then. Just the giving of your heart to me."

They had reached the dais and the queen cleared her

throat. Korl let his hand drop, his face reddening as the spell of intimacy between them broke.

Master R'in climbed the mosaic step and bowed to the rulers, then turned and faced her and Korl. "Proof of the Bond must be given before all assembled, before the ceremony that will turn this Wilding into one of Royal blood can be performed." His voice had risen with each word, swelling to a boom of authority that echoed down the cavernous hall.

Mahri's knees wobbled and her head spun and she wanted to slow everything down. First, she'd thought she went to her death and she hated Korl with a passion. Now, she wanted to kiss him with gratitude for saving her life, and give him a good hard kick for trapping her this way.

She felt Jaja stroke her cheek and sighed. She'd almost forgotten his comforting little presence.

Mahri found herself being turned around by the pressure of Korl's warm fingers. She faced the assembled throng and a sudden weakness assailed her, so that she had to lock her knees to keep upright. So many people, so many different expressions. Surprise, disbelief, hatred, fear.

She froze inside herself and heard the snap of zabba between Korl's teeth as he crunched the root. She watched the assembly stare at him, their heads bobbing when his eyes sparkled with the Power, then felt them pierce her with expectant gazes.

"Share my Power," whispered Korl.

Mahri couldn't move, could barely breathe. Thoughts and emotions swirled through her brain and she couldn't make sense of any of them. Jaja slapped the back of her head, setting the crown of pearls around her brow askew.

"They don't believe we're Bonded," he continued. "It hasn't happened in generations and they seek proof. Do you think they'd let just *any* water-rat become their princess?"

She groaned. A princess, that's what she'd be? By-the-moons, she couldn't do this! Mahri felt as if the bars of a cage had settled around her and with each passing moment they'd contract until her breath was strangled from her lungs. She bunched her muscles to flee and knew Korl must've sensed her near-flight.

He caught her face with his hand, yanked it around to face him. "I love you," he growled. "Let that be enough for now." And bent his head down to kiss her.

Another sigh swelled the room; an occasional titter and an embarrassed clearing of the throat. But Mahri was dimly aware of it, trapped in the fire of his mouth, the feel of his breath on her face, the smell of his skin invading her senses. She had no control when he touched her, even in front of others.

Mahri lay open to him and didn't need to take, for he fed her Power. It tingled through her pathways, shivering up her spine.

Jaja chirruped with delight, right in her ear, and she jumped away from Korl. They stared at each other, both panting in the quiet room, both their eyes now spitting sparks of green Power.

"I am witness," boomed the voice of Master R'in. "That this woman had no access to zabba this day. Are there any here who deny this Bond?"

The hall exploded with noise, but no voices cried out to say nay.

She heard King Oshen rise from his chair and the

room became still. "So be it," rumbled a voice very familiar to Mahri. He sounded much like Korl. "Let the ceremony begin!"

He came forward, placing a hand on each of their shoulders. "And none too soon," he muttered at them.

Korl still held Mahri with his gaze and wouldn't let her go. The Power thrummed in her system and helped to heat the fire in her body. She'd missed his touch, had forgotten the effect it had over her. Had it only been two days since she'd last seen him? In that room of treasures it had felt like forever so that she ached for him now with an intensity she couldn't fight while he kept looking at her.

The king cleared his throat and spoke to Korl, low enough so that only they could hear. "By-the-Power son, get a hold of yourself! You'll bed her soon enough."

Korl blinked, his face suffused with red, making the scars on his cheek stand out, then busied himself with straightening the front of his jacket. Mahri breathed a sigh of relief and controlled the fire in her loins by sheer force of will.

"Not if I can help it," she mumbled with false bravado.

The king's eyebrows rose almost up to his hairline and he looked from the two of them with puzzled speculation. "There are some things you haven't told me, Korl."

"She's a challenge, to be sure." He shrugged, his face all arrogance. "But you know I always get what I want."

King Oshen threw back his head and laughed, while Mahri fisted her hands and glared. She Saw into the red carpet at their feet and before Korl could stop her Mahri Changed it to blue, with swirls and eddies woven throughout, like her beloved waterways. Fish and monsters and the wonders of her swamps formed beneath their feet and she grinned with delight, now feeling more at home.

Jaja chirruped with glee and scampered down the lace of her dress, pointing at the designs in the new carpet for the benefit of the astonished crowd. Master R'in gaped and muttered something about the power of a Wilding. Queen P'erll frowned thoughtfully and stole a glance at her daughter. S'raya clutched the arm of a man dressed in black, who patted her hand and appraised Mahri with a look that felt as if he peeled back several layers of her skin.

There's more undercurrents here, Mahri realized, than in all the channels of Sea Forest.

"I understand," said Korl as he studied the new carpet, grinning with recognition at a many-tongued monster. He threaded his arms through hers and signaled at the Master Seer to begin the ceremony.

Mahri wondered if he truly did. "It's where I belong," she whispered, gazing at a school of silver-fish that swam around her dress.

"You belong with me," growled Korl.

And while R'in droned on and they were wrapped in vines of heart flower, then blessed with the salty waters of Sea Forest and crowned with diadems of crystal coral, Mahri stared longingly at the weave of her carpet and Korl held her to his side as if he'd never let her go.

Her surroundings became a blur as she remembered her first ceremony when she'd taken Brez, how she'd thought they'd be together forever. But Mahri was wiser now and although she smiled at people that were introduced to the new princess of Sea Forest, inside she felt like she was dying. Perhaps this, then, was her execution.

They entered another room and sat at a table laden with more food than she'd ever seen in her lifetime. The aroma of succulent meat and spiced bread made her mouth water, yet when Korl forced a bite on her she had to swallow several times before she could get it down. Conversation swirled around her and she heard little of it, wrapped so inside of herself that even Jaja had given up reaching her. Instead her pet proceeded to snatch food from Mahri's plate then crunch with a regal air, challenging anyone to deny him the meal.

She barely noticed the snickers and whispers of "water-rats" and "animals at their tables." Then Korl called Jaja onto his lap, let him sample the foods from his own plate, and the snide comments ceased.

Prince Charming, thought Mahri. Always doing something that makes me admire him even more. I wish he'd just stop it.

Her enticed gaze traveled along the firm slope of his shoulder, to the hollow of his throat, and she remembered the softness of his skin there.

What've I done? she cried. I'll be chained to this man for the rest of my life. I'll have to fight every day against falling in love with him. Korl's right, I'm afraid to give him my heart and mind, for if I make him a part of me as I did Brez, I'll never survive if I should lose him.

Korl's full mouth spread while he laughed about something with his father, creating that dimple in his cheek, drawing Mahri's mesmerized stare to those parallel scars.

No, she thought, it'll be worse than it was with Brez, for I always held a part of myself separate from him. I'll be more vulnerable than ever before, because Korl does things to me, touches places inside of me, that have always been my own. If I fall in love with him we'll be so entwined that there'll be no "me" and "you." Only "us."

Mahri's chest fluttered and she stifled a moan.

The room grew quiet and still when a bone dancer began the evening's entertainment, all eyes glued to the instrument that whirled in deadly precision around the girl's head, all ears straining to catch the song that keened through the holes of the bone *'ka*. As enraptured as the rest, Mahri started with surprise when she felt a soft tap on her shoulder and looked into the soft black orbs of a native, the scarlet band of a palace worker wrapped around its throat.

Where'd it come from? she wondered, scanning the room. Natives were everywhere, serving dishes and clearing plates and filling glasses. She just hadn't noticed them before. Perhaps because they hadn't wanted her to.

Then she caught the gaze of Master R'in as he studied the native and her, frowning at both of them with puzzled alarm. So, she wasn't the only one aware of the native's presence beyond their shadow of servitude. It gave her small comfort.

"What do you want?" she hissed. "Seems to me that your plan is going along just fine, whether I like it or not."

The native's bush of fine-scaled fur lifted around its head and those black eyes tried to speak to her. Mahri felt it tap upon the barricade around her mind and Jaja turned and snapped at the creature. For a moment the two stared at each other, Jaja's tail fanning out into a bristle, in some silent battle of wills. Then the native sighed and her monk-fish nodded his head with indignant satisfaction and turned back to his half eaten candied pom-poms.

He won't destroy the mind-barrier for them, thought Mahri with relief, and stroked her pet's tail back down into a smooth coil.

The native then pointed across the table, at the pale head of Korl's half-sister and her black-attired companion, then drew a webbed finger across Mahri's throat and bared its teeth at her. And then disappeared.

Mahri blinked. Where had it gone? She glanced around the room and couldn't see any of the natives, except as a dark blur passing among the courtiers. Then she Saw with the small dregs of Power left from Korl, and this time could make them out more clearly, as their structure was slightly different from a human's. She knew if she could get access to more zabba, and if she cracked her mind-shield, that not only would she See them but could Speak to them as well.

She wondered if Master R'in could too, and resolved to seek him out, for some reason feeling that she could trust the old man. In the meantime, the native had aroused her curiosity.

"Korl."

"Aah," he turned toward her and smiled. "You're not mad at me anymore?"

Drat his dimple, she thought. "Mad doesn't begin to define what I feel—no wait—I want to talk to you, but only under one condition."

"And that being?" He leaned toward her.

Mahri leaned back. "Just don't look at me."

"You would deny me even that pleasure?"

"And I won't look at you," she added, staring past his shoulder. It was her only defense against his allure and she knew she'd best get in the habit of avoiding his gaze if she wanted to keep any of her self control.

His voice gentled to a whisper. "What happens when I look at you water-rat? What are you so afraid of?"

Mahri didn't appreciate the husky tone of his voice, even if her body did, already responding to it with shivering warmth.

"As if you don't know," she snapped. She pointed at his half sister, hoping to distract him from his determined attempts to stroke her arm. "Is that S'raya?"

Korl turned and looked across the table while he joined in the applause as the bone-dancer finished her performance.

"How did you know?"

"She's been looking at me with enough venom to make a viper proud."

Korl laughed. He'd been doing that a lot, this evening. "She's been foiled again, you see."

"No, I don't. I don't know anything about anyone around here. I sense all kinds of currents but can't fathom them. I don't belong here, Korl."

His fingers traced a pattern through the fine hair along her arm. "You will—just give it time. And I'll help you in any way that I can."

He caught her hand and cradled it in his own. Mahri stared at her palm while he traced a finger lightly along the creases. It pleasure-tickled.

"Your arrogant self-confidence will get you killed one of these days," she predicted, hoping to shake him up, just a little.

He laughed again. "It's what keeps me alive." His voice deepened. "It's what got me you." His fingers traced a circular pattern on her palm and against her will she spread out her hand to give him better access. She hadn't known her skin could be so sensitive there.

Korl stroked and caressed while he spoke, but as she wished didn't look at her. "The king named S'raya as successor when they couldn't find me. As first-born with Master Tolerance I will inherit the crown. I have a younger brother, older than S'raya, but he doesn't have Master tolerance for zabba. As next eldest with enough Power to rule, S'raya would inherit." He grinned. "They all assumed I'd died after so long in the swamps. They couldn't know I had you to look after me."

Mahri humphed. He'd saved her life more than once and he knew it. Was he trying to remind her of that? If so, he was more devious than she'd ever thought, this charmingly sincere man.

"Anyway," Korl continued, "I'm the only one in the way of S'raya's schemes for the crown. When you kidnapped me she thought her dreams had come true. And she didn't even have to kill me herself."

Mahri gasped. He said it so matter-of-fact.

Korl shrugged. "She would've you know, with that boyfriend of hers, when they chased after us in the cove. If it weren't for you." His fingers stilled on her palm. "But now I'm back and all her plans for power are ruined. Father plans to announce the change of succession tomorrow."

"Aren't you afraid she'll try to... kill you again?"

"No. Are you?" She pulled away her hand. He caught it and settled it back on his thigh. Strong fingers stroked her palm again. "Sorry. Couldn't help but wonder. Anyway, if I should die within the confines of the palace, with wards of Power everywhere, she'd be the first suspect and wouldn't stand a chance for the crown, even if somehow proven innocent. S'raya's unscrupulous, but not stupid."

Mahri fought against him a moment, their hands struggling under the table, both of them looking anywhere but at each other. Then Korl realized that she wanted his hand on her own thigh and began to stroke *her* fingers across *his* palm.

His breath caressed her ear for a moment. "That feels incredible."

Mahri bit her lip. He still obeyed her, not looking at her face anyway, but his eyes were fastened to where the neckline of her gown arched in a deep vee. She'd thought her chest had felt uncommonly warm.

"Stop that," she snapped.

He let out an exaggerated sigh.

"That doesn't explain," Mahri continued, stroking his palm in an almost-apology, "why S'raya looks at me with such hatred."

"You were her only hope."

Mahri's fingers stilled when he didn't continue and began to stroke only when he spoke again.

"All right. She thought that my marrying a water-rat would change my father's mind about the succession."

She dug her nails into his palm. "How so?"

"Let go of my—you've got claws like a treecat!" He shook his hand in mock pain and laughed. "I'll be scarred all over from loving you."

"Aya."

"And enjoy every minute of it. Don't think you scare me, little girl. Now, somehow S'raya thought that the people wouldn't accept a root-smuggling-water-rat-Wilding as their future queen, that marrying you would ruin my chances for the succession."

Mahri frowned, glancing around at the group of Royals who looked at her as if she were some wild animal, waiting to pounce on them. "And it hasn't?"

"Of course not." A layer of hauteur settled over his shoulders. "The people know that I'll make a better ruler than S'raya, regardless of my chosen lifemate."

Mahri jerked to her feet. She'd never felt so belittled. Her mouth gaped like a fish out of water as she gathered the breath to tell him exactly what she thought of him. Korl's face tightened and he caught her arm and dragged her to the dance floor. An orchestra had started playing sometime during their conversation, the bone instruments creating a haunting melody that floated around the ornately carved wooden walls.

Korl twirled her around the polished floor, faster than the music called for, making her pant with the effort of keeping up while she struggled in vain to get free from the circle of his arms.

"Let me go."

"Not until your temper cools."

Mahri noted with satisfaction that he gasped for breath as well. Faces spun around her, eyebrows raised and mouths aflutter with speculation.

"People are staring!"

She'd almost twisted free when Korl flung her backward in a dip, and she scrambled to hold onto him instead.

"They're trying to figure out this new dance of ours." He yanked her upright, Mahri pushed away from his chest but he caught both her arms, slammed her back against him and they both grunted.

"Being with you," he panted, "is like waiting for a whale's spout to blow."

Mahri opened her mouth to curse and he dipped her again.

"The trick is to anticipate the moment of eruption," he paused while he spun her twice, "and divert the spray," another dip, and she heard the bones in her back pop, "in a different direction."

The musicians had watched their prince and struck up a tune that had them stomping their feet with the liveliness of it. When Korl whirled her past the stage, Mahri flung the players the filthiest look she could summon.

"Will you listen now?" panted Korl.

Mahri didn't have the wind to reply, so she just nodded her head.

"S'raya thought, they all thought, that we weren't really Bonded." Korl threw her away and back, using her arm like a whip. "After all, it hasn't been done in generations."

He did a sort of trot around the room, bouncing her right along at his side, then came to an abrupt stop and bowed to her. "Now, you've made my right for succession even stronger, for you've doubled my root-Power. That wouldn't exactly make you a friend to my sister."

Mahri curtsied, aware of all the eyes on them, and tried to stretch out the stitch in her side.

"I see," she gasped.

So that was why he took her as lifemate. To secure the throne. And he thought this confession would make her feel better? When she'd already thought he'd taken her as lifemate just to save her?

Mahri couldn't stop the sinking feeling when she realized this, but she could, as always, take refuge in her anger. She cursed him roundly, even using a few of Vissa's most colorful expressions, until she realized that the music had stopped and her voice echoed throughout an abruptly silent room.

Korl's face turned hard as bone, and he nodded toward Master R'in. The old man's eyes glittered with Power and she found her muscles contracting into an awkward curtsey.

"You're overly tired," announced the prince for the benefit of the watching Royals. "I'm sure you'd like to retire to our rooms."

Mahri felt the muscles in her neck wobble, glared at the old man when she felt him lock her jaw. Korl took her hand and kissed it, grazing her skin.

"If you cannot behave like a lady," he muttered, "then I must help you do so."

Mahri could only glower at him, helpless against Master R'in's Power. Did he think to turn her into his puppet? To avail himself of her root tolerance when needed, then parade her through the palace under someone else's control? The bars of her cage were more confining than she could've ever imagined.

Chapter 16

MAHRI PACED THE SPLENDID LENGTH OF KORL'S ROOMS, ignoring the feel of chi-fur beneath her naked feet, the sumptuous tapestries that covered the walls, the glittering mosaics that adorned picture frames and table legs and wardrobes. All she could think of was the humiliation of being marched from her own reception with her muscles controlled by the Power of Master R'in.

If she'd harbored any hope that her life in the palace would allow her any amount of freedom, Korl had thoroughly squashed it by giving that command to the Seer. She had to escape this luxurious prison and the man who sought to make her into something she wasn't. She had only to figure out how.

Mahri strode over to the balcony, giving the lace dress a savage kick where it lay on the floor. She'd stripped it off so that she only wore the silk pantaloons and thin top of underwear, feeling more comfortable with the ease of movement, but yearning for the sturdier snar-scales of her traveling clothes. She didn't care who might see the new princess of Sea Forest so scantily clad; she hung onto the railing and let the breeze ripple through her unbound hair while she breathed in great gulps of it.

The moons had just come out and the canopy of trees glowed beneath their light, throwing shadows in multiple directions. The Palace Tree was the largest, oldest one in the forest and the rooms were carved out of the outer bark at nearly the very top of it, making the view breathtaking with its scope.

Trapping her within the tree walls with extraordinary effectiveness.

Jaja, thought Mahri, *any luck?*

Her monk-fish answered with a muffled chirrup, dropping an oyster shell full of whipped seaweed. She turned and looked at him.

You were supposed to be sniffing out zabba, you little scamp. Not your next meal!

He held out his webbed hands in a helpless gesture and shrugged, his whiskers dripping green goo. He sat on another pink table, much larger than the one in the other room they'd been imprisoned in, with an even greater selection of cold foods and drinks. Mahri sighed. Too much temptation for such a small monk-fish.

I need zabba to escape, she chided. *And your nose is better than mine in seeking it out. Did you try the connecting rooms?*

Jaja shook his head, stole one last look of regret at his interrupted feast, and bounded through an arched entryway.

She watched him go with a sad smile. It amazed her how easily she took for granted their ease of communication. Before, she knew her pet sensed her feelings and caught a glimmer of her needs, yet she was now convinced that he understood every word she thought at him. And since her overdose, she knew that she'd understand him just as easily if she allowed the removal of that barricade from around her mind.

Mahri shook her head, still trying to comprehend the alterations within her. It had to be the overdose and the new pathways that had been forged inside her that allowed her to See the thoughts of the creatures of Sea Forest. At first she'd thought that it might be the Bonding that had changed her, but Korl could only See into her mind, he'd never shown any ability with anything or anyone else. Maybe that was why he was so intent on entering her mind again, but she couldn't allow herself to yield to that final possession. She'd been very… content, with her life. Before Korl.

As if she'd conjured him up, the double doors opened and the prince of Sea Forest entered the room. He'd removed the jewel-studded jacket, loosened the ties of the silk shirt so that the golden smooth skin of his chest peeked through. His leggings outlined every muscle before disappearing into the top of tall, black boots. Mahri tried very hard to retain her anger at him.

Korl removed the ceremonial sword from his hip and tossed it outside the room before shutting the doors. "Do you intend to destroy every room I put you in?" he asked as he surveyed the shambles of his apartments.

Mahri shrugged. She'd desperately searched for zabba before giving up and hoping Jaja would sniff some out. She hadn't paid any attention to the clothes she'd tossed out of wardrobes, the drawers she'd left open, the cushions she'd overturned.

Korl grinned and removed the crown of crystal from his head, setting it on a small table shaped like a curled ocean wave and topped with a slab of polished shell. He advanced on her, his face alight with purpose, every movement of his body speaking of his intent to possess her, his words an afterthought to this goal.

"You have an astonishingly filthy mouth, Mahri Com'nder. Quite inappropriate for a delicate princess."

"I'm not…" began Mahri, and then he shook back his head, strands of pale gold curling across his brow, whispering along the collar of his shirt. His lids half-closed, thick lashes shadowing them, smooth neck exposed and vulnerable. She wished she knew how he did that.

"I'm not a delicate anything, and if that's what you wanted you should've taken a courtier for a mate." She fisted her hands and advanced on him, refusing to let his virility distract her from her rightful anger. "And if you ever, ever, allow someone to control me again, your next taste of zabba will be your last. For I swear I'll rip the Power from you so fast you won't have time to—"

"I apologize."

"Fight me off, and then I'll—"

"I said I'm sorry," he injected again, this time lowering his voice to that deep timbre and brushing his fingers across her cheek.

Mahri stepped back. "What?"

"I had to do something and it was the only thing I could think of. Do you have any idea what you were saying?"

"No."

She suddenly realized that a Royal, a prince, no less, was apologizing to a water-rat. A lowly born smuggler and Wilding that wouldn't even be considered fit to lick his boots. The entire situation reeked of absurdity.

Korl raked his fingers through his gold hair. "You made Lady Katra faint."

"Over just words?"

"Well, she faints over something at every ball,

probably laces her corset too tight, so don't let it bother you too much. But you had half the men in the room stunned with admiration and every woman red with embarrassment. Where'd you learn to curse like that, anyway?"

"Vissa."

Korl scowled. "I should've guessed." His fingers went from cheek to the side of her neck, and on to play with the thin material across her shoulder. "By the way, you looked beautiful tonight in that dress. But I like you in pants the best."

Mahri shivered. His fingers moved so gently across her skin that she gritted her teeth against the pleasure of it. "Don't try to change the subject. I want your promise that you'll never do that again."

"Agreed, but you'll also have to make me a promise."

"Aya?"

His hands traveled down her arms, his eyes held her in thrall, and she watched his lips moving with an intense fascination. "Try to control that temper of yours and quit jumping to the wrong conclusions."

"Such as?"

"Thinking that I took you for lifemate for your Power! It's obvious to anyone with half a brain that the succession is mine and that would be the last reason I'd take anyone for my mate, Bonded or no. Do you know what the Royals are doing right now?"

Mahri shook her dark red hair.

His hands lowered to both sides of her waist, enclosing her with their heat. "They're placing wagers on us."

"Wagers?" Mahri's eyes were half-closed, her lips opened in unknowing invitation as his hands curved around her back, pulling her forward into the hardness of his body. He'd charmed the anger from her again with his silken words. Or was it that her passion smoldered so close to the surface of her rage?

"Mmm hmm," breathed Korl, pulling her pelvis against his loins. "Odds are that one of us won't survive the wedding night."

Mahri reached up and twined a curl of gold around her finger, then plunged her fingers into the mass of his hair with an overwhelming feeling of wicked luxury.

"That's ridiculous," she murmured.

"Aah, but they think you're a savage, my dear. Capable of quite anything. They saw lust in your anger, but no love in your eyes. Can you blame them for what they're thinking?"

And he didn't wait for a reply, so impatient with words that he swung her into his arms and carried her through the archway.

"Jaja, get lost," he commanded.

Her pet looked up, saw the edge of that pink food-laden table through the doorway, then lifted an inquiring brow at his mistress. Mahri held onto Korl, her arms wrapped around his neck and the musky scent of him filling her senses. They'd come so close to joining again that she should've known it would only be a matter of time. But she'd always imagined them together in the swamps, not in a palace bed... in a place where she no longer felt like she knew him.

Jaja chirruped with impatience, wanting that food but unable to move until she reassured him that she wanted him to go. She felt Korl's eyes on her but refused to meet them, instead her gaze focused on the carvings on the headboard of the bed. Swirls of water and a pod of narwhal floated across the surface of it; fisjewels, glittering scales, and pearls embedded in the design. The open sea, where no boundaries limited freedom.

"I don't know who the prince is," she said.

Korl's breath when he answered stirred the hair over her ear. Again, he seemed to understand what she was saying. "He's the Healer, who helped save your village. The man who loosed you from the tongues of a sea monster and who loved you on a flower bed and in the warm waters of a crystal cave."

Mahri smiled. When he spoke the images flitted through her mind, and more. His face when the claws of a treecat ripped through his shoulder, the feel of his soul melding with hers when he followed her into root-madness, the wholesome warmth of his mind in hers. This man in fine clothes, who would be king, was still all of those things.

And, ach, how her body wanted him.

"Jaja, get lost," she breathed.

Korl set her down and ripped the flimsy top from her shoulders, burying his face in the curve of her neck. Mahri sucked in a breath while he tasted her skin like a starving man who feared that the feast would be snatched away.

"Korl." She had to tell him before he turned her will into mush. "My mind and heart are my own. Don't try to break that barrier."

He growled and ripped her trousers in half, letting the silk pieces flutter to the floor.

"You're all mine," he ground out, his eyes burning over her naked body. "You just don't know it yet. But

I promised never to take from you what's not given freely. I've had no zabba, your mind is safe from me, and as for your heart… it's a matter of time."

You arrogant man, thought Mahri, and smiled. Korl's smile widened with appreciation but he stood still, waiting.

Mahri sighed in exasperation. She closed the small gap that separated them, unlaced his shirt and slid it off those broad shoulders. And that seemed to be all the invitation he required. His hands caressed her everywhere; hungry, demanding, near frantic with need. And then his mouth followed and she let the liquid heat of it consume her, crying out when he found her breasts, shuddering as he suckled and sent waves of pleasure shooting down between her legs, where she throbbed for him with an ache that made her moan his name over and over.

He'd taken control of her.

Mahri coiled her fingers in his hair and drew his face to hers, her body so tense that she sought to calm it with the tender feel of those warm lips. Korl's pale-green eyes met hers and she lost herself in their depths until her nipples hardened in the cool breeze that blew from the open balcony doors.

"Mahri," he groaned, and lowered his mouth to hers, strong fingers running through her hair, down the length of it until he cupped her bottom and brought her against the hard silkiness of his body. She caught at his waistband and dug in her fingers, pulling down the last barrier between flesh on flesh, breaking away from their kiss, knowing she left his mouth hungry for more.

She remembered the feel of him in her hands and uncovered him without a thought of shyness, sinking to her knees, filling her gaze with the sight of him. Korl mumbled something that sounded like a curse and yanked her to her feet, lifted her in his arms and then brought her down gently on the softness of a featherbed.

"I'm going inside of you," he said, "and nothing will stop me."

Mahri's heart stumbled in her chest.

He caught her knees and spread them, stared at the sight of her open and waiting and she saw him pant and his eyes turn feral with desire, pride, and too many other emotions for her to separate them. He knelt before her and she cradled his throbbing need for her in her hands and brought it closer to the center of herself and when that hot skin touched her own wet core she screamed.

Korl slid inside of her slowly, as if to make the length of her his own, to brand her with his heat, and Mahri continued to scream, until he filled her completely and then stopped with his body rigid and his arms trembling against her shoulders.

"Korl?" she panted, full of him but wanting more, raking her fingernails across his round, smooth bottom, reveling in the hard muscles that tensed beneath her hands.

"I want to move," he said through clenched teeth. "Are you going to scream again?"

"I... I don't know."

He groaned and swore. "Fair enough."

And he pulled back, then plunged forward even faster until he caught her up in the rhythm and made her scream his name again and again. Nothing existed but this feeling of complete connection, this rightness. This striving for the glorious feel of his release throbbing in her, and her own, rippling through her body in waves of unbelievable pleasure.

When Mahri came back to reality he lay on his side next to her, his arm thrown over her waist possessively, his face relaxed in slumber. She didn't know why, but for the first time in years, since Brez and little Tal'li had died, she cried. But she did so silently, so she wouldn't wake him. So he wouldn't know.

"Water-rat."

A ghost of a whisper in the darkness. Mahri sat up with a start, reached for a bone staff that was no longer there, and tried to make sense of her surroundings. Memory flooded back and she looked down at the man at her side.

"Korl? What is it?"

"My enemies… S'raya. Boyfriend."

Mahri ran into the adjoining room and grabbed a light globe. Did he always dream in nightmares in his palace? She placed the ornate globe next to the bed and gazed at his face with a frown. His eyes were wide open but that didn't necessarily mean he was awake, and she saw fear in their depths, as if he struggled against some evil thing.

"Korl, are you awake? What's wrong?"

His broad chest heaved as if he ran a race. His eyes wouldn't blink and Mahri felt a small trickle of fear blossom in her chest.

"Wake up!" she commanded.

"Not… asleep." Korl panted. "S'raya… stupid."

Mahri frowned. What did that mean? Then she remembered their conversation during that strenuous dance, when he'd said that S'raya was unscrupulous, but not stupid. Stupid enough to attack him with Power in the guarded Palace Tree? Is that what he means?

"Jaja," she called, hoping her pet hadn't eaten his way into a complete stupor. But he already stood at her shoulder, those huge brown eyes watching Korl with concern. "Zabba—I need root. Did you sniff out any earlier?"

He looked from her to Korl.

"I think he's being attacked with Power, Jaja. He needs root!"

Her pet chattered and scampered down the bed, through a small archway into the bathing room. Mahri had already searched it, but Jaja stopped before a tall chest of carved bone and pointed at it. She opened it again, spilling shells of soap and baskets of herbs onto the floor, their sharp scent combining into an overpowering aroma.

"Where?"

Jaja climbed up the shelves like a ladder and tapped on the back of the chest. Mahri felt a small seam, and an even smaller hole where a key could be inserted. She ran back to the bed.

Korl hadn't moved, but the golden tan he'd acquired in the swamps had faded to white, so that the scars on his cheek stood out in relief. His breathing had slowed, but that didn't reassure her, for it looked as if he struggled still—but weakly now.

"Where's the key, Korl? The key for the chest in the bathing room. You need Power."

"Yesss... no. Mas... R'in."

Mahri spun. "Jaja, fetch Master R'in. I don't care how, but find him and bring him here."

Jaja chirruped and slipped out the balcony.

"He won't get here in time, Korl. Where's the—" and she added some colorful descriptions, "key?"

His chest heaved again. By-the-moons, thought Mahri, nothing can happen to him. Not now.

"Pink," he gasped, and lay still, as if that one word had taken all the strength he had, his chest now rising and falling painfully.

Goosebumps prickled Mahri's skin in the chill night air, the sound of falling rain a muted roar from the open balcony doors. Pink, she thought furiously. What could that mean? Was it the name of someone, the name of some kind of filing system, the color of a pocket on one of his jackets?

Color?

And she remembered the pink table that Jaja loved, and sprinted into the other room, banging her shin against a chair and yelping a curse. She swept the feast from the table, fruits and shells of candies and cheese and cold fish crashing into a messy heap onto the floor.

Mahri uncovered all the light globes and used her fingers to search the legs, top, and sides of that shiny table. Nothing. Not a seam or crack or anything to indicate a secret drawer. And she couldn't think of anything else pink. She'd always hated that color, anyway. Looked horrible with red hair. By-the-moons, what could she do? How could she help him without zabba?

Korl began to moan and call out senseless things. How did someone kill another with the Power, anyway? She'd never conceived of such a thing. One body organ would be all it took for someone with a Healer's knowledge. S'raya wouldn't know such things, but that Seer?

Would he know how to deliver the longest, most agonizing sort of death?

"Korl!" she screamed in frustration, and fear turned to rage.

Where would that arrogant man put the key? What if he didn't hide it? What if he—a typical male—had just laid it on the table? Mahri dove into the pile of food, searching through the muck, squeezing cheese through her fingers and flinging it away, picking apart fish filets and tossing them aside until her fingers felt the hard shape of a bone key.

Mahri wiped it as she ran back into the bathing room, inserted it into the hole after several attempts, and grunted with relief when she heard a click. A panel sprang open. Her mouth gaped at the amount of zabba in that space, enough to supply her entire village for a year, before she snatched the nearest pouch of it and dashed back to the bed, stuffing zabba into her mouth and gagging at the bitter taste of it.

Korl's beautiful green eyes darted around the room in terror, his mouth slack and babbling meaningless phrases. Her own eyes sparked Power, the root rushing through her system, and she fed it to Korl through the pathways, feeling him eagerly draw it from her. His face showed reason for just a moment and he looked up into her own.

"I know what… love is. It's you Mahri. Simply… you." And his eyes glazed, his next words meaningless drivel about monsters and murderers and horrors she couldn't begin to imagine.

Mahri clenched sheets in her fists. Hard. What were they doing to him? She could only guess that somehow they attacked his mind, not the body.

She hadn't even known it was possible to enter another's mind unless there was a Bond, until it had happened to her with the overdose of root—and even then she only accessed the native life of Sea Forest. And they seemed to all possess an exclusively natural mental connection. Could someone acquire that ability another way? How could she possibly know?

Mahri grabbed up a blanket from the bed and wrapped her naked body in its warmth. All she knew was that the only way to help Korl was to break down the mind-barrier and meld with him. Again, she'd be forced to an action that she'd only take to save another, and although she could refuse to do so, she knew she couldn't watch Korl die and do nothing. How did she manage to get into these situations?

She chewed as much zabba as her stomach would hold down, cracked her mind-barrier and reached into her pathways, following the sparkles of green light when it connected with his, until she reached the nub where the Power entered his own mind. She hesitated a breath, then followed, surrounded once more by his thoughts and memories, the essence of this man.

Korl, she thought-whispered, trying to ignore the black shapes that darted through his mind. *Focus on me. Link with me.*

Mahri? So weak, that call. *It's hard to stay with you, so much of my mind is gone. Get out while you can, before they twist you too.*

Who? she demanded. *S'raya and that blackrobe*?

Yessss. So faint.

Korl! Remember when you melded with me, when I Saw too deeply into the essence of matter? Our souls joined and we survived. Join again with me now and hold on to that part of you.

No. Firm denial in that. *Then if they destroy me, they take you too.*

You arrogant—just do it!

No answer.

Mahri raged with fear that she'd lost him, hoped beyond hope that he'd do what she'd told him to. A golden form took shape in her Sight, in the maelstrom of his mind, and began to float toward her. But two of the black shapes solidified, blocked his path, and Mahri knew one to be his sister.

Korl said you were stupid, she mind-spat. *If he dies you're the first they'll suspect and I'll make sure to tell them what happened.*

Laughter; loud, long, and echoing, screeched through Korl's mind.

Think they'll believe your word, you ignorant water-rat, over mine? S'raya's mental voice sounded old and evil. *Especially after that scene at your so-called joining. They know you hate Korl, that you kidnapped him and he forced you as lifemate. They'll think you made him insane somehow through the Bond. Thank you, Wilding, for the opportunity—again—to destroy my brother.*

Mahri drew on the Power, not knowing how it would affect the body she'd left behind, only caring that she needed as much as possible to save Korl. She fisted a hand and looked down with astonishment. In his mind she shimmered as a ruby-red shape, and in her hand she held a fireball of green Power.

She ignored the two solid black shapes and started hurling green balls at the other monstrous things that whirled around her. The Power flared when it hit one, and the shape vanished.

Ha! thought Mahri.

Stop her, screeched S'raya, and the black shape next to her own lifted a hand and green lightning flared and shot towards Mahri. When it hit her she reeled with the pain of it, but gathered more Power and flung it at the Seer.

He flickered to ghostly black and his thought-words wavered. *This Wilding has more tolerance for the Power than I've ever seen! No wonder he Bonded with her. Give it up, S'raya.*

And within the beat of a heart he left Korl's mind.

No! S'raya screamed and her black shape rushed at Mahri, hit a fireball straight on, and her cries died into nothing.

So quickly, thought Mahri, *had she defeated them. Yet, they could have just as easily snuffed out her during that timeless battle.*

Then all Mahri could See was green and she felt her own mind thud back into her body.

Drained but thankfully not root-fried, she sank her head onto Korl's chest. The warm, smooth skin of it rose and fell in an easy, steady pattern and she sighed with relief as she listened to the strong beat of his heart.

Jaja chattered from the adjoining room and Mahri rose to her feet, clutching the blanket around her and trembling more from fatigue than the cold. She leaned against the archway and watched with hooded gaze as Master R'in surveyed the shambles of the room.

"You did it again," he said in disbelief as he gazed at the seaweed that dripped from tapestries and the fruit that splattered framed artwork and the shredded fish that littered silk cushions. "And to think I was curious to see what you'd do with Power."

Mahri's eyes flashed sparks from the dregs of zabba still in her system. "I was looking for something."

The old man entered the room, skirting the worst of the mess, and motioned the guards at his back to stay at the door. "Did you find it?"

"Aya."

"And my prince?"

Mahri shrugged. "He's still abed."

"Your pet dragged me from my own," Master R'in replied with a frown, "as if the Royal couple were in need of my services. Am I correct?"

She hadn't the strength to answer, just turned and stumbled back to the bed and collapsed next to Korl. She felt the old man follow and use the Power to probe her, give a satisfied grunt then do the same to Korl. His gnarled hands paused over that head of pale hair.

"Who dared?" he gasped.

"His sister," mumbled Mahri. "And that Seer. You'd best see to them, old man, for they'll be the ones needing your 'services' now, not my lifemate."

R'in gasped again. "*You* saved him?"

Mahri felt familiar strong hands sift through her hair and looked up into Korl's face. No madness there now, but a tenderness that made her shiver and forget even the presence of the old man.

"Of course she did," said Korl.

He pulled her face to his using a fistful of dark red locks. His mouth captured her own, with a reverent inquiry that Mahri knew the meaning of. That he could want her again, so soon, and after what they'd just went through… perhaps even because of it. She groaned into his mouth and his hand fought beneath her blanket, hot fingers ripping up her back and down, lower, to her bottom…

Master R'in cleared his throat. "Er, well, then if you don't need me your Highness, perhaps I will check on your sister."

Mahri heard the words through a haze of arousal. Korl only needs to look at me, she thought, and no one and nothing else exists for me. And when he touches me, it's even worse, the total domination of my senses.

She whimpered and Korl growled.

The old man picked up the ends of his robe and ran from the room, with quite an astonishing display of agility for one of his age.

Chapter 17

MAHRI KNEW SHE'D AGAIN HAD TOO MUCH ZABBA, FOR an overdose had brought her to this same place before. She walked along an enormous branch of the Mother Tree, the curls of mist parting to again reveal that door of strange carvings.

As she entered into that cavernous room hollowed in the bark of the tree and that circle of light, she tried to remember how much root she'd chewed before she'd entered Korl's mind. Surely not enough for an overdose. But had her body continued to ingest zabba while she'd fought that inner battle? Had it provided her with what her mind needed to survive, without thought of the ravages it would cause in her system?

Mahri shrugged, making Jaja scramble for purchase on her shoulder. "Too many unanswered questions," she muttered in disgust.

It's why you've called me, answered an alien voice inside her mind. The Speaker entered the circle of light and Jaja immediately hopped to her shoulder to rub cheeks.

"Me? Call you?"

The Speaker nodded, the scarlet and deep blue feathers of her headdress fluttering with the movement. *You... angry with us. Feel like... we play with you?*

"Aya, a pawn that you spy on, to move at your whim."

The Speaker shook with almost human indignation. *No, no! We help... guide.*

Mahri began to pace that circle of light and noticed that just like the last time it already started to shrink. "You said that before. Maybe what you consider guiding, we consider manipulation."

Do not know word. No understand.

Mahri sighed in exasperation. If they couldn't communicate with each other, how did these aliens expect to guide them, anyway? They made decisions based on their concepts, not a human's.

"Why don't you just explain everything, as you see it. Then I can decide whether you're right or not." By-the-moons, she sounded as arrogant as Korl. But she didn't care. They seemed to want her cooperation—why else try to communicate with her—and she wasn't going to just go along with their plans. Regardless of what had passed between her and Korl already.

Then she grimaced. Not that she'd had any luck fighting their control anyway.

The Speaker stroked Jaja's ears, and her pet extended them into the huge fins they were, brown eyes wide in appeal as he wagged them at Mahri. She fought back a grin at the sight of that tiny face surrounded by those huge, waving fins, her anger fading a little.

I already... yes, I try harder to make understand. You come from above, yes?

"You told me that before, however hard it is to believe. I'll accept that my ancestors came from another place than this."

Good. Now, Sea Forest wild... death easy for your kind. We help, give root, but problem. Only some can

chew zabba, others die. But good too, your...differences.
We all same, us natives, peaceful... but go nowhere.

Mahri nodded, wishing the native would hurry up, for the smaller the circle of light got, the quicker it seemed to shrink. It might've helped if she'd talk back with mind-speech, but she wasn't willing to break down that barrier, to allow them access to her in anything other than this dream-talk.

Your species also...mad-angry-war. Always one with more power than other, seek to have all. But we choose to let you become part of our world anyway. See long... future. No war, our people become your servants, to guide, protect, choose path to peace.

Mahri nodded, remembering what the Speaker had told her before. That these natives had given up a part of their world, worse, made themselves virtually slaves to her people, to avoid war and the annihilation of her kind. They truly were aliens to her people. She couldn't imagine humans going to such lengths to preserve another species, even if it were for their own good. Still, she couldn't see what her and Korl had to do with any of this.

The alien fluttered impossibly long lashes in excitement. *But we must all become one with Sea Forest! Your minds all... closed. Must have equal root... knowledge for to happen.*

"And if we don't?" asked Mahri, unable to imagine her own mind left open to mingle with the thoughts of thousands. Would it be even possible to retain one's identity? The aliens seemed to have done so, but her own people?

The Speaker bowed her head. *Your kind will not... survive-live-continue. But your people may come again, and then be war, for will not understand Sea Forest and number of you too great to... reach all.*

Mahri's heart pounded. Of course, if her ancestors came from somewhere else, it made sense that more people were out there, among the stars. And they wouldn't understand the Power or the dependence this world had on everything in it. "But how can a Bond between Korl and I help all our people become one with Sea Forest? He can only touch minds with me. If I let my barrier down I can reach your native life, but he can only touch mine."

Many connections can be made. Sometimes... twisted.

Mahri nodded, remembering the forced entry into Korl's mind by his sister. She knew she should ask if the native knew how they'd done it but...

No evil. Must go slowly. The Speaker continued on, shaking her head again. *Not so much at one time. Little things add to greater good. You make Prince of Changes choose path that lead to greater good.*

Mahri still didn't understand. Maybe she never would, their minds were so unalike. Fear fluttered in her stomach, at the thought that if they didn't someday understand each other, her kind might not survive.

Jaja folded his ears and chattered. The circle of light had shrunk so that Mahri and the Speaker had to stand almost nose-to-nose to stay in it. There wasn't much time and Mahri didn't relish the thought of another overdose just to answer her one burning question. When she woke, if she woke, who knows what damage she might've caused herself this time. The memory of that mind-trip through the essence of all things made her clutch at the Speaker's narrow shoulders and squeeze.

"Did you make him love me?" she blurted.

Then cringed at her own selfishness. The fate of all mankind seemed to rest with her and Korl, yet all she could think to ask was if he truly loved her.

But without that, nothing else seemed to matter.

The Speaker grunted a wheeze that could only be laughter. *This is true reason angry? Fight us?*

"Aya." Shame in that admission, but defiance also. The circle of light had shrunk until she could barely see the alien's face surrounded by those brilliant feathers.

And then only blackness and the sound of the Speaker's mind-voice. *We only chose the door. The rest... up to you.*

The door? wondered Mahri. Aya. At the Healer's Tree, when she'd chosen a door seemingly at random, and later cursed herself for the ill fate of choosing a Healer that turned out to be a prince.

Not so random a choice, after all.

———

Mahri walked through the elegant corridors, trying to remember the directions she'd overheard to Master R'in's rooms. Between her recovery from another overdose, and then Korl's persistence in making sure she was healthy again (in mind and especially body) she hadn't left their apartments for almost three turnings of the moons. And she had no idea of the palace layout.

She'd been walking for some while before she noticed that laughter had erupted several times after she'd passed an open door. Mahri wondered if it had anything to do with her and back-tracked to the last doorway she'd just footed by.

A circle of busily sewing women dropped their skeins and hastily rose to their feet and bowed.

"Your Highness," greeted a raven-haired woman. "How may we assist you?"

They didn't ask her to join them, and although Mahri hadn't expected them to, she still felt a bitter twinge of disappointment. "I'm looking for Master R'in's chambers."

A young girl giggled behind a gloved hand at the hoarseness of the princess's voice. Mahri felt her face turn red and swallowed hard on the gravelly feel in her throat. It seemed her screams had been heard beyond her and Korl's apartments and she blushed again at the memory of the delicious cause of them.

The raven-haired woman shushed the girl before replying. "He's two levels below us, Your Highness. Third turning on the right. Do you not have a guard to escort you?"

Mahri shrugged. She needn't tell them she'd given the guard Korl had assigned to her the slip. Besides, they hadn't been for her protection, or status either. They'd been ordered to keep her a prisoner. "I didn't want one."

"Of course not," whispered a small thin woman amidst sudden muffled snickers.

"Do you sew, my lady?" asked someone else in the group. Mahri felt them advance on her like a pack of vulture-rays.

"No."

"Of course not," said the same woman, this time much more snidely.

"I mean, yes," snapped Mahri. They made her so nervous she could barely answer a simple question.

"I mean, I sew seams and such, but nothing like what you're working on." She gestured at the skillfully embroidered tapestry that lay stretched on its frame in the middle of the room.

"No matter, Highness. I'm sure your talents lie in other areas."

Another round of giggles followed. Did they think her stupid, wondered Mahri, that she didn't understand their game of words? For all their friendly smiles and manner, she detected the underlying hostility within their jesting.

"Aya, I'm also quite skillful with this." And she pulled her bone staff from her belt and flicked her wrist in the subtle yet complicated pattern that extended it. With much persuasion on her part, Korl had returned her weapon and had her snar-scale leggings and top copied in silk for her to wear when she refused the dresses that had been sewn for her. She regretted the decision to wear the boating outfit now, despite the comfortable familiarity of it, for it made her more of an alien to these women.

She swung the bone and managed to at least back the women away from their predatory advance on her. So they wouldn't accept her—no surprise that—but at least she'd make them show a little respect. Mahri made three successive moves and snapped the top of a swan-shaped table in half.

"I'm quite skillful at killing," she growled, and managed to bare her teeth without bursting into laughter.

As one, the women sucked air through their teeth and backed away from her in horror. Except for the young girl, who eyed the Wilding with awed fascination. "Have you really killed? Do you truly have Master tolerance of zabba? What's it like to pole a boat? Are the swamps really full of monsters?" Her questions poured forth so quickly Mahri had no chance of answering them, even if she'd had a mind to. The small woman pinched the girl's arm and brought her to heel.

Mahri sighed. Perhaps, if she had a mind to try very hard, it might be possible to make a few of these women her friends. But it wouldn't be worth the effort, for she didn't belong here, and wouldn't be staying once Korl came to his senses and realized he could never make her into a princess.

Mahri spun and left the room, snapping her wrist to shorten her staff and slamming it back into her belt with feeling. And a ridiculous belt it is, she thought as she caught sight of the gleam of crystal imbedded into it. Worth a small fortune, the gilded thing, just to carry her worn old staff. But it seemed that if she refused to wear the crown, Korl had to identify her as Royalty somehow, and the belt was his attempt at a compromise.

She ignored the peals of laughter and half-frightened imprecations of "savage" and "barbarian" that echoed down the corridor—and no longer had to wonder about the laughter that greeted the sight of her. The courtiers were having a grand time at the expense of the prince's new bride.

It didn't make her feel any better that she'd expected their scorn and derision.

How she hated this place! So he loved her—so what? He still chose to keep her a prisoner and no matter the elegant trappings, the palace was still her prison. His definition of love—again—was greatly different from her own.

After her dream with the Speaker, she'd decided to help Korl rule if it came to that. But she'd admitted to herself that she didn't know how to help him. She knew how to be herself, and every ounce of her being rebelled at staying in the palace. As long as she lay in Korl's arms she could be happy, but they couldn't stay abed all the time, no matter how much she longed to do so, and Mahri wondered how long it would be before her hatred for this place extended to him as well. She didn't want it to come to that.

Mahri took the circular, carved stairwell down the two levels, aware that the Royal Family had their own Powered elevator, but refusing to take advantage of it. Only in these small denials could she exert some semblance of her vanishing independence.

She wished Jaja were with her. He'd done an admirable job of distracting the guards for her though, and she'd bet that afterwards he'd gone back to gorging himself again. If he kept it up she'd have to roll her pet out of the Palace Tree.

After Korl had allowed her to leave their bed, her first thought had been to seek out Master R'in, and she wasn't quite sure why. But she felt for some reason that he might be her friend.

"Your Highness?"

She stopped, stunned to see the lined face of the Master Seer, as if she'd conjured him up from thin air.

"May I be of assistance?"

"Aya. I came to see you."

It was his turn to look stunned. "Me?"

"Aya. Korl said you'd answer my questions, help me to learn about the palace… and other things." Mahri just hoped her lifemate hadn't had a chance to talk with R'in yet. Although he had suggested she see the Seer, she didn't know how much Korl would allow the old man to tell a water-rat. This might be her only chance to learn as much as she could.

He stroked his beard thoughtfully. "Makes sense. A bit dangerous to have a Wilding, er, an untrained Seer, running around the palace."

Mahri smiled and nodded. She needn't tell him Korl didn't allow her near any zabba and had hidden that stash in the bathing room in another place. He didn't want her using it to escape, for without it he knew she'd barely make it to the base of the Palace Tree, much less through the guarded channels. She'd been counting on his pride to keep the knowledge that his bride was a prisoner only to his own personal guard.

Master R'in's eyes sparkled with more than just the Power of root. "Perhaps you'll even teach me a few things."

Mahri shrugged. All she knew were the swamps. Could he really be interested in her home?

The old man waved her toward an open door and when Mahri crossed the threshold she stopped in stunned amazement. Shiny boxes of silver lay everywhere, piles of round discs—of some pearly substance that rivaled the inside of Caria's most beautiful seashells—littered the spaces in between. Walls of wooden shells held stacks of Leviathan bones, and Mahri threaded her way through the chaos to finger the flat pieces.

As she'd thought, words were inscribed on each surface, the same way Caria had scratched her notes about Mahri's adventures. But whereas, by necessity, her sister-in-life had worked with soft bone, Leviathan had been used for these tablets, and only Power could shape that substance. They'd last forever.

Mahri eagerly picked up several and began to read, mentally thanking Caria for teaching her that skill.

The old man had his own private library... and some of the tablets had the yellowish-brown tinge that spoke of great age! This was surely the greatest treasure to be found in the Palace Tree.

"You're welcome," said R'in, "to come here anytime and read the records, although not much might be of interest to you." He sighed. "Only an old man seems to have interest in the First Records. Like most, you'll probably find the main library more appealing."

Mahri looked up from what appeared to be a personal account of someone called the First Commander. "You mean there's more?"

Master R'in nodded, fought a rather condescending smile unsuccessfully. "My collection contains only those records no one else had any use for."

Mahri laid a hand over her heart. More bone books! To imagine such a thing, why, Caria would have fits.

Some water-rats were literate, those that kept track of goods for trade, but they usually had no need of records of any permanence, and to be in possession of anything other than private accounts would be cause for arrest by the Royals. Even Caria's scratches, if discovered, could get her family into more trouble than they were worth.

"You'd get arrested for allowing a water-rat to read books of knowledge."

He threw back his head and laughed, a throaty chuckle that Mahri immediately liked. "You still think of yourself as that, do you? My dear child, you're a

Royal now, and may read whatever you wish. Besides, I would not deny anything from the woman that had saved my prince."

Mahri frowned. She'd asked Korl and he'd refused to answer… perhaps the old man would tell her what had happened to his sister. "How is S'raya anyway? And that blackrobe."

R'in's beard wiggled. "You don't know? You should have been warned!"

"Warned about what?"

The Seer frowned. "I can't imagine why my prince… well, perhaps he thought to protect you. No matter, you should be told. S'raya went quite mad and killed herself. But the blackrobe has disappeared, and taken with him several of the palace monk-fish."

"For what purpose?"

The old man shrugged. "We only recently discovered that he'd been performing experiments on them. We assume that's how he learned to See into the mind of our prince—something I'm still having difficulty believing. And since you thwarted his plans I think you should be wary of him, at least until he's been found."

Mahri nodded. Knowing Korl's arrogance, he probably felt that they'd catch the blackrobe, and in the meantime he'd keep her safely imprisoned in the palace. Why bother telling her anything when he'd take care of her anyway?

She sighed. Would he ever consider her his equal?

Mahri turned back to the shelves and feather-touched the stacks of bone. "But Caria can't learn," she whispered.

"Eh? What's that?"

"Why can I learn, but none of my family or friends

can? I'm still the same person I was before I took Korl as lifemate."

Master R'in shook his head. "Customs, dear. Traditions that started with the first taste of zabba. And they die hard."

"So, no matter how hard I study, I'll never be Korl's equal. Water-rats are considered inferior beings by law and nothing I do can change that."

"I'd hoped that you'd wish to study for its own sake." He hobbled over to one of those shiny boxes and rapped the top of it. A boom-rattle noise followed. "Curiosity, perhaps. If you wish to know the beginnings of the law, you've come to the right place."

Mahri sighed. So he wouldn't discuss the stupidity of Royal Law. She'd have to approach him within the boundaries he expected. "All right, I give. What is that thing?"

He smiled at her, as if to say he'd judged her rightly. "It's a compu'tor, and these shiny round things are books that it can read." A dawning excitement showed on his face. "They're artifacts left over from the original Landing, but the crash destroyed much of the equipment, and age the rest." His face fell for a moment. "They don't work anymore so all the knowledge contained here cannot be read and only a small portion was recorded on Leviathan tablets."

"So it's true," breathed Mahri as her fingers flitted from tablets to discs. "Our ancestors did come from the stars, in a boat of fire?"

Master R'in's eyebrows rose, the beaked nose twitched. "I didn't think you'd understand what I was even talking about. Where'd you learn such things?"

A product of his time, his voice shook with

indignation, that a non-Royal would know of such things. Mahri tried to forgive him his ignorance, as she hoped he would hers. "In dreams."

"Then they were dreams of Power. My prince was right in sending you to me. We have much to teach each other, you and I."

"Aya. You teach me the beginning of our history…"

The old Seer smiled. "And you teach me how you fought a battle of the mind."

And so it began.

Mahri stood on the balcony of her apartments, let the breeze lift her hair and bring the smell of the open sea, salty fish, and spicy plant life to her. A hugull cried it's mournful "rraaa-kay-raa" and her stomach twisted with longing for the swamps. Only birds ventured this close to the city. The sound of humans replaced the roar of swamp animals and she didn't like it.

It had been many turnings of the moons since she'd been imprisoned here and she'd learned a great deal from Master R'in. That her ancestors had come from another planet, one where there was something called land, which R'in thought could be what lay at the bottom of the sea, but unattainable to those of Sea Forest so of little use for study. They had, however, metal from this land, something that equaled Leviathan bone in strength, yet could be shaped with a different sort of power. They called it teknologee.

This power had allowed them to study the affects the zabbaroot had on mankind. How the chemical in the root reacted with the DNA (the smaller components of what made each human unique, explained Master R'in) of certain humans to open pathways into untapped areas of the brain. Allowing eyes to See on the molecular level. And for those with enough immunity to the root's poison, an increase in the brain's electrical output to the point where the resulting electro-magnetic waves could actually manipulate those molecules. At least, those were the words he used to explain her question. Half of which she understood.

Much of what R'in taught her of her ancestors she didn't understand, wasn't sure that even he did. But the knowledge from them—of the shape and structure of things, of the inside workings of the human body, of the sea and plant life and animals—she grasped quickly.

Mahri smiled. Master R'in seemed to take her brightness personally, as if he were responsible for the intelligence of her mind.

She wanted to concentrate on Healing, but he'd hear none of it. Although most Seers specialized in one area he felt she could encompass them all and therefore become a Master herself.

Jaja hopped on her shoulder and chirruped. "You scamp," she whispered, and scratched the scales beneath his chin. The monk-fish cooed, looked mournfully out over the canopy of trees. "You too? No matter how much I learn, how hard I try, I still don't feel at home here. We belong in the swamps, Ja."

Mahri sighed. She knew the beginnings of the hereditary laws of learning, how the First Commander, who showed the most tolerance of the root, had set up his little kingdom on this new planet, ensuring that his sons would continue to rule by controlling knowledge and zabba. Power made some men cruel, and hungry for more.

But it didn't change the way of things now and to this house of people she'd always be the "savage." The prisoner.

Jaja nodded his head and patted her cheek.

Master R'in, in return, had indeed learned from her. She shared her knowledge of mind-connecting and how the overdose had allowed her this ability. They speculated on whether or not the same had happened to S'raya's boyfriend, or if he'd discovered another way to reach the mind through the monk-fish. For only with one of those small pets could the Bonding ceremony be performed, although no one was quite sure how it worked. Even a Bonded.

But Mahri didn't share her knowledge of the natives with him, she didn't trust R'in that much, and although he knew they had a purpose other than the serving of humankind, he'd only guessed at what it could be.

They'd become close, she and the old man, but not that close. And besides Korl, and the ever-present guard (who'd given up trying to keep her penned and now just watched over her), he was her only companion. Mahri sighed and longed for Caria's laughter and no-nonsense advice. And the company of her swamps.

"You're miserable here, aren't you?"

Korl's deep voice startled her, made Jaja hop from her shoulder to look about with a lolling tongue, to see if the man had been accompanied by a servant with their dinner tray. Mahri had been so lost in thought she hadn't heard anyone come in. "Do you care?"

"How can you ask me such a thing?"

He spun her around, captured her with his gaze, and she felt her knees go weak. He never failed to mesmerize her. Nor could she lie to him while he looked into her soul.

"I'm happy when I'm in your arms," she snapped, as if it were a curse. For although her words to him were often devoid of warmth, her body never was. All he had to do was touch her and all thoughts flew away, only the heat of his skin and the hardness of his own body existed for her.

And their bodies had become very familiar to each other over the past moon-turnings, so that now when he smiled, causing one cheek to dimple and the other to pull at his scars, her hand reached up unerringly to finger that line of damaged skin, to wrap itself within the pale silkiness of his hair.

He tried to pull his head away. "But I can't be with you all the time."

"Aya." She pulled his mouth to hers, always hungry for the taste of him, and he kissed her most thoroughly, always responding in kind. Their groans mingled in their mouths while Mahri ran her hands across the broad expanse of his chest, around to the lower curve of his back.

"I'm trying," he panted, "to talk to you."

"Why bother? You know what's in my mind."

He frowned, pulling down the curls at the edges of his mouth. "But I really don't, now, do I?"

Mahri forced her hands down and fisted them at her sides, because she couldn't pull the rest of her body away from the welcoming warmth of him.

He always pushed for more. No matter the physical ecstasy of their joining, he always pleaded for her to let their minds meld as well, to become one. And she couldn't do it, remembering how she'd lost herself within him whenever she'd allowed that kind of closeness, and too fearful to risk such a thing. For she knew that in truth he searched for the possession of her heart and she wouldn't surrender it to him.

Even now.

Chapter 18

KORL GRABBED HER ARM AND BEGAN TO DRAG HER from the room.

"Where are we going?" said Mahri.

"I want to show you something." He flung open the doors with one hand, the other keeping a firm grip on her.

"Jaja!" Mahri didn't know why, but she wanted her pet with her. The monk-fish looked up from a turtle-shell bowl filled with some sugary concoction, a glob of the stuff atop one small finger, poised before that little brown mouth. A long, pink tongue flicked out and licked his finger clean, the small body trembled with delight, and he looked beseechingly from her to the bowl. His shining brown eyes told her that this was some new treat never before experienced.

I don't care, she thought-spoke. The pooch of Jaja's stomach extended beyond his webbed toes and he'd become awkwardly heavy on her shoulder. Nothing had threatened his loyalty to her like the culinary delights from the palace kitchen, and she'd had enough. *It's me or the food, Jaja. Choose now.*

He rolled his eyes to the turtle bowl with regret, let out a dramatic sigh, and managed to waddle after them as Korl yanked her past the door.

They made their way down corridors she hadn't seen before, her hand clasped within Korl's, Jaja and the prince's personal guard trailing behind. Mahri had managed to escape those guards a few times, but the one that had captured her at Vissa's was a wily fellow with a healthy tolerance for the root, which meant that she usually had an escort to Master R'in's rooms that discouraged any exploring.

They piled into the elevator, crowding the Seer who Pushed it, the fall of it raising her stomach to about the area of her throat, and got out when they reached water-level. Mahri glanced out a passing window, felt her heart do a joyful flip at the sound of a channel so near—that a quick hop over the sill would land her in its warm depths. She twisted her hand within his, struggling for a moment to get free.

"I knew if you were this close the water would call to you," grumbled Korl.

He threw open a double door and she gasped at the garden that lay before them. Enclosed within walls formed from a weave of living tree branches, the garden sparkled with the fall of water from numerous fountains, gave off a heady aroma from the combination of thousands of blooming flowers, and sounded with the squeals and growls of hundreds of small animals.

Korl slammed the doors on the frowning faces of his guard, allowing Jaja to barely squeeze through—but near smashing his fin-tail. Then the prince crossed his arms over that broad chest, a frown marring his face.

He's lost his tan, thought Mahri. And for some reason he's angry—very, very, angry. She'd felt it building in him on their way to this place, could see it now in the rigid set of his shoulders, the hardness of his pale face. And yet she should be the angry one, that a place such as this existed, and instead he had kept her up in the heights of the tree.

"It's akin to the swamps," she breathed.

He only raised his eyebrows and watched her. She felt so many conflicting emotions from him underneath that fury, and knew he sensed her own in kind. For although she'd refused to mind-join, the results of the Bond, or perhaps from the times that they had touched each other in that way, had made them both sensitive to the others' emotions.

Had he felt her misery so clearly then, that it prompted this excursion to forbidden ground? Why else take her here now, and for what purpose?

Mahri opened her mouth, then shut it again. Best go slowly, for the most prominent feeling she sensed beneath his anger was fear. She took two steps, turned, and raised a brow at him. He said nothing and she continued on, taking his silence as consent to explore. Jaja puffed alarmingly in trying to keep up with her, the little glutton, so she scooped him up into her arms.

It wasn't like the swamps, this enclosed garden. It was a prison also! The animals she'd heard were all caged, in cunning twists of branches yes, but caged nonetheless, pacing against the confines of their prisons, lounging with dull eyes or scraping, digging at the walls with bloodied paws. Jaja climbed to her shoulder and cooed mournfully at them while Mahri caressed the handle of her bone staff, aching to snap those confining branches.

She felt the heat of his body behind her.

"This is what you wanted to show me?" she asked, her throat tight with horror. "The way you Royals keep your wild things around you?"

"No."

The deep throb of his voice pulled her toward him and she fought it. Mahri's traitorous body responded to him even in his fury, wanting his hands in her hair, his breath in her mouth. He'd taught her something new, her prince. That as long as he was near her, nothing, nothing, could stop her desire for him. Even if he hated her, she would still want him.

Mahri fed on his anger to fuel her own. "What then, did you want to show me, in this... place?" And she gave that word all the disgust she could.

"Something Master R'in pointed out to me."

Mahri frowned. What had that old Seer to do with this?

She followed Korl through a twisting pathway, dodging the leaves of a stingvine until she realized that all the thorns had been somehow plucked from it, making it look a pathetic, naked thing. Was there no end to the control of the Royals? How she wished for the Power to set this garden aright!

When she unconsciously drew Power from Korl he held up his hand. "Not yet," he commanded, and stopped the flow.

Yet? Did that mean he would allow her zabba? She sensed a change in him and met his look with a searching stare of her own. He shuttered them against her and this act shook Mahri enough to follow him without another word, for she'd always been the one to look away from his soul-reaching gaze.

The sculpted archway of vines opened onto a small clearing that rivaled that corridor of white flowers they'd traveled through in the swamps. But it also recalled her bird-cove, for the flowers wore the same sheer variety of colors that graced the plumage of that noisy flock. In the middle of this velvet color stood a spindle bush, the skeletal branches shaped by Power to form an oval of a cage atop the thin trunk.

Mahri felt the maker's design of this flower-enclosure as a place to display the contents of this cage, as if the setting must honor what lay within. She walked forward with a mix of curiosity and horror, trampling fallen petals of purple-red-yellow that released even more ambrosial perfume into the already sweetened air.

Jaja hopped from her shoulder and waddled over to a cradleplant, crawled into one of the welcoming blossoms and curled up for a nap. Mahri ignored him—except to acknowledge that he again sought to sleep off another eating binge—and pushed her face against the branch-bars of the cage.

She spun, her hair slapping into her face. "It's empty," she accused Korl.

He stepped forward, the spicy scent of his skin over-whelmed for a moment with the fresh release of perfume. His hand shook as he smoothed the red strands away from her face, then he moaned and buried his fingers in the mass of it behind her head, thereby trapping her within the circle of his arms.

"Master R'in brought me here last night," he began, the anger in his face masked for a moment by something else as he studied her, tracing a path from the heart-shape of her brow, down her freckled nose to the fullness of her lips, along the curl of her chin to the ridges of her cheeks. As if he wished to memorize every detail of her.

"I didn't even know this place existed… too many gardens are created by bored courtiers to keep track of them all. But it seems that this particular courtier had a taste for the swamps and the creatures rare and wild." His frown told her that he considered her one of those creatures as well, as they traveled from the hollow of her neck to the swell of her breast.

Mahri blinked, aware that her hands lay on his waist—that even now they plucked the laces from the holes of his shirt, to remove that barrier to the warmth of his skin beneath—yet she was so intent on unraveling his words that her body moved without thought from her mind. "What creature does this cage hold?"

"A bird," he growled, for her questing hands had reached the small peaks on his chest, had rubbed them to hardened sensitivity. "Rare indeed, said to have come from the Unknown treelands, beyond even the swamps of your people."

Mahri's hands eased the shirt off his broad shoulders. Caria would be more interested in a new species than she would. But she'd been to the Unknown a few times, and pride prompted her to ask the name and kind of bird, for perhaps she'd seen it herself.

Korl shook his head in response to her questions, the pale strands of his hair slipping across his naked shoulders, tickling the backs of Mahri's hands. "The courtier named it a qa'za, for it's rarity made it precious beyond price. I doubt if even your far wanderings brought you close to where it's said to nest."

She shrugged, knowing full well the many surprises her swamps had still yet to reveal to her. Every journey she made brought her new and amazing discoveries, so

it didn't surprise her that others had found their own as
well. But why had he brought her to see an empty cage?
"Why isn't the qa'za in the cage?"

"It died."

Mahri felt the muscles in his back tighten and she
kneaded them with the pads of her fingers. He'd brought
her to see an empty cage. But more mysterious was that
Master R'in had brought him here first. She held on to
her patience and waited for Korl to explain, waited for
the fury that still boiled deep within him to be released.

Korl's eyes had widened to huge, mournful proportions, and the mask of arrogance he wore like a second
skin had slipped. Mahri stared at him in fascination, her
hands stilled, for he didn't let her see his true self very
often. She'd have to link minds with him for that.

"R'in told me," he half-whispered, "the story of the
qa'za. And I understood his meaning, as I'm sure you will
also." And he took a step back, those long legs making it a
wide space between them, and her hands fell to her sides,
fingers spread as if his skin still lay beneath them.

Korl's voice took on the singsong quality of a traveling bard. "A gypsea tribe brought the bird to the palace,
for the pleasure, and bribery, of the king. He gave it into
the keeping of Lista, a courtier who had a fondness for
rare things, and with her Power she made this garden
for the bird; all paths leading to this flower-place, to its
cage. She cared for it well, fed it the choicest of seeds,
water purified and sweetened with Power. And for a
time, it lived."

Mahri blinked. She knew why Master R'in had
brought him here, and until now hadn't realized how
well the old man had come to know her.

The anger had started to seep back into Korl's voice. "No matter how much she cared for it, how often she talked and petted those silky feathers, no matter how much she loved…" and his voice broke on his rage and he had to swallow it before he could continue. "Every morning more of its feathers would be missing, for it beat at the bars of the cage all night long, until even the small downy scales were sloughed off. And though its beauty was gone, Lista kept the qa'za, for to her it was still a rare and precious thing."

Korl paused, his breathing harsh as if he'd poled all night long, and removed the circlet of crystal he wore, studying it as if he'd never seen it before. "They told her it wouldn't live in captivity, that some creatures had to be free to survive, but she wouldn't listen. Instead she tried to Heal it with the Power, to grow it new feathers, to calm its mind so it wouldn't beat senselessly against the walls of the cage."

He threw the circlet into the petals at Mahri's feet. "She gave it everything… everything!" Korl raked his hands through his hair and he looked at her, anguished rage twisting his face. "But you know what happened, don't you?"

Mahri couldn't move, couldn't speak. She hoped that Lista had set it free, that the tale had a happy ending, but knew from the expression on his face that it didn't. It was only a bird, she thought, yet she knew they spoke of more than the qa'za.

"It beat," and he ground the words out, one by one, "at the bars of the cage until it lay bloody and dead."

Mahri lifted out a hand to him, slowly, carefully. Did he understand, then? Could she hope that the story of a captured qa'za had somehow made him realize how useless it was to keep her imprisoned here?

She managed to speak. "At least it was free."

His face turned red. "It was an exceptionally stupid bird!" he bellowed.

"Aya."

"Come here."

She walked forward, stepping over the circlet, unable to disobey. To get anywhere near him seemed the most foolish of things to do, for his body radiated his fury, his eyes sparked with more than the zabba in his system. For the first time Mahri felt weak when compared with his strength.

But she couldn't quench that flare of hope that he might, just possibly, let her go.

Korl read something in her face that enraged him even more and his muscles tensed and he reached for her clothing and with a violence that took Mahri's breath away he ripped the silk from her body. Strong arms enclosed her in a grip that pulled her from her feet and slammed her against his rigid torso.

"You will love me," he commanded, crushing his mouth to her own, plunging his tongue inside to possess her, and she couldn't fight him off. Wouldn't even if her body had let her. For this one moment in time he wouldn't be denied and she knew it, and although startled at first, something inside of her responded to him so that, like the first time they'd made love, Mahri was more than ready for him.

She must be the savage the Royals accused her of being, because his need to dominate excited her beyond reason. When she pulled back from her to tear his own leggings from him, and kept one hand fisted in her hair so that she couldn't escape, she whimpered not from pain but from the sheer animal desire that swept through her. Mahri reveled in the knowledge that he wanted her with a mindless passion, that he'd fight an army and win if it got in his way between them.

Had any woman a man that wanted her this much?

He shoved her down in the carpet of fallen petals and plunged inside of her and Mahri raked her nails across his back. She matched him thrust for thrust and when he growled his release a cry tore from the back of her throat as a wave of ferocious pleasure ripped through her entire body with contractions that made her arch her back again and again.

Mahri relaxed in complete fulfillment. A drop of wetness hit her cheek, and she looked up in surprise to see Korl's face twisted with horror.

"What've I become?" His face reddened with shame and he pushed away from her, scrambled in the colorful softness for her clothes and tossed them at her.

"Korl…"

"Get dressed."

Mahri held the strips of shredded silk up in the air, a grin tugging at the corners of her mouth. "In what?"

His mouth hung open while he struggled into his leggings. "I did that?"

"Aya." Mahri giggled.

Korl straightened, hands on hips, leggings slouched just below that, covering him halfway so that her eyes strayed to the curls of dark gold hair shimmering over the tops of them. "How can you laugh after what… what I just did to you?"

"Oh, quit being so patronizing. Do you really think you did anything that I didn't want?"

That arrogant mask fell back over his features and Mahri sighed with relief. Better that, than…

Korl flexed and crossed arms that bulged with muscle over his hard, broad chest. "I suppose you think you're stronger than I am, too?"

Mahri shrugged, wondering what the "too" meant but so satisfied in her bed of spent flowers that she could only grin back up at him. "Of course not, your Royalness. But I did have my staff within reach." She rubbed the top of her weapon that still lay securely in its loop from her waist-belt, having withstood the shredding of her silk outfit.

He gave an imperious nod, acknowledging her skill with the weapon against his own brute strength, but with enough skepticism to let her know she'd have to prove it for him to believe it.

"You couldn't have stopped me," he growled.

Mahri sniffed and scooped handfuls of multi-colored blossoms over her skin, refusing to reply. She knew a thousand armed warriors couldn't have prevented him from taking her, but she'd be drowned before she'd admit it. The man already thought too highly of his physical prowess.

He grinned at her, watching the petals that blew across her navel. "I'll never look at another flower without imagining the velvet of your skin hiding beneath. You are a wild thing, aren't you?"

"Mmm," sighed Mahri contentedly.

And then he frowned. "Like the qa'za."

She hesitated. "Aya."

"It was a stupid bird." Korl spun and left the clearing, returning moments later with a pack made from otter skin. He tossed it down next to her with a negligent flick of his wrist.

Mahri sat up, dark red hair covering her like a cloak. She reached into the pack, pulling forth newly stitched snar-scale leggings and vest, a hand-tooled belt of such fine scales that it lay fluidly across her palm, a full bag of zabba attached to it. She looked up at Korl through her lashes.

"The qa'za should've been happy."

She nodded.

"It had the best of everything."

"Aya." Mahri's heart soared with happiness, and Korl felt that rise of feeling and swayed in reaction to it. But she couldn't suppress that flare, for she knew that he'd decided to free her. To let her return to the swamps. She scrambled into the snar-scale clothing, replaced the gem-studded belt for the plain, scaled one from around her waist, settling her staff into it without a hint of regret.

She clucked at Jaja to wake, who blinked sleepily before emerging from his petaled cocoon to scramble onto her shoulder. Mahri fished zabba from her pouch and crunched into the bitterness while she followed Korl to a leaf-shrouded door that opened onto the wide channel that surrounded the Palace Tree. The low-lying branch the garden had been made on sat just above the surface of the water, and Mahri looked over the edge to see her boat anchored below.

Jaja squeaked in glee and dove, popped up near the bow of her craft and crawled aboard, inspecting the inside as if to be sure that it was indeed, their own little boat.

Mahri turned and looked into a face rigid with grief and rage. She didn't need the Bond between them to feel Korl's soul. But the joy that spread through her own overshadowed her empathy for him, no matter how hard she tried to suppress it.

"I'm truly free?" Sparks of Power flashed from her eyes and she could feel the tiny explosions that rippled through her pathways.

His hand shot out, wrapped in her hair and dragged her up against his chest, belying his words. "Yes. You're free to go, but that doesn't mean you have to."

She stiffened beneath his warm lips against her ear. Her next words dripped sarcasm. "Ach. So just knowing I'm free should be enough?"

"Yes. No. Water-rat, let me in." He slid his mouth along the side of her face and her traitorous body responded to his need, pulling toward him even while her wit fought against that draw.

"Just this once, let me feel your mind within my own," he continued. "Then you'll understand why you can't leave me."

Although she couldn't fight the lure of his skin she had no trouble battling his will, so that when he entered her pathways to tap at her mind-barrier she held it firm.

"Don't," she snapped. "Isn't it enough that we're Bonded? That we've forged ties that can't be loosed? My thoughts are my own and will stay that way!"

His entire body sighed, and she felt the mourning within him overwhelm all other emotions.

"You ask too much, more than I am willing to give." Her hands sought the silk of his hair, twined within that pale mass and drew his mouth to her own, apologizing for the hurt she gave him in the best way she could.

"That's why I have to leave," she murmured when they drew apart.

Rage surfaced again and Korl pushed her away, his face rigid, the parallel scars along his cheek standing out in high relief. "Go then, water-rat. I don't know what got into me anyway, allowing scum like you into my bed."

Mahri knew he meant to hurt her, to use words like knives to give her back some of his own pain. And he'd succeeded admirably, throwing her own insecurities at her; that she wasn't worthy to be a princess, that she belonged in the swamps with the rest of the peasants. She wanted to defend herself, but swallowed the nasty words, knowing his pain to be greater than her own.

Mahri bowed to him instead, a parody of a courtier's obeisant sweep to the ground. "This scum was honored, Your Highness, to be allowed into that most Royal of Chambers." Her olive eyes twinkled up at him, and he fought, ach, how he fought the tug of a smile at the edge of that handsome mouth.

"I didn't mean it," he sighed, raking his fingers through the waves of his hair.

"Aya, you did. But it's all right, for I know what I am, and it's why I must leave."

It no longer mattered what the natives demanded of her, nor her own intentions to stay and help him rule, for she knew the truth, that she'd never be his equal, nor allow him to so control her mind and body that she'd cease to exist. The gulf between them lay too wide to cross.

Mahri turned to leave but he reached for her again and she couldn't refuse, knowing this may be the last time she'd ever see him, certainly the last time she could ever touch him. So she allowed her hands to feel every inch of her prince, to glory in the liquid texture of his hair, the warm curve of his neck, the firm muscles of his shoulders and the tight mounds of his bottom.

She tried to memorize each glorious part of him, and felt the exploration of his own fingers as if he sought to do the same.

And then the liquid heat of his mouth across her own made her sob his name. How could she leave him? How could she purposely seek to be anywhere but within the wondrous circle of his arms? Korl felt her sudden indecision for his hold tightened and he traced a fiery path to her ear and whispered and growled his love for her.

Fear shivered a path up her spine. If she didn't take control she'd be bound to him for certain. Mahri yanked his head back with a tug on his hair, and he allowed her to, the muscles in his jaw rigid as she stroked her tongue up his neck and across his own ear, whispering back to him, "I'm sorry," before rising on her toes and grinding her mouth atop his with a ferocity that stunned them both.

Feeling that it was the hardest thing she'd ever have to do in her life, she let him go and dove into the water, heaved herself into her craft and loosed the anchor. Mahri grabbed her staff and flicked her wrist in the pattern that extended it to poling length and pushed away from the Palace Tree branch.

She drew on the Power and Saw into the water, churning it beneath her to aid the current, reveling in the feel of that welcome, familiar liquid. Then she felt another inflow of strength and looked up to where Korl stood above her, Power flashing from his eyes, legs parted and head thrown back.

He fed her Power, helping her to be free.

Mahri held the wave beneath her, felt it churn to be set loose and propel her boat forward.

"You'll be back," Korl shouted at her.

She memorized the proud, strong look of him.

"I'll leave a light burning in the window of my old room in the Healer's Tree."

Mahri smiled sadly. She'd never forget that she'd thought it had been her bad luck to choose that door, when in reality she'd had no choice—the natives had led her to it. Would he truly leave a light burning for her there?

The Wilding shrugged, vowing she'd never know, feeling something inside of her tear apart at that surety.

Mahri released the wave and her craft shot forward, Jaja in the bow, his tiny webbed fist raised forward and his tail finned out behind him.

Chapter 19

KORL MADE HER BREAK EVERY VOW SHE'D EVER SWORN.

He'd been true to his word and had kept a light burning in the window of his small room in the Healer's Tree. A light that screamed like a beacon across the water, for he'd used the Power to create such a blaze; no light-globe could have produced such brilliance. Mahri had been drawn there night after night, had sat in the shadows and stared at that beckoning warmth, cursing herself for her weakness, cursing him for his stubbornness.

She thought he'd soon forget to set the light; she thought she'd eventually cease to go check. When neither happened, she realized that the only way to stop this tugging on her heart was to get as far away from him as possible.

But it seemed that Mahri couldn't get far enough away from the draw of that light, for it stayed in her mind while she traveled through the swamps, to the very outskirts of human-settled trees, through the Gap Channel—that dividing river of water that must be crossed to reach the Unknown tree forests.

And after several weeks of travel through those wild regions, she still saw that beacon of light whenever she closed her lids.

"What's wrong with me?" Mahri asked Jaja as she poled through an unusually calm channel. "How far must I go until the hold this man has on me is broken?"

Her pet shook his head and slapped his forehead with a webbed hand. The pooch of his tummy had shrunk to a tiny sag of scale-skin as they'd traveled, and he hadn't been a particularly good companion. She knew he dreamt of sugared fruit and fish pies and blamed her for the lack thereof.

He'd spoiled so easily, thought Mahri. Soft beds, gourmet food. Aya, it's a good thing we'd left when we did. Otherwise we might've been trapped there forever.

The current slowed, almost reversed back on itself, and her mouth dropped open. Before them lay the open sea, a smooth expanse of blue-green that shimmered beneath a sun unhindered by any canopy of trees, and beyond that, another line of forest, arising from the water to stand no bigger than her thumb because of the distance.

Mahri anchored the boat before it reached that open expanse and stared. By-the-thirteen-moons, how far had she come? She'd never heard of an end to the Unknown, had just assumed that it faded to open sea, yet beyond lay another cluster of tree forest that bespoke of another place. A Beyond the Unknown.

"Would that be far enough?" she mused aloud.

Jaja chattered and shook a finger at her.

"Ach, it's not that far. We could make that line of trees before nightfall."

He slapped a tiny webbed hand against his scaled forehead and fell backward.

"Dramatics won't change my mind." And Mahri flicked her wrist and the pole shifted back into a short staff. She eased it into her belt, lifted anchor and grabbed the oars. When she sat, Jaja hopped over to her and took both her cheeks into his scaled palms, those brown eyes luminous and compelling.

That barrier around her mind cracked a tiny portion, a testament to the panic of her monk-fish, that he did so without her permission, and the gentle thoughts of her pet trickled into her awareness.

No, no, spirit-friend. No native go there, no protection for you.

"Jaja," whispered Mahri. "I can hear your thoughts."

This wasn't like when she'd mind-melded with Korl, or when she'd been bombarded with the senses of the Sea Forest. His thoughts were such tiny things, no threat to her own identity, just a sharing that she welcomed as if a part of her head had been empty and only now felt whole.

You ready now friend.

"Wha… what do you mean?"

Lots zabba open way. You strong now, no hurt. He make you strong.

Mahri knew that Jaja referred to Korl, but she still didn't understand. "How long have you thought I'd be strong enough to breach that mind-barrier?"

Jaja hung his head as if ashamed. *For long now. But not happy with you.* He looked back up at her and sighed. *Good food at Big Tree. Humans make fish warm, make tender. Like stay with prince, foolish friend.* And he shook his head with disgust as he thought those last few words.

Mahri's head swam. Could she be dreaming all of this? Had she chewed too much root again? But she felt the sun's heat on the top of her head, felt the breeze caress her skin and smelled the salty tang of the ocean too clearly for this to be anything but reality.

She frowned down at her small pet. "So why now?"

Make choice. Go this way, and he pointed at the enormous expanse of open sea, *no come back. Prince of Changes need you. Future of Sea Forest need you. You other half of soul, must join.*

His thoughts had started to fade so Jaja dug in her pouch and pushed a piece of root into her mouth and she crunched it between her teeth. Bitterness flooded her throat and Power sparked through her pathways, and Mahri widened that crack in her mind-shield with caution, remembering the overwhelming surge of sensations she'd experienced before.

But it seemed Jaja was right, for she could now control that flood of thought, could sense the hunger of a stingray without getting pulled into the creature's own little awareness, could feel the cold of the deep ocean through the narwhal without getting sucked into that ancient sentience. Mahri could tap into the wealth of life that teemed throughout the forest without it overwhelming her.

"How?" she wondered aloud.

Jaja shrugged. *Always could, just too afraid. Too easy to go,* and he stopped his thought, spun a webbed finger in a circle at the side of his head. *Humans not strong always like my people. Must use lots root, and sometimes kill you.*

Mahri thought of her own nearly fatal overdoses and nodded.

Jaja released her cheeks, fanned out his ears and tail once in happiness and hopped to the bow of the boat. *Go back now.*

Mahri ignored him and continued to explore Sea Forest with this new ability. So much had been closed off to her!

It was as if she'd been blind and could suddenly see, yet more than that for all of her senses expanded to encompass the brilliance of the forest. She experienced each small life and plant, but still embraced the forest as a whole harmonious throbbing entity. And rather than being overwhelmed and lost in it all, she kept her own identity apart. Even while knowing the smallness of her place in the whole, Mahri retained the enormity of her own being.

"Jaja, it's wondrous!" She tried to form words for what she felt, and knew that they couldn't come close. "This is what the natives wanted, isn't it? For all humans to feel the oneness of Sea Forest—to respect our dependence on the whole pattern."

Jaja turned and gave the equivalent of a mental snicker. *Takes long time for all to See. Few, then more. Must all Bond, be equal. Prince of Changes start the chain. You must show him. Go back now?*

Mahri released her awareness and centered on her own self, concentrated on the monk-fish's words. "Just because I can lower my barrier for you and the forest doesn't mean that I could for him."

You strong enough now, foolish-friend.

She shook her head in negation. This new sensation was nothing like what she'd felt with Korl. Jaja couldn't understand the power of the human soul, the risk when two people sought to share minds. Maybe the alienness of Sea Forest and its natural inhabitants allowed that keeping of herself apart, but what she'd felt the few times she and Korl had done such a thing had been the near extinction of her own self.

I can't go back, she thought, and Jaja gaped in disbelief. *You're wrong, Jaja. I'm not strong enough to join with Korl in the way your people want. And I'm not strong enough to resist him, so I must get as far away from him as possible.*

Jaja pointed with his webbed finger. *Go that way, no come back!*

Mahri picked up the oars that she'd let fall during their conversation and began to row out to the open sea.

"So be it," she muttered. She wasn't sure she wanted to come back from the Beyond, knowing that fear goaded her yet somehow not caring. "You don't have to come with me if you don't want to."

She waited for Jaja's reply, afraid that he'd take her up on the offer, then breathed a sigh of relief when he threw a small webbed fist forward over the bow in that familiar gesture of "onward." But he threw one last thought at her, before retreating behind a stubborn wall of silence.

Silly, silly human.

Mahri had thought the open sea would be just like her channels, just bigger. She couldn't have been more wrong. When she Saw into the waves, the strings were broader, stronger, and refused to change into the shapes she strove to form. Chewing more zabba seemed to help a bit but she didn't know these waters and until she did all the Power in the forest wouldn't help. Her muscles ached from rowing and she used the zabba to enhance their strength instead.

The sun lay hot on her shoulders as they crested wave after wave, their goal of tree lines never seeming any closer. Mahri fell into the rhythm of her rowing, wondering if Jaja were right, if this journey would take her on a path she'd never return from. If that were true... she'd refused to think of Korl for so long that she had to fight to bring up the memory of him. Perversely, Mahri felt safe to do so now. Now that he lay beyond her reach.

His eyes were the easiest to remember, that pale green fire that had always drawn her right into his arms. The soft strands of golden hair, whispering across her fingers. The curve of his mouth and the tilt to his nose, broad shoulders rigid with muscle, skin velvet beneath her palms. Mahri sighed and shifted where she sat.

Her memories stoked smoldering embers and she told herself that her body had gotten used to being loved again, that was all. The ache to feel his arms around her was a physical response to thoughts of his nearness.

Something twisted inside of her at the idea of never touching him again, never feeling the strength in his hands as they caressed her shoulders, her breasts, down, past her belly, making her suck in her breath, as they reached for the place that needed his touch the most...

Mahri swore, her voice bouncing across the waters to be absorbed by the sheer mass of it. How could she be doing everything in her power to put as much distance as possible between the two of them, yet still torture herself by the mere thought of him touching her? Seasons of travel separated them, and soon a large breadth of ocean, and yet she could still feel him in this boat. Still feel that he was a part of her.

Spirit-friend.

Mahri looked up, blinked as if coming awake from some dream. "Why do you call me that, anyway?" she thought to ask Jaja.

We one, too. He shrugged, as if that was the best explanation he could relay to her. *Uh, night comes.*

The sun had indeed set with a glow of orange and she realized that they'd only made it halfway to that line of trees. They'd be forced to stay all night on the open sea and as night rain began to fall Mahri hoped that it wouldn't bring any heavy storms with it. She dropped the oars, her fingers so cramped around the handles of them that it took an agonizing while to force them open. Blisters had popped on her palms and she chewed zabba and healed them, then covered her craft with the narwhal tent to sluice off most of the rain.

All the while, her thoughts stayed on Korl. She'd been so certain that distance would dull her desire for him and now that it hadn't she felt even more confused about her feelings. Could it be possible that she'd given her heart to him, as well as her body? Even though she'd tried so desperately not to? Her fingers fumbled with the rope she'd been tying, amazed that she'd allowed herself to even form that idea.

Thunder cracked overhead and she looked up with a frown. "That's what I get for hoping."

Waves that had formed small troughs before, now grew to create one deep abyss after another. It was like the Royal's elevator, making her stomach fly up to her throat, then slam back past her knees. Jaja attached himself to her waist by a death-grip on her belt as the storm continued to grow.

Mahri couldn't allow herself to crawl beneath the tent and just let the fury of the tempest control her fate. She had to stand beneath the deluge of rain that felt like shells being pelted against her skin and chew more root.

She'd thought to go easy on zabba tonight as it always weakened one after the Power was spent, and she needed the strength to row again tomorrow. As she looked far up to the crest of another mammoth wave she knew that without the Power there wouldn't be a tomorrow for her.

Mahri shifted her sight and Saw into the rebellious water, knowledgeable enough about the sea now to not even try to Push the whole of it, just manipulate the surface so that her craft skimmed with the curve of the dips. When a wave threatened to break above them and drag the boat down she used the Power to skim beneath and rise up to the next curve.

It would be a fight to see who could last the longest. The storm or her Power.

"More root, Jaja," shouted Mahri over the roar of the sea, afraid to let go of the sides of her craft now, it bucked so alarmingly. Her little pet dug into the pouch and fed her the rest of the bag for the next few hours, sustaining Mahri and allowing the Power to flow. But the tempest continued—if anything it seemed to grow in proportion—and she wondered at the ferocity of it. It seemed that without the shelter of the trees the fury of a storm could grow unabated.

Spirit-friend.

Mahri started. It would take some getting used to, this new ability to hear her pet's thoughts.

Jaja, I'm busy.

No more root, he thought-answered.

Mahri Twisted and Pushed another wave. Thank-the-moons they'd stumbled onto a tree that grew the zabba vine when they'd traveled through the Unknown. One did not ignore such a find. They'd harvested as much as they could store to supplement the zabba that Korl had provided her with.

Do you think you can reach the secret compartment?

Sure, sure, came the confident reply. But Jaja still had a death-grip on her belt against the bucking and rolling of their small craft.

Mahri felt the Power draining from her too quickly as she fought the rebellious water for control.

"Sometime soon, Ja!" she shouted, her words lost in the thunder of the sea.

Lightning cracked and Jaja leaped beneath the tent. Mahri felt a sudden shudder of fatigue sweep through her body, the first sign that her system faltered from lack of root. Another tumbling crash of wave broke over them and this time when she Pushed at the water it responded stubbornly. The deluge caught them halfway out from under it.

The force of the water slammed across her shoulders and head like a giant wet hand, shoving her to her knees. Mahri heard the timbers in her boat crack before she saw the flying pieces, and then for a moment only muffled sound as she sank beneath the water.

She fought against the weakness of zabba use and made her trembling muscles kick for the surface, opened her mouth and screamed Jaja's name. Nothing lay around her but water, no small head bobbed within her sight, not even a piece of wood to be seen from her destroyed craft. But her pet had more chance of surviving than she, for he swam like the fish he was, and could stay submerged for a long time without coming up for air.

But the supply of zabba went down with her craft and she had barely enough Power in her system to keep herself afloat. Mahri tasted the sourness of true fear, and choked and swore at the way it sapped her of hope.

She closed her eyes against the salty sting of spray and told herself to think. She had to find Jaja. Maybe he managed to get some root before that wave hit. It could be their one chance. And she opened her mouth to scream his name again when she remembered that they now had another method of communication.

Jaja? Jaja!

No answer, and she didn't know enough about this thought-speech to know how close he needed to be to hear her. Did distance matter, is that why he didn't answer? Or could he have gotten hurt from the force of the wave, a splinter of wood through his small body? Mahri told herself to stop imagining such things.

Another heave of water lifted her into the air and for a moment she rode the top of a gargantuan wave. Lightning cracked and lit the stormy night, but nothing lay below her but dark swells. And then the wave threw her back down.

Jaja!

Water slammed into her mouth like a fist, forced its way into her lungs. Ach! How it burned! The pain of it made her panic, gave her new strength, so that she kicked for the surface with renewed vigor. But Mahri no longer knew in which direction the surface lay.

It should take longer than this to die, she thought wildly, and used the dregs of Power left in her to force oxygen into her abused lungs. She wouldn't give up so quickly!

Then the water surrounding her calmed and she floated in tranquility. Her vision faded to an inky blackness so she sought the inner one, cursing herself for not using the rest of the Power to See with her mind. But oddly enough she realized that she did See a light, beckoning to her through the black, and she went toward it, sluggishly at first and then with a speed that hurtled her straight into it.

Mahri blinked, or thought she did, unsure if she had lids to blink with. The Healer's Tree stood before her and the light that beckoned had been the beacon that Korl had sworn to leave burning for her. She walked— no, floated—into that room and seemed to hover somewhere near the ceiling.

Vases and pots and baskets of flowers covered the room, so that only a small space of floor from the door to the bed lay bare. But even that small area lay covered in white flower petals, with mounds of them heaped atop the bed.

She felt choked with some unnamable emotion, some new sensibility created by the thought of Korl spreading freshly plucked petals in the hopes that she'd return to share them. How could she not love him? Cowardly to admit it when she knew she was about to die, but finally admit it she did. And Mahri opened her inner self, like one of those flowers unfolding to seek the warmth of the sun.

The door opened and he stood there, the light shining in his golden hair, casting shadows along his profile. Korl walked over to the window then back to sit on the bed, his hands clenching into sudden fists, crushing several unfortunate petals.

Korl?

His head snapped up and he looked toward the window. "Mahri?"

Aya. She'd forgotten the sound of his voice, they way it made her shiver. And how the feel of his golden mind inside her head created another warmth that spread like a comforting balm. Yet, there was something else…

"Where are you?" He strode to the window and looked out.

I… I think I'm a ghost.

"A what? What happened?" And he clutched at his head, as if just now realizing that her voice came from within.

I've drowned, I think, in the sea Beyond the Unknown. But Korl, there's something here…

His face had turned as white as the petals, then flushed with renewed arrogance. "No," he commanded. "I do not give you leave to die!" Then he fumbled at a pouch strung at his waist and determinedly began to chew handfuls of zabba. His eyes flashed with the fire of root Power.

"Stupid bird," he muttered between mouthfuls. "Should've kept you caged, instead of letting you go off to die in some Unknown place."

A dark speck that had crept inside Mahri's mind when she'd opened herself to Korl began to expand into a filthy cloud.

Through the open door strode another figure, a monk-fish perched on each black clad shoulder.

Behind you! Mahri thought-screamed. *The blackrobe!*

Korl reacted with the speed of a warrior, pulling the ceremonial sword from the scabbard at his hip and whirling to face the shadow behind him. But then he froze, held in thrall by the Power of the two monk-fish.

The fog in Mahri's mind expanded, tendrils of inky slime beginning to trace a path along the green pathways of her Power. The blackrobe tried to use his pets to *force* a Bond with her!

"No!" bellowed Korl, knowing what the man attempted to do, his own link with Mahri keeping open the door that allowed it to happen.

From you to me, thought Mahri. *Jaja said I'd have no protection in the Unknown. Break the link, let me go, or he just might succeed.*

"You finally seek me out and I have to let you go?" Korl vibrated with frustration. "I want to keep you inside of me always!"

The contrast between the prince's golden presence and the foulness of the blackrobe was balanced only by the monk-fish. However they'd been forced to participate in this Bonding it wasn't willingly and they did what they could to stop the advance of the evil one. But what Mahri had always feared would happen with Korl began to overcome her in that blackness. She began to lose herself.

Korl felt her fade, renewed his struggle against the Power binding him, and swung his bone sword in a wide arc, straight for the throat of the blackrobe. "I'm always allowing you to leave me!"

A scream of pure agony rent the air as Korl's sword swept the blackrobe's head from his body, the two monk-fish barely avoiding that flash of blade.

At the same instant, Mahri felt both of them leave her mind, allowing her to be blissfully alone again. And she felt a pull on her that became a brutal yank as the room faded in her Sight to be replaced by a glowing brilliance of green fire.

Power! Korl fed her discarded body Power that swept through her system and brought her soul slamming back into it. Mahri felt the pain again, of lungs drowned and unmoving, and wondered what he'd gained her. Perhaps some more time only, for how could she reach the surface, still not knowing in which direction it lay? But even more, if she managed even that feat, without her boat she had no chance of ever crossing that large expanse of sea into the shelter of the trees.

Through almost numb skin she felt the touch of her monk-fish. *Jaja?*

Bump head. Back now. See big fins?

Mahri's head spun. Big fins? What did he mean? She couldn't See anything, with the Power or otherwise… and then she remembered that new ability, and quested with her thoughts. Yes, a school of narwhal swam far beneath the fury of the stormy sea. Big fins, indeed.

Jaja's thoughts broke through her own. *You speak. No listen to little me. My mind like gnat-fish on such big back.*

Mahri shuddered. To touch the thoughts with a creature as old as the sea—they knew things her mind couldn't encompass. But what choice had she? She sent out a plea, tentative at first, then stronger as she met no resistance. Down to the depths spiraled her thought-quest, and she sensed one, two, three of the beasts. They ignored her as slightly more of a nuisance than a gnat-fish.

Again, demanded Jaja.

So she held strong, sending until she touched a youngling, who answered her out of sheer curiosity.

Who are you?

One who needs help.

Aaah. A long, thoughtful pause followed. *You're one of the aliens, yes?*

Mahri had always thought of the natives as the aliens, not her own kind. But the creature was right. *Aya*.

You break my peace.

Mahri waited. Evidently peace was the order of their universe and his thoughts radiated her disruption of their placidity. Would his youth be in her favor, that he'd seek a little diversion? That he'd answered her at all seemed a miracle.

I like your mind, responded. *New, different ways of thought. And there is another strong one, who calls to you. Can you not hear?*

Mahri wondered—could it possibly be Korl?

Aah. Another long sigh. *Names are meaningless, souls are all. I will help you. Such a shame for one so loved to die.*

And after what seemed an eternity she felt the smoothness of the whale's skin beneath her, lifting her up to the surface of the ocean, into a night that slowly calmed as the storm passed. Mahri used the Power to Push her lungs and heaved up enormous amounts of saltwater. She gasped for air and fought against the pain until she could Heal herself and then blinked, unbelieving, as the huge creature beneath her began to move through the sea.

Jaja patted her cheeks and chirped small, joyful noises at her as they headed toward home.

Chapter 20

IT SEEMED THAT GOING AROUND THE UNKNOWN ON A narwhal was faster than going through twisted channels on a boat; only a few days passed before they reached the outskirts of the swamps that sheltered her sister-in-life's village, and Mahri was forced to make a decision sooner than she'd thought.

Stay, or continue on to the Palace Tree?

She ran her palms across the rubbery hide of the narwhal, small rivulets of water from their passage through the sea flowing over her fingers. Just because she'd admitted her love for Korl didn't mean anything had changed. He was still a Royal, the heir to Sea Forest, and she just an ignorant water-rat. A smuggler of root who stood for everything the Royals did not—freedom of knowledge and Power.

And she still feared Korl. His demands that she become one with him in every way, through a merging of minds that threatened the individuality of her very soul, were intensified by the encounter with the blackrobe. She'd felt what it would be like to be consumed by another and Korl offered her no compromises. It would be all or nothing.

Jaja slapped her upside the head. *Go back now?*

She scowled, knowing he didn't refer to the village but to the Palace Tree. Although one thought away from deciding to return to the warmth of Korl's arms, she just couldn't bring herself to do it. Their entire world would have to change for them to be together and she didn't believe it ever could.

My thanks, great one, for your help, she thought to the massive beast beneath her.

Cold, lazy thoughts touched her own. *Anytime, alien from the stars. Your thoughts are most... interesting.*

Mahri flushed, leaped down to the whale's flipper and dove into the sea, Jaja chattering angrily, but only a splash behind. How much of her thoughts had the great creature shared? That crack around her mind-barrier felt wider and made her feel a bit more vulnerable, yet oddly enough she had no desire to seal it again, as if the gift of communication with the narwhal was worth the price of her own privacy.

She reached the roots of a small sea tree and crawled across it, wishing she had zabba to heal the injuries she'd acquired during that storm. Her lungs ached from the exertion of that short swim and she'd suffered from shortness of breath even while sitting still.

Mahri used the tree trunk to gain her feet and looked up at the narwhal as it swam out to sea. She swallowed. That black shiny hide gleamed in the sunshine, still towering over her even at this distance, and she marveled that she'd dared to ride atop such a magnificent wild being. The snout rose briefly, the silver horn that lay embedded there raised as if in silent salute, and a fountain of water sprayed from the blow hole, droplets glittering like crystals in the sun.

Farewell, drifted a final thought. *Let us play again, soon.*

She nodded, a sickly grin across her lips. Being drowned wasn't exactly her idea of a game she'd like to play again.

The village still lay some distance into the trees and Mahri began to walk the branches, trying hard not to mourn the loss of her craft. It had been formed by her Wilding mother for her father, many moons ago, and she didn't possess the skill her mother had with the Shaping of wood, her own affinity with water predominant. Any boat she made would be lucky to float.

She reached for a vine, tested the strength, then swung across to another tree, careful to avoid a nest of firebugs on landing. Jaja rode her shoulder but refused to speak to her, his thoughts vibrating with disgust at her decision to return to the village instead of the palace.

When they reached their destination they were met with a bustle of activity. Mahri wiped a tired hand across her brow and blinked at the rows of boats filled to bursting with gear. It had been some time since the village had moved, why were they packing up now? They hadn't harvested all of the zabba in this area yet.

Mahri desperately hoped it wasn't because Korl had betrayed their location.

She sought Caria's home and pushed open the skin door. Except for a few broken seashells scattered across the floor, the rooms were bare. Too tired to even seek out her sister-in-life among the throng of people around the boats, she sat outside the shelter and leaned against the wall-branch and dozed.

Tiny fingers patted her face. "Jaja, stop it."

A high, feminine giggle responded and Mahri woke, unaware that she'd even drifted off, and looked into the impish face of her niece. "Hello, Sh'ra."

"Hi," the little girl replied, her gaze lowered to the ground, a small, brown toe prodding at a bit of leaf.

"Where's your mother?"

The child shrugged and Mahri sighed.

"You do remember me, Sh'ra?"

"Oh, yes." Her niece raised her eyes and Mahri sucked in a breath. "You're my auntie who saved me from the fever."

Mahri nodded, still unbelieving. Sh'ra's eyes sparkled with the Power of zabba!

"You chew root, child?"

"Aya, just like you. That's why we're going to the city."

"You're what?" Mahri's voice had almost shouted that question, and she'd risen to her feet, making her head spin so badly she had to shut her eyes. By the time she'd opened them again the girl had disappeared.

What had she meant, they were going to the city? Why would they leave the swamps? What had happened while she'd been gone?

"Jaja, find Caria and bring her to me. Now!"

The monk-fish flew from her shoulder in response to the demand in that voice and disappeared over the side of the branch, to return after what seemed a long time later with her sister-in-life in tow.

"Mahri!" exclaimed Caria. "Where on Sea Forest have you been?" And she captured her in a hug of welcome that caused tears to roll down both their cheeks.

It was some time before Mahri could disentangle herself from Caria's hold. "Never mind that—tell me what's going on here."

Caria dropped her arms and stood back to study the redhead. "Well," she said, "you don't look like a queen to me."

"What… What are you talking about? And when did you test Sh'ra for root tolerance? You know how dangerous it is to expose her at such a young age! And by-the-moons, what's all this talk about going to the city?"

Caria took a deep breath. "Sh'ra discovered a small patch of zabba herself and she scared me to death after we discovered she'd chewed it but she had the tolerance and thank-the-moons you're back, we now have a guide to the city and you'll have to wait for the answers to the rest of your questions until we're on the boat." And with those hurried words she spun and ran back to the dock, leaving Mahri no other choice but to follow.

Then she was swept into a crowd of confusion, people saying goodbyes, for only a third of the village was going to the city. Mahri caught a glimpse of Trian, one of the few that were staying behind, and the man had his arm wrapped protectively around a pretty blonde woman.

"His lifemate," hissed Caria, appearing at her shoulder. "He gave up on you after hearing of your own joining with the prince."

Mahri met Trian's gaze and smiled, hoping she conveyed her happiness for him with that look. He responded with a grin, and the blonde smiled back at her too, then huddled closer to the big man at her side.

Mahri felt Caria's hand push her forward and she lost sight of the couple in the crowd.

"Come along, we'll follow your boat," said her sister-in-life. "Everyone's so grateful that you're going to be our guide."

Mahri felt dazed. Had she agreed to lead this excursion? But her assent didn't seem to matter, and it seemed to be the only way she'd be able to get the answers to her questions.

"I don't have a boat… any longer."

Caria's mouth gaped, then she snapped it shut. "Well, then. You'll ride in ours." And maneuvered her toward the most heavily laden of the tiny fleet.

"Which way?" asked Wald, his big frame balanced in the middle of the boat, a wooden pole clutched in one beefy hand.

"To the city?"

"And sure, where else?"

Mahri shrugged weakly and gestured at the third branching channel on the right. With a grunt Wald set their craft in that direction, the rest of the fleet following right behind.

The deck lay so crowded with belongings that Mahri had to weave her way to where Jaja sat in his usual place at the bow. The monk-fish kept striking his fist forward over the water and turning back to look at her with a triumphant gleam in his brown eyes.

Just because we're going to the city doesn't mean we're returning to the palace, Mahri thought at him.

Jaja shrugged in a "we'll see" motion and stuck his fist defiantly forward again.

Mahri spun, spied the top of Caria's head just behind a tall box, and crawled over to her. "I'll be having those answers, now."

"Of course, if you're sure Wald won't be needing your guidance?"

Mahri frowned. "It'll be a while before we'll need to change passages."

Caria shooed Sh'ra up to the bow with a promise that Jaja would play with her, then folded her hands into her lap and cocked her head. "First, just answer me one question. Where have you been?"

"To the Unknown, and Beyond."

Blonde eyebrows rose in amazement and Mahri was tempted to tell her that she'd ridden a narwhal. But even Caria's imagination had its limits, and besides, she had too many questions already, to invite any more.

"Why?"

"No you don't. You said one question and that's it. My turn. What's possessed you people, that you'd go to the city?"

Caria leaned beneath the opening of a tent and emerged with a handful of dried fruit and fish. "You eat while I talk, deal?"

Mahri reluctantly agreed, but after her first bite she realized how hungry she was for a cooked meal. and ate with relish.

"The king has changed the laws."

Mahri's eyebrows rose but she continued to chew.

"He's decreed that all knowledge is now available to anyone who wishes to seek it, and has turned the Seer's Tree into a public place of learning."

Mahri choked. That hallowed of all places, open to water-rats? Years of secrecy suddenly exposed—had the king gone mad?

"Furthermore," continued her sister-in-life, as if she quoted from the document of decree herself, "although zabba will continue to be regulated to those qualified to use it, it's no longer illegal for a non-Royal to have it in their possession without special permission from the king."

Caria leaned over and pounded Mahri on the back

when another fit of choking overtook her. Her damaged lungs made her wheeze and she couldn't speak. Generations of hoarding zabba and the Power had come to an end, yet she couldn't imagine the king making those kinds of decrees unless something dire had happened.

Their entire world had changed while she'd been roaming the Unknown.

Mahri froze at that thought, understanding dawning on her. What had Caria said earlier? About her being a queen? "It's Korl, isn't it? He's become King of Sea Forest and made all these changes, hasn't he?"

Caria nodded. "The old king died and named Korl as successor. And sis," her voice lowered, "the decree not only forbids the Hunting of a Wilding, but orders them welcome to learn from the Masters."

Indeed. Mahri's head swam. Prince of Changes, wasn't that what the aliens had called him? Didn't they hope that he'd set in motion the means for all humanity to have the ability she'd gained, to See with her thoughts into all of Sea Forest? And she'd played right into their hands, with her strong will and need for freedom. Had they known all along that she'd leave him, that he'd make these changes so that she'd come back to him?

And she'd thought they didn't know humans at all.

Mahri shook her head, amazed at her own arrogance. What made her think he did all of this for her? And she'd accused him of being conceited! He could've made these laws in response to his time in the swamps, perhaps because the natives had sought him out while she was gone, to convince him of the need for change.

No, no. They couldn't speak with him! As far as she knew, that dubious honor had only been bestowed on her.

She shivered with a sudden, manic surge of joy. Could it be possible that he had changed their world for them, to one that they could share together?

There was one way to find out.

Mahri crawled over boxes. "Wald."

"Ya."

"Move over." And she flicked her wrist, extending her bone to pole length. Wald sat down, acknowledging her greater experience in poling, and drew a long swig from the flask at his belt. Caria sat beside him.

"Do you have any zabba?" asked Mahri. Wald tossed her a pouch and she grinned. "Is there anyone else in this fleet with enough Power to Push the water?"

"Sh'ra has that affinity," announced Caria, her voice full of pride.

Jaja, thought Mahri. *Bring the child to me.* And then she said aloud to her sister-in-life, "Is that why you're going to the city, to have Sh'ra taught?"

Caria nodded. "But even though Wald and I don't have enough tolerance to Push, only to sometimes See, we still want to learn anything they'd be willing to teach us. Two hands will always be useful, don't you think?"

"With minds like yours behind them," assured Mahri. She chewed root while she continued to pole, felt the Power flow through her pathways and turned sparkling eyes on her niece. "Your instruction will begin now, little one. For there is swamp-knowledge, too. Which is just as important as book-learning, aya?"

Chestnut curls nodded and Mahri shifted her Sight and helped the girl See into the water.

"Sh'ra?"

"Aya, Auntie?"

"Look into the trees. Do you, ah, See anyone?"

Her niece's head snapped upward. "Just leaves and birds. And vines, and stuff. Am I supposed to See something more, Auntie?"

Mahri swallowed.

"No, child," she whispered as her olive-green eyes closed for a moment. When she opened them the natives still stood there, lined along the bank of the channel, strings of coral and feathers decorating their scaled bodies, webbed fingers spread in gestures of farewell.

And as her boat passed their ranks, they each bowed to Mahri, with most elaborate sweeps of respect, like the ripple of a brown wave.

***

The waterways around the Seer's Tree were clogged with boats of all sizes and descriptions. Robed Masters walked along the root banks and through the mass of people, trying to bring some semblance of order. Mahri stared in open-mouthed wonder, not until this moment actually believing it. Water-rats to be trained as Masters! Those of non-Royal blood with high root tolerance no longer to be hunted down like criminals, but to be taught in the Tree of Learning!

"Do you suppose we'll have to live on the boat?" wondered Caria.

Wald shrugged. "Seems like there's a lot more people here than the king expected. We'll make do."

Sh'ra clapped her hands. "Ooh, we'll sleep on the water just like Auntie."

Mahri smiled down at her niece. All of her family had so readily accepted these changes—ach, all of Sea

Forest, it looked like. But her own head still spun with the changes Korl had wrought as king. Perhaps because she'd felt the disdain of the Royals when she'd lived in the palace, could she really understand the enormity of what had happened.

"Now then, who have we here?" rasped a voice from the bank. A hood covered the head of a Master, his face lowered over a bone tablet that he scribbled furiously on. "I'll be Seeing into you, to study your pathways, see what level of root-tolerance—"

He had looked up, his gaze alighting on Mahri's stunned face. "Your Majesty!"

"Master R'in!"

The old man bowed to her with such an elaborate swoop that her family turned and stared at her, as if just now realizing that she was some kind of Presence.

"Stop that, R'in," snapped Mahri.

The old man looked up with a grin on his face. "You'll have to get used to it, Wilding."

"No, I don't."

R'in ignored her. "The king will be overjoyed that you're back, and to think that I will be the one to escort you to him! Where did you go, Your Majesty? And why did you stay gone so long? The rumors that have buzzed through the palace…"

"Would you stop calling me that?"

"What?"

"Your Majesty! I'm not your anything ach, never mind. I've not decided if I'm returning and would ask for your word that you'll not reveal my presence to anyone."

The wrinkles on his face sunk into even deeper grooves. "I don't understand. Why wouldn't you return?

Isn't the reason you didn't stay because you could never be accepted as an equal? Has not my king decreed that you will be treated as such?" His voice lowered into incredulity. "By-the-Power, could it be that you don't realize he's done all of this for you?"

"Has he?" Mahri's voice sounded very small.

Master R'in frowned in annoyance. Caria and Wald stared from her to the old man with the most astonishing looks on their faces that Sh'ra giggled at the sight of them.

Mahri shrugged. She wished everyone would stop staring at her, for even those that anchored next to their craft had stopped and turned to gape. "There's more to this, Master R'in, than the equality of my people."

"You do not feel welcome at the palace." He scratched through the scraggly bush of his white beard. "You must know, Your Majesty, that many would welcome your return, including this old man. For the story of the attempt on Prince Korl's mind by his sister and that dark Master has circulated throughout the courtiers, and now that he has become king, well. It might be considered treasonous not to accept the woman that had saved the life of our king."

Mahri sighed. All the walls between her and Korl kept tumbling down. Except the one she most feared.

"My thanks, Master R'in, for your support and words of welcome." Already she sounded so formal, unlike herself, as if being Royalty was a cloak one could don. "But I would still ask you not to reveal my presence. Can you do so?"

He opened his mouth, then shut it again.

"If I... command it?"

The old man sketched another brief bow. "As Your Majesty wishes."

Mahri looked around. More people were staring, the chatter and noise that had surrounded them reduced to an almost eerie silence. "And don't call me that," she whispered, ducking her head.

Master R'in cleared his throat and turned to Wald and Caria. "May I have the honor of testing your family for tolerance?" They nodded their heads, looking bemused. "Depending on your affinity, we'll be sending you to the Healer's, Artist's, Merchant's or Warrior's Trees. Should you have the potential for Mastery, you'll come with me to the Seer's Tree. Is that agreeable?" His eyes turned to Mahri seeking permission and she nodded.

At least the people surrounding them had gone back to whatever they were doing before R'in had made such a fuss. Although they still whispered and glanced in her direction, the old man honored her wishes and appeared to act as if he were going about his normal duties. At the end of his testing, he bade them follow him to the Seer's Tree.

"It seems to run in the family," he said, indicating Sh'ra. Mahri smiled at her niece, knowing Caria and Wald were excited to be going to the Seer's Tree.

"You know," continued Master R'in in a whisper as the family packed their belongings to carry with them, "the king would banish me to the root farms if he knew I saw you and allowed you to go. But you won't be coming with us, will you?"

"Not now."

He sighed. "At first I thought him mad, when he brought home a Wilding. But look at the changes you've wrought." The sleeves of his robe flapped as he waved his arms around at the myriad boats clogging the channel. "Never in my lifetime would I have thought that the Royal line would risk their control of Sea Forest. And do you know the very best thing?"

Mahri shook her head.

"Some of these water-rats want to learn of the First Records!" Those faded eyes sparkled with more than zabba as he reached out and surreptitiously kissed her hand. "Thank you, Your Majesty. And... come back to us."

Then he straightened, old bones popping, and waved at a group of guards to come help her family with the rest of their belongings. Mahri kept her head lowered in case she'd be recognized, although she didn't think any of the king's personal guard would be among that number.

"What will you do?" asked Caria amid the hugs of parting.

"I'm not sure. Can I borrow your boat?"

"Of course."

And so they left, little Sh'ra waving goodbye until they disappeared behind a forked branch, and Mahri maneuvered the craft away from the congestion, occasionally tripping over the scattered seashells that had fallen out of Caria's bundles.

What would she do?

Mahri had no idea and fought a ridiculous feeling of abandonment by the one family she could lay claim to. She'd always left them, before. This was the first time they'd left her. Surely therein lay her sense of loss.

A huge raft drifted up ahead, surrounded by small one-person boats and canoes, a building erected in the middle which spewed forth sounds of revelry. She anchored her boat to a post and hopped aboard, smiling at the sign that flapped over the doorway of this floating tavern. Jaja rode on her shoulder and clapped his hands in anticipation.

Mahri opened the door and felt as if she'd been sucked right into the midst of the celebration. A shell of quas-juice appeared in her hand and Jaja chattered a demand for a sip. She held it up to him while she surveyed the small room, standing on her tiptoes to see over the shoulder-to-shoulder crowd.

A husky voice warmed her ear. "I knew ya' would escape."

Mahri leaned back into the warm body plastered behind her. "Did you now?"

"Ach, no one could keep my gal imprisoned for long."

She laughed, looked over her shoulder into the glittering black eyes of Vissa. He licked full lips as he stared at her mouth, his hands already roaming the contours of her body. "So the conquering heroine returns to me, eh?"

Mahri tried to move out from underneath those searching fingers but too many bodies hemmed her in, sealing them in a web of privacy. "What do you mean—heroine?"

"Darling, everyone knows the king made free of the zabba for the Wilding he took for lifemate. And after that fight in my place—and how was I supposed to know it was the prince I pounded, I ask ya'? Anyway, yer a heroine to the swamp-rats, don't ya' know?"

A shiver of something went up her spine. If they only knew that events had come about because of her fear of the prince, maybe the water-rats wouldn't be so eager to call her a heroine. She ignored that ridiculous title, just as she ignored the other that R'in had labeled her with.

"Seems to me that you caught the bad end of that fight, Vissa."

He threw back his head and laughed, the sound booming over the rest of the noise. "A good thing, too. Else I'd not be here now to welcome ya' to my new place. Come on, let me show ya' around."

Mahri allowed him to grab her arm and pull her through the crowd, releasing her hold on the shell of juice to Jaja, who slurped in greedy pleasure. The place looked to be nothing more than a shack on a raft, but it did sport a bar in the far corner and Vissa brought her around to the back of it.

"This is only the first one, mind. And I've still got the tavern on the docks. But my new plan, see, is to build floating taverns all over Sea Forest, to bring my happy-brew to those poor unfortunates that can't make it to my permanent place. What think ya'?"

Mahri shrugged. "Sounds good, but why bother?"

"Ach, girl, ya' don't know how ya' have turned the world around now, do ya'? Zabba's legal now, darling, and profits will go down cause of it. But there's other ways to earn a bone." She nodded and he grinned lazily, played with the ties of her vest before running a finger across the swell of her chest. "I can take good care of ya', girl. If ya' have a mind to stick around."

Mahri studied that handsome face and saw to her surprise that he meant what he said. He lifted her up and set her on the back of the bar, planting himself between her thighs and cradling her with those large, muscular arms.

Jaja jumped from her shoulder and scampered down the bar, sampling drinks as he went. The crowd was in such good cheer they allowed the little moocher to do it.

Vissa lowered his voice. "Are ya' going back to him, then?"

Mahri shook her head no.

"Then stay with me."

She shook it again. His hands on her body told her one important thing. It wasn't just any man she desired, for only Korl's touch could make her shiver with lust.

He kissed her nose. "I told them, it was only the swamps for ya'."

"Told who?"

Those black brows rose almost to his hairline. "Don't ya' know the entire forest's waiting to see if ya' go back to him? And I told all who'd listen that my girl's too independent to shackle herself to a man. Although, if ya' chose a king over me, I'd find it in my heart to forgive ya'."

Mahri grinned. "Would you now?"

"Aya. I also told them that the woman I knew wouldn't give up her freedom for nothing. That she'd never let herself fall in love again, especially to no Royal. No matter that they'd changed their ways now, they still can't bring back the dead. 'Why,' I said, 'she's making them pay now, ain't she?'"

The grin had frozen on Mahri's face. Is that what Vissa truly thought, that she was making Korl pay for the death of her former lifemate and child?

"I have to hand it to ya', girl. Ya' sure have made a fool out of that prince. Why, it wouldn't surprise me none that that's why us here swamp-rat's really think yer a hero—"

Mahri slapped him. One minute she sat stock-still, and the next she looked at the red brand of her hand appearing on that handsome face.

Jaja, she called.

Her pet wove through shells of quas-juice and tried to hop on her shoulder while she and Vissa continued to stare at each other in horrified fascination. The monk-fish wobbled and tried to hop again, gave up with a drunken shrug of scaled shoulders and crawled to his perch, his tail anchoring him as he swayed.

Mahri stormed out of the shack and Vissa let her go, a smile of pure satisfaction across his handsome, albeit thoroughly slapped, face.

Chapter 21

MAHRI'S TOES CURLED AGAINST THE WOODEN DECK OF the boat while she waited for nightfall, the water current threatening to push her through the screen of bamba fronds that she'd anchored behind across from the Healer's Tree.

While she waited, she considered that if the Royals wanted to eliminate all those with a tolerance for zabba, this would be the perfect plan. Bring them out of hiding and then… Only her belief in Korl dismissed those awful thoughts from her mind. He wouldn't do such a thing—and then Mahri laughed at herself. What a long way she'd come, that she believed in the honor of a Royal!

She frowned, knees bent with the ebb and flow of the water, eyes intent on one particular window in the Healer's Tree. Had she changed so much, then? When she'd first developed this new ability to Hear with the Power it had terrified her, so much so that Jaja had built that black wall around her mind to protect her. Yet, first she'd allowed a crack in it to speak with Jaja, and she must've developed some control, for the life-thoughts of Sea Forest had not overwhelmed her when she'd done so. And then it had widened to allow her to Hear the narwhal, and when she realized that her thoughts also lay open to that great one, she'd actually accepted it.

She'd also shattered the mind-barrier to save Korl,

even after knowing the terror she'd felt the first time she'd allowed their minds to merge, in that brief connection when Bonding. And later, when the overdose had thrust her into a world of nightmare... but that had been more than thought-sharing.

Their souls had joined.

Mahri shivered and absentmindedly popped a tuber of zabba into her mouth. Yes, she'd changed. But would it be enough?

Dusk darkened the sky and she watched that window with even more intensity. Perhaps Korl had grown tired of setting that beacon for her, had found another woman to love, one more willing to give him all that he demanded. Perhaps his love had turned to hatred, if he knew his subjects called him fool because of her.

Mahri clenched her fists. Korl was many things—many wonderful, warm things—but never a fool. She couldn't allow anyone to think that of him.

The light that burst from the window near blinded her, and when Jaja leapt for her with jabbers of excitement he knocked her off-balance and they both ended up sprawled in the bottom of the craft. To lose her footing on any boat, even one not her own, was a first, and she could feel the shockwaves from Jaja's mind as he stared at his mistress with tiny mouth agog.

With the joy that sprang from the thought that he still wanted her also came a frisson of fear. For a moment she felt that she'd rather face a white water channel of skulkers—even that many-tongued monster—than pole across that stretch of water to the window.

I'm a coward, she thought.

Jaja slapped her upside the head. *No, no spirit-friend.*

Seen you fear many times. But coward's only one who runs away.

And that's exactly what Mahri felt like doing. She scowled at the monk-fish. *Ach, you're a clever little thing.*

Jaja batted wide, innocent eyes at her.

Mahri snorted, then stood and flicked her wrist, her staff lengthening with a soft whoosh of sound that mingled with the slap of the water and the swish of the fronds. She poled across to the underneath of the balcony where that beacon of light called, weighed anchor and pulled the grapnel from her pack. When she threw the hook upward, she remembered the first time she'd done this, and smiled.

The zabba in her system gave her the strength to near fly up the rope and over the railing, and she crouched for a moment, checking for any guards. Odd, that none patrolled about to challenge her. She'd think that after the last time they wouldn't be so lax in guarding the prince's—no, the king's, room.

And then another thought struck her. What if the guards had orders to keep clear of this area, in the event that their... queen might return? Mahri swallowed. How could she, an ignorant water-rat, even think of herself as a queen? She'd be an imposter, a pretender on the throne. Korl could change many things, except for what she was.

And what he was. For if she entered that room, there would be no holding back. Fear again tingled its way up her spine. She'd left him once and knew she couldn't do it again. If she walked through that door there would be no turning back, and she knew, no holding back. He wouldn't accept any compromises. He'd want all of her and nothing less.

Mahri lifted her chin. Yet he hadn't asked for anything that he hadn't been willing to give himself. Korl had changed their world for her, making them equals in the eyes of Sea Forest. She swayed in indecision. All… or nothing?

Jaja grunted and leapt toward the light, right through the open window.

Mahri leaned forward and still couldn't make her body move, but her thoughts swirled like the tide. Every time Korl had her in his web he'd let her go—hadn't he proven that he wouldn't take away her freedom? She'd been so concerned with making everything fit so that they could be together… yet when she wasn't with him nothing else seemed to matter. Not the laws of Sea Forest or the well-intentioned motives of fur-scaled aliens.

She smiled when she realized that she'd had it all backwards.

They just needed to be together and make everything else fit *them*.

Mahri didn't bother with the door either. She cursed softly and followed her pet, one leg after another over that sill, then stood and stared in astonishment.

It hadn't been a dream, or some death-induced hallucination, as she'd half-suspected. Mahri had been in this room with Korl, for it still lay covered in flowers, as she'd last seen it. But then only her spirit had been here and she couldn't smell the perfume, nor appreciate the myriad brilliant colors of the blossoms.

She stepped toward the bed, her hands reaching out of their own will, gathering an armful of the spent petals that covered the mattress, burying her face in the shades of white, inhaling their sweet scent. For although pots held scarlet, indigo, pale-lavender flowers, the petals on the bed were only from white blooms; the tiny curls of shi, the thin cups of the tea plant, the palm-sized spray of the cho-vine. All of them caressed her with their velvet down.

Fresh! she thought. The petals were fresh, as if they'd just been plucked this morning. She dropped her armload in awe. Korl had hundreds of flowers harvested for this bed every single day? In the hopes she might, possibly, return and share it with him?

Had any man ever wanted a woman this much?

And then the inner door opened, Jaja squealed with glee and jumped into the arms of the man standing there, and for the first time in a very long while Mahri looked on the face of her lifemate and thought: had any woman ever wanted a man this much?

The beacon of light that surrounded the windowsill flared for a moment before fading away, as if its purpose was now complete, leaving only the twinkling glow of the miniature light-globes that lay scattered around the room like so many stars, to combine their radiance in a diffused glow. But in that brief flare Mahri had taken notice of every detail of his features. From the waves of pale-golden hair that strayed over his forehead—lines of worry etched there which she didn't recall—to the white scars that lined his cheek, making her fingers itch to trace them. And the curl of his lips, the tilt of his nose, the warm fullness of his mouth.

Mahri's legs turned to water and she went down. Fortunately the bed was close enough so that she sat instead of fell, while errant thoughts continued in a stream of fire. The broad shoulders of his naked chest, the silk leggings that outlined long, muscular legs. The glow of light gold skin and the texture of his silky chest hair that created a dark line between his ribs that wandered down to where it spread to nest that which made her throb with the mere thought of its promise…

Ach, how she'd missed the sight of him!

Korl petted and scratched Jaja as if he couldn't believe the cool-scaled bundle lay in his arms, and the small monk-fish closed his lids and purred with delight. The man's voice, when he spoke, took Mahri's breath away. How could she have forgotten how the low deep timbre of it made her insides melt?

"Down the hall, to your left, old friend, is a pink table laid out just for you. With what I could remember of your favorite delicacies."

Jaja opened one brown eye and fixed it on Mahri. *His head's like a block of wood. Ask him, spirit-friend, if it's the same pink table?*

Mahri opened her mouth, shut it, then stammered, embarrassed by her shyness. "I… I don't know why it matters, but Jaja wants to know if it's the pink table that was in… our apartments."

Korl didn't look at her, hadn't since he'd walked into the room. Instead, he continued to smile down at Jaja. "The very same."

With a chirrup of delight Jaja sprang to the floor and disappeared down the hall. Korl stepped all the way into the room and shut the door behind him. "So, you've learned to talk to Jaja?"

Mahri shrugged. She didn't know what to say, and neither, obviously, did he. Or did he really care that she'd cracked that mind-barrier? Hoping that she'd let him in as well. She filled her lungs, wishing it were courage instead of air. "I can talk to other wildlife now, too. And of course the natives."

He took a step toward the bed and she inadvertently drew back. He reminded her of a treecat on the prowl.

"Humans too?"

Mahri shook her head. "Only you, because of our Bond."

And then he stood before her, she could feel the heat of him radiate like a small sun. Strong fingers cupped her chin and lifted her head to finally meet her eyes with his own.

"I always knew you were special," he said.

Mahri blinked, the feelings she read in his look twisting something inside of her, slamming that unnamable reaction into her stomach. "You don't seem surprised to see me," was all she could think of to say.

"I knew you'd come back," he replied with a husky sigh, a hint of arrogance, a trace of anger. "I'm just annoyed that it took you so long."

As always, his eyes were her downfall. She couldn't look away, couldn't move or breathe against the chemistry that flared between them. And although it hurt with the intensity of it, at the same time a soaring excitement ripped through her that made her weak from its passing.

The king went down on one knee before her, his large hand cradling the back of her head, pulling her toward his mouth. But she still couldn't look away from those eyes, the lights in the room reflected there with the pattern of a star-lit sky, because he hadn't released their hold on her yet, hadn't tasted enough of her soul.

"You've always been mine," he murmured. "You'll be happy, now that you know it in your heart."

"Will I?" she sighed, his lips so close to her own she could feel the breath of his words.

He moved his mouth atop hers, a gentle questioning at first, as if time had made him somehow unfamiliar with her. But then his fingers twisted in her hair and his kiss became demanding, hungry, as if that same stretch of time had also taken his body beyond the limit of endurance and now the need was a wild frenzied thing that he couldn't, wouldn't, control.

Mahri's body mirrored his, caught the fire of his passion and made of it a raging inferno when it combined with the flame of her own desire. She caught a handful of his hair and pushed his head closer to her own, plunging her tongue into his mouth, trying to crawl inside of him with a fierce need that would've frightened her if she'd still had the ability to think.

When Korl ripped the ties of her vest she felt the scales dig into her skin with a scrape before tearing free and she laughed at the small pain of it. When her leggings came off in the same impatient way, Mahri responded in a like manner with his own silk pants, the thin stuff of it shredding in her grip.

The sight of his need for her, the throbbing, hard length of it, made her swallow a scream, for she didn't want everyone in the Tree to know she'd returned—at least, not to announce it in quite that way.

Korl, watching her look at him, growled.

And Mahri again compared him to a treecat, wondering how he could make that spine-tingling sound. Then there were no more thoughts, no more words, nothing but the feel of Korl's smooth skin beneath her fingers, the liquid silk of his hair against her breasts while he tried to devour them, the hot palms of his hands as they branded every one of her curves. He pushed her down among that bed of white petals, the crushing releasing a wave of fresh scent that Mahri was dimly aware of, for his own musky aroma already filled her nostrils, wove a heady path through her lungs, making her dizzy with the sheer potency of it.

He surrounded her, weighted her with the force of his lips and his thighs pressed against her own, that hardness of him sweeping across the nub of her own center in a hot, wet promise of fulfillment. And Mahri wanted more, scraping her nails across his back and the tense mounds of his bottom, demanding to be a part of him, thrusting her tongue inside his mouth in a parody of what she craved.

With mindless rapture Korl drove into her, pulled out by necessity and snarled at the need for it, before plunging into her again and again until they both reached that peak of timeless suspension that begged to be shattered into waves of ecstatic pleasure.

Mahri trembled at the apex of fulfillment, knowing the brilliance that followed, relishing in the anticipation as much as the actual experience itself.

But she hadn't been aware of the Power that throbbed through her pathways, so overwhelmed by the physical magic between her and Korl. Yet she felt it now, shivering through her, more than could be accounted for in the small amount of zabba she'd chewed. She realized that Korl had been feeding her Power, that he'd Seen into those green pathways and had waited patiently at where they forked and then spread into her mind.

Waiting for this moment.

Mahri had known that he'd ask this of her, to be one in all ways, yet still she balked at his entrance. Even now, with her body tensed like a bow for release, she couldn't do it. Couldn't give up her inner mind-self to him.

Korl thrust at her, his rhythm now slow and purposeful, knowing just where the peak lay so that neither of them tumbled over the edge.

"I can't wait," he ground out, "much longer, water-rat. I don't have any control with you, but by the Power…" he slammed his teeth together with a grimace and grit out his next words. "This is nothing! Nothing…" and he couldn't go on, overcome by ragged gasps for air, his body trembling with the control he tried to exert over it.

But she'd already understood what he'd tried to tell her. That this physical connection between them wasn't enough for him, couldn't compare to what he sought from her. Yet, if this were nothing, what awaited them when their minds met?

He widened that small crack already in her mind-barrier and she let him. When she sensed his presence, that wholesome goodness that could only be Korl, she invaded him in kind, sweeping up his pathways into that familiar golden place she thought of as his mind. Mahri had been here before, but then she'd battled evil and he'd been shuttered against her. And the time before that the touch had been so brief she'd only caught wisps of himself and his memories.

This time he lay open to her, a warm welcome that felt as if she'd come home. She'd wanted to crawl into his skin, had been frantic with a desire to become one with him. This is what she'd sought—unknowing. The physical aspect of it just a sliver compared to the overwhelming oneness of this mind-joining.

Ach, how he loved her! And trusted her, for she hadn't realized how lonely his life had been, how even a crown prince never could afford to completely trust anyone. She hadn't forgotten that glimpse of memory from his mind before, and knew now that a knife in the dark was the least form of assassination that threatened one direct in line for the throne. Especially when there were other siblings who sought that power.

Korl thrust once, twice; hard enough to let them become aware of their almost forgotten bodies, and when her own body mercifully convulsed into waves of pleasure, the rest of that mind-barrier shattered as well. For a moment of sheer bliss she encompassed it all: the strength of Korl's mind, the merging of their souls into one whole, the essence that was the world of Sea Forest—from the smallest slug to the greatest of the leviathans—and the heights of passion.

Mahri's mouth dropped open in awe. This was what the natives had wanted for all of mankind. This was why they'd brought her and Korl together, for her to bring the king that awareness of humanity's connection with this world, to make him one with Sea Forest. For too long the Royals had used the Power to Shape this world to their own will, but in order for humanity to survive they must learn to shape their will to that of Sea Forest.

Mahri snapped her mouth shut and studied Korl's face, the wonder that they'd just experienced also reflected there. She laughed with the sheer exuberance of life and he grinned back at her, understanding shining on that handsome face.

She traced the scars from cheek to jaw and wondered
that she'd ever been frightened of this moment. Afraid
that she'd lose herself in him. But sharing the mind was
like making love, the connection burned but there still
lay a separateness, an oneness of identity that became
more enhanced by the joining, not overwhelmed.

Mahri sighed. She'd worried about giving him her
heart, and yet, all along, it hadn't been hers to give. For
he'd taken it the first time he'd looked into her eyes.
And the fear that he'd leave her, as had Brez and little
Tal'li, that it would tear her asunder again… that had
also been laid to rest. So simply.

"You think too much," drawled Korl, his hand sweeping the hair away from her face.

She turned into his palm and kissed it. "Aya. We'll
never leave each other, will we?"

He frowned, but knew what she meant, for as it occurred to her mind, it had to his. "With the Bond it's not
possible. If you should die, so shall I."

Mahri nodded. *I love you*, she thought.

I know, he responded.

Arrogant man.

Korl lowered his head and kissed her nose. *You know
my thoughts, now, water-rat. Know I can't live without
you. But if you wish…* And when he spoke, he used words
as if he were a guard taking sword-oath to his king.

"Mahri Zin—now Com'nder, know that without the
Bond, you are the other half of my soul, and without
you I'm incomplete. My heart has always been and will
always be yours, and for that alone, I couldn't live without you."

Tears burned at the back of her lids and she blinked

them away. *I know*, she thought at him. A little of his own arrogance would never hurt. He had an ego big enough for a narwhal to swim in, as she'd always suspected, but knew now for certain.

You don't have to be tough with me.

Mahri's hands played through the mounds of petals on the bed as she answered aloud, "Aya, I do," and wondered if she'd ever get used to this new mental form of communication. Vocalizing her words came more naturally to her and it felt more satisfying to spit them out of her mouth, rather than her head. Her roving fingers fetched up a torn piece of her clothing buried in soft petals and she seized upon it.

"You've got to stop doing that," she told him, waving the ragged scales before his face.

He tossed back his head, shook the hair from his face in a blatantly masculine, self-satisfied manner. "I can afford to rip the clothes from your body every night for the rest of our lives."

Did he think to arouse her with that promising threat? Surely he knew he already had her with that shake of his head. And then she wondered how much those moments of shared thought revealed. The mind held layer upon layer, some thoughts so deep they were near unreachable. She could read the thoughts he directed at her but she'd have to probe with the Power to delve deeper.

"It's a good thing that we can't know everything about each other."

"Mmm," murmured Korl, absorbed in covering her naked body with flower petals. "Time will reveal the rest of your faults to me soon enough."

Mahri scowled and she opened her mouth to curse

when she looked into his amused gaze and Saw herself mirrored there.

You're so easy to arouse, he thought at her with contented satisfaction. *Life with you will never be dull.*

Her eyes widened at what she'd seen in his mind. If Korl saw any faults in her they were so overwhelmed by his belief of her perfection that they scarce existed. She wondered if they'd always See each other this way.

Of course. Now lay still woman, I forbid you to move unless I command it.

And Mahri obeyed, if only because it felt so good as he slowly removed each petal that he'd covered her with. Korl unveiled her skin bit by bit, sometimes lifting a white blossom with shaking fingers, sometimes blowing them from her with a gentle puff of air from those full lips, and then licking away the whiteness with a wet heat that sent shivers through her.

It took the king a very, very, long time to uncover her completely. And when he made love to her again it was such a gentle, prolonged sort of thing that Mahri didn't even have the breath to scream. They fell asleep from sheer exhaustion, a tangle of arms and legs and wilted petals.

"Jaja?" Mahri stared at her pet through slitted eyes. It was the middle of the night; she could hear the rain patter on the outside balcony and pound atop the sea tree's massive leaves. Her body ached and tingled all over and she sought nothing but more sleep. She snuggled closer to the radiant heat of Korl's body.

I want to share, spirit-friend.

"Huh? Ach, Jaja, just go away."

Here, taste.

And Mahri felt something gooey stroked across her lips. She licked and woke up just a bit more. It was sweet and exceptionally good.

See? Yummy stuff. Want more?

Mahri moaned. She might be able to speak with her pet now but she'd never understand the odd quirks to that little mind. Had he gotten tired of gorging alone, or what? "I want to sleep," she mumbled.

Jaja let rip a loud burp. *Okay. But you eat for two now, need extra foood.* And he drew out that last word, like a fishing line over still waters.

Her eyes flew open, all traces of sleep banished by her pet's thoughts. "What do you mean, eating for two?"

Her pet shrugged, his tail a fan of dark scales in the muted light of the twinkling globes. *You. Prince. See well. But not as much as Jaja, hey?*

Mahri brushed hair away from her face and rubbed her eyelids. By-the-thirteen-moons! Had she and Korl really Sensed all life on Sea Forest, yet missed a tiny spark that she carried inside her? Could it possibly be true?

Sure, sure. Go eat now?

The king's eyes flew open. "Is he telling you what I think he is?" They glowed with that brilliant pale-green, even without the sparkle of zabba.

Mahri started at the sound of Korl's deep voice. She hadn't known he was awake, hadn't enough zabba left in her system to See into his thoughts either, and surprised herself by feeling a twinge of regret for the lack.

"Aya, I'm carrying your child," answered Mahri, marveling that she even spoke such words. She had to think about this, it had happened so quickly. How could she adjust to another one to love, when she still wasn't even used to Korl? Too many thoughts swirled through her tired self and when the king reached for zabba she stayed his hand, not wanting the chaos of his own mind as well.

He acquiesced to that silent request, turned, and enfolded her in the warm comfort of his arms.

"You think too much," he told her again.

"Aya."

"You will learn my definition of love," he commanded, "and forget your own notions."

Mahri nestled her face into the curve of his neck and breathed in the musky scent of him. His was such a more simplified version that perhaps she should give it a try. Just hold the joy of love in her heart and share it with each other and everything else be cursed. Yes, she just might be able to do that.

Go eat now? came Jaja's impatient demand.

Mahri sat up. "I think I am kind of hungry."

Jaja clapped his hands and scurried through the open door. He was joined by two other monk-fish, the ones that the blackrobe had forced to his dark purpose. Now that S'raya's boyfriend was dead they seemed to have completely recovered from the twisted way he'd used them, jumping and bouncing in play as they followed Jaja. Still, they reminded Mahri of the dangers that lurked in this elegant palace. And of how much the king, and now their child, needed her.

Korl threw back his head and laughed, rose from the bed and tossed her a shirt from a chest. His body shimmered like pale gold in the light, all curves and planes and hard ridges. He laid back down and Mahri fought the urge to join him. She had all kinds of hungers.

And now, all kinds of ties. The thought snuck into her like a guilty thief and she couldn't help the feeling of entrapment that followed. Yet surely, Korl understood her, more than anyone else ever could. Their minds had met and he knew what she needed. Would a child change all of that?

"I'll be back," she promised him, making more of the words than they seemed.

His deep voice answered solemnly. "I know."

She froze, her hand on the edge of the door. Did he understand her aright? Did he know that she spoke of more than just this moment, that her soul demanded freedom as much as his demanded complete union? Mahri thought of zabba, then shook her head. The words must be spoken aloud.

"Sometimes," she whispered, "I'll need to return to the swamps."

"I know."

"With… with my child." Mahri held her breath. Would he allow the little one's freedom also?

"With *our* child," he corrected her.

Mahri's heart soared with joy. But of course, there was never any compromising with Korl, she knew that. It was all or nothing. And she had it all. Her stomach rumbled and she skipped from the room, seeking Jaja, and almost didn't hear his next words.

"You'll always come back to me, Mahri Com'nder. And I'll always leave a light burning in the window for you."

Acknowledgments

A special thank you to my agent, Christine Witthohn, whose efforts will allow this book to reach a wider audience.

About the Author

Kathryne Kennedy is a multipublished, award-winning author of magical romances. She's lived in Guam, Okinawa, and several states in the U.S., and currently lives in Arizona with her wonderful family—which includes two very tiny Chihuahuas. She welcomes readers to visit her website where she has ongoing contests at: www.KathryneKennedy.com.

For more from Kathryne Kennedy,
read on for an excerpt from

THE
FIRE LORD'S
LOVER

Now available from
Sourcebooks Casablanca

"YOU'VE HEARD THAT HE HAS WON THE KING?"

"Of course."

Cassandra didn't need to name her intended. They both knew of whom she spoke. And suddenly her doubts overwhelmed her. If only she had inherited some of that elven beauty, perhaps she wouldn't be so unsure of winning him over. Her brown hair had a hint of red, her brown eyes a touch of gold, but her appearance held nothing unusual enough to tempt him. Fie, the nuns likened her to a little brown wren. She lowered her voice to a near whisper. "The very thought of him frightens me sometimes. I think he is more elven than human. I worry I shan't be able to please him."

"Cass." Thomas's own voice lowered to a husky timbre. "Look at me."

She never should have spoken of her fears. Not to him. Truly, not to anyone. But her marriage had always seemed a distant thing, something she needn't worry about for a long time. The day had come faster than she had been prepared for.

When she didn't turn around, Thomas clasped her shoulders and spun her, forcing her to look at him. "You don't have to go through with this."

She looked into those gray eyes and saw to her utter astonishment that he meant what he said. "Do not allow me to give in to a moment of cowardice, Thomas."

"I'm serious." His hand brushed her cheek.

When he'd first come to tutor her, she would have given her life for that touch. But Thomas had kept himself aloof, recognizing her infatuation for what it was. Or so she had thought.

"Come away with me," he said. "You don't have to go through with this. The Rebellion will find someone else to marry the bastard."

Just the thought that she would stray from the path laid out for her dizzied Cassandra for a moment. Nearly every day of her life had been in preparation for her marriage to the Imperial Lord's champion. The thought that she wouldn't fulfill her destiny set her adrift. "It would be impossible."

He misunderstood her. "No, it wouldn't. I've given this a lot of thought over the past few days. I'm the most skilled spy in the Rebellion, Cass. I can get you out of Firehame into one of the neighboring sovereignties before anyone suspects you're even missing. I can keep you safe."

She shook her head and his temper flared. "You are going to your death, Lady Cassandra."

Her own temper retaliated in response. "You've known this for years. Need I remind you that you are the one who taught me the death dances? You are the one who swayed me to the Rebellion's cause. How dare you take advantage of my cowardice to offer me this false hope."

"It's not false." He picked up her hands and went down on one knee. "Marry me."

"I cannot."

"Why?"

"Because I don't love you."

His breath hitched. She hadn't meant to put it so baldly. "You don't love the bastard either. And you can't marry *him*."

She pulled her hands out of his. "I can. I will. That's different and you know it. It's a path I decided to take long ago. I've made my peace with God and am willing to risk my immortal soul."

"Don't spout that holy drivel at me, Cassandra. This priestly garb is nothing but a disguise, you know."

She couldn't help the half smile that formed on her mouth. "And well do I know it, Viscount Thomas Althorp."

He stood, raking his gold hair away from his eyes, scowling at her stubbornness. "You used to love me, once."

"I admit I was infatuated with you. How could I not be? Besides my father, you're the only man with whom I've spent any company." She didn't mention her betrothed. She'd been allowed out of the confines of the school to meet with him on several occasions. But it had all been formal functions, and Dominic Raikes barely seemed to notice her.

Thomas made a strangled sound, stepped forward, and roughly took her into his arms. And then he kissed her.

Cassandra had never been kissed before. He caught her completely unawares and at first she could do nothing but study the peculiar sensation of having a man's mouth on her own. Warm, wet... and decidedly odd. She couldn't quite decide whether she liked the experience or not.

Thomas pulled back his head and stared down into her face. "You don't feel a thing, do you?"

She frowned. "What exactly am I supposed to be feeling?"

He let out a sigh of exasperation and kissed her again.

Cass wondered if it would feel the same when her intended finally kissed her. Although she couldn't be sure if he would, not knowing if it was necessary for the act of... procreation. He'd made it very clear he would do only his duty and nothing more. That he viewed her as his breeding stock.

The thought made her try to respond to Thomas. This might be her only chance to experience a true kiss. She cautiously curled her hands around his shoulders, which made him moan and lean even closer to her, nearly bending her backward with the force of his mouth.

Cassandra could think of nothing other than the pain in her back and the need to breathe.

Thomas pulled away and raised his golden brows. "Despite your lack of enthusiasm I know you aren't frigid," he muttered.

"What do you mean? I'm not the slightest bit cold. Indeed, your hold is nearly suffocating me with warmth."

He straightened and set her away from him. "You could come to love me, you know."

"I'm not destined for love. I knew that the moment I decided to join the Rebellion."

He spun and sought out the chair by the fireplace, sat with his elbows propped on his knees and stared into the embers. "You've always been stubborn. Once you set your sight on something, there's no changing your mind. I had to try though." He glanced up at her, gold hair tumbling over his brow. "Do you know how many assassins we've set on the elven lords? And they've all failed, Lady Cassandra. Every last one of them."

The look in his eyes frightened her. She prayed to God for courage and took a moment to compose herself. She smoothed her sleeves, fluffed her skirts. Their lesson today had not gone as she had thought it would. Fie, she had never imagined having such a conversation with Lord Althorp. Had never imagined that the man who'd always reassured her would now require that same sentiment back.

She folded her hands in front of her and gave him a cheeky grin. "How many of them managed to nearly strangle you to death, Thomas?"

He couldn't seem to resist smiling back at her. "Confound it, girl. I can't help but admire you. There's nothing I can say to change your mind, is there?"

"No." She felt her smile falter as she thought of the enormity of her task. "I cannot think of myself, Thomas. Nor you, nor my father… or the elven bastard, for that matter. The freedom of the people of England is at stake. And just the chance"—she clasped her hands tight—"the mere chance of ending these ridiculous war games and setting the king in power once more is worth my soul."

"Not to me." She opened her mouth again and he held up a pale hand to quiet her. "Enough. Do you know your eyes glaze over like a nun at prayer when you say such things?"

"Had I not been chosen for this task, I would have liked to have taken the vows."

Thomas laughed at her, slapping his knees. "Oh, no, my girl. Becoming a nun is not for the likes of you."

Cass raised her chin, miffed at his opinion of her. "I would make a very good nun."

He laughed harder, wiped the tears from those wicked gray eyes. "Sometimes I think I know you better than you know yourself. There's a fire within you, Lady Cassandra. I felt it in your kiss. And one day it will be set free, and heaven help the man who stokes it." He motioned her to the chair across from him and Cassandra took it, although her back stayed as stiff as a rod. He eyed her for a time in silence, only the crackle of the fire and the muted sounds of a carriage rumbling past the window disturbing the quiet.

All trace of humor vanished from his expression, and he leaned forward, his brow creased in earnestness. "I do not think your father did you a favor by having you raised among all this religious dogma. You've taken it to heart and I'm not sure if it will help or hinder you."

Cass frowned. She'd always considered Thomas's lack of faith a peculiarity, another oddity to his character compared to those she'd always been surrounded by. She pitied him for it.

Thomas sighed. "Well, then, there's no help for it. Despite my teaching, the nuns have managed to keep you pure, anyway. What a paradox you are, my dear. The court won't know what to make of you."

"Unless they get in my way, they hardly matter."

"I dare say. Now, this will probably be the last time we will be able to meet privately."

Cassandra felt her stomach twist. In many ways, Thomas had been her only friend. How would she manage without his company?

He patted her hand then snatched his away, as if he had to force himself not to hold onto her. Their conversation today, that kiss of his, had changed their relationship, it seemed. Perhaps it would be better if they did not meet again.

"Don't worry," he assured her. "You shall still see me. But not as Father Thomas. Viscount Althorp, however, will reappear at court, to the surprise and delight of all, I am sure." He gave her that crooked grin that had once made her younger self swoon. "But it wouldn't be safe for us to talk often, or privately, so listen closely."

She nodded, relieved they had resumed their familiar roles as tutor and student.

"I don't know," he said, "if having the king's court in Firehame will make your task easier. See if you can aid Sir Robert Walpole, but do not risk your task for his sake. We've never had an assassin this close to an Imperial Lord before. Your mission is far more important than the leader of the Rebellion, do you understand?"

Cassandra nodded.

"Your magic for the dance will not be enough. You never would have returned home after your trials if you had enough magic to truly threaten the elven lord. Only surprise and skill will overcome him."

Although Cass vaguely remembered her trials, she knew her father had been disappointed when she hadn't possessed enough magic to be sent to the elvens' home world, the fabled Elfhame. His friend, Lord Welton, had bragged for years that his son had been a chosen one, and the duke had been decidedly put out when he could not say the same of his only child.

It had soothed her father somewhat when she'd become affianced to General Raikes. And now that her intended had won the king…

"It may take you years to get close to the Imperial Lord," continued the viscount. "It will help you immensely if you can manage to make your new husband trust you. But even then, do not rush forward blindly. Remember your most important lesson."

The words fell from her mouth without thought. "Patience."

"Just so. Practice it with Dominic Raikes. I'm sure he will tax it."

Cassandra smiled. Thomas did not return it this time. Instead he leaned forward, his gray eyes hard as steel. "Make sure of your opportunity before you seize it. If nothing else, remember that, my girl."

"I will. I promise."

The bell rang, signaling the end of prayer, and made both of them jump. Thomas smiled at her rather sheepishly, and Cassandra feared the smile she gave him in turn held too much sadness in it.

He walked her to the door, bowed low over her hand. "If you ever need me, leave a message for Father Thomas. I will come... if it's safe."

She understood. From this moment forward, she should depend only upon herself. She turned to leave, but he would not let go of her hand.

"Are you sure?" he murmured.

"Yes." Oh, how confident she sounded! Was it false or true? She supposed the next few days would tell.

His grip loosened and she felt her entire body grow cold. Would she ever be truly warm again?

"Farewell, then, Lady Cassandra. You have been a most excellent student."

She might never see him again, at least in this guise.

She wondered what he would be like in the full role of Viscount Althorp. "Goodbye, Father Thomas."

Cass slipped out the door almost as quietly as she'd entered. Some of her training had become pure habit. The hall flowed with the colorful skirts of the ladies of quality and she insinuated herself within the crowd of students with barely a notice. She knew she should go to her rooms, that her father had sent his servants along with her wedding gown so she would be prepared for tomorrow.

But the entire encounter with Thomas had shaken her belief in the path she had chosen to take. Her widowed father had no idea of her involvement with the Rebellion; he would have disowned her, since he stood to gain status and funds with her union to the champion.

She'd missed her mother over the years, but never as much as she did at this moment.

So when Cass passed by the chapel she slipped inside and closed the door behind her. She'd always had God to talk to. For a moment she enjoyed the silence, the chatter of the girls muffled behind the walls. Prayer time had ended and so she had the entire place to herself.

She passed the pews and went straight to the altar, sinking to her knees on the bare stone, as close to the cross as propriety would allow. She bowed her head, pressed her palms together, and continued her interrupted prayer, her words barely above a whisper.

"Almighty God, please let my new husband be happy with me tomorrow so I can murder his father."

———

Cassandra sat within the carriage, trying not to rumple the

silk of her wedding dress. The sunshine streamed through the windows and struck the silver edging decorating the cream fabric, and shot tiny sparks of light around her. Father had insisted on the silk, had chosen the pleated gown himself. He wanted his daughter to shine.

Cass wanted only to disappear.

She glanced across the coach at her father. The press of traffic to Westminster Abbey impeded their progress, and the Duke of Chandos grumbled again.

"Devilishly foolish of the lot. They're all here to see the wedding and they can't have one without the bride. We shall be late because of all the gawkers."

He checked his gold watch for the hundredth time. Age had not diminished her father's handsome looks. His silver white wig made his hazel eyes appear lighter and they made a striking contrast against his tan face. He loved to hunt, spent a great deal of time outdoors, which had kept up his youthful physique. He had not mourned Cassandra's mother for long, although she supposed she couldn't blame him, when women kept throwing themselves at his feet.

He'd inherited only a pretty face from his elven blood.

"Please, Father, don't be concerned. They will wait for us."

"Eh?" He glanced up, as if he'd forgotten her presence. "Yes, quite right." The Duke of Chandos leaned over and patted her hand. "As you are my only child, your son will inherit the title. Of course they'll wait."

Cassandra gave him a weak smile and turned to stare out the window. Her new stays itched. And Father had insisted she wear the most outlandishly wide hoops; as a consequence, they kept popping up in her seated position. She gave a sigh of relief when she saw the Gothic arches of the Abbey. The carriage stopped in front of the ornately carved entry. The area had been roped off to hold back the crowd, and a line of uniformed officers standing in rigid military attention created an aisle for her to walk through.

Their uniformed escort leapt down from the back of the coach and opened the door, stepping aside to create another barrier against the watching crowd. Cass felt as if she were on display and confined all at the same time.

A sudden flare of cool white fire highlighted the officers and the entrance to the church, dancing upward past the tops of the spires in curling waves of crystal scintillation. Cass could feel the strength of the Imperial Lord's magic like a shiver in the very air. Her hands began to sweat inside her silk gloves.

Father stared out the window and swallowed. "Don't worry, my dear. We'll do just fine."

She couldn't be sure if his words were to reassure her or himself.

Father exited the carriage first, adjusted the lace at the sleeves of his satin coat, and held out his hand to her. Her fingers trembled as she clasped it. The sweep of her gown preceded her from the carriage and when she raised her head a sudden beam of fire touched her satin pinner, radiating outward to join the already swirling beams. Her knees felt like pudding and for the first time in her life she thought she might swoon.

Cass muttered a prayer, took a deep breath, and walked forward to her doom.

But the moment she entered the grand abbey, the

carved images of saints and apostles calmed her. Statues of angels stared lovingly down at her, the feathers in their wings, the very folds of their robes, appearing softly real from the skill of the artisan that had sculpted them. Father led her down the nave and she ignored the hundreds of staring eyes of the nobles who sat in the pews, keeping her gaze focused on the great cross over the high altar. The music of the choir soared above and beyond the Imperial Lord's magical fire that had led them inside, and she let the melody carry her slippered feet down the very, very long aisle.

She didn't trip on her gown. Father didn't stumble in his new high-heeled shoes. Cassandra thought she might manage this public display without too much fuss after all, until they neared the altar. And she saw her intended. And his father.

General Dominic Raikes's handsome features had always flustered her. But today she realized the elvenkind had brought the beauty of angels to earth for them... and Dominic looked so strikingly similar to his elven-lord father. Her intended stood with military precision; indeed, he'd worn his uniform, although she doubted he wore this version in battle. The red wool had been replaced with red velvet, with gold trim about the sleeves and flared skirt of the coat. Dozens of gold buttons trimmed the wide cuffs of the coat and down the opening, although only one clasped it closed at the waist. His cravat and sleeves dripped with black lace and that color matched his shiny boots and the velvet cloak slung over his shoulders.

Not the normal dress for a marriage, but it suited him well.

He wore no wig, of course, since after all, the reason the gentry wore them was to copy the elvens' silver blond hair, and the general had inherited the original. As she drew closer to him, she noticed he wore his battle braids in his hair, but they'd been drawn back and fastened behind his head, revealing his pointed ears and the high cheekbones in his face.

Cass had her attention riveted on him, but he didn't return the favor. Indeed, his gaze roamed the vaulted ceiling and he looked... bored.

She glanced over at Imperial Lord Mor'ded. He'd dressed in the same manner as his son, although Cassandra imagined he'd never fought on a real battlefield in his life. His face looked slightly paler than his son's, his shoulders narrower, his legs less muscular. And his black eyes...

Cass's face swiveled between the two of them. Large elven eyes, as shiny and black as coal, they almost looked like they had facets in them. Both their eyes would be beautiful—glittering like exotic jewels—if they hadn't looked so very cold. So very cruel.

Instead of the angels to whom she'd compared them, she should have been thinking devils.

Cass turned her attention toward the archbishop and kept it there as her father brought her to stand next to General Raikes. He didn't so much as blink to acknowledge her presence. Her head just topped his shoulders and she fancied she could feel the heat of his body.

She refused to allow her intended to intimidate her by his mere presence.

The entire wedding party waited in a frozen tableau while the choir finished its song. Yet beneath Cass's dress her toes continued to tap in time to the music. She felt the dance swell inside of her, seeking direction. A brief thought came to her and made her stomach flip. Could she kill Mor'ded now and put an end to this farce? She'd resigned herself to the knowledge that she wouldn't survive the assassination. Surely the Imperial Lord's son would kill her if she moved now. What better way to send the sovereignty into chaos and advance the tide of the Rebellion?

Her heels lifted. Her knees swayed.

General Dominic Raikes leaned down and whispered in her ear. "Do you have an itch?"

The archbishop frowned at them. Imperial Lord Mor'ded fastened those cold eyes on her.

Cass froze. Had she detected a note of mockery in the general's deep voice? She stole a glance at him. His emotionless eyes stayed fixed on the archbishop as well, but the corner of his mouth twitched. She vowed she'd seen it twitch.

She felt a flush creep from belly to nose and knew her face had turned a deep red. And knew her opportunity to act had passed. The choir ended with a crescendo of glorious song, and without further ado the archbishop began the ceremony.

Perhaps it was just as well. Thomas had cautioned her for patience and she'd almost rushed forward. And as she stood through the painfully long ceremony and went through the motions required of her, she chided herself.

Imperial Lord Mor'ded's body nearly vibrated with tension, his eyes watching the assembled guests without appearing to. His white fire magic still swirled among the guests and she suddenly wondered if it had all been for show. Could he search for hidden dangers with it? Could he sense an attack, whether magical or physical, with his power?

Cass couldn't be sure. The information that the Rebellion had on the elven lords was sketchy. Thomas had done the best he could, but she suddenly realized she'd been ill-prepared for her task. She could feel the power of Mor'ded's magic, and the tiny bit she possessed seemed negligible by comparison. Perhaps the wiser course would be to discover all she could about the elven lords and their magic before she acted at all.

Cass now stood facing her... new husband. She supposed she'd have to get used to that idea. Although she didn't think she could ever get used to the coldness of his beautiful eyes. She'd hoped she could use the general to gather information about the elven, but right now he did not look like a man who could be used. Indeed, when his eyes met hers for a moment, a shiver of dread went through her.

The few times she'd visited him, he had treated her with a disinterest bordering on contempt. She'd foolishly thought that when she became his wife that might change, but it appeared the ceremony affected him not at all. Faith, how would she manage to share his bed tonight? Best not to think of that.

She blanched as her new husband slid a ring on her finger. A band of gold with a rose carved atop it. But the rose looked so real, the edges of the petals as delicate as the true flower. Cass couldn't resist the impulse to bring it closer to her face, then nearly jumped when the petals curled closed, changing the carving to a tight bud.

He'd given her a ring crafted with elven magic.

Her eyes flew up to his in alarm.

General Raikes lowered his head. "It won't harm you," he muttered, a note of exasperation in his velvety voice. And then he lowered his head and kissed her, signaling an end to the ceremony.

Cass's heart flipped over. She stood quite frozen, unsure of what had come over her. The general had done nothing more than press his lips to hers. And her entire body had shivered. From that one dispassionate touch.

As the onlookers broke into polite applause, Mor'ded leaned close to his son and said, "Surely the champion can do better than that."

She watched her husband glance at his father. Saw his face harden with challenge. Then the general wrapped his arms around her and roughly pulled her against his chest and Cass could only pray.

Her new husband kissed her again. But this time, he kissed her like Thomas had, bending her backward in his arms, moving his mouth over hers as if he sought to eat her alive. But the experience was totally unlike the one she'd shared with Thomas.

The world seemed to fall away. Cass became aware of nothing and no one but the man holding her in his arms. The heat of his mouth, the fire that ran through her body, the sheer exhilaration of the taste of him. Her senses heightened. She felt her breasts tighten and strain toward him. Felt a wetness between her legs that frightened and excited her all at the same time. His tongue pressed against her lips and lacking any experience of what to do, she opened her mouth and he invaded it, stroking and tasting until she just forgot to breathe.

Her new husband abruptly let her go and set her away

from him. Cass swayed. The applause in the room had risen in volume and she blushed again to realize she'd behaved in such a manner in front of an archbishop, half the country, and in the house of the Lord, no less. She couldn't account for what had come over her.

General Raikes gave his father a heated look. "Will that do?"

Mor'ded chuckled.

When Dominic took her hand and led her back down the nave, Cass could do nothing but weakly follow. But she noticed the rose in her ring had come unfurled, spreading out into a glorious open blossom.

THE
FIRE LORD'S
LOVER

BY KATHRYNE KENNEDY

IF HIS POWERS ARE DISCOVERED, HIS FATHER
WILL DESTROY HIM...

In a magical land ruled by ruthless Elven lords, the Fire
Lord's son Dominic Raikes plays a deadly game to conceal
his growing might from his malevolent father—until his
arranged bride awakens in him passions he thought he had
buried forever...

UNLESS HIS FIANCÉE KILLS HIM FIRST...

Lady Cassandra has been raised in outward purity and
innocence, while secretly being trained as an assassin. Her
mission is to bring down the Elven Lord and his champion
son. But when she gets to court she discovers that nothing is
what it seems, least of all the man she married...

---

*"As darkly imaginative as Tolkien, as richly romantic as Heyer,
Kennedy carves a new genre in romantic fiction."*
—Erin Quinn, author of *Haunting Warrior*

"Deliciously dark and enticing." —Angie Fox, *New York
Times* bestselling author of *A Tale of Two Demon Slayers*

978-1-4022-3652-5 • $7.99 U.S./$9.99 CAN/£4.99 UK

My
UNFAIR
Lady

BY KATHRYNE KENNEDY

A WILD WEST BEAUTY TAKES
VICTORIAN LONDON BY STORM

The impoverished Duke of Monchester despises the rich Americans who flock to London, seeking to buy their way into the ranks of the British peerage. Frontier-bred Summer Wine Lee has no interest in winning over London society—it's the New York bluebloods and her future mother-in-law she's determined to impress. She knows the cost of smoothing her rough-and-tumble frontier edges will be high. But she never imagined it might cost her heart…

"Kennedy is going places." —Romantic Times

"Kathryne Kennedy creates a unique, exquisite flavor that makes her romance a pure delight page after page, book after book." —Merrimon Book Reviews

"Kathryne Kennedy's computer must smolder from the power she creates in her stories! I simply cannot describe how awesome or how thrilling I found this novel to be."
—Huntress Book Reviews

"Kennedy is one of the hottest new sensations in the romance genre." —Merrimon Reviews

978-1-4022-2990-9 • $7.99 U.S./$9.99 CAN